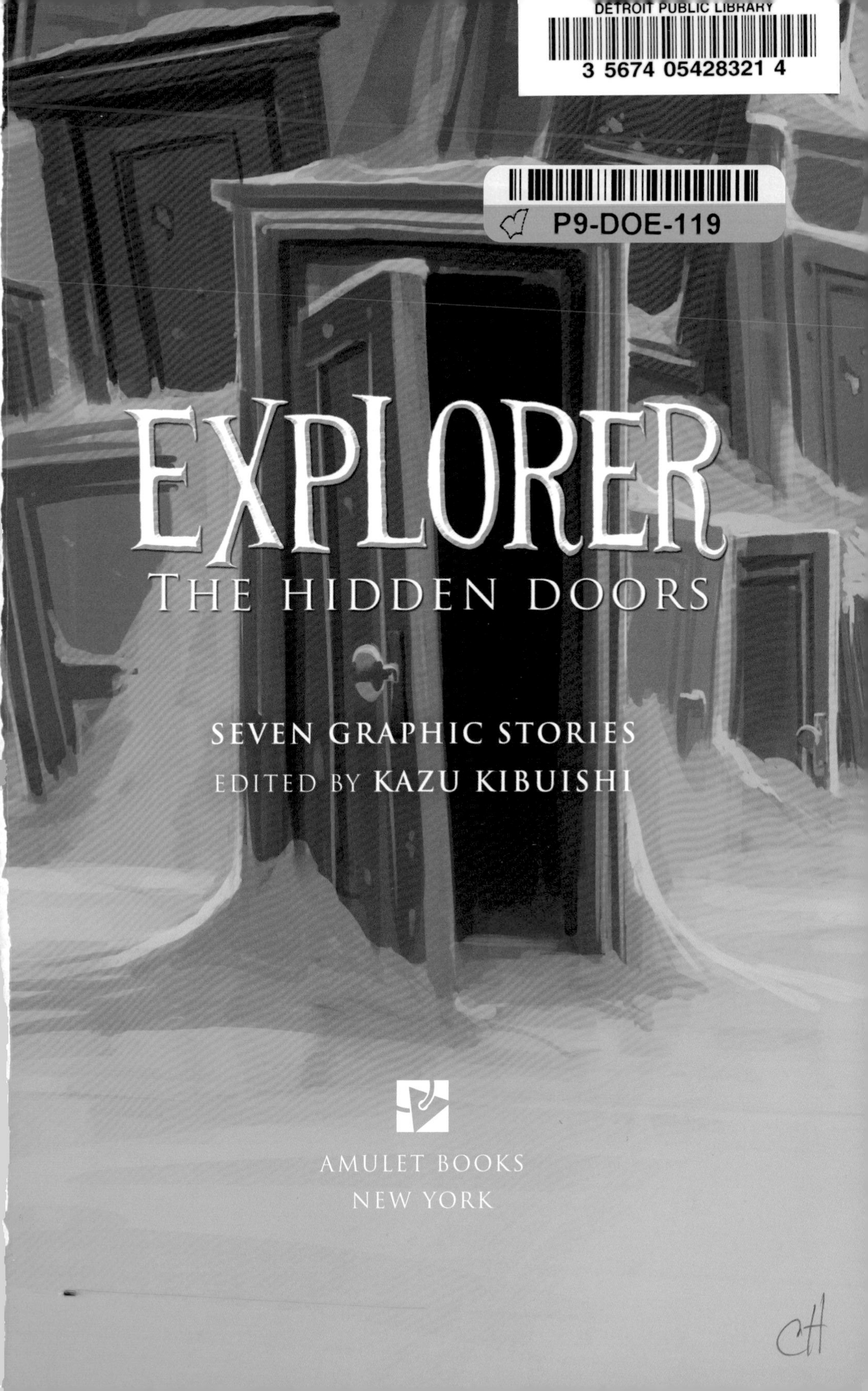

# EXPLORER
## THE HIDDEN DOORS

SEVEN GRAPHIC STORIES

EDITED BY KAZU KIBUISHI

AMULET BOOKS
NEW YORK

THANKS TO MY COEDITORS,
CAROL BURRELL AND JASON CAFFOE
—K.K.

Publisher's Note
This is a work of fiction. Names, characters, places, and incidents are
either the product of the author's imagination or are used fictitiously, and
any resemblance to actual persons, living or dead, business establishments,
events, or locales is entirely coincidental.

Library of Congress Control Number: 2014938941

Paperback ISBN 978-1-4197-0884-8
Hardcover ISBN 978-1-4197-0882-4

Cover art © 2014 Kazu Kibuishi
Compilation © 2014 Bolt City Productions
Book design by Chad W. Beckerman and Jessie Gang

Text and illustrations © 2014 by the individual artists as follows:
"Asteria Crane," pages 4–23, © 2014 Kazu Kibuishi
"The Giant's Kitchen," pages 24–41, © 2014 Jason Caffoe
"Luis 2.0," pages 42–57, © 2014 Jen Wang
"Two-Person Door," pages 58–75, © 2014 Faith Erin Hicks
Fish N Chips in "Spring Cleaning," pages 76–93, © 2014 Steve Hamaker
"Mastaba," pages 94–109, © 2014 Johane Matte
"When Is a Door Not a Door?" pages 110–127, text © 2014 Jen Breach
and Douglas Holgate; illustrations © 2014 Douglas Holgate

Printed and bound in China
10 9 8 7 6 5 4 3 2

Amulet Books are available at special discounts when purchased in quantity
for premiums and promotions as well as fundraising or educational use. For
details, contact specialmarkets@abramsbooks.com, or the address below.

**ABRAMS**
THE ART OF BOOKS SINCE 1949

115 West 18th Street
New York, NY 10011
www.abramsbooks.com

# CONTENTS

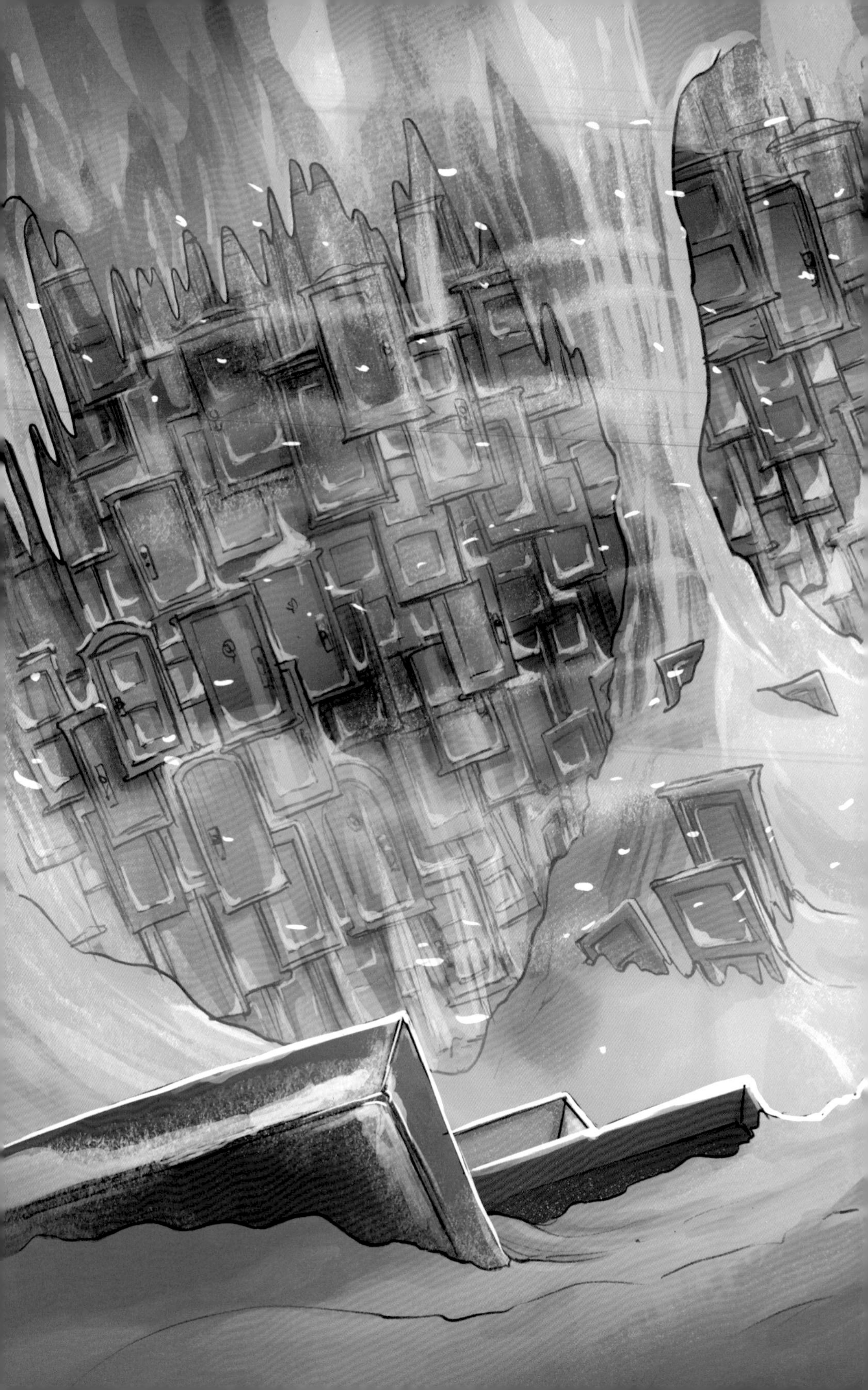

DOCTOR, CAN YOU HEAR ME?
YES, I CAN HEAR YOU, LEN...
ASTERIA CRANE
BY KAZU KIBUISHI
COLORS BY DENVER JACKSON

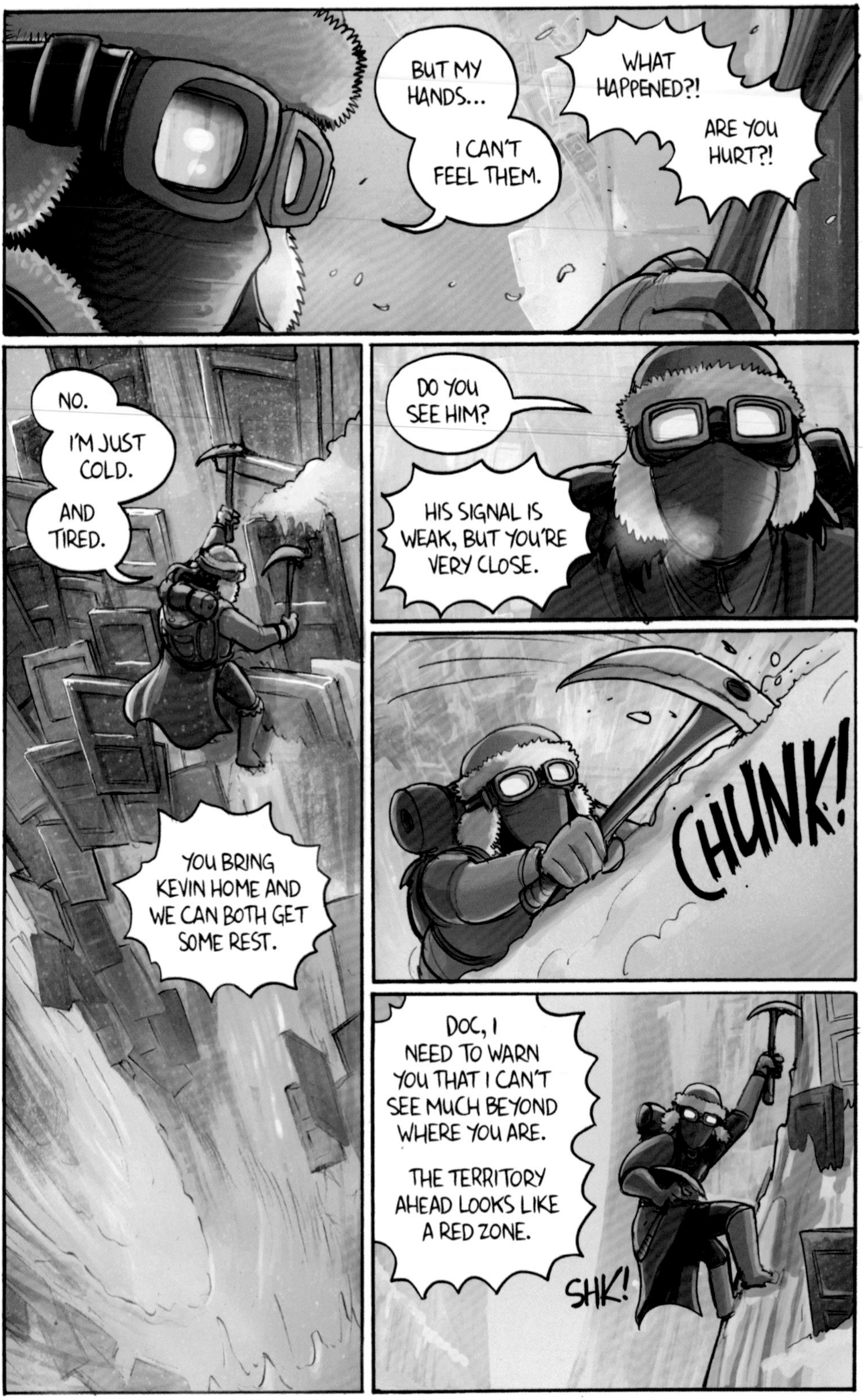
BUT MY HANDS...
I CAN'T FEEL THEM.
WHAT HAPPENED?!
ARE YOU HURT?!
NO.
I'M JUST COLD.
AND TIRED.
YOU BRING KEVIN HOME AND WE CAN BOTH GET SOME REST.
DO YOU SEE HIM?
HIS SIGNAL IS WEAK, BUT YOU'RE VERY CLOSE.
CHUNK!
DOC, I NEED TO WARN YOU THAT I CAN'T SEE MUCH BEYOND WHERE YOU ARE.
THE TERRITORY AHEAD LOOKS LIKE A RED ZONE.
SHK!

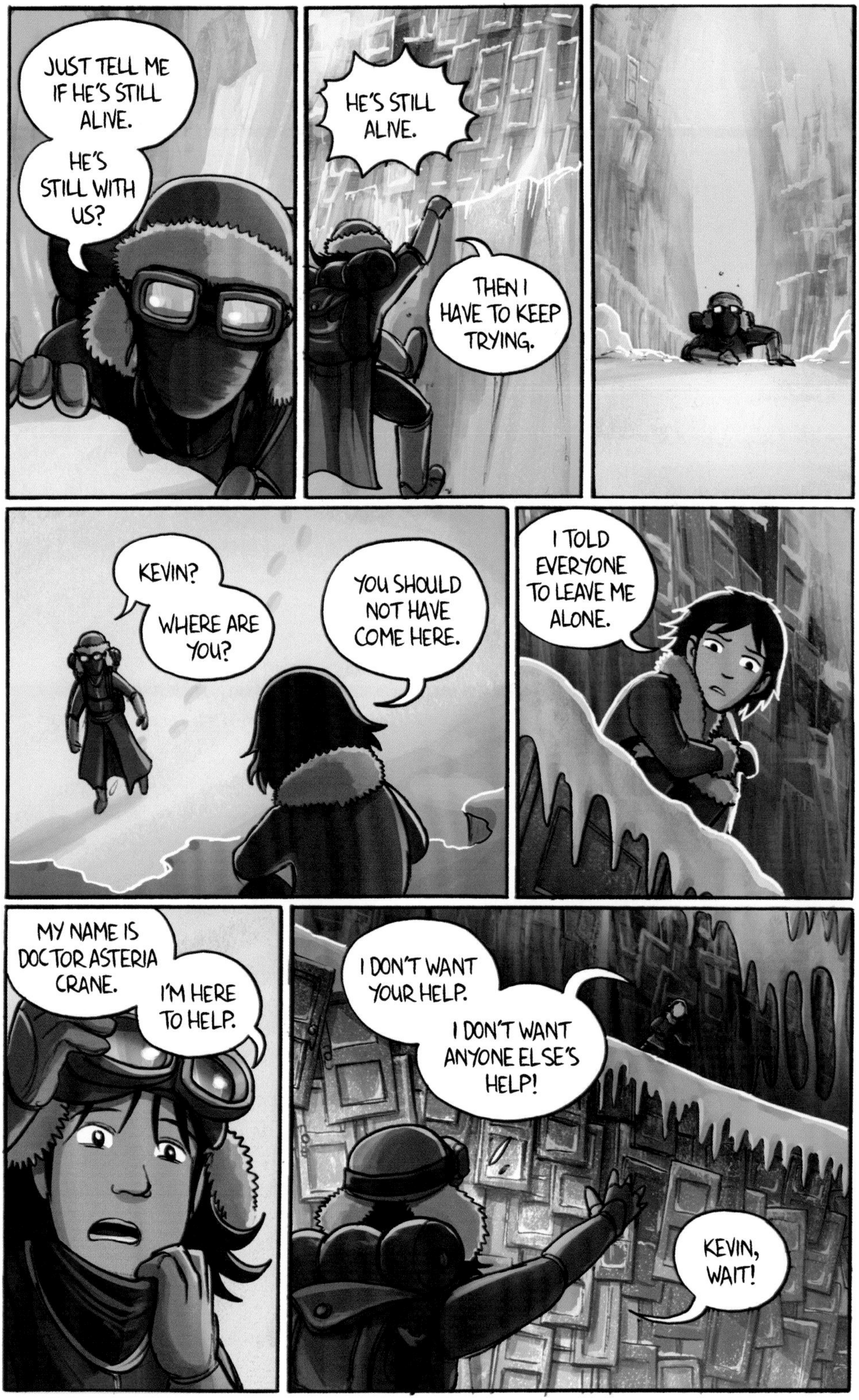
JUST TELL ME IF HE'S STILL ALIVE.
HE'S STILL WITH US?
HE'S STILL ALIVE.
THEN I HAVE TO KEEP TRYING.
KEVIN?
WHERE ARE YOU?
YOU SHOULD NOT HAVE COME HERE.
I TOLD EVERYONE TO LEAVE ME ALONE.
MY NAME IS DOCTOR ASTERIA CRANE.
I'M HERE TO HELP.
I DON'T WANT YOUR HELP.
I DON'T WANT ANYONE ELSE'S HELP!
KEVIN, WAIT!

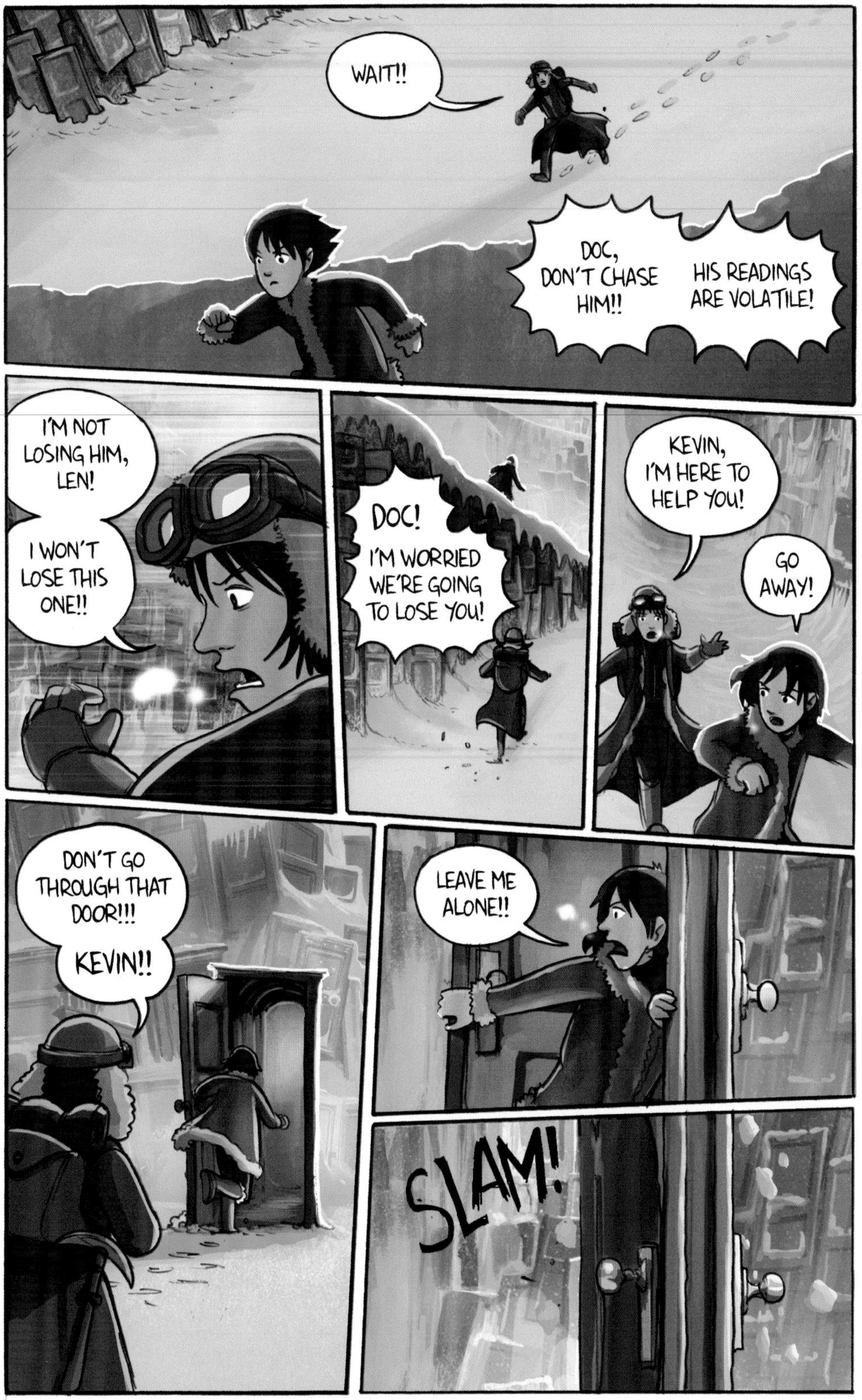
WAIT!!
DOC, DON'T CHASE HIM!!
HIS READINGS ARE VOLATILE!
I'M NOT LOSING HIM, LEN!
I WON'T LOSE THIS ONE!!
DOC!
I'M WORRIED WE'RE GOING TO LOSE YOU!
KEVIN, I'M HERE TO HELP YOU!
GO AWAY!
DON'T GO THROUGH THAT DOOR!!!
KEVIN!!
LEAVE ME ALONE!!
SLAM!

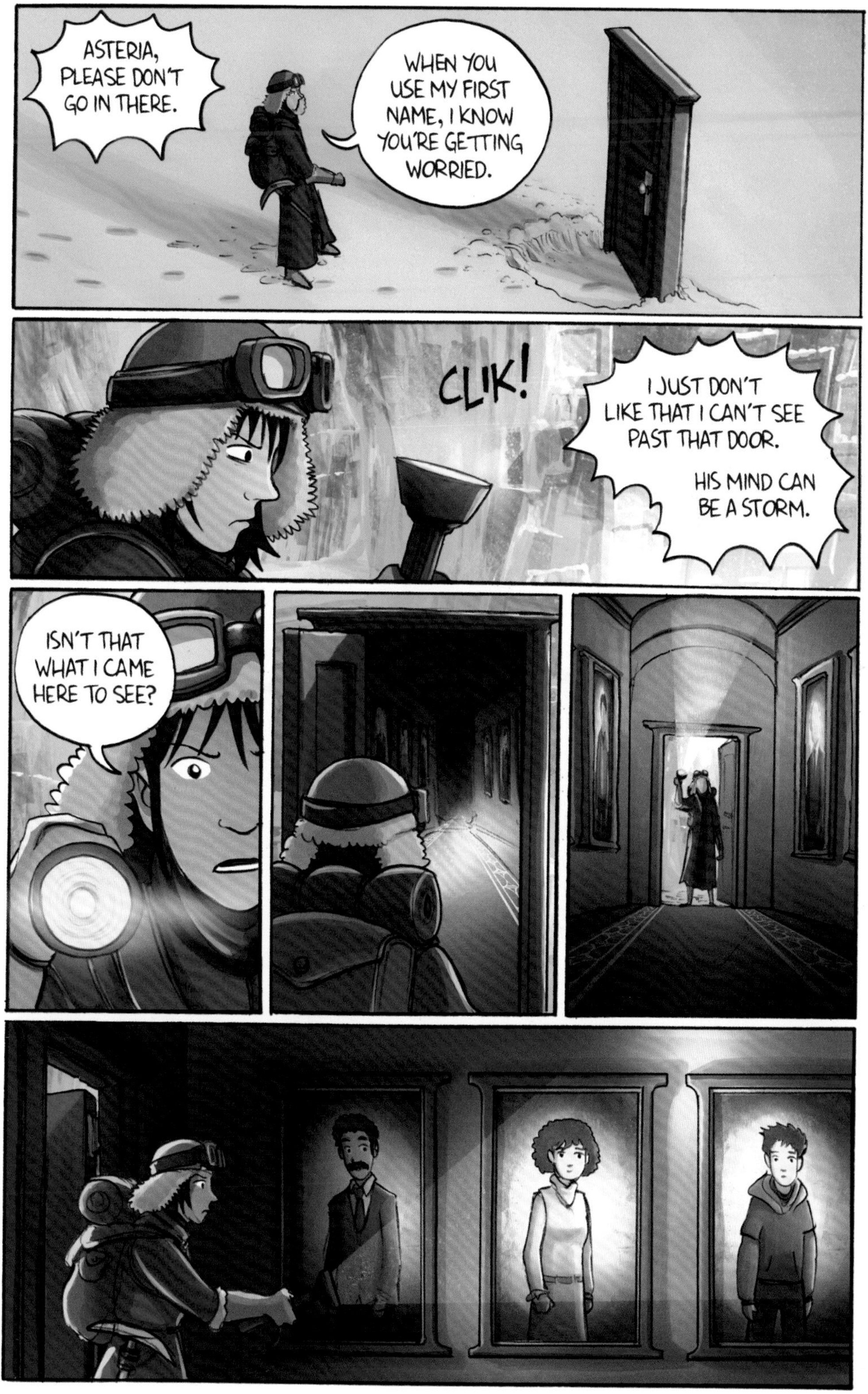
ASTERIA, PLEASE DON'T GO IN THERE.
WHEN YOU USE MY FIRST NAME, I KNOW YOU'RE GETTING WORRIED.
CLIK!
I JUST DON'T LIKE THAT I CAN'T SEE PAST THAT DOOR.
HIS MIND CAN BE A STORM.
ISN'T THAT WHAT I CAME HERE TO SEE?

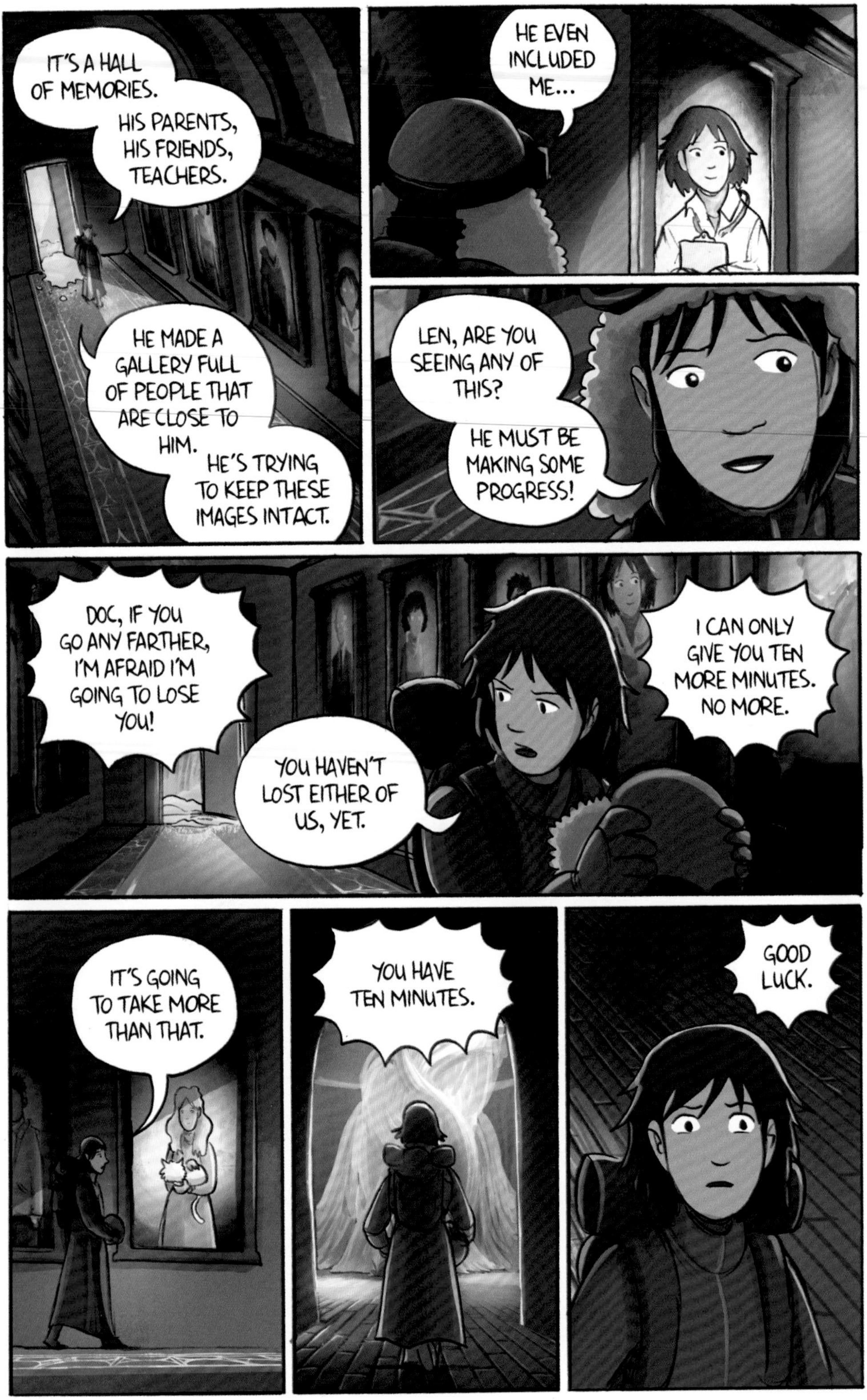
IT'S A HALL OF MEMORIES.
HIS PARENTS, HIS FRIENDS, TEACHERS.
HE MADE A GALLERY FULL OF PEOPLE THAT ARE CLOSE TO HIM.
HE'S TRYING TO KEEP THESE IMAGES INTACT.
HE EVEN INCLUDED ME...
LEN, ARE YOU SEEING ANY OF THIS?
HE MUST BE MAKING SOME PROGRESS!
DOC, IF YOU GO ANY FARTHER, I'M AFRAID I'M GOING TO LOSE YOU!
I CAN ONLY GIVE YOU TEN MORE MINUTES. NO MORE.
YOU HAVEN'T LOST EITHER OF US, YET.
IT'S GOING TO TAKE MORE THAN THAT.
YOU HAVE TEN MINUTES.
GOOD LUCK.

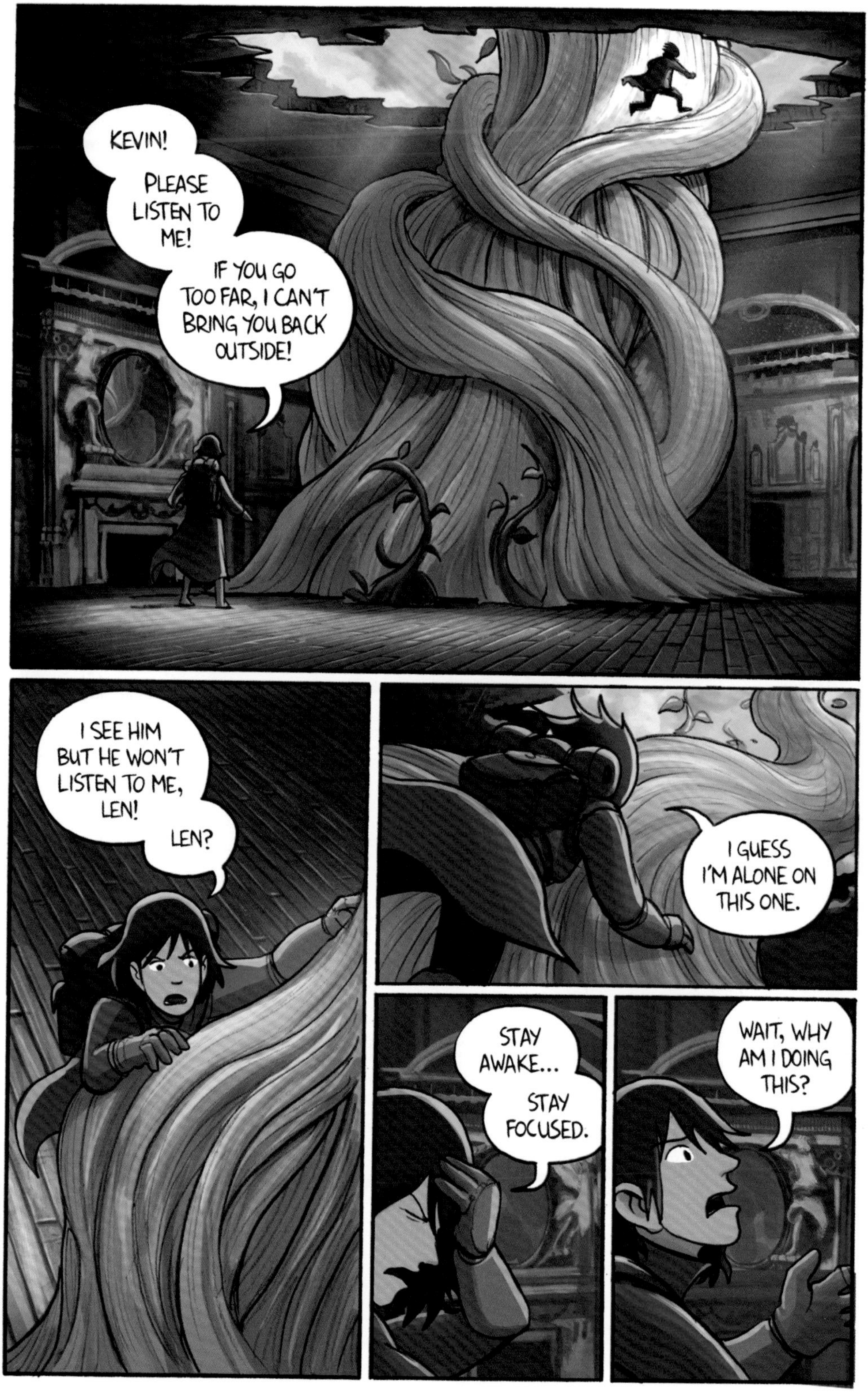
KEVIN!
PLEASE LISTEN TO ME!
IF YOU GO TOO FAR, I CAN'T BRING YOU BACK OUTSIDE!
I SEE HIM BUT HE WON'T LISTEN TO ME, LEN!
LEN?
I GUESS I'M ALONE ON THIS ONE.
STAY AWAKE...
STAY FOCUSED.
WAIT, WHY AM I DOING THIS?

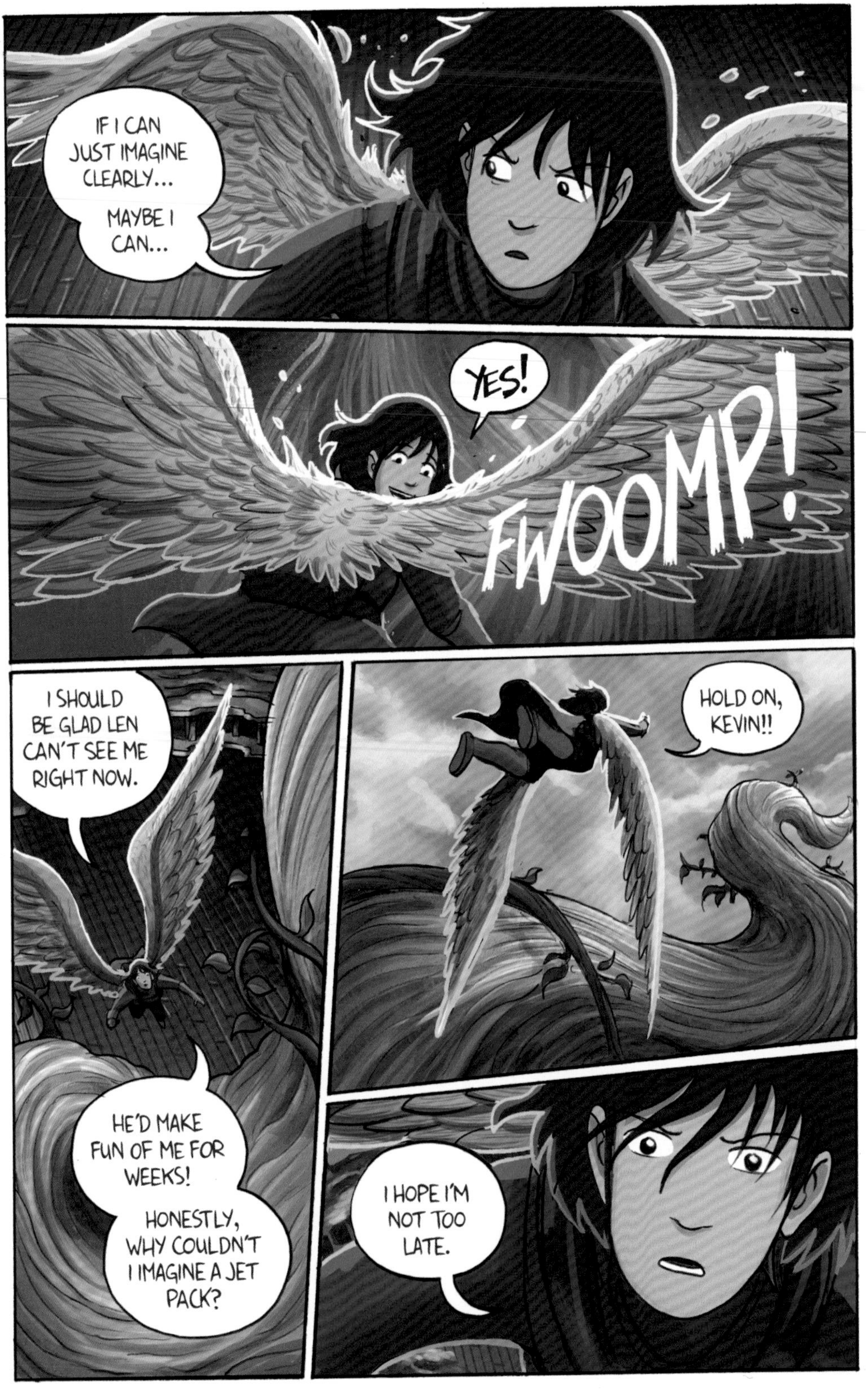
IF I CAN JUST IMAGINE CLEARLY...
MAYBE I CAN...
YES!
FWOOMP!
I SHOULD BE GLAD LEN CAN'T SEE ME RIGHT NOW.
HE'D MAKE FUN OF ME FOR WEEKS!
HONESTLY, WHY COULDN'T I IMAGINE A JET PACK?
HOLD ON, KEVIN!!
I HOPE I'M NOT TOO LATE.

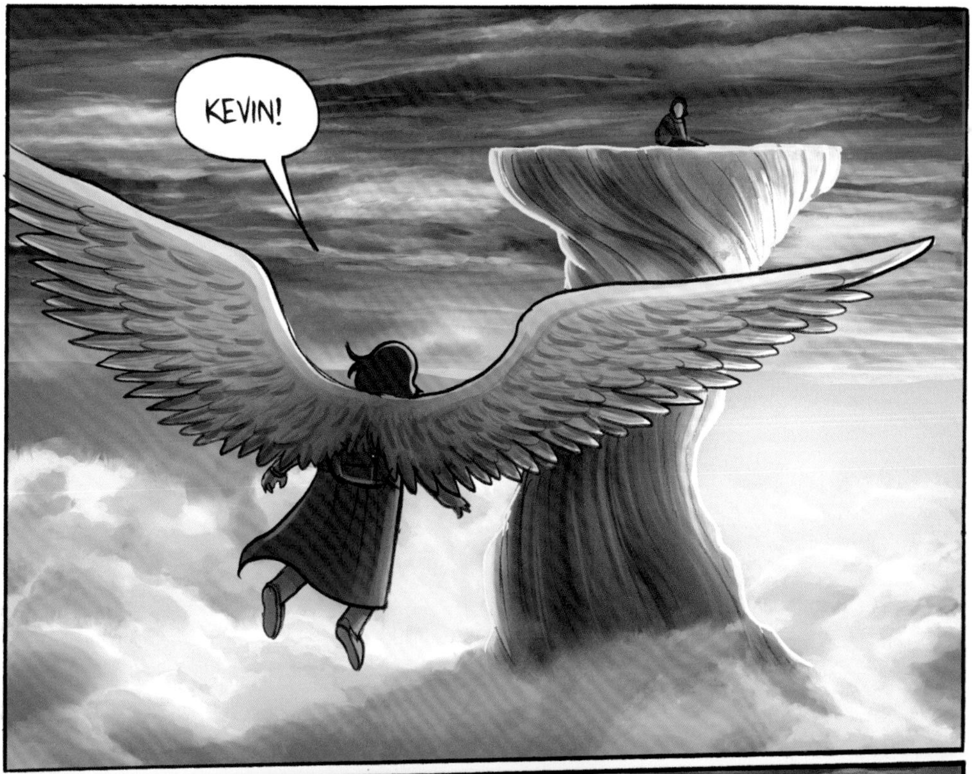
KEVIN!

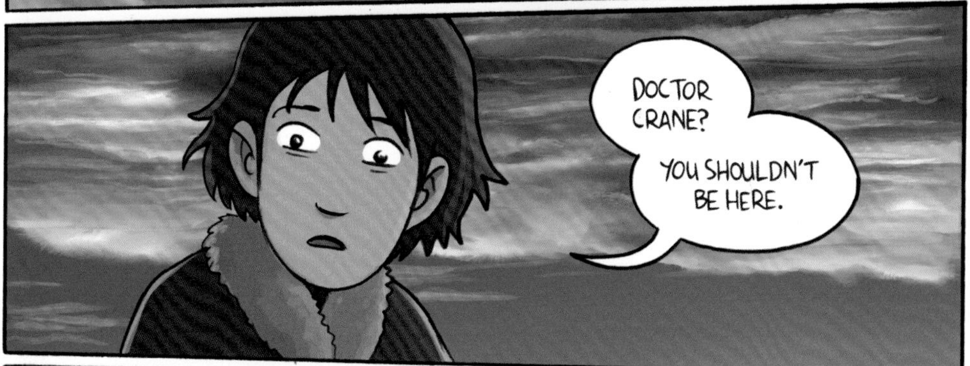
DOCTOR CRANE?
YOU SHOULDN'T BE HERE.

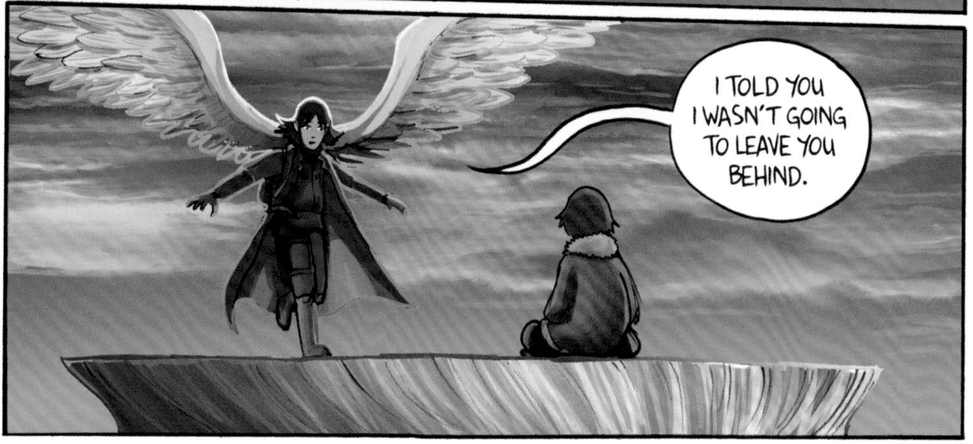
I TOLD YOU I WASN'T GOING TO LEAVE YOU BEHIND.

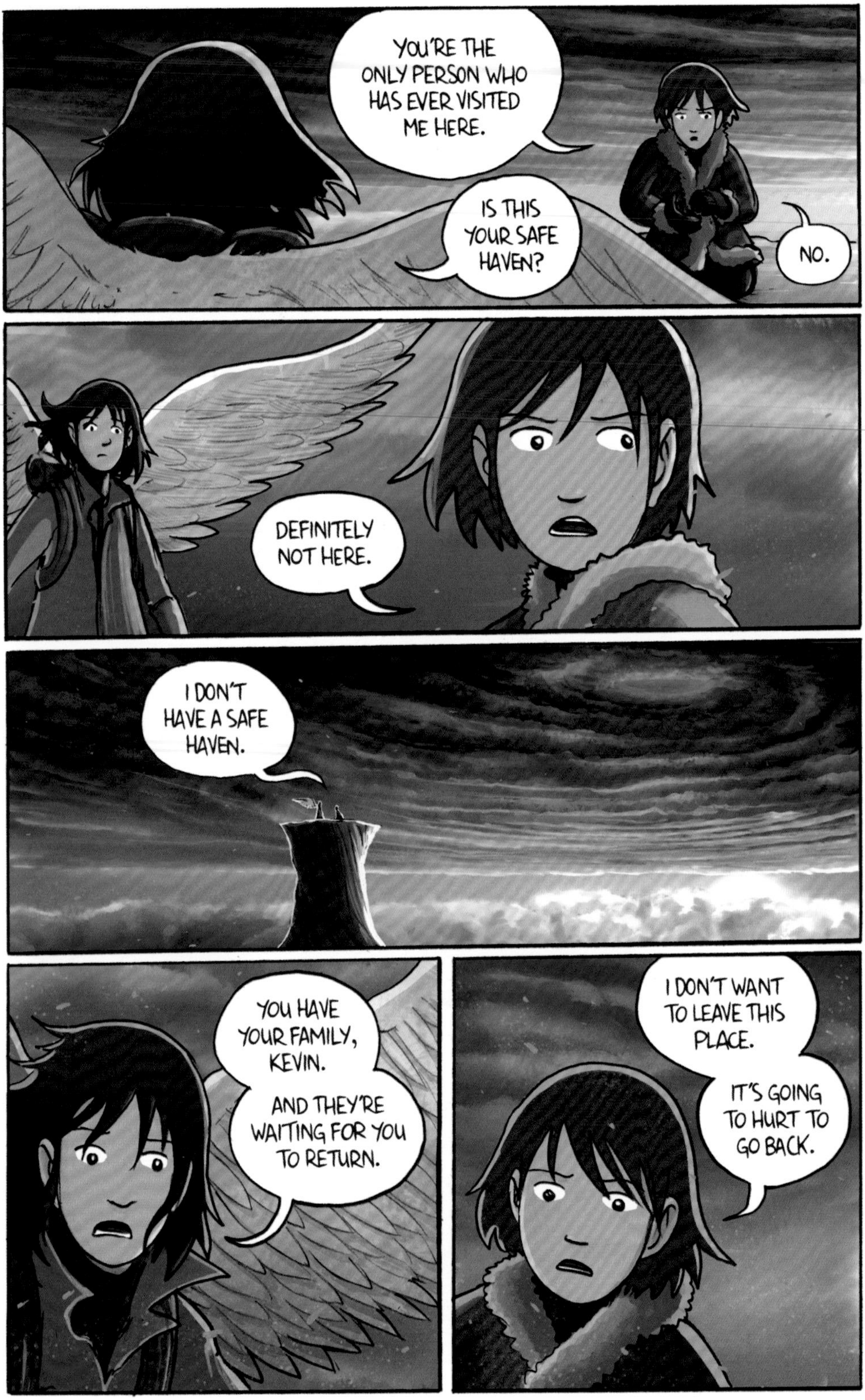
YOU'RE THE ONLY PERSON WHO HAS EVER VISITED ME HERE.
IS THIS YOUR SAFE HAVEN?
NO.
DEFINITELY NOT HERE.
I DON'T HAVE A SAFE HAVEN.
YOU HAVE YOUR FAMILY, KEVIN.
AND THEY'RE WAITING FOR YOU TO RETURN.
I DON'T WANT TO LEAVE THIS PLACE.
IT'S GOING TO HURT TO GO BACK.

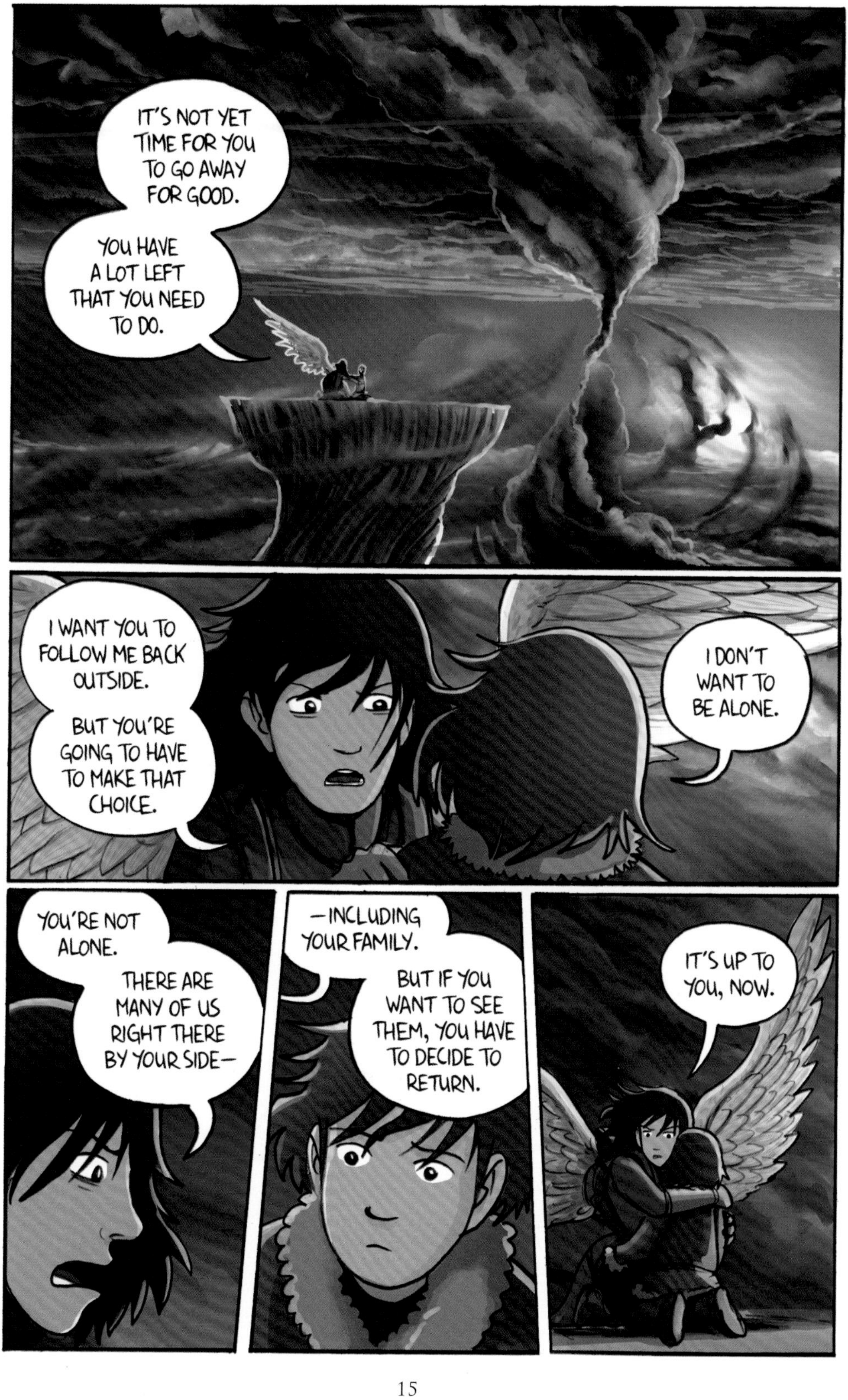
IT'S NOT YET TIME FOR YOU TO GO AWAY FOR GOOD.
YOU HAVE A LOT LEFT THAT YOU NEED TO DO.
I WANT YOU TO FOLLOW ME BACK OUTSIDE.
BUT YOU'RE GOING TO HAVE TO MAKE THAT CHOICE.
I DON'T WANT TO BE ALONE.
YOU'RE NOT ALONE.
THERE ARE MANY OF US RIGHT THERE BY YOUR SIDE—
—INCLUDING YOUR FAMILY.
BUT IF YOU WANT TO SEE THEM, YOU HAVE TO DECIDE TO RETURN.
IT'S UP TO YOU, NOW.

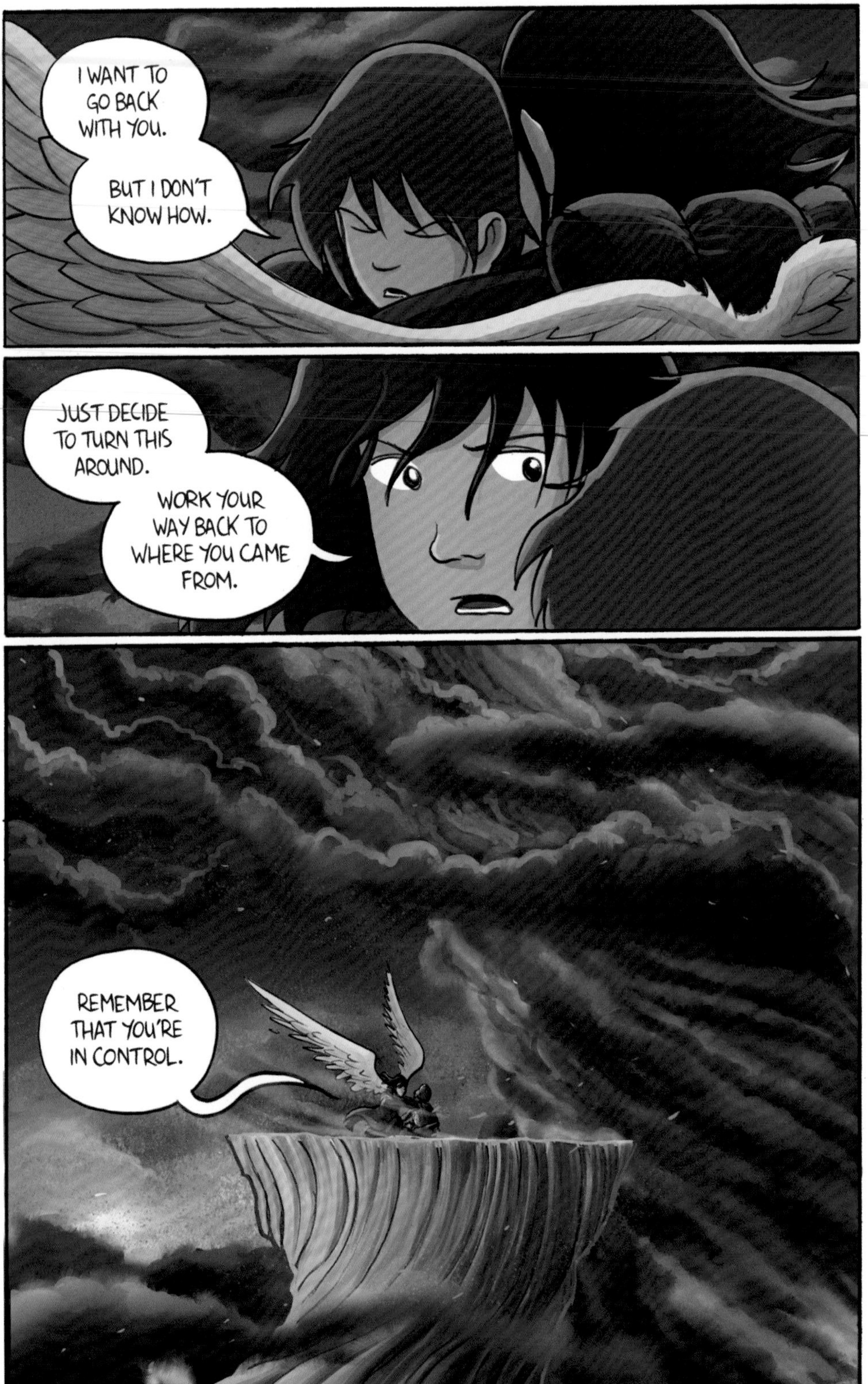

I WANT TO GO BACK WITH YOU.
BUT I DON'T KNOW HOW.
JUST DECIDE TO TURN THIS AROUND.
WORK YOUR WAY BACK TO WHERE YOU CAME FROM.
REMEMBER THAT YOU'RE IN CONTROL.

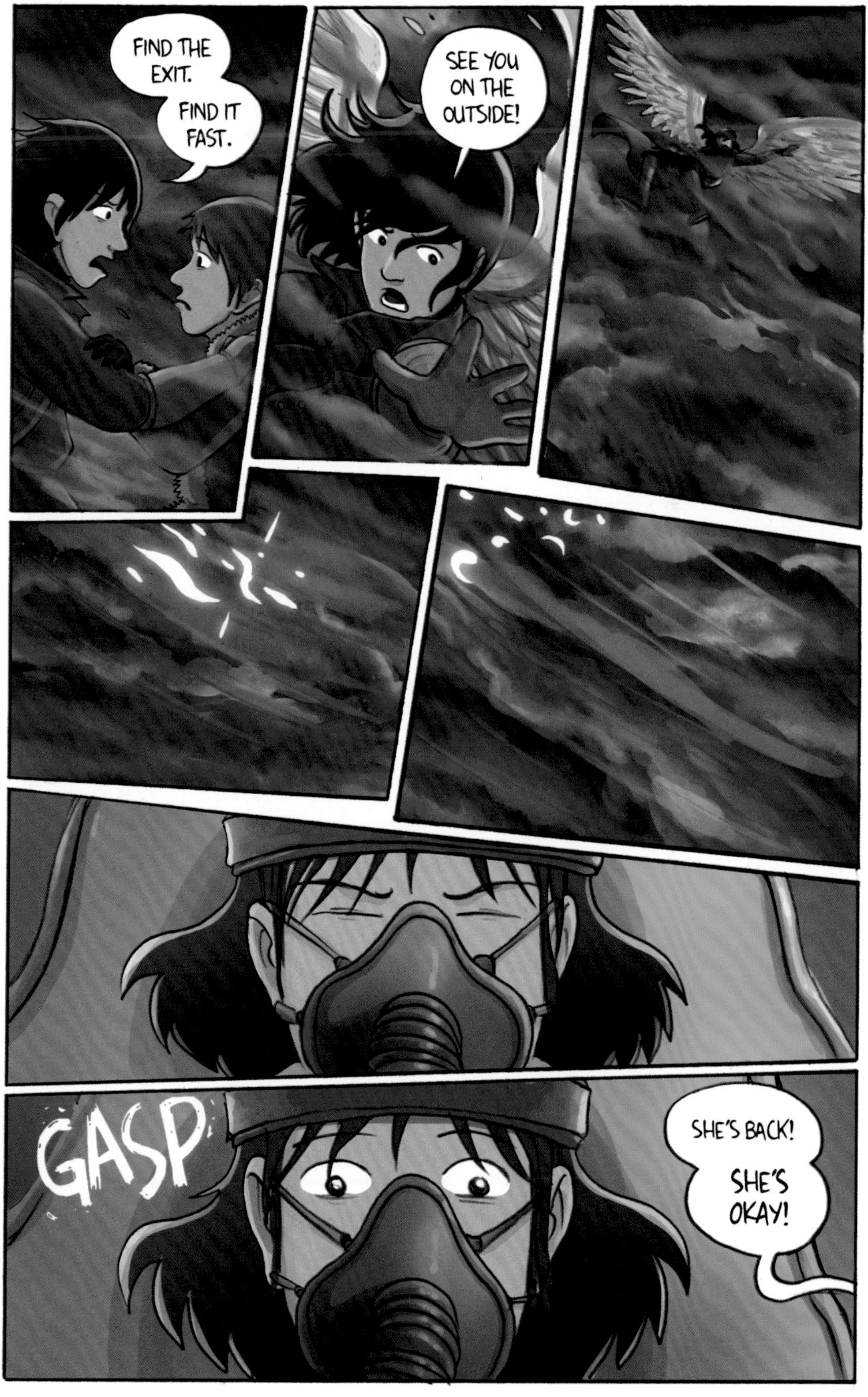
FIND THE EXIT.
FIND IT FAST.
SEE YOU ON THE OUTSIDE!
GASP
SHE'S BACK!
SHE'S OKAY!

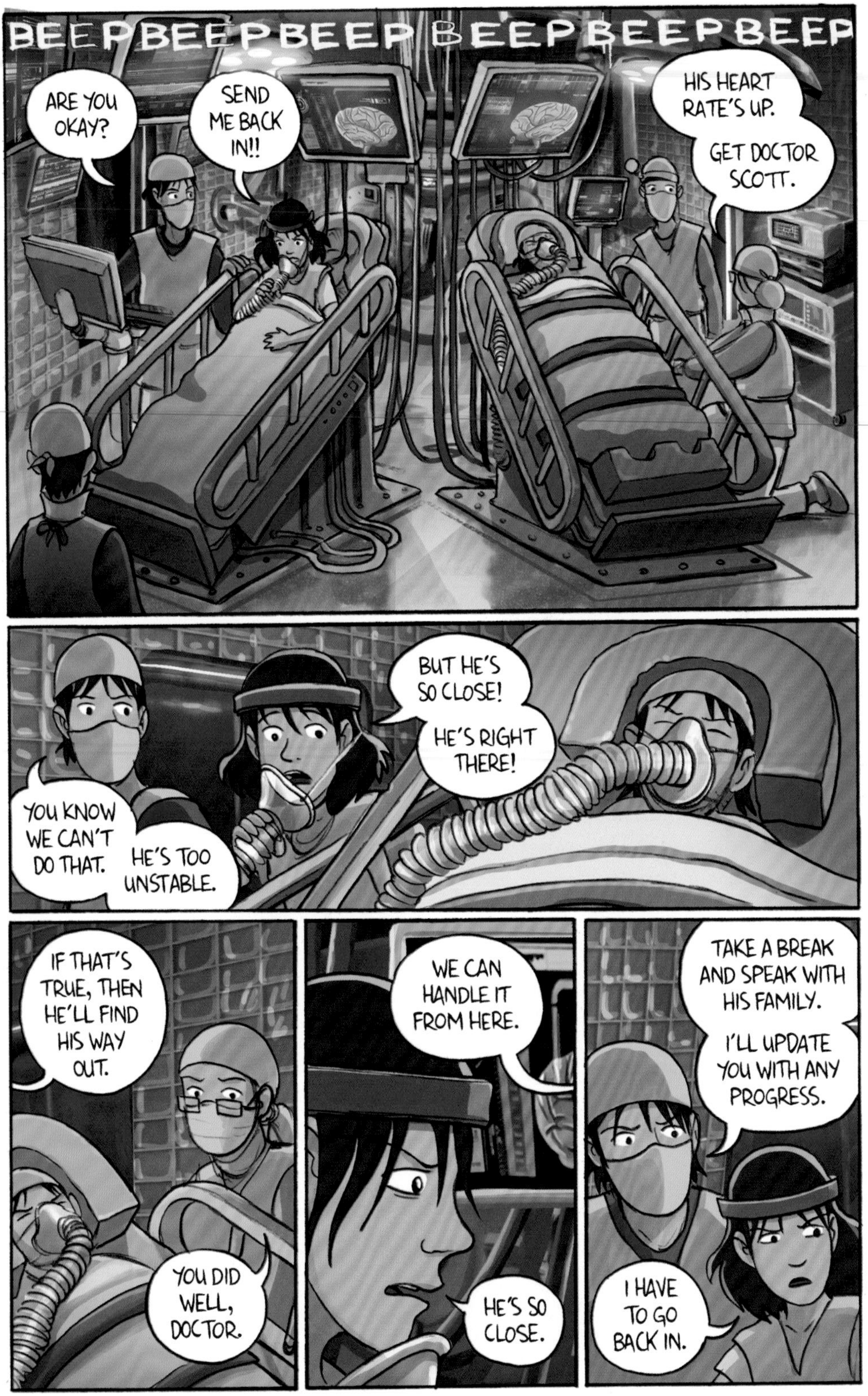
BEEP BEEP BEEP BEEP BEEP BEEP
ARE YOU OKAY?
SEND ME BACK IN!!
HIS HEART RATE'S UP.
GET DOCTOR SCOTT.
YOU KNOW WE CAN'T DO THAT.
HE'S TOO UNSTABLE.
BUT HE'S SO CLOSE!
HE'S RIGHT THERE!
IF THAT'S TRUE, THEN HE'LL FIND HIS WAY OUT.
YOU DID WELL, DOCTOR.
WE CAN HANDLE IT FROM HERE.
HE'S SO CLOSE.
TAKE A BREAK AND SPEAK WITH HIS FAMILY.
I'LL UPDATE YOU WITH ANY PROGRESS.
I HAVE TO GO BACK IN.

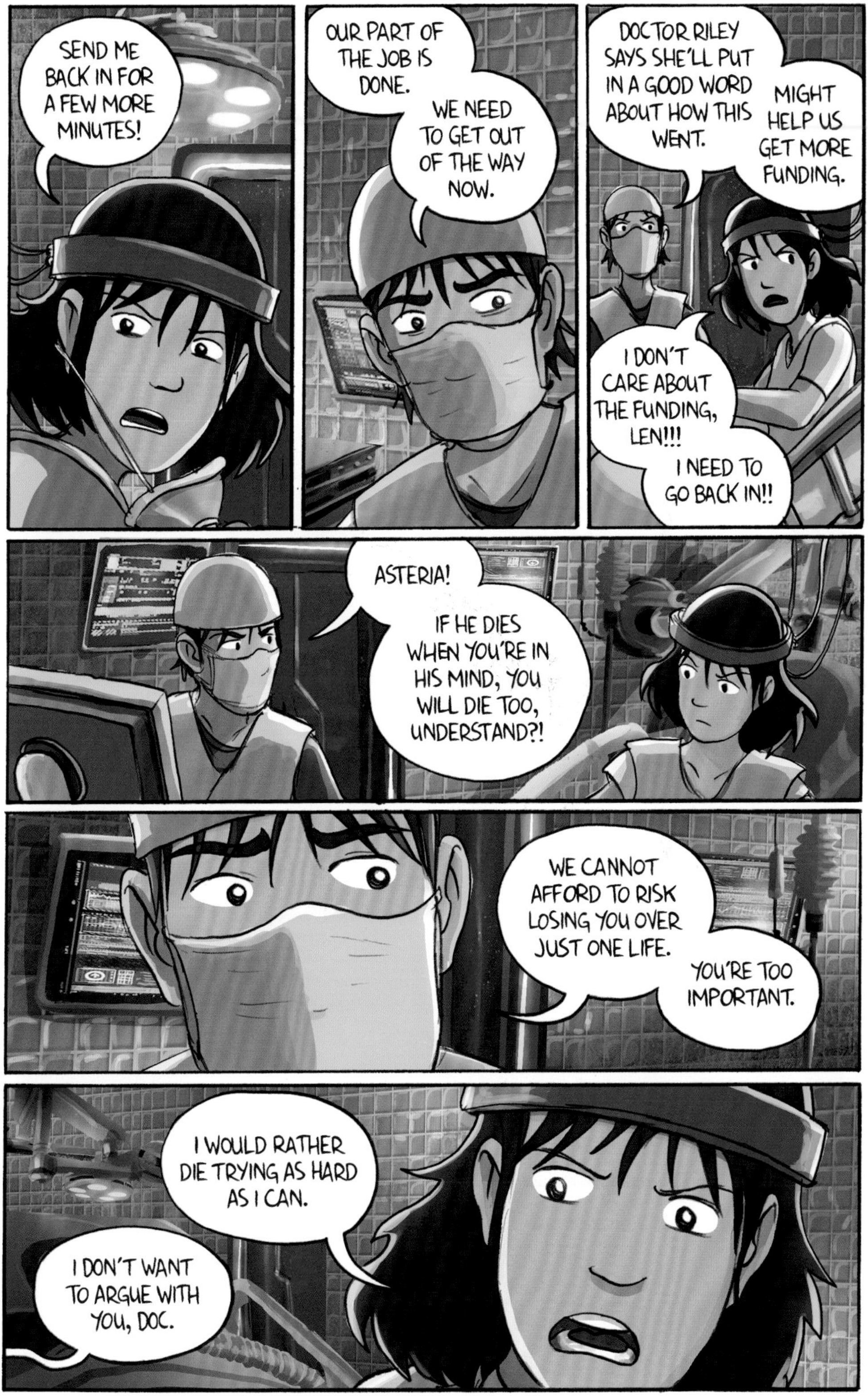

SEND ME BACK IN FOR A FEW MORE MINUTES!
OUR PART OF THE JOB IS DONE.
WE NEED TO GET OUT OF THE WAY NOW.
DOCTOR RILEY SAYS SHE'LL PUT IN A GOOD WORD ABOUT HOW THIS WENT.
MIGHT HELP US GET MORE FUNDING.
I DON'T CARE ABOUT THE FUNDING, LEN!!!
I NEED TO GO BACK IN!!
ASTERIA!
IF HE DIES WHEN YOU'RE IN HIS MIND, YOU WILL DIE TOO, UNDERSTAND?!
WE CANNOT AFFORD TO RISK LOSING YOU OVER JUST ONE LIFE.
YOU'RE TOO IMPORTANT.
I WOULD RATHER DIE TRYING AS HARD AS I CAN.
I DON'T WANT TO ARGUE WITH YOU, DOC.

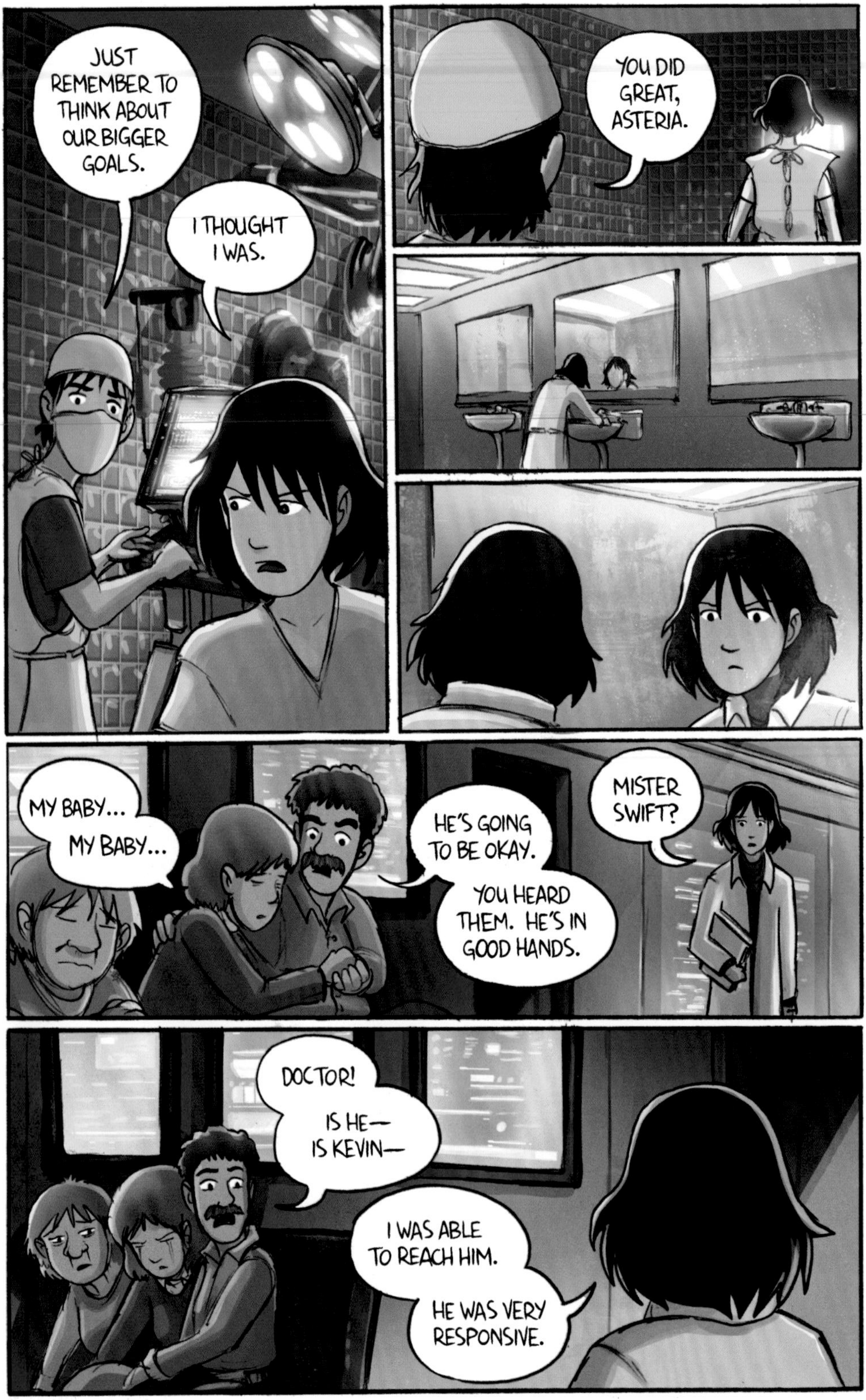
JUST REMEMBER TO THINK ABOUT OUR BIGGER GOALS.
I THOUGHT I WAS.
YOU DID GREAT, ASTERIA.
MY BABY... MY BABY...
HE'S GOING TO BE OKAY.
YOU HEARD THEM. HE'S IN GOOD HANDS.
MISTER SWIFT?
DOCTOR!
IS HE— IS KEVIN—
I WAS ABLE TO REACH HIM.
HE WAS VERY RESPONSIVE.

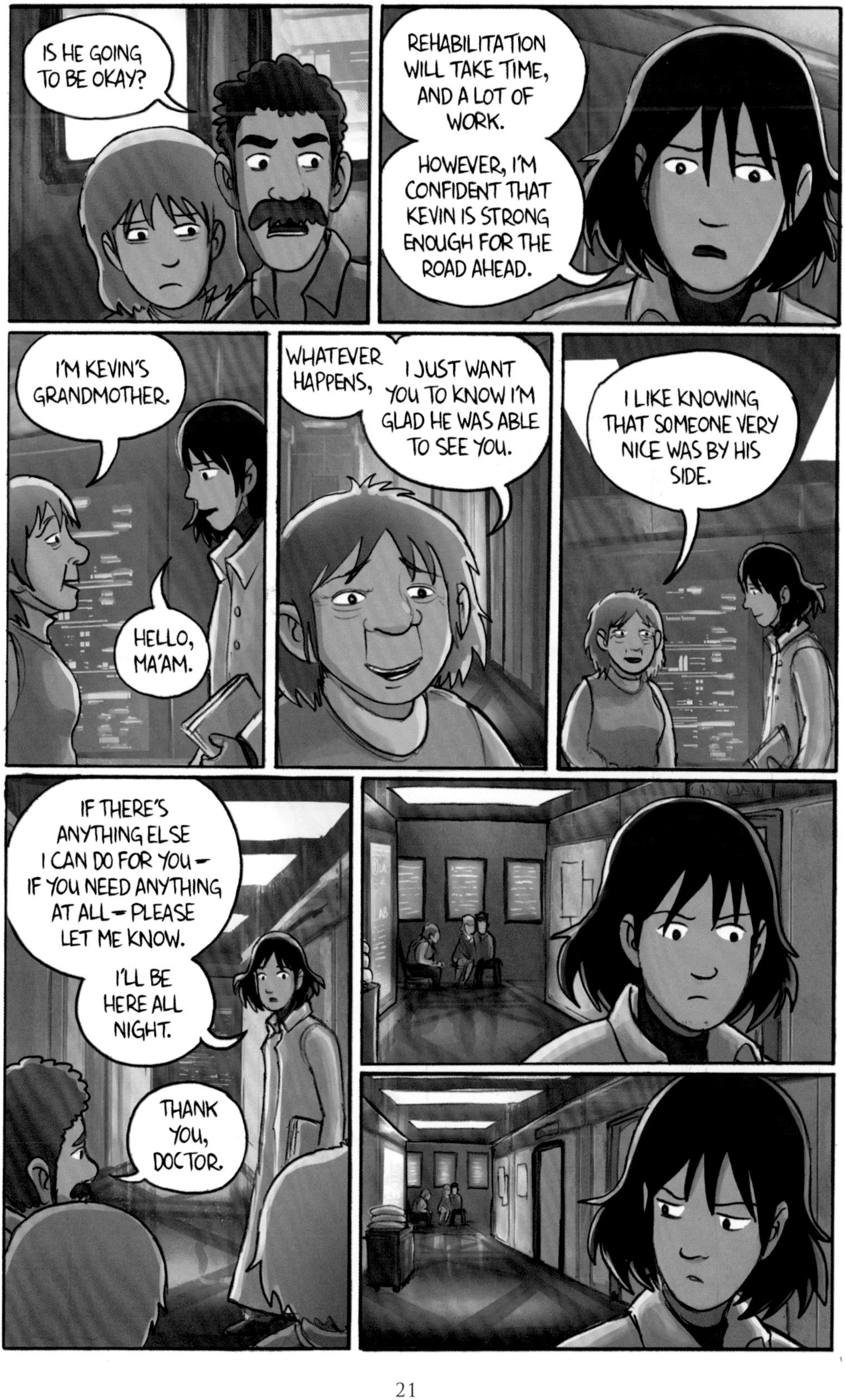
IS HE GOING TO BE OKAY?
REHABILITATION WILL TAKE TIME, AND A LOT OF WORK.
HOWEVER, I'M CONFIDENT THAT KEVIN IS STRONG ENOUGH FOR THE ROAD AHEAD.
I'M KEVIN'S GRANDMOTHER.
HELLO, MA'AM.
WHATEVER HAPPENS,
I JUST WANT YOU TO KNOW I'M GLAD HE WAS ABLE TO SEE YOU.
I LIKE KNOWING THAT SOMEONE VERY NICE WAS BY HIS SIDE.
IF THERE'S ANYTHING ELSE I CAN DO FOR YOU — IF YOU NEED ANYTHING AT ALL — PLEASE LET ME KNOW.
I'LL BE HERE ALL NIGHT.
THANK YOU, DOCTOR.

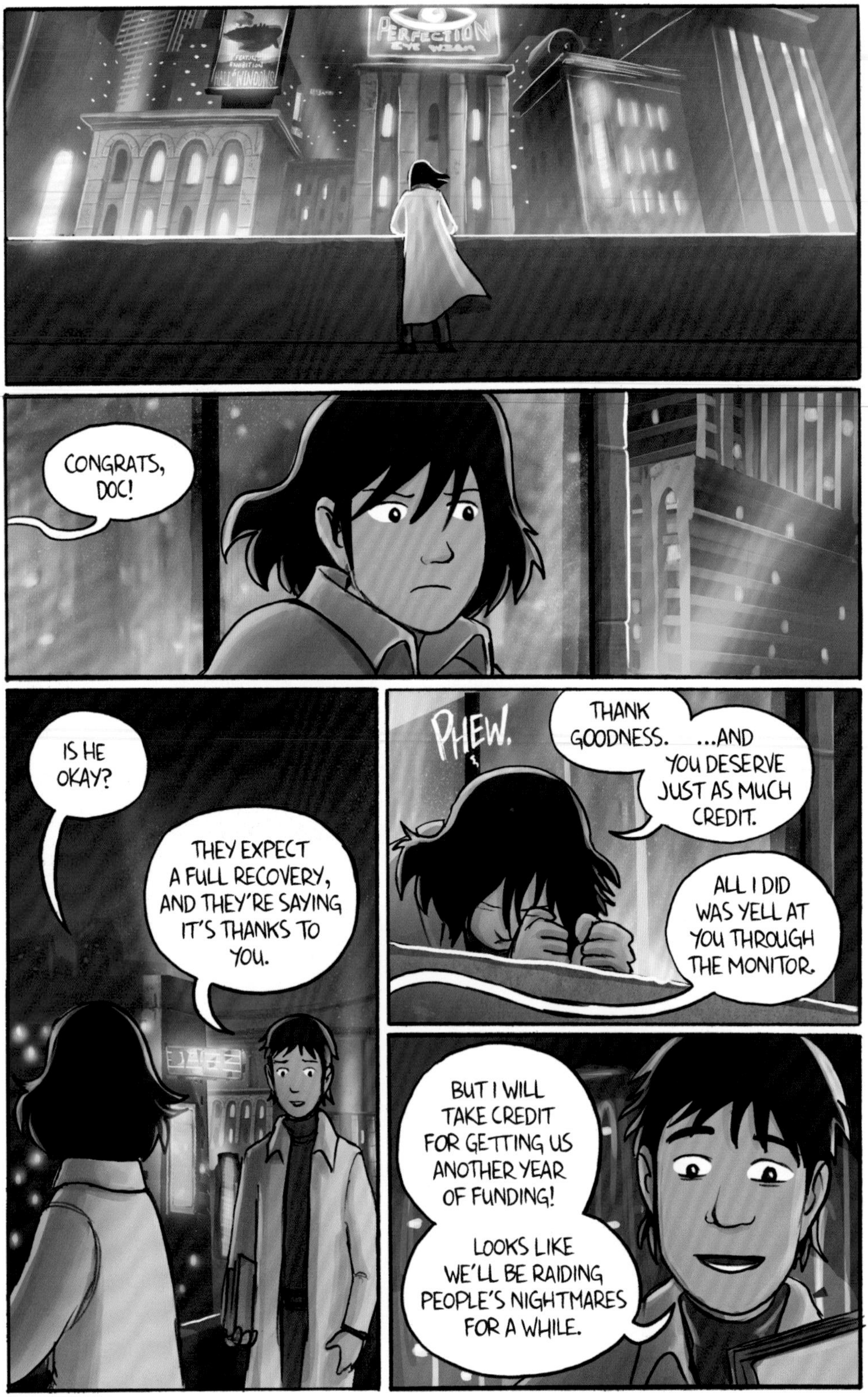
PERFECTION EYE WEAR
HALL OF WINDOWS
CONGRATS, DOC!
IS HE OKAY?
THEY EXPECT A FULL RECOVERY, AND THEY'RE SAYING IT'S THANKS TO YOU.
PHEW.
THANK GOODNESS. ...AND YOU DESERVE JUST AS MUCH CREDIT.
ALL I DID WAS YELL AT YOU THROUGH THE MONITOR.
BUT I WILL TAKE CREDIT FOR GETTING US ANOTHER YEAR OF FUNDING!
LOOKS LIKE WE'LL BE RAIDING PEOPLE'S NIGHTMARES FOR A WHILE.

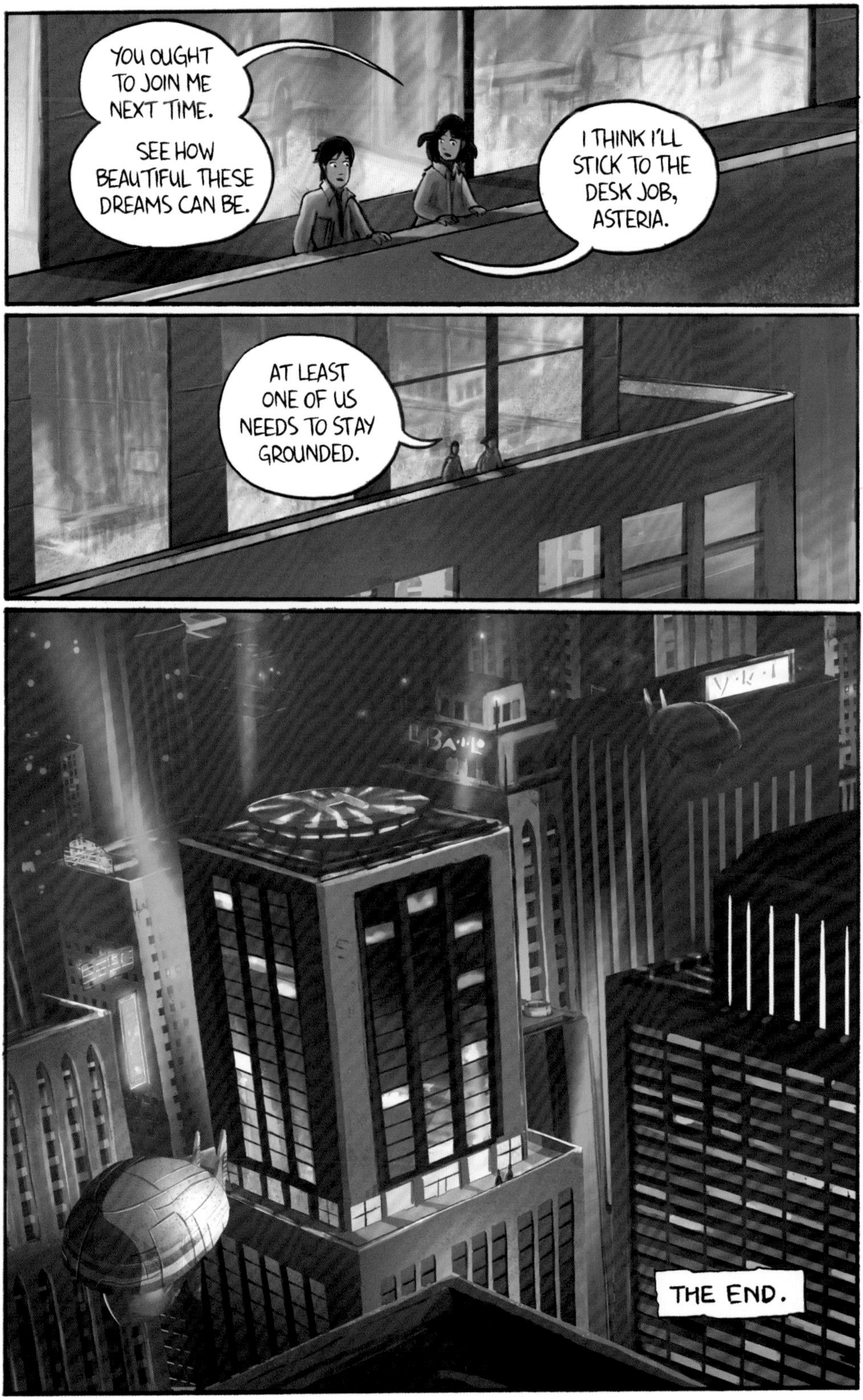
YOU OUGHT TO JOIN ME NEXT TIME.
SEE HOW BEAUTIFUL THESE DREAMS CAN BE.
I THINK I'LL STICK TO THE DESK JOB, ASTERIA.
AT LEAST ONE OF US NEEDS TO STAY GROUNDED.
THE END.

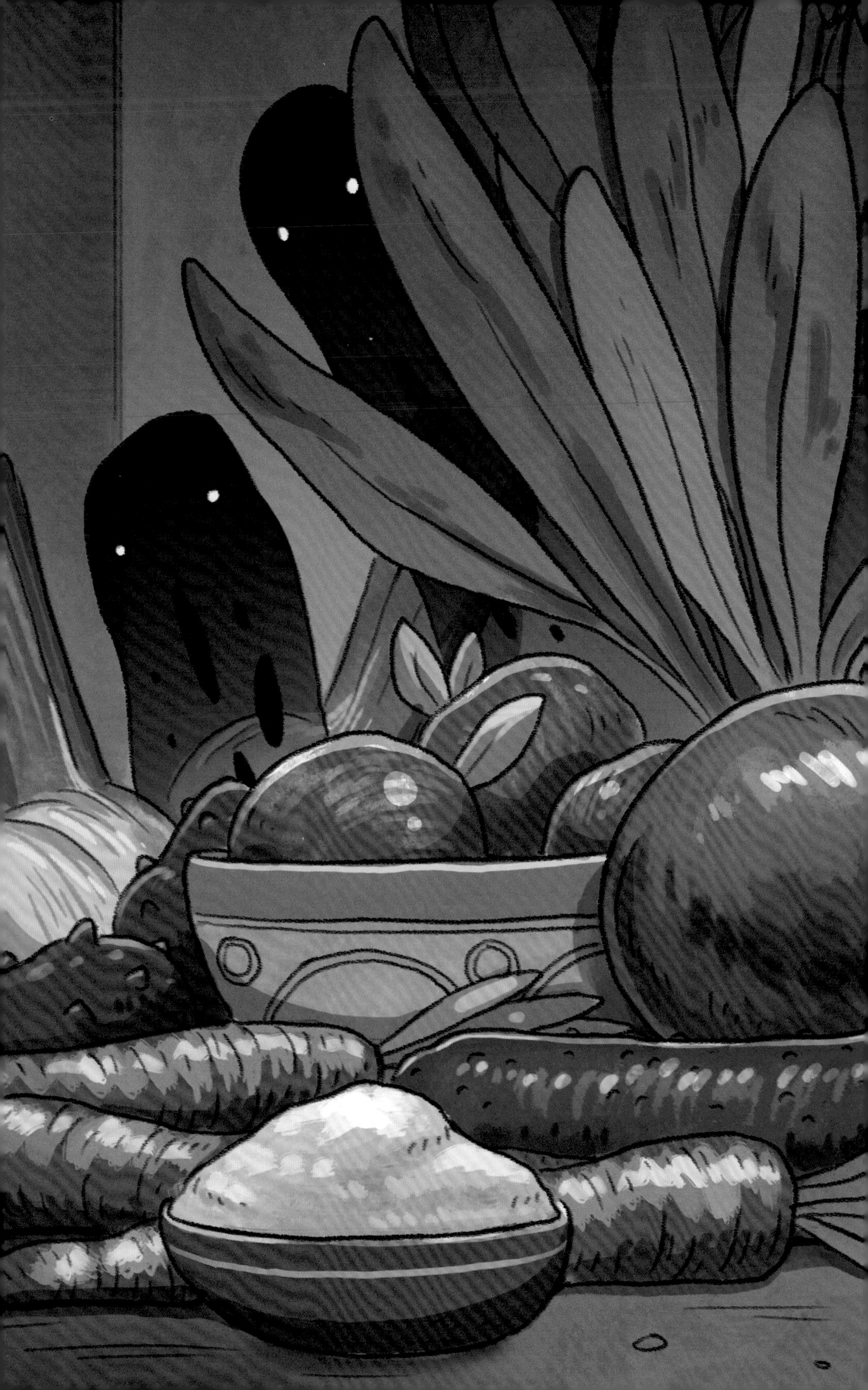

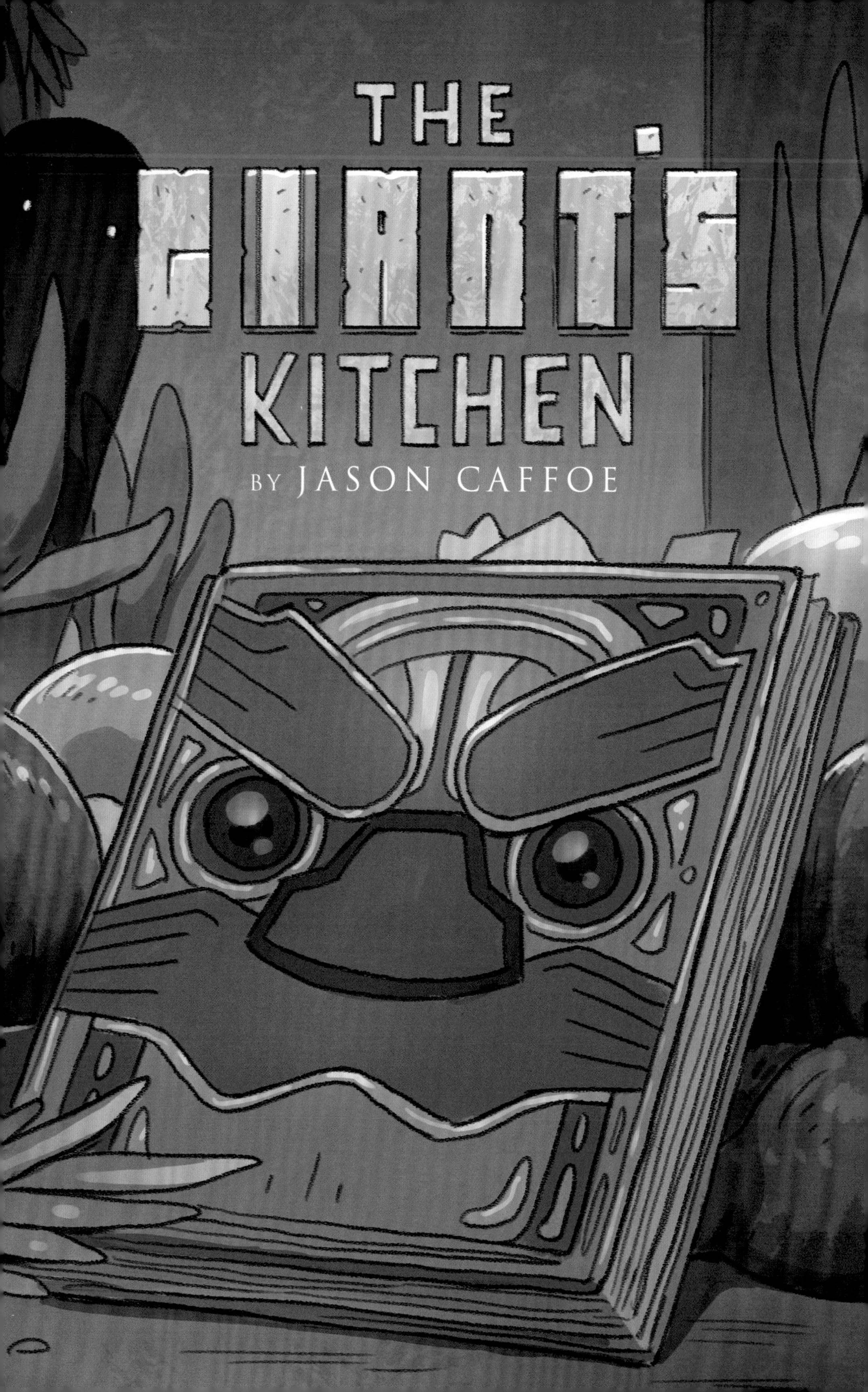
THE GIANT'S KITCHEN
BY JASON CAFFOE

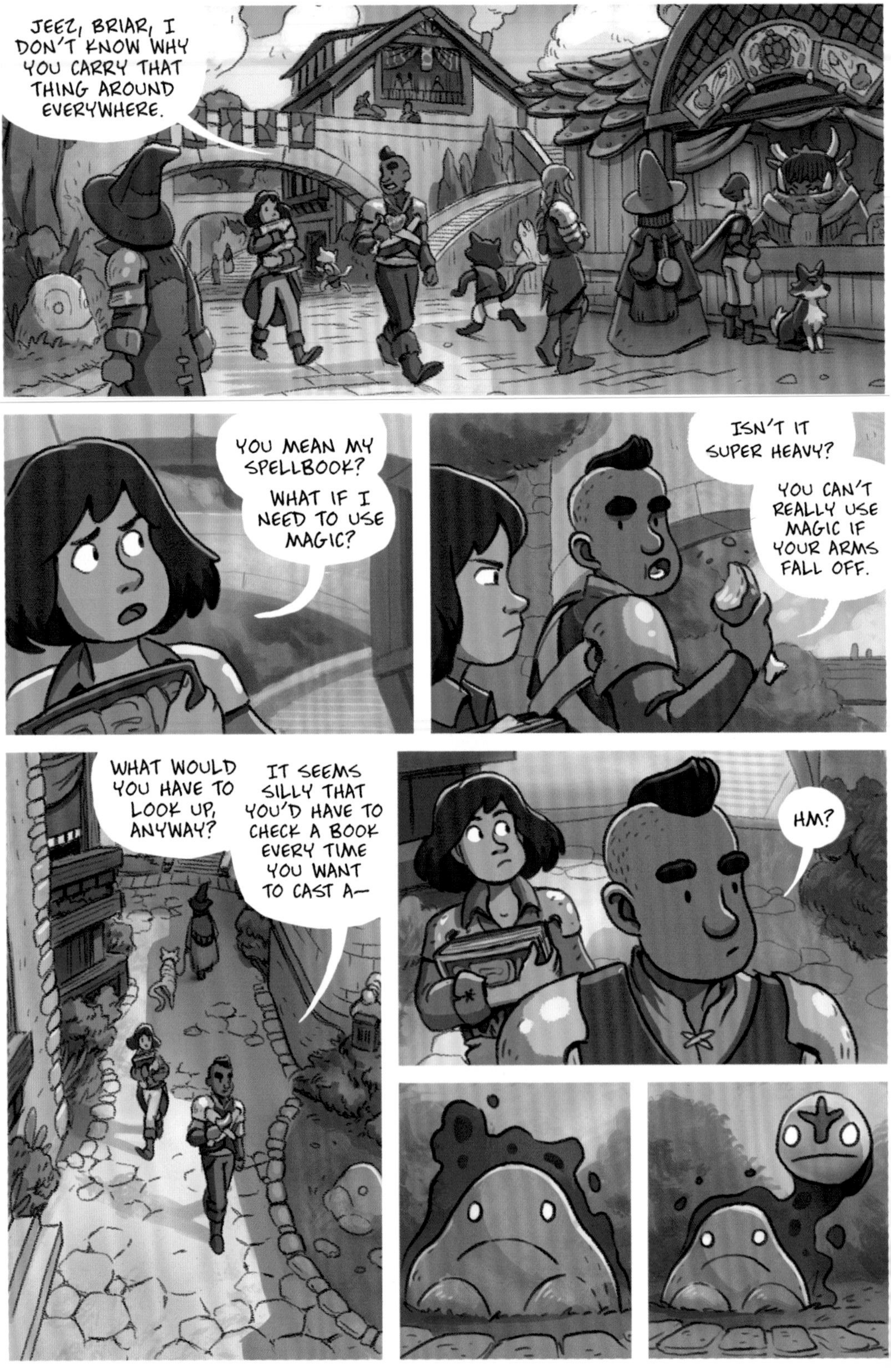
JEEZ, BRIAR, I DON'T KNOW WHY YOU CARRY THAT THING AROUND EVERYWHERE.
YOU MEAN MY SPELLBOOK?
WHAT IF I NEED TO USE MAGIC?
ISN'T IT SUPER HEAVY?
YOU CAN'T REALLY USE MAGIC IF YOUR ARMS FALL OFF.
WHAT WOULD YOU HAVE TO LOOK UP, ANYWAY?
IT SEEMS SILLY THAT YOU'D HAVE TO CHECK A BOOK EVERY TIME YOU WANT TO CAST A—
HM?

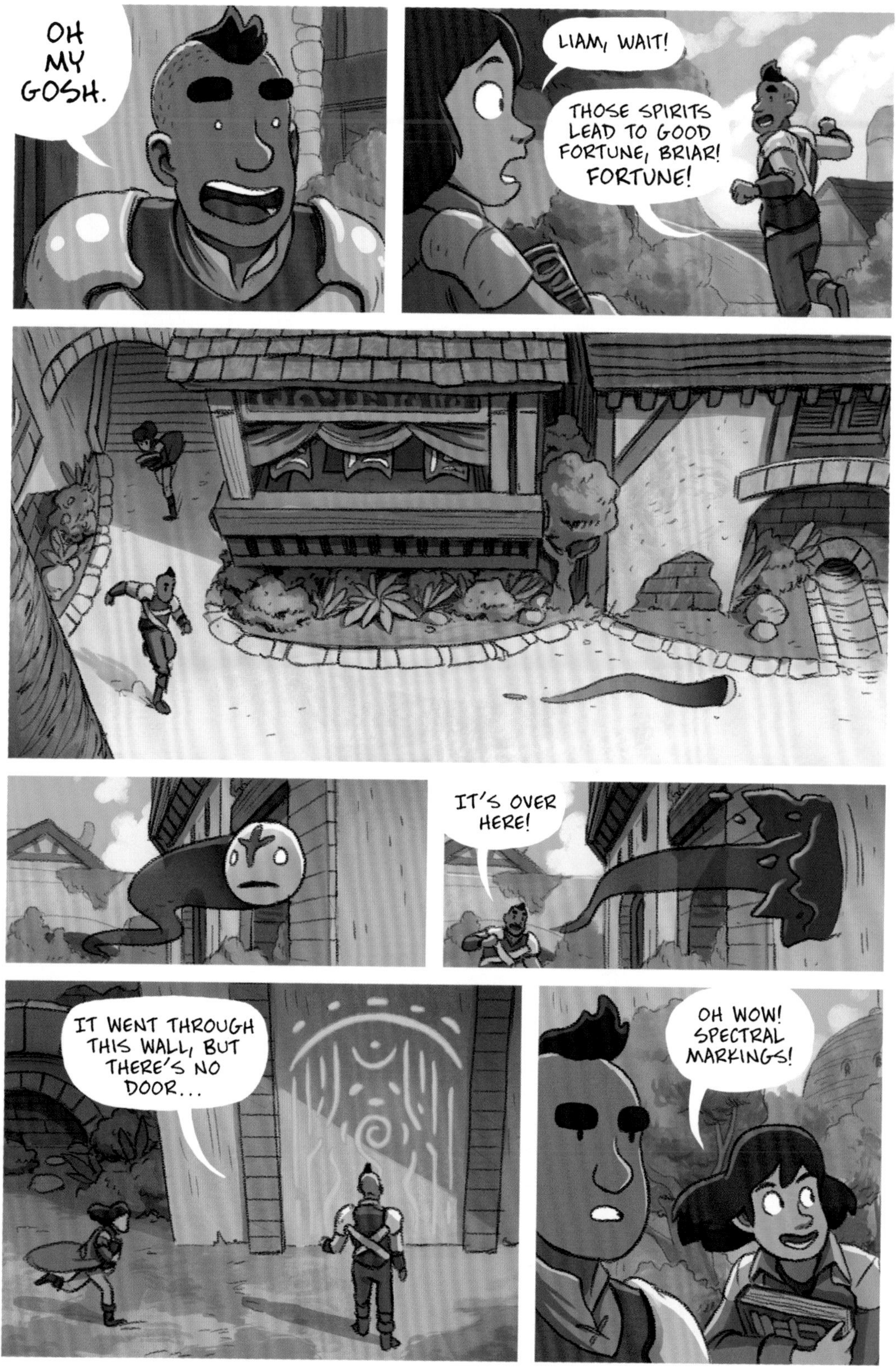
OH MY GOSH.
LIAM, WAIT!
THOSE SPIRITS LEAD TO GOOD FORTUNE, BRIAR! FORTUNE!
IT'S OVER HERE!
IT WENT THROUGH THIS WALL, BUT THERE'S NO DOOR...
OH WOW! SPECTRAL MARKINGS!

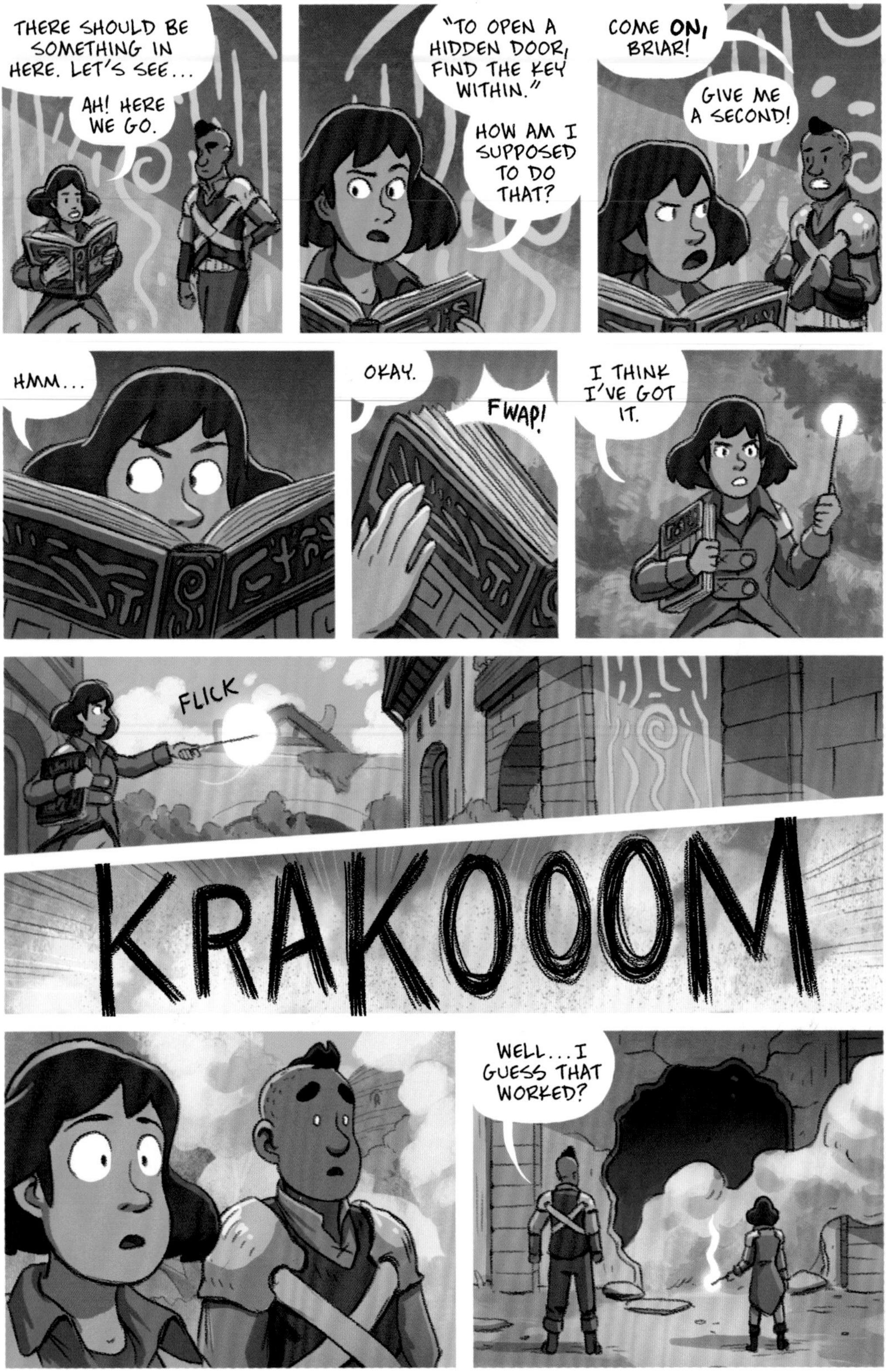
THERE SHOULD BE SOMETHING IN HERE. LET'S SEE...
AH! HERE WE GO.
"TO OPEN A HIDDEN DOOR, FIND THE KEY WITHIN."
HOW AM I SUPPOSED TO DO THAT?
COME ON, BRIAR!
GIVE ME A SECOND!
HMM...
OKAY.
FWAP!
I THINK I'VE GOT IT.
FLICK
KRAKOOOM
WELL... I GUESS THAT WORKED?

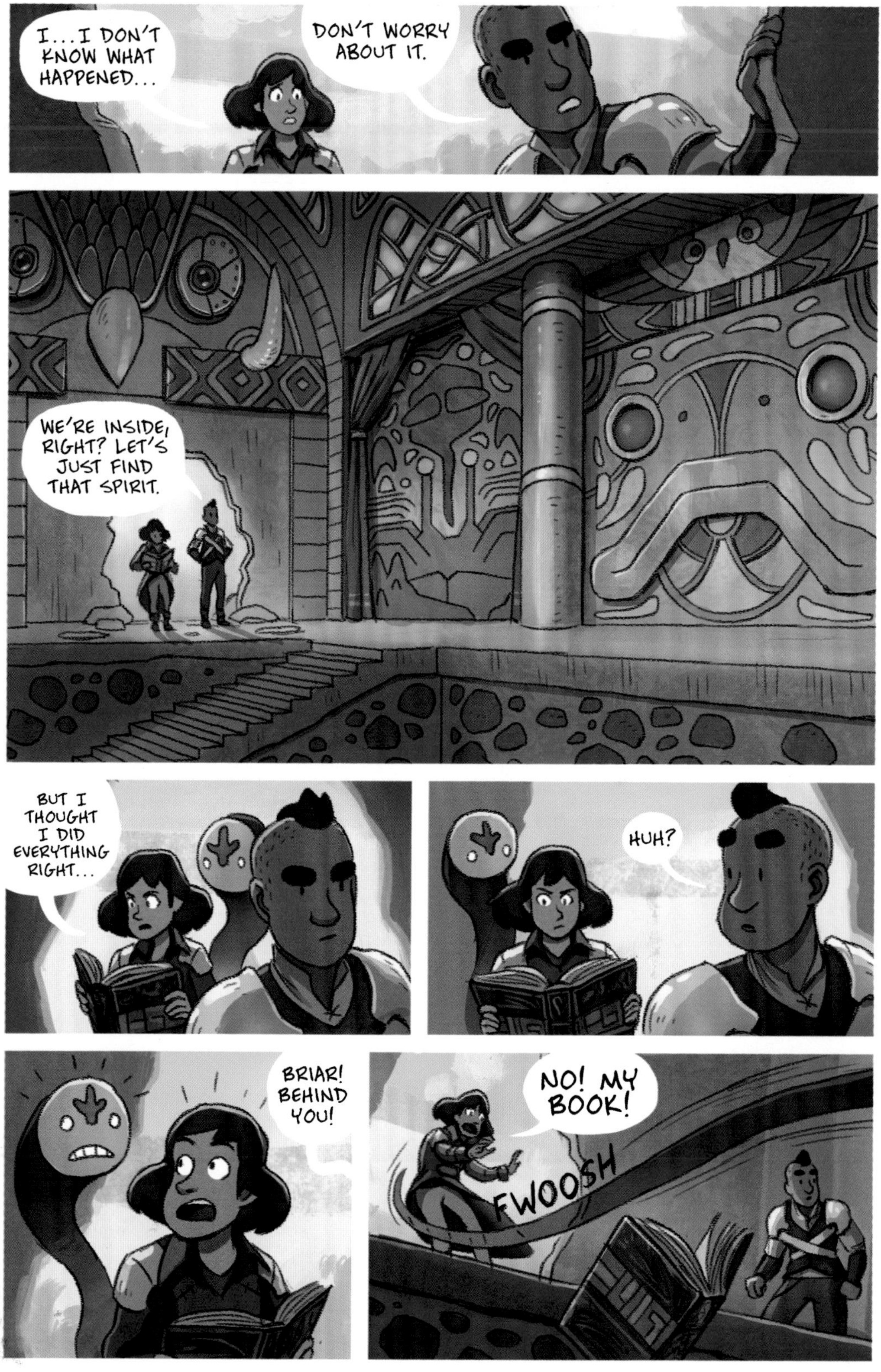

I...I DON'T KNOW WHAT HAPPENED...
DON'T WORRY ABOUT IT.
WE'RE INSIDE, RIGHT? LET'S JUST FIND THAT SPIRIT.
BUT I THOUGHT I DID EVERYTHING RIGHT...
HUH?
BRIAR! BEHIND YOU!
NO! MY BOOK!
FWOOSH

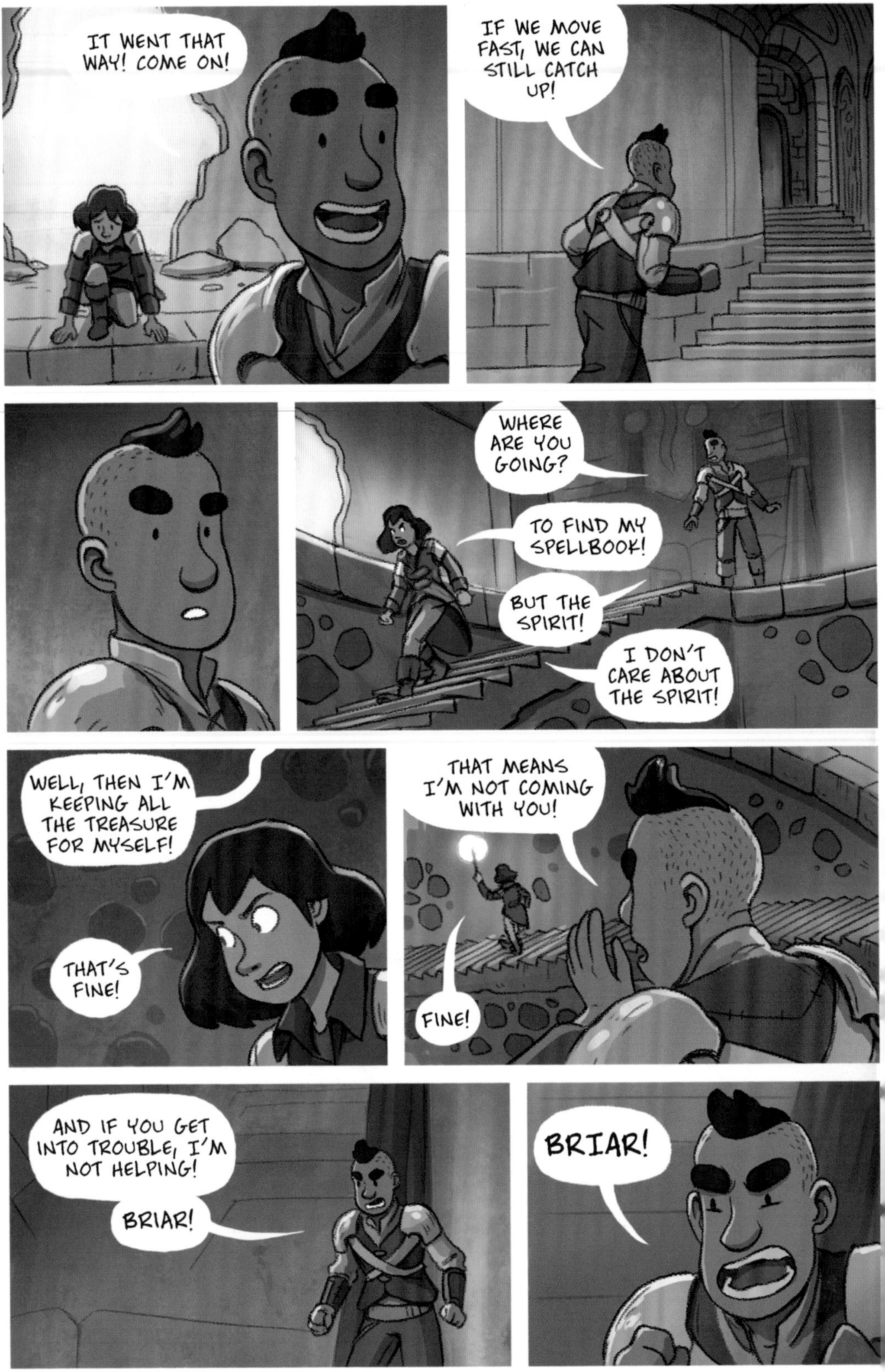
IT WENT THAT WAY! COME ON!
IF WE MOVE FAST, WE CAN STILL CATCH UP!
WHERE ARE YOU GOING?
TO FIND MY SPELLBOOK!
BUT THE SPIRIT!
I DON'T CARE ABOUT THE SPIRIT!
WELL, THEN I'M KEEPING ALL THE TREASURE FOR MYSELF!
THAT'S FINE!
THAT MEANS I'M NOT COMING WITH YOU!
FINE!
AND IF YOU GET INTO TROUBLE, I'M NOT HELPING!
BRIAR!
BRIAR!

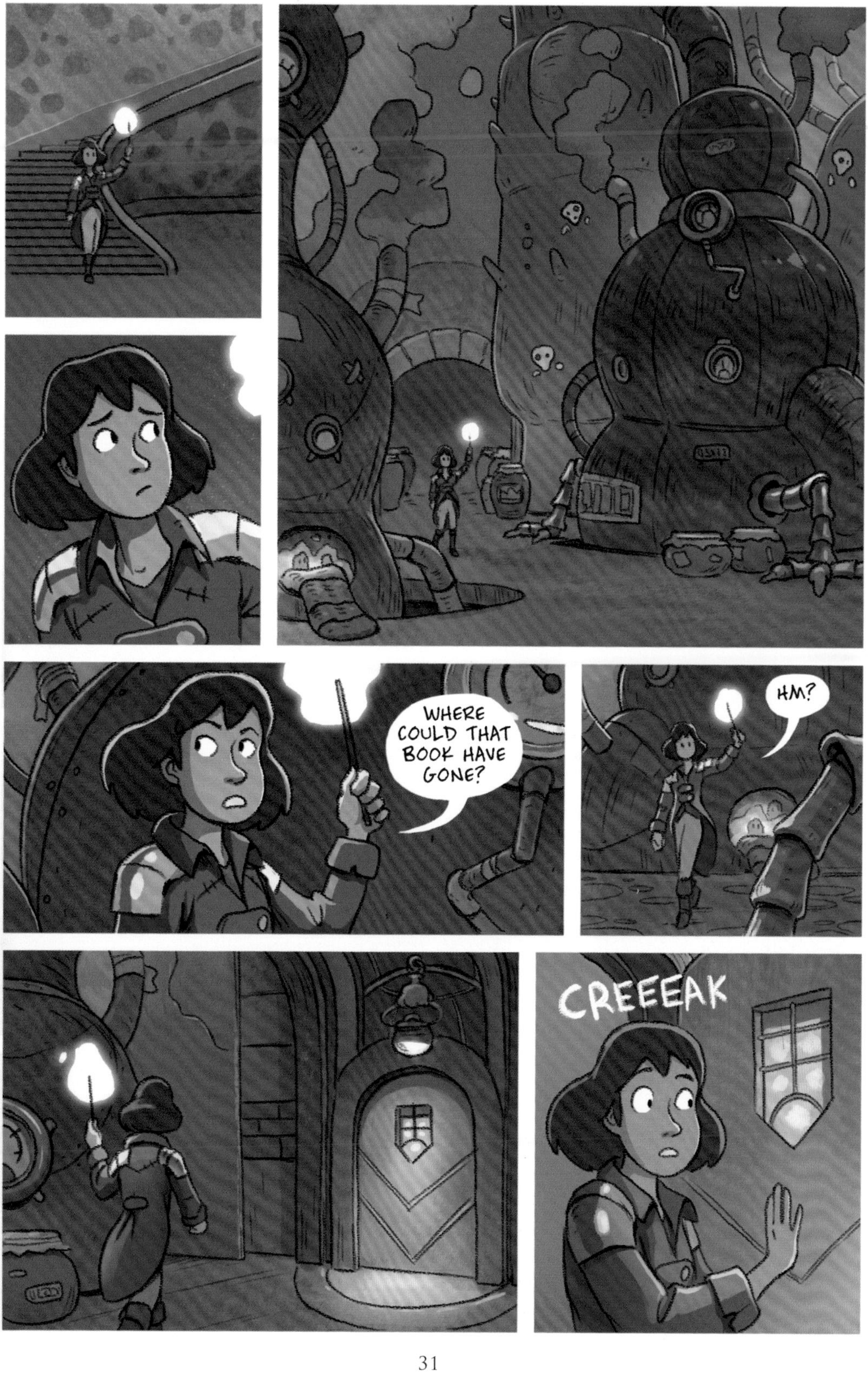
WHERE COULD THAT BOOK HAVE GONE?
HM?
CREEEAK

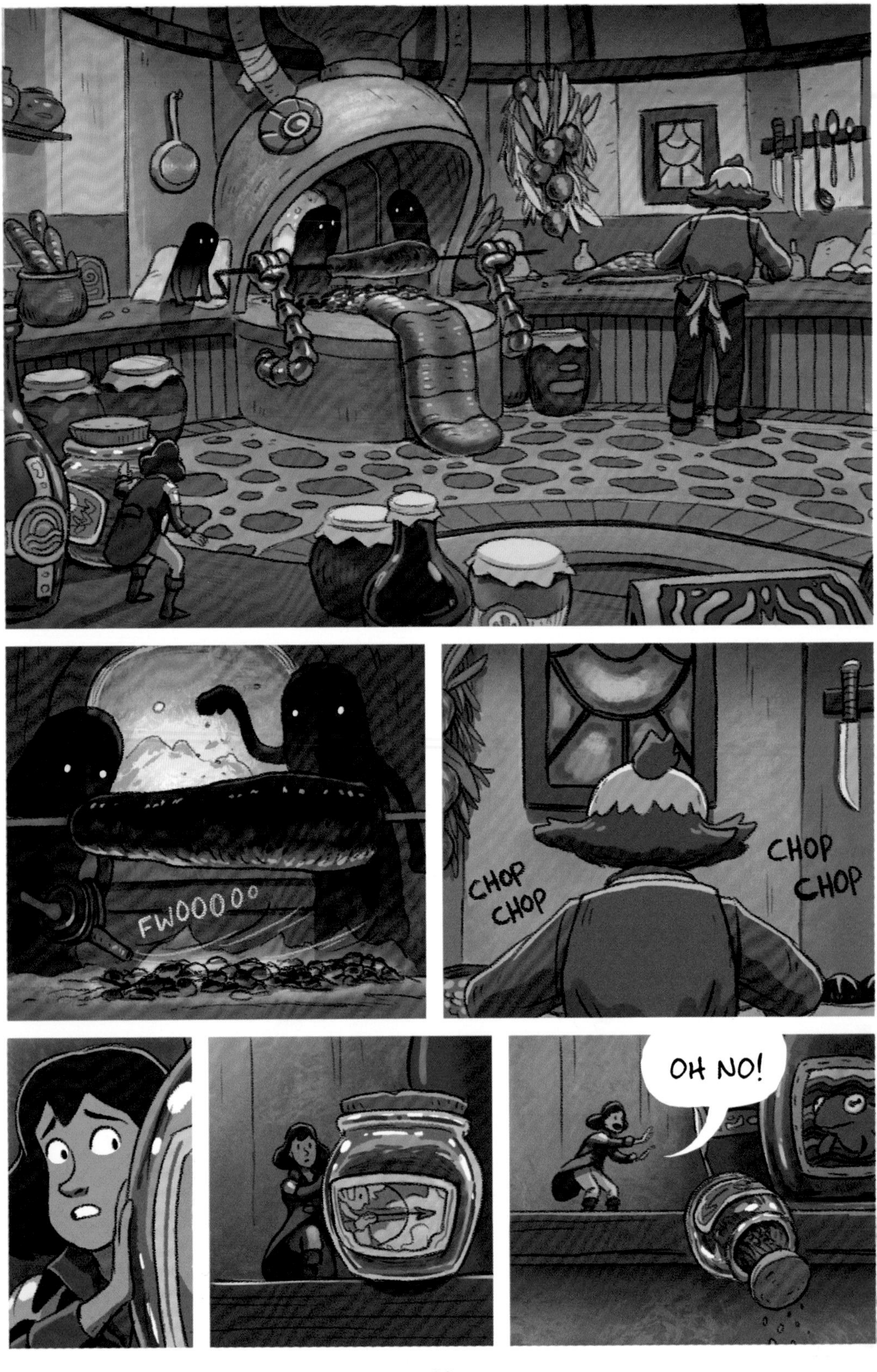
FWOOOOO
CHOP CHOP
CHOP CHOP
OH NO!

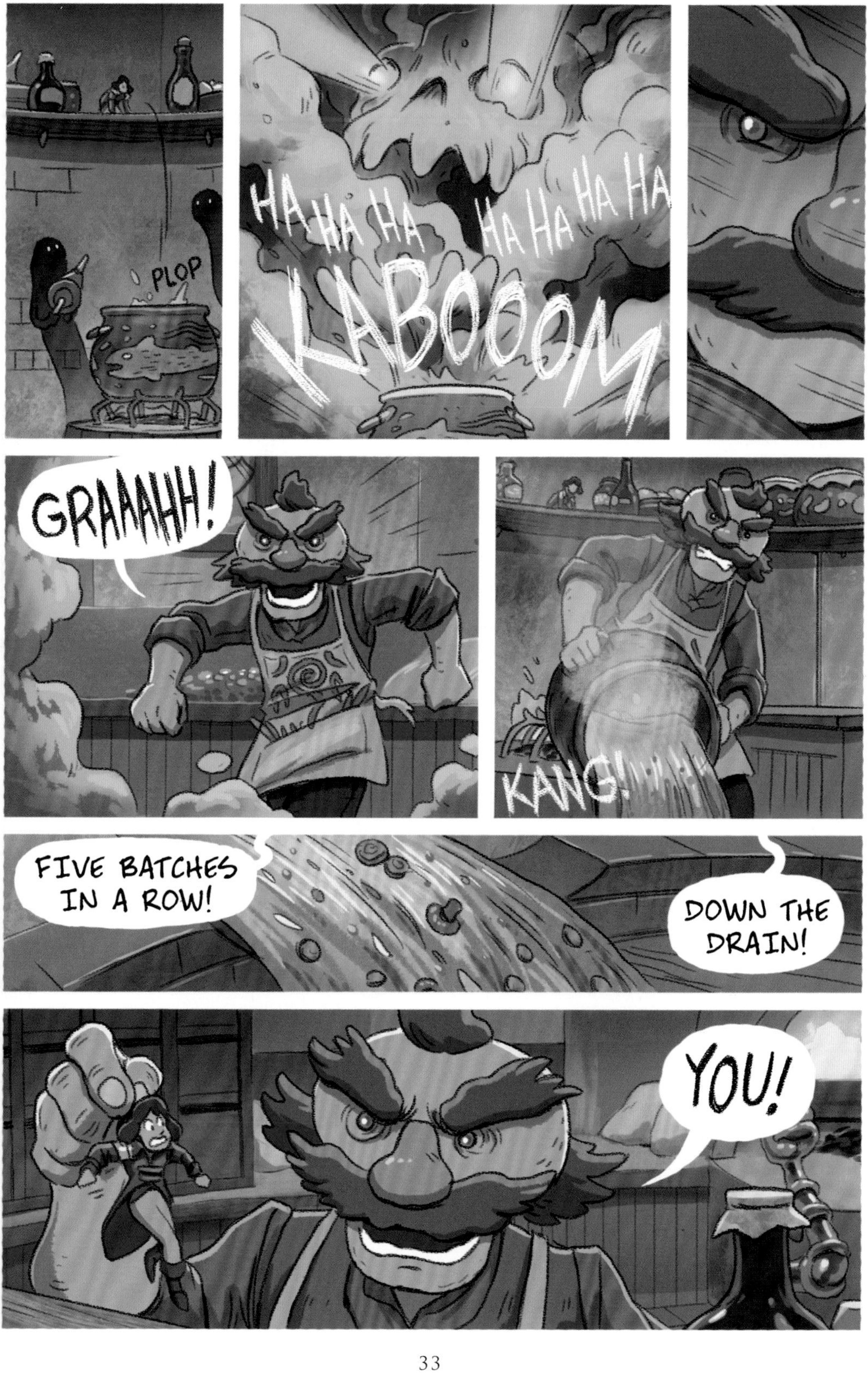
PLOP
HA HA HA
HA HA HA HA
KABOOOM
GRAAAHH!
KANG!
FIVE BATCHES IN A ROW!
DOWN THE DRAIN!
YOU!

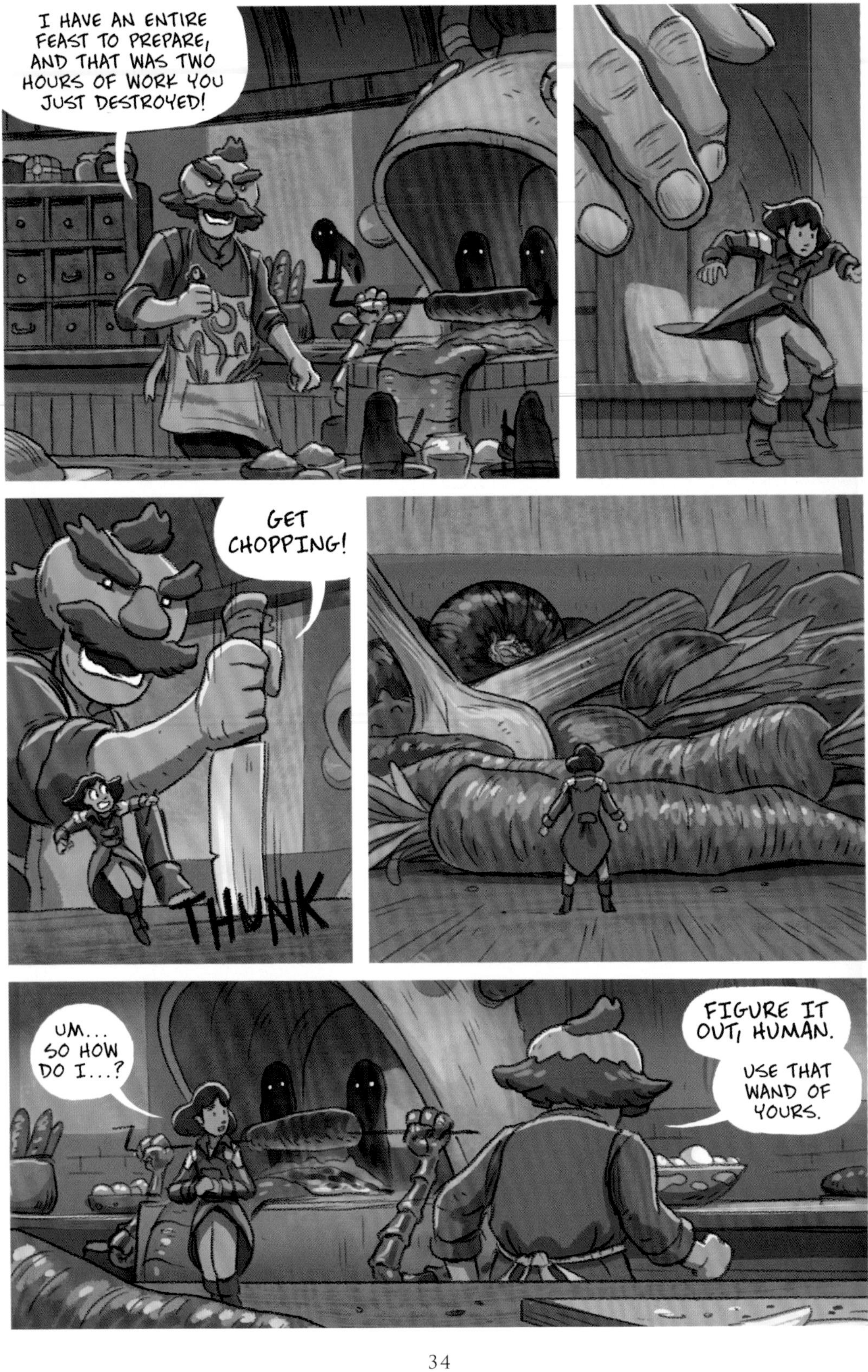
I HAVE AN ENTIRE FEAST TO PREPARE, AND THAT WAS TWO HOURS OF WORK YOU JUST DESTROYED!
GET CHOPPING!
THUNK
UM... SO HOW DO I...?
FIGURE IT OUT, HUMAN.
USE THAT WAND OF YOURS.

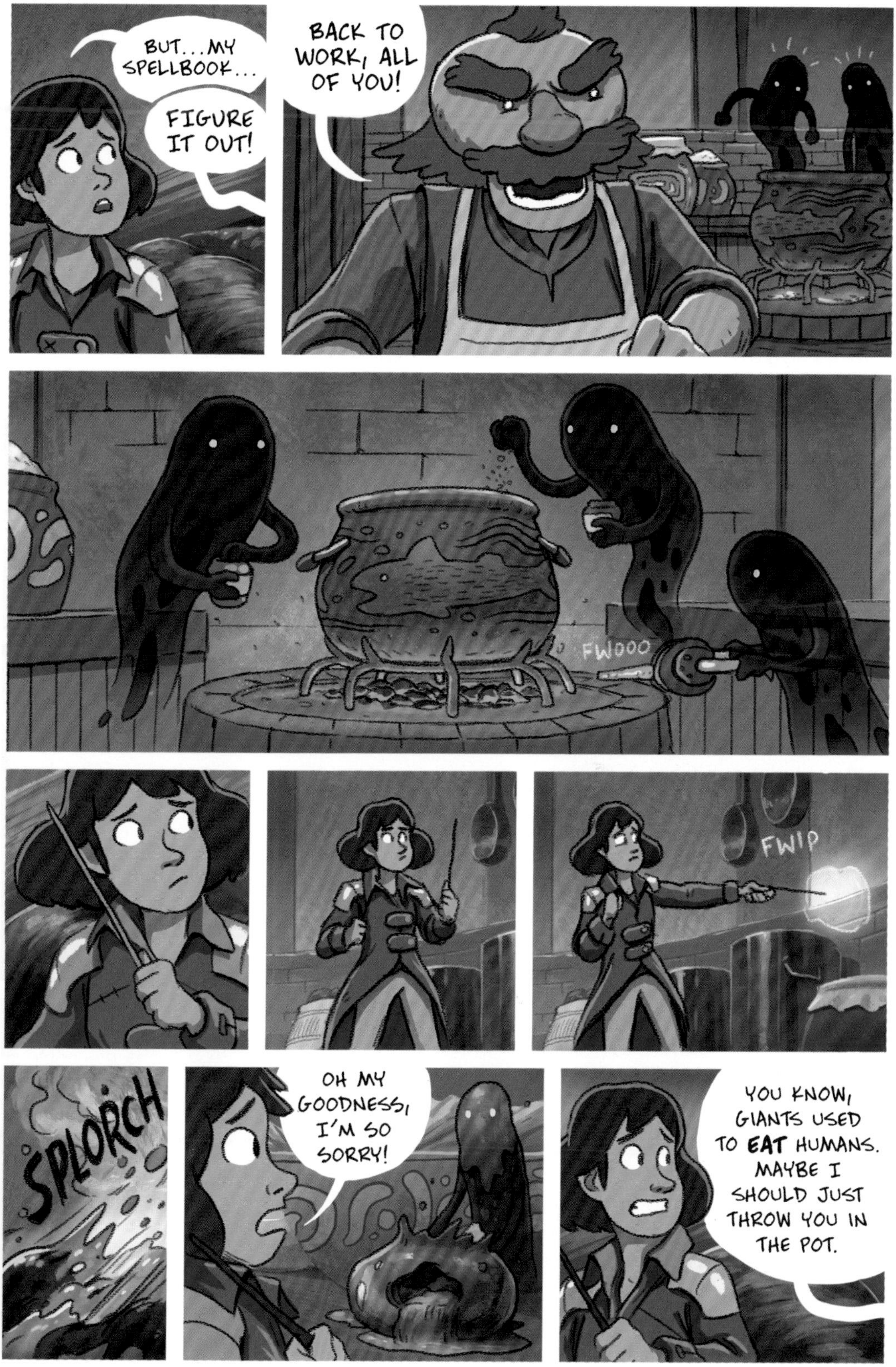
BUT...MY SPELLBOOK...
FIGURE IT OUT!
BACK TO WORK, ALL OF YOU!
FWOOO
FWIP
SPLORCH
OH MY GOODNESS, I'M SO SORRY!
YOU KNOW, GIANTS USED TO EAT HUMANS. MAYBE I SHOULD JUST THROW YOU IN THE POT.

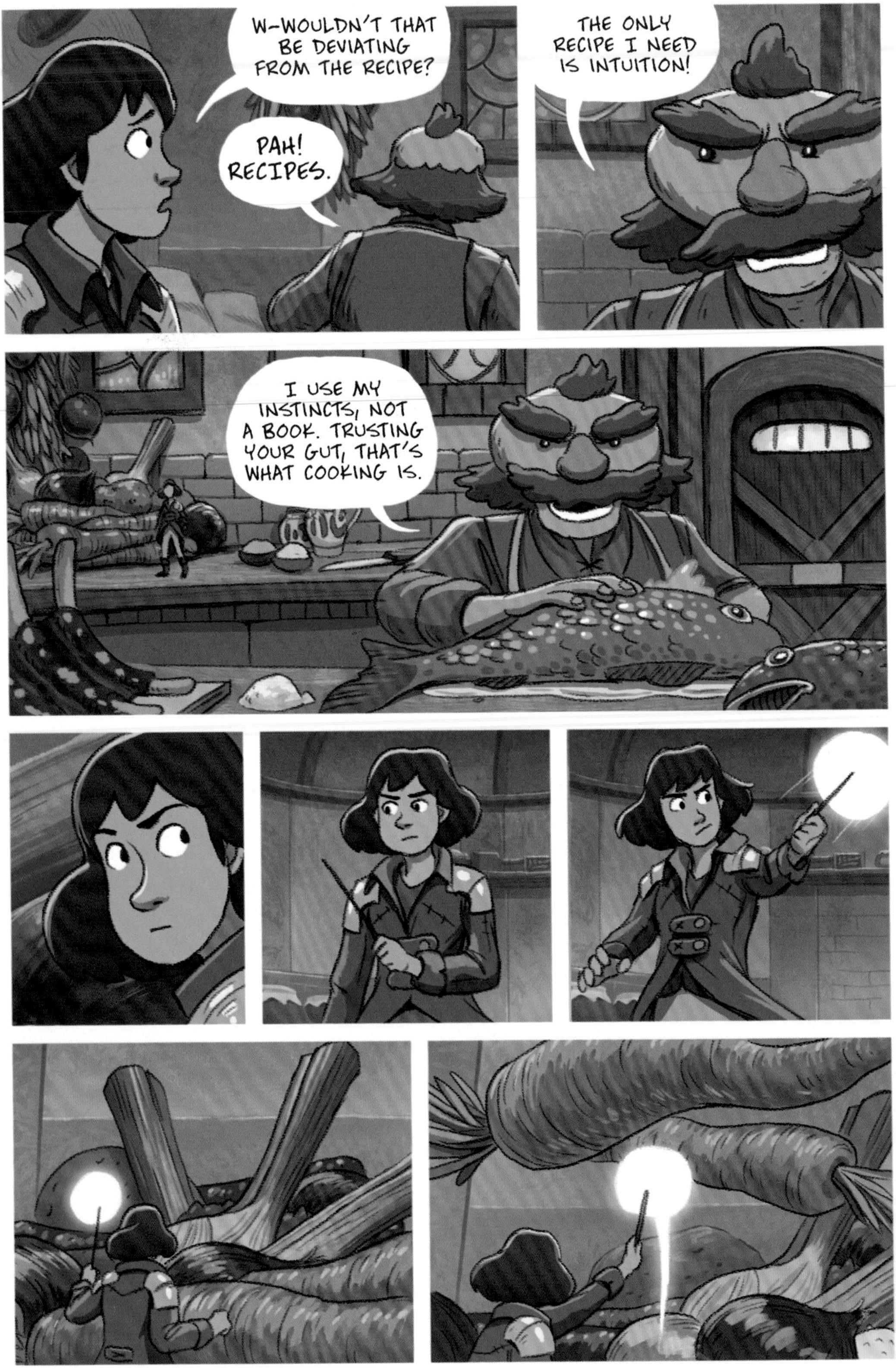

W-WOULDN'T THAT BE DEVIATING FROM THE RECIPE?
PAH! RECIPES.
THE ONLY RECIPE I NEED IS INTUITION!
I USE MY INSTINCTS, NOT A BOOK. TRUSTING YOUR GUT, THAT'S WHAT COOKING IS.

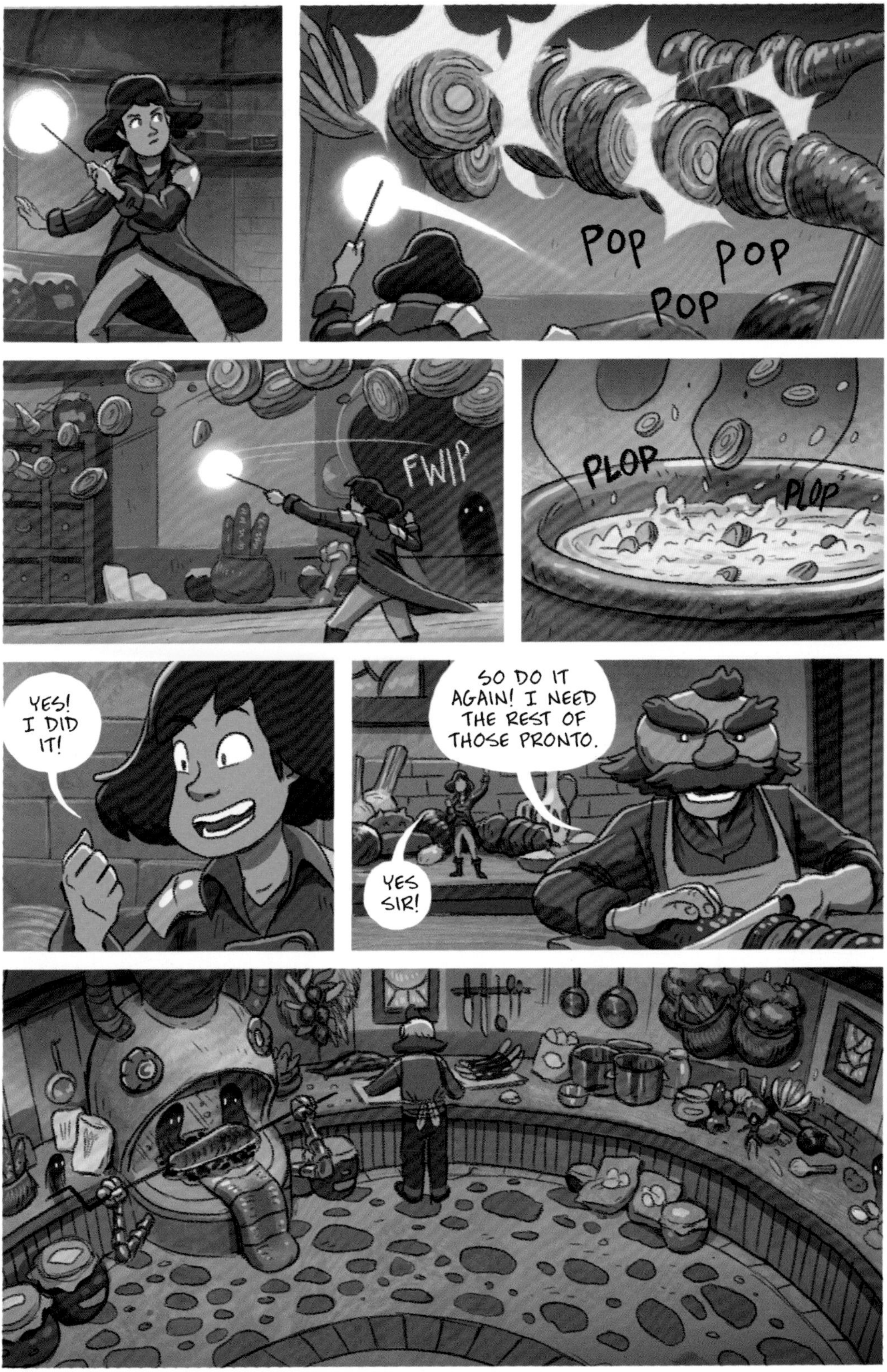
POP
POP
POP
FWIP
PLOP
PLOP
YES! I DID IT!
SO DO IT AGAIN! I NEED THE REST OF THOSE PRONTO.
YES SIR!

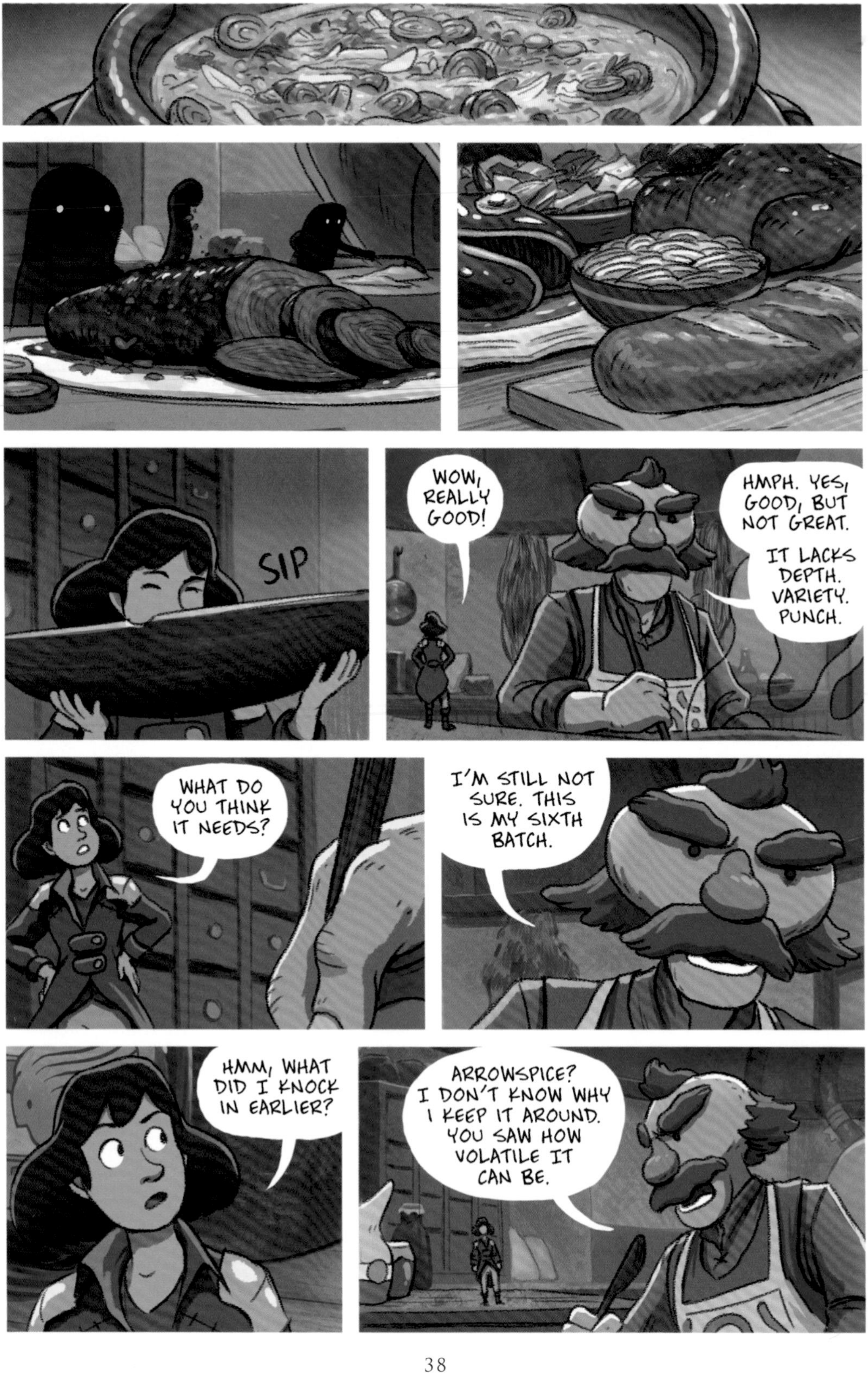
SIP
WOW, REALLY GOOD!
HMPH. YES, GOOD, BUT NOT GREAT.
IT LACKS DEPTH. VARIETY. PUNCH.
WHAT DO YOU THINK IT NEEDS?
I'M STILL NOT SURE. THIS IS MY SIXTH BATCH.
HMM, WHAT DID I KNOCK IN EARLIER?
ARROWSPICE? I DON'T KNOW WHY I KEEP IT AROUND. YOU SAW HOW VOLATILE IT CAN BE.

WELL, I KNOW IT SUMMONED A GIANT LAUGHING SKULL, BUT I THOUGHT IT SMELLED PRETTY GOOD FOR A SECOND!

HMPH.

SHUFF

CHOP CHOP CHOP

HA HA

POOMF

HA HA HA

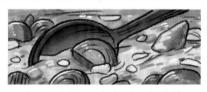

SIP

HAHA! WELL, WHAT DO YOU KNOW. THIS IS TREMENDOUS!

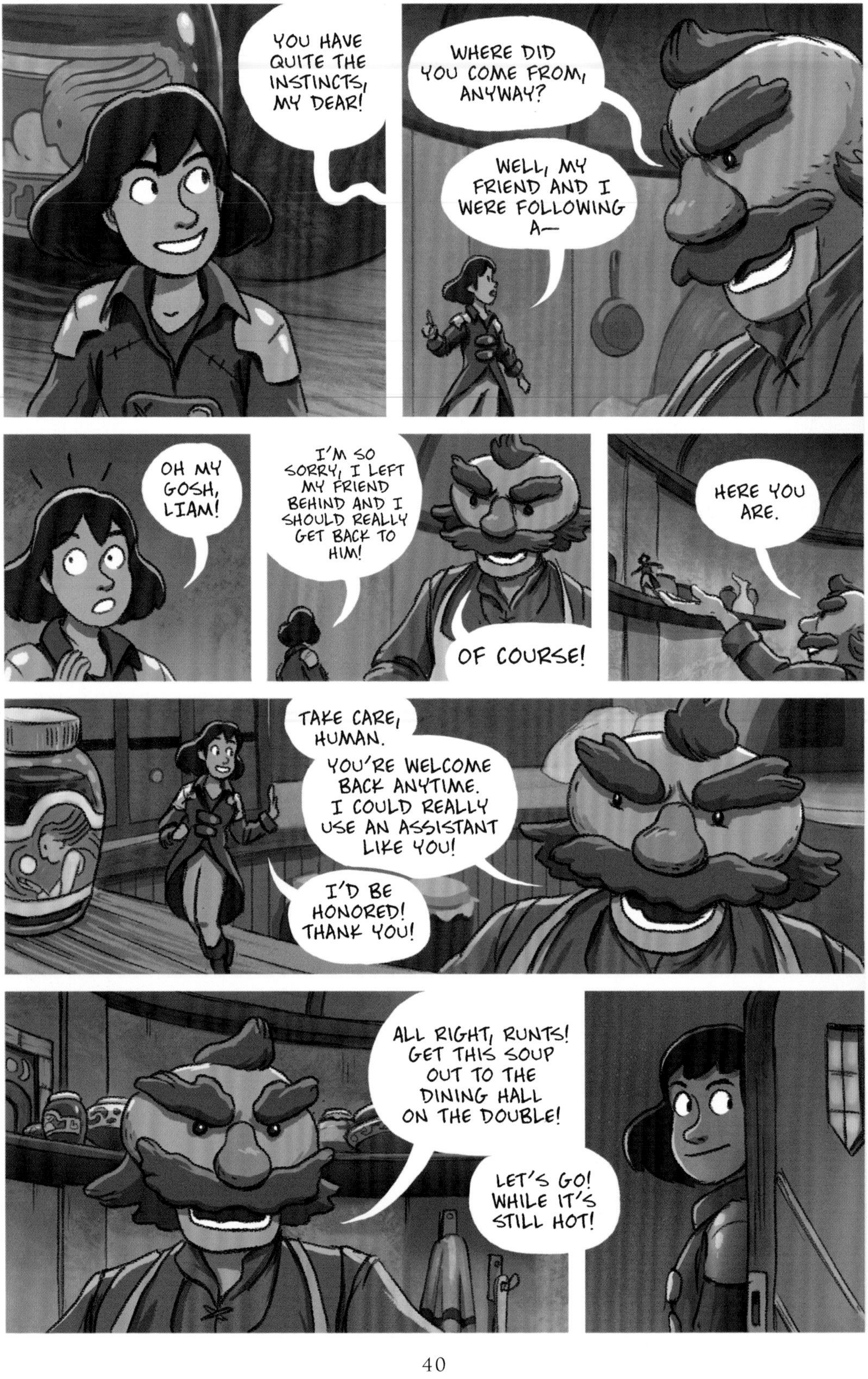
YOU HAVE QUITE THE INSTINCTS, MY DEAR!
WHERE DID YOU COME FROM, ANYWAY?
WELL, MY FRIEND AND I WERE FOLLOWING A—
OH MY GOSH, LIAM!
I'M SO SORRY, I LEFT MY FRIEND BEHIND AND I SHOULD REALLY GET BACK TO HIM!
OF COURSE!
HERE YOU ARE.
TAKE CARE, HUMAN.
YOU'RE WELCOME BACK ANYTIME. I COULD REALLY USE AN ASSISTANT LIKE YOU!
I'D BE HONORED! THANK YOU!
ALL RIGHT, RUNTS! GET THIS SOUP OUT TO THE DINING HALL ON THE DOUBLE!
LET'S GO! WHILE IT'S STILL HOT!

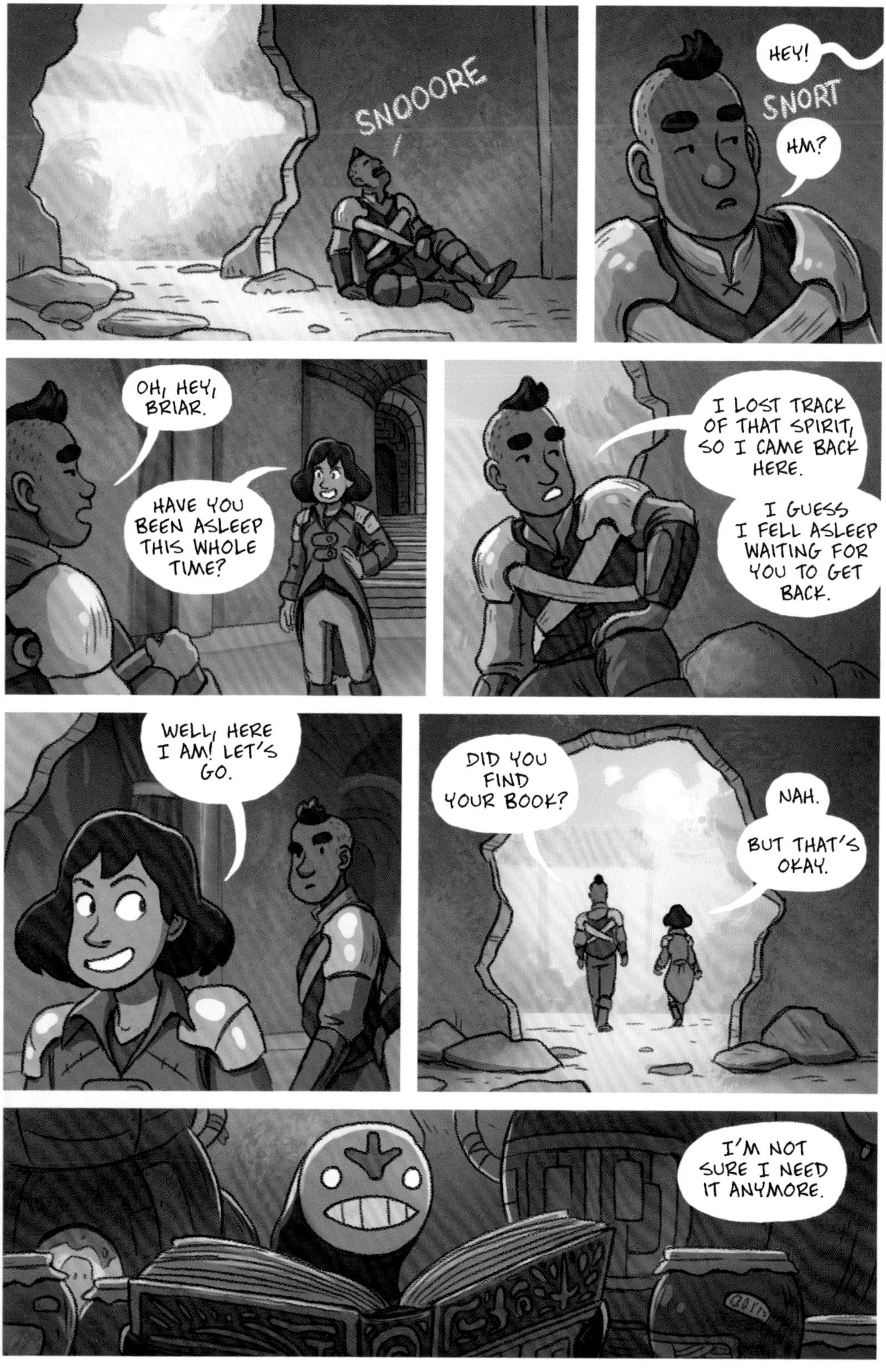
SNOOORE
HEY!
SNORT
HM?
OH, HEY, BRIAR.
HAVE YOU BEEN ASLEEP THIS WHOLE TIME?
I LOST TRACK OF THAT SPIRIT, SO I CAME BACK HERE.
I GUESS I FELL ASLEEP WAITING FOR YOU TO GET BACK.
WELL, HERE I AM! LET'S GO.
DID YOU FIND YOUR BOOK?
NAH.
BUT THAT'S OKAY.
I'M NOT SURE I NEED IT ANYMORE.

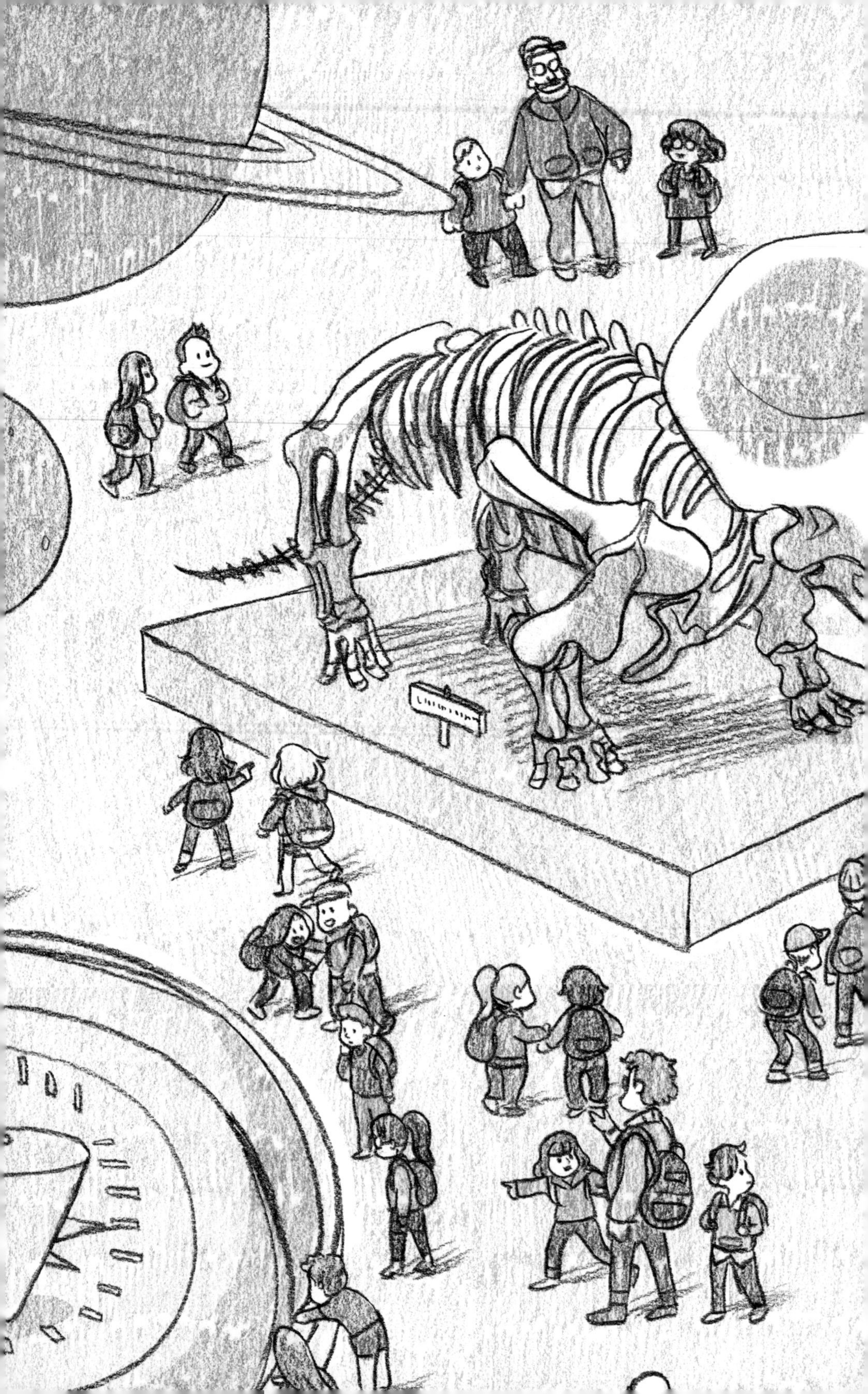

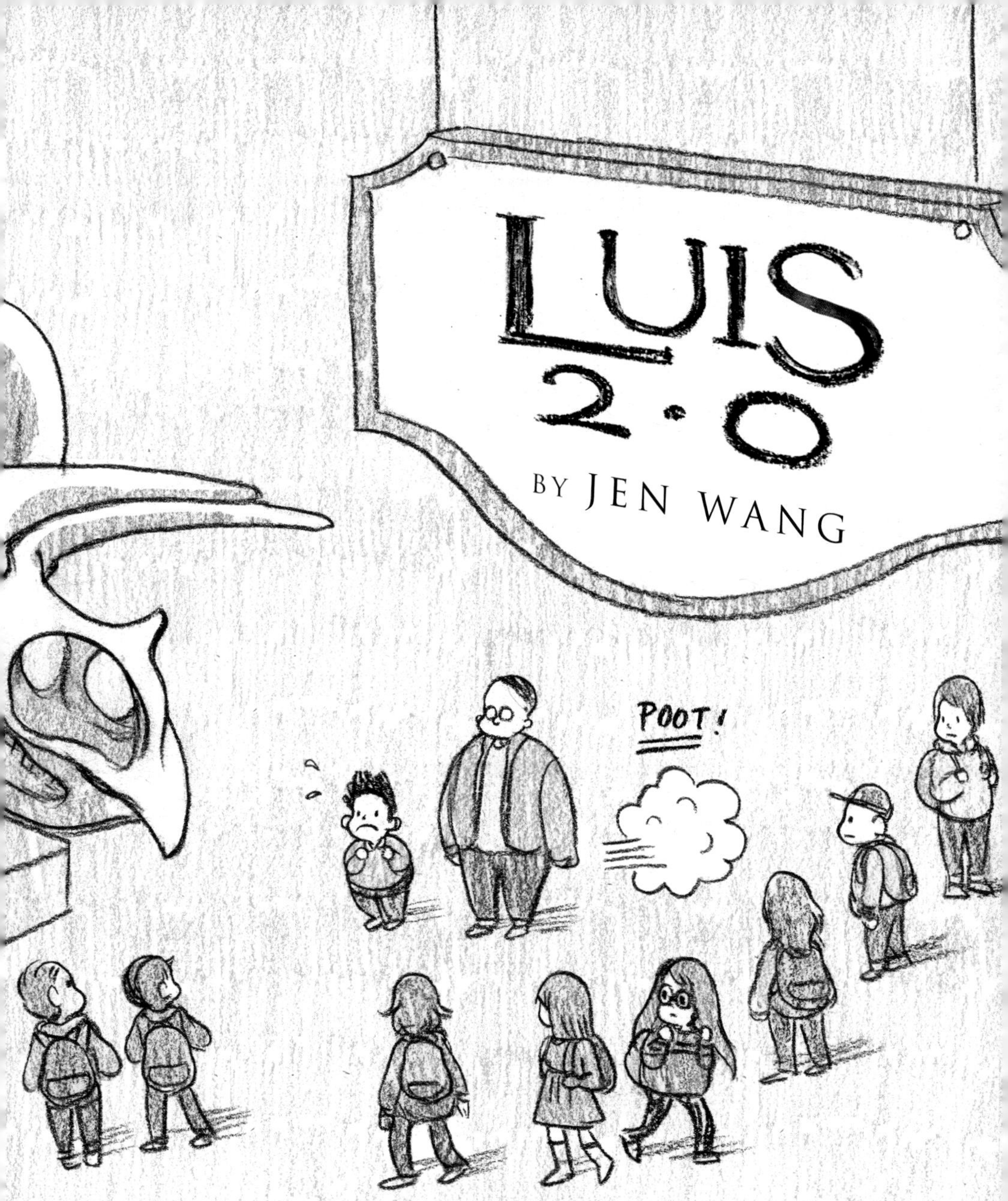
LUIS 2.0
BY JEN WANG
POOT!

It probably started the time my dad farted in front of everybody on our field trip to the Science Academy.

It wasn't his fault! He has a condition, I swear!

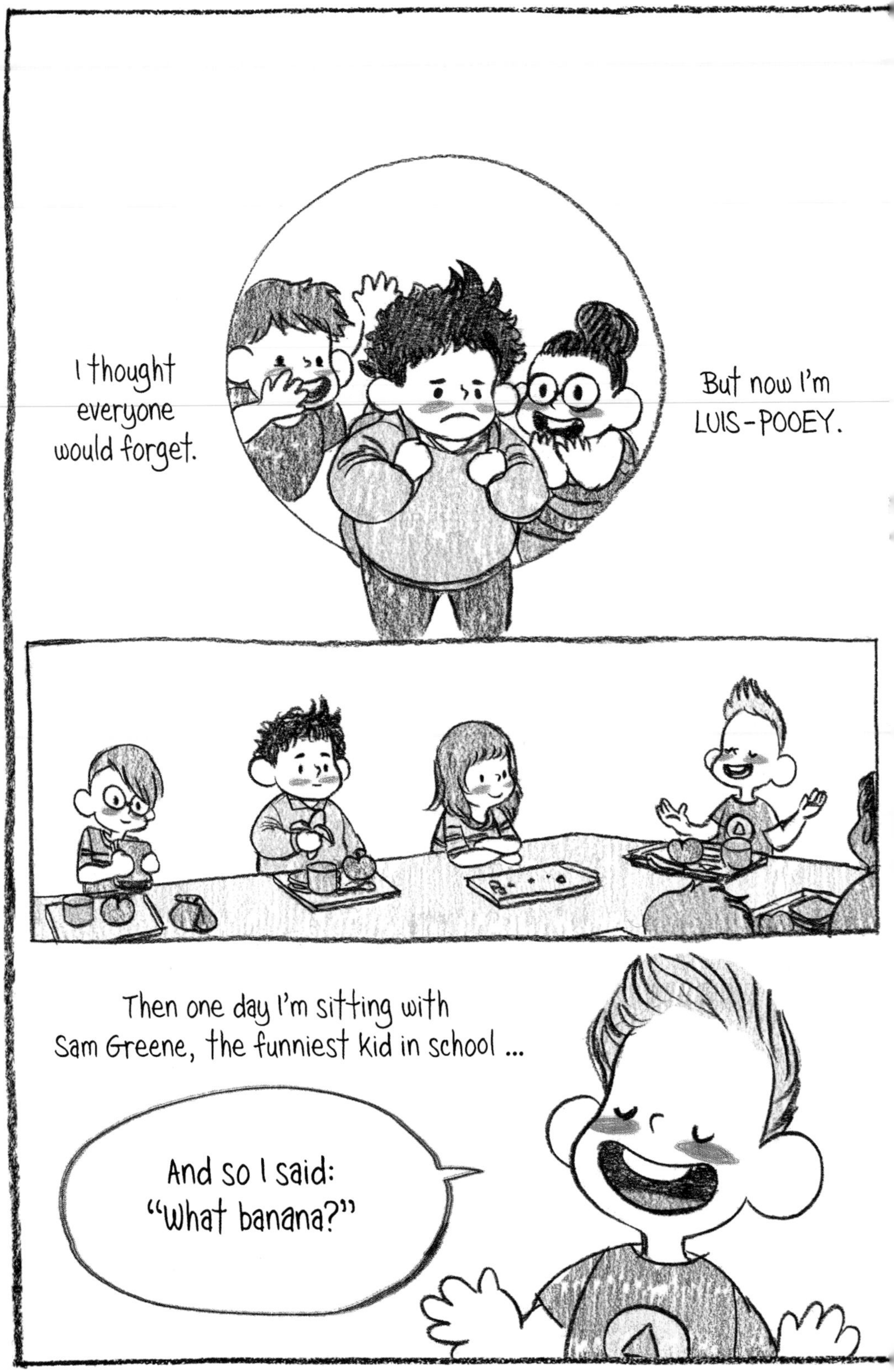
I thought everyone would forget.
But now I'm LUIS-POOEY.
Then one day I'm sitting with Sam Greene, the funniest kid in school ...
And so I said: "What banana?"

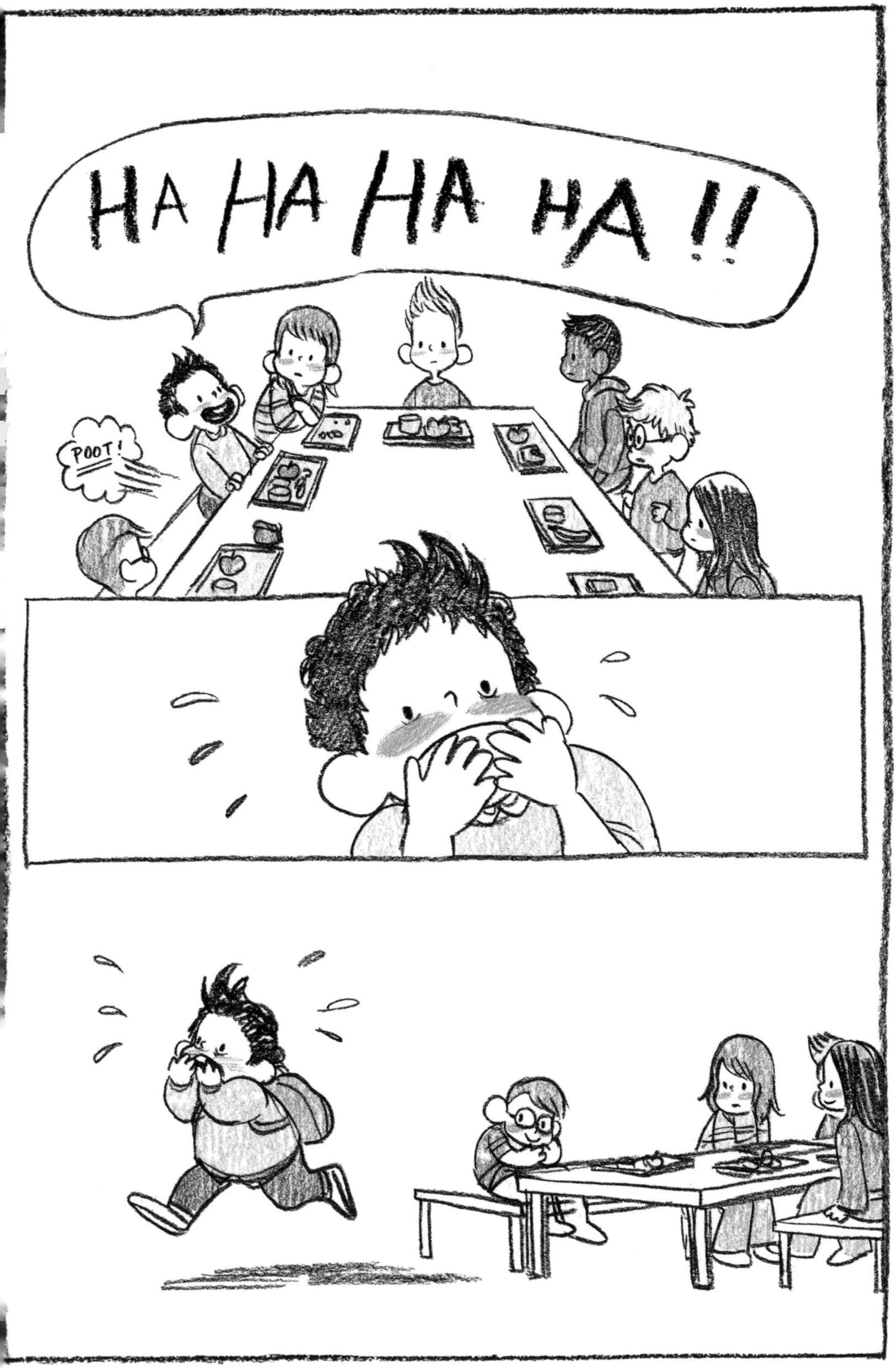
POOT!
HA HA HA HA!!

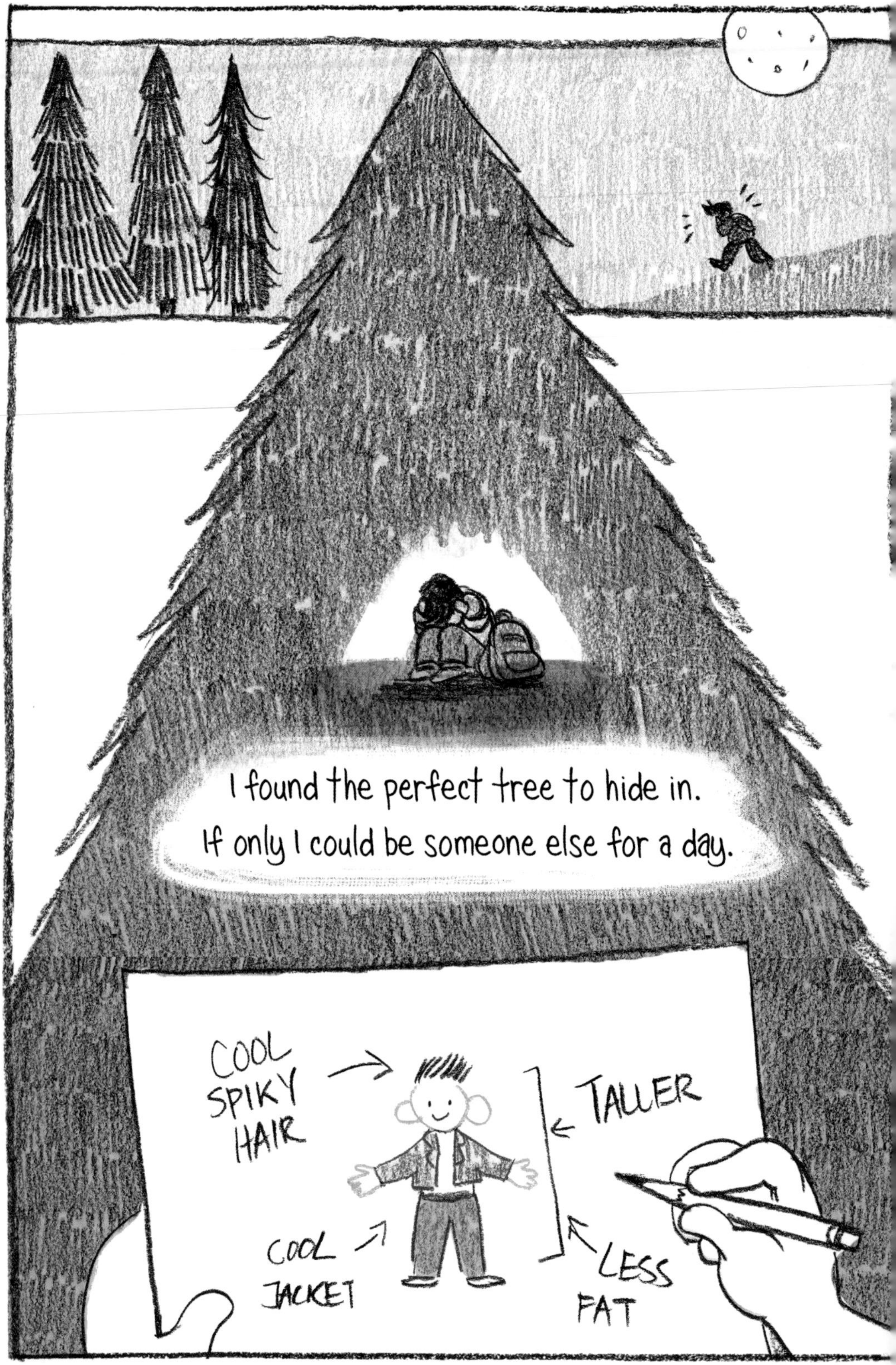
I found the perfect tree to hide in.
If only I could be someone else for a day.
COOL SPIKY HAIR
TALLER
COOL JACKET
LESS FAT

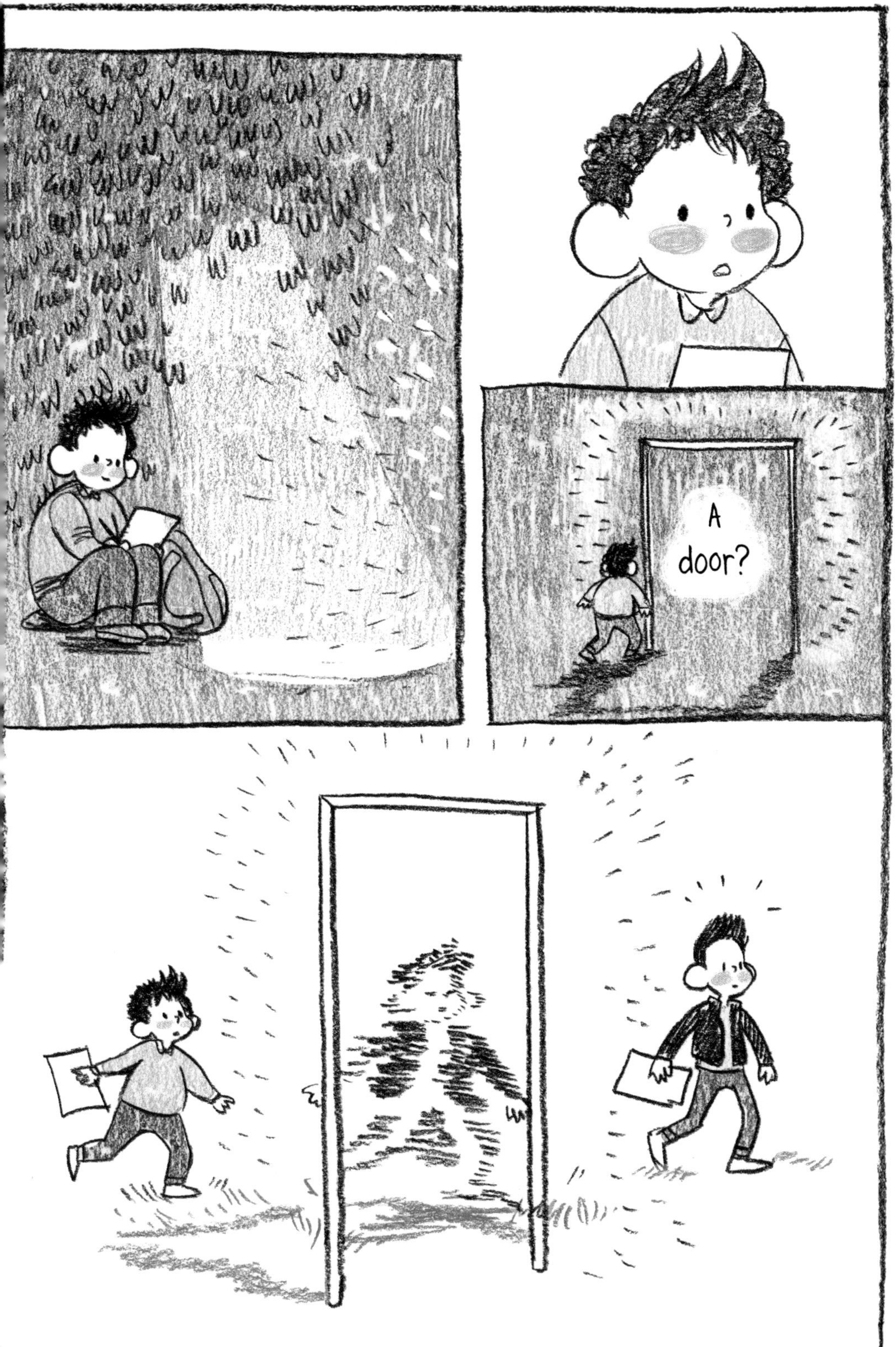
A door?

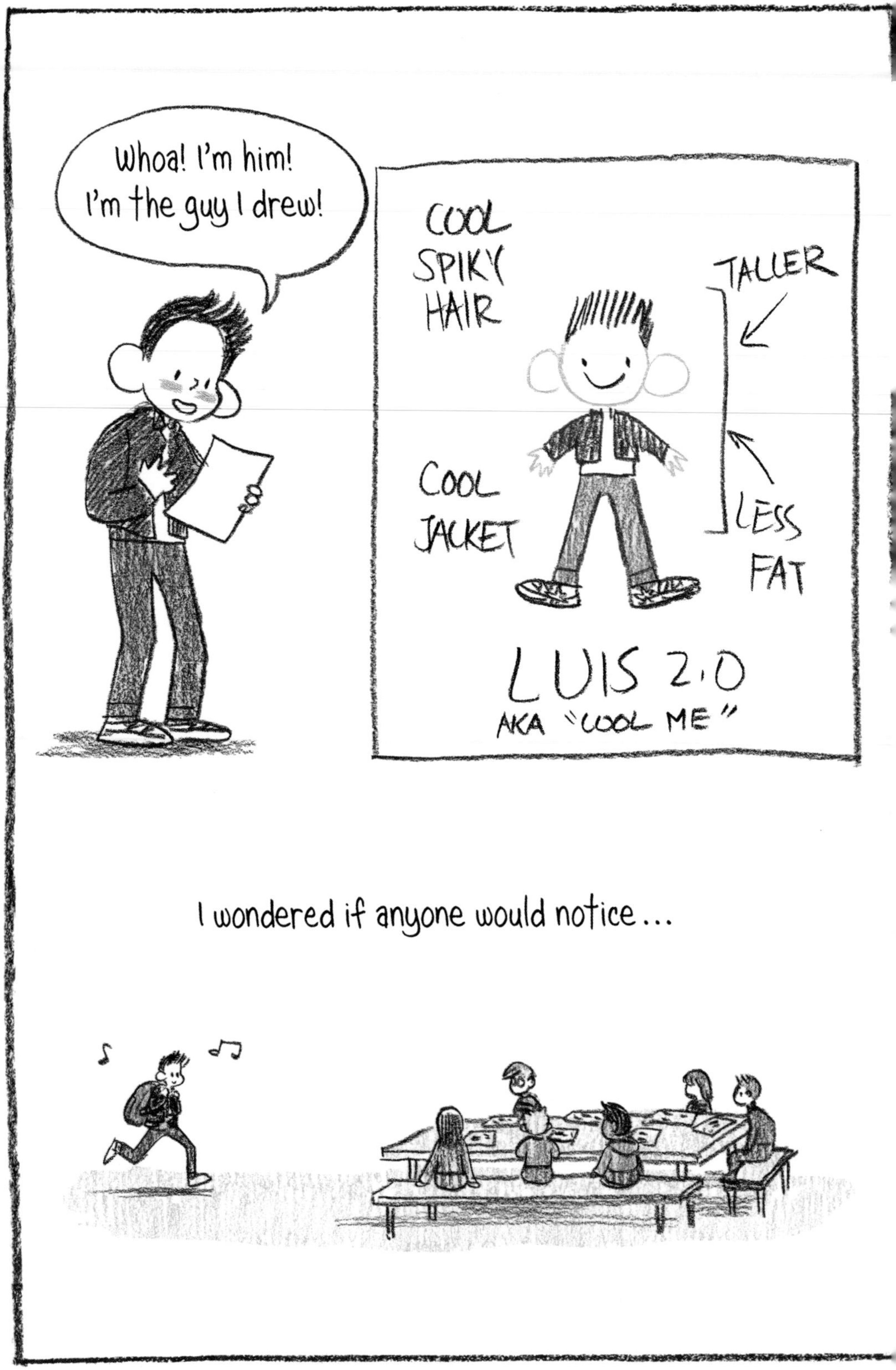
Whoa! I'm him! I'm the guy I drew!
COOL SPIKY HAIR
TALLER
COOL JACKET
LESS FAT
LUIS 2.0
AKA "COOL ME"
I wondered if anyone would notice...

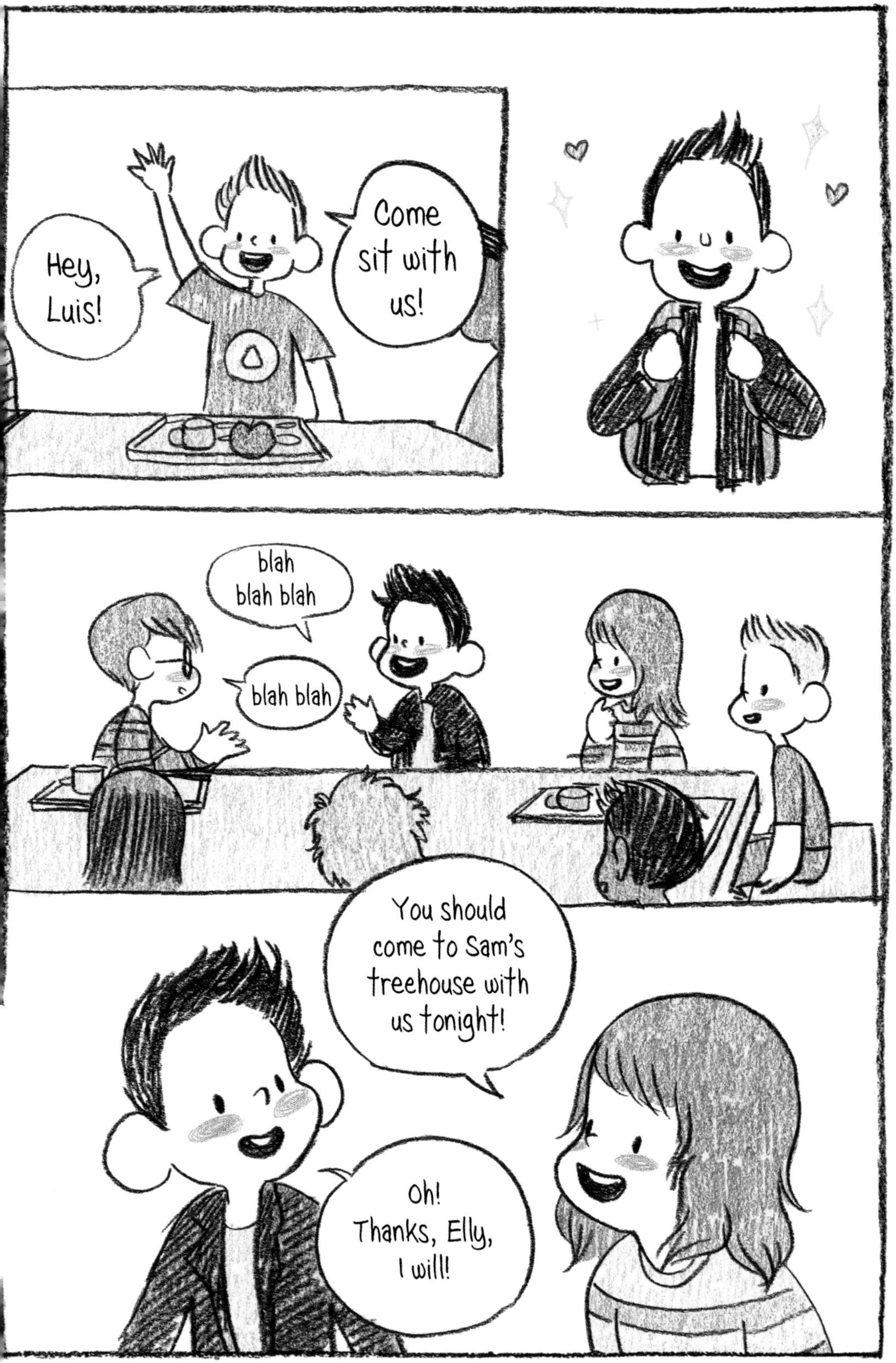

Hey, Luis!
Come sit with us!
blah blah blah
blah blah
You should come to Sam's treehouse with us tonight!
Oh! Thanks, Elly, I will!

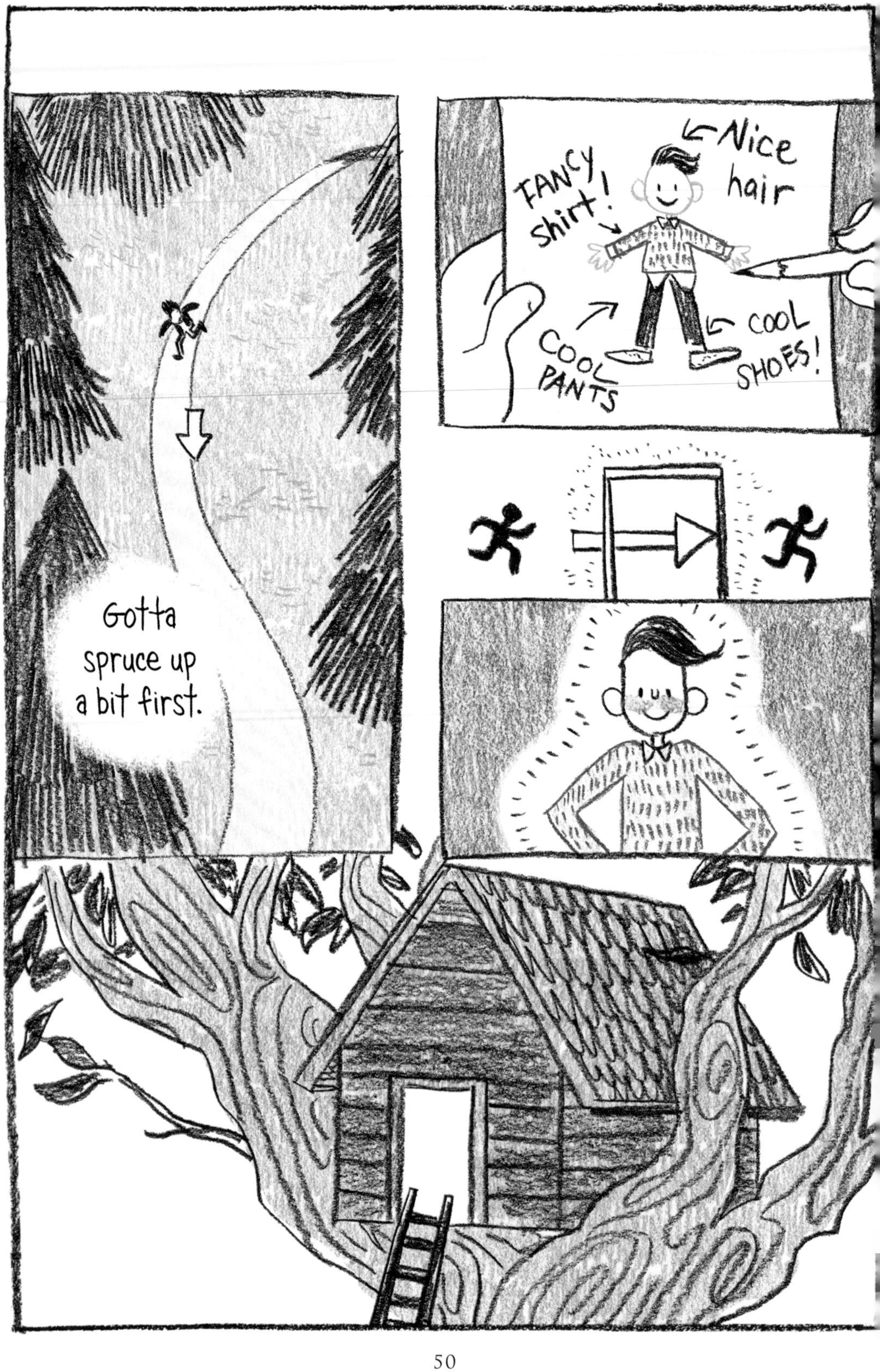
Gotta spruce up a bit first.
Nice hair
FANCY shirt!
COOL PANTS
COOL SHOES!

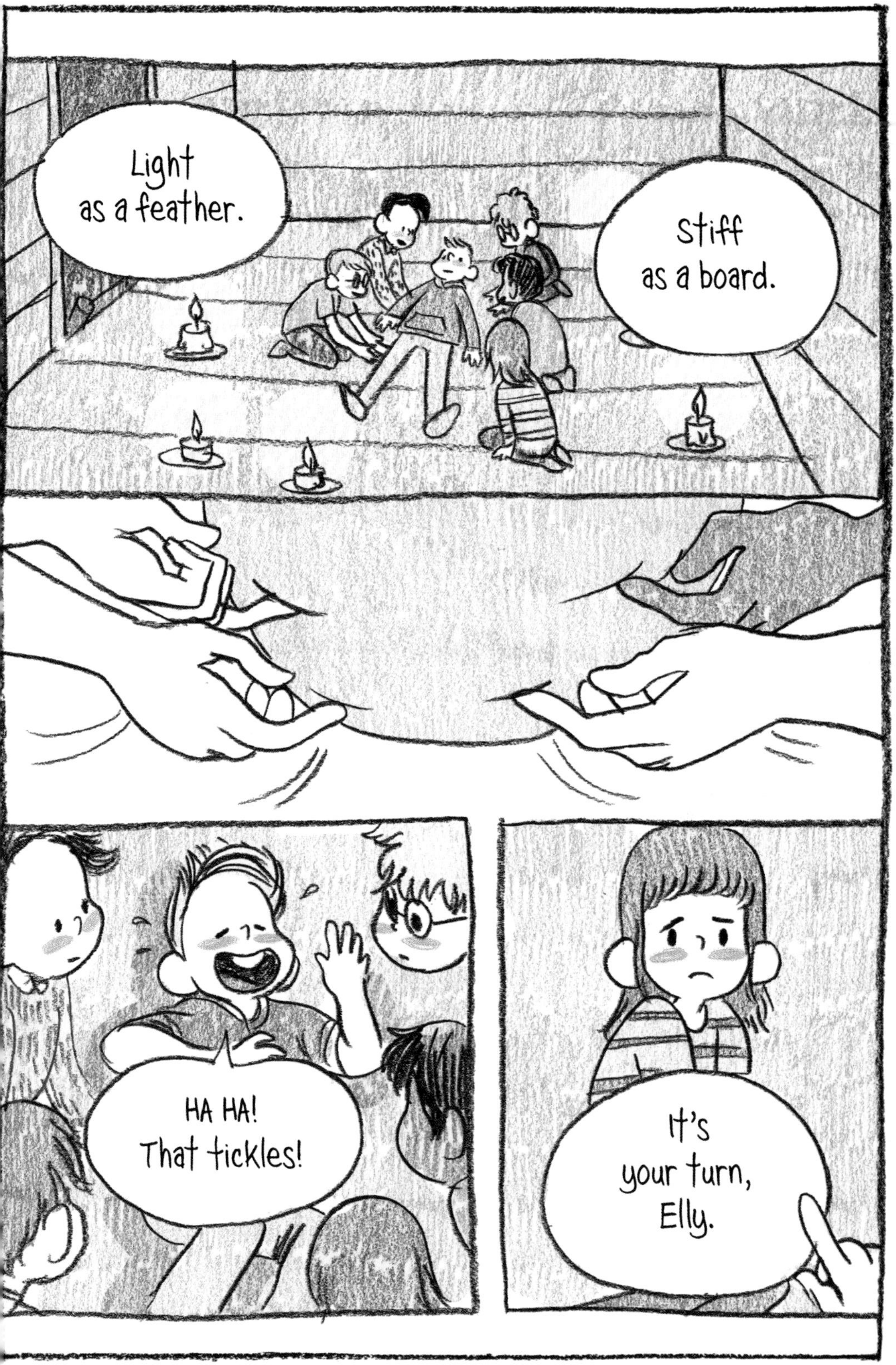
Light as a feather.
Stiff as a board.
HA HA! That tickles!
It's your turn, Elly.

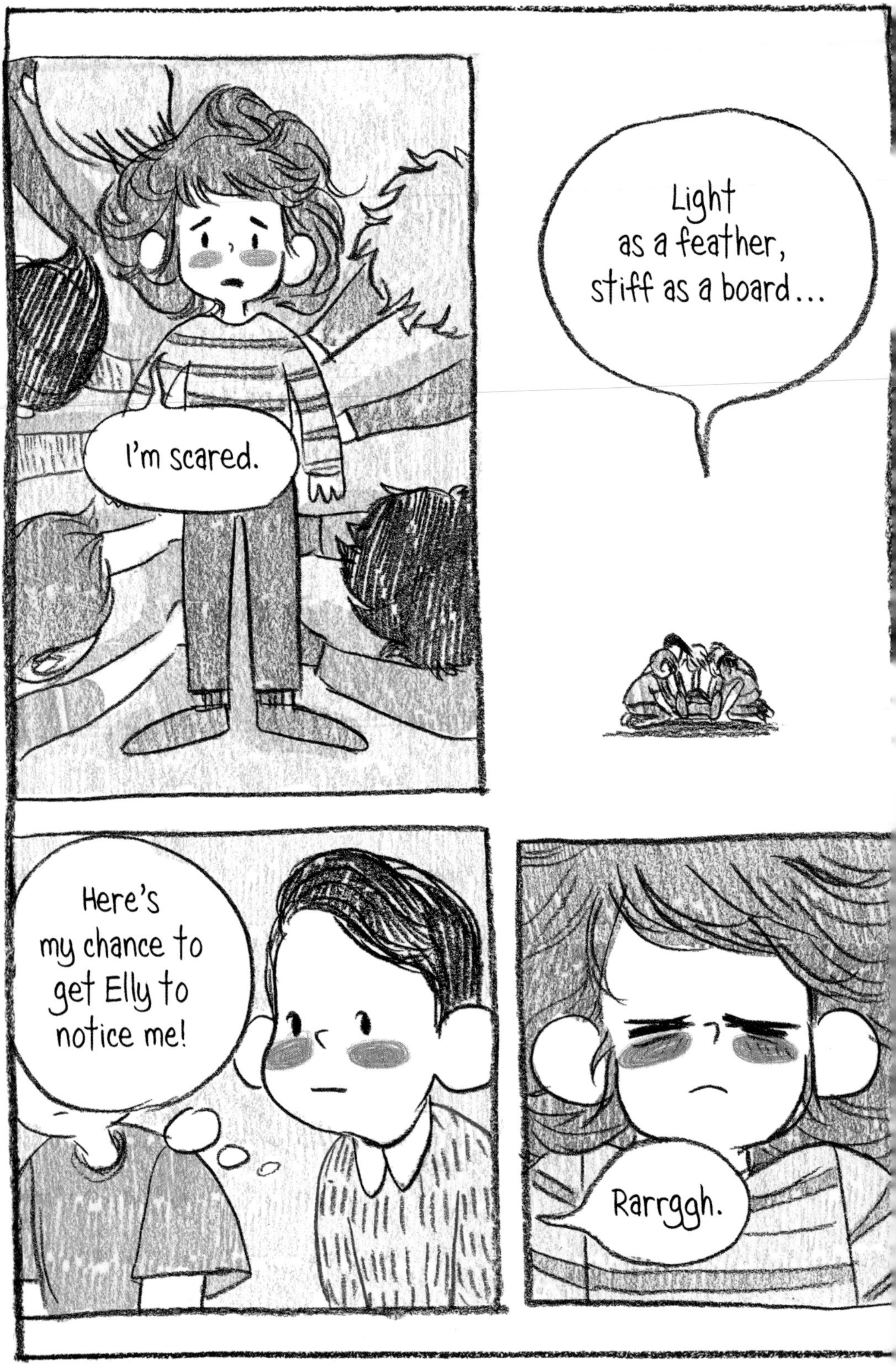
I'm scared.
Light as a feather, stiff as a board...
Here's my chance to get Elly to notice me!
Rarrggh.

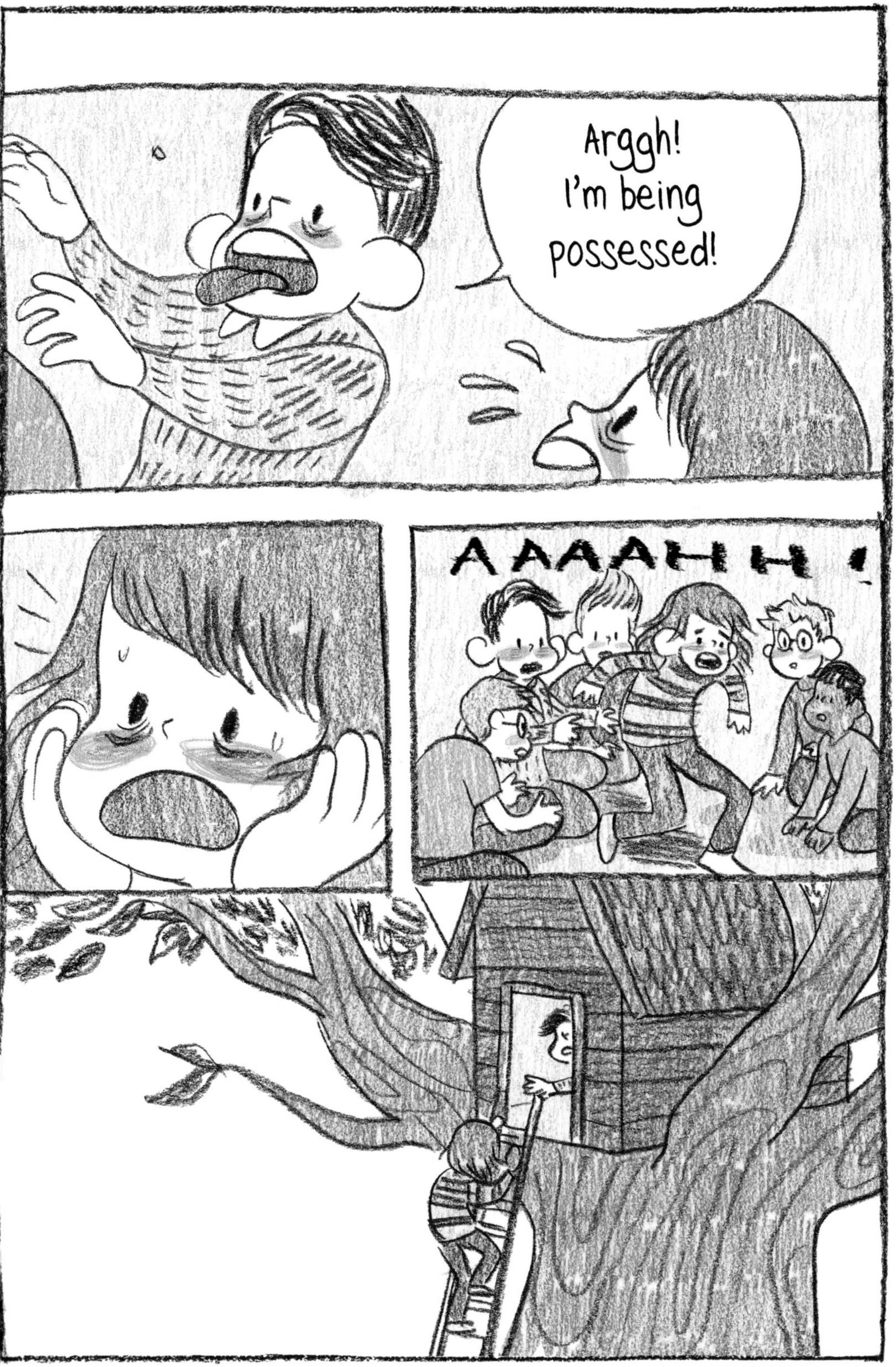
Arggh!
I'm being
possessed!
AAAAHH!

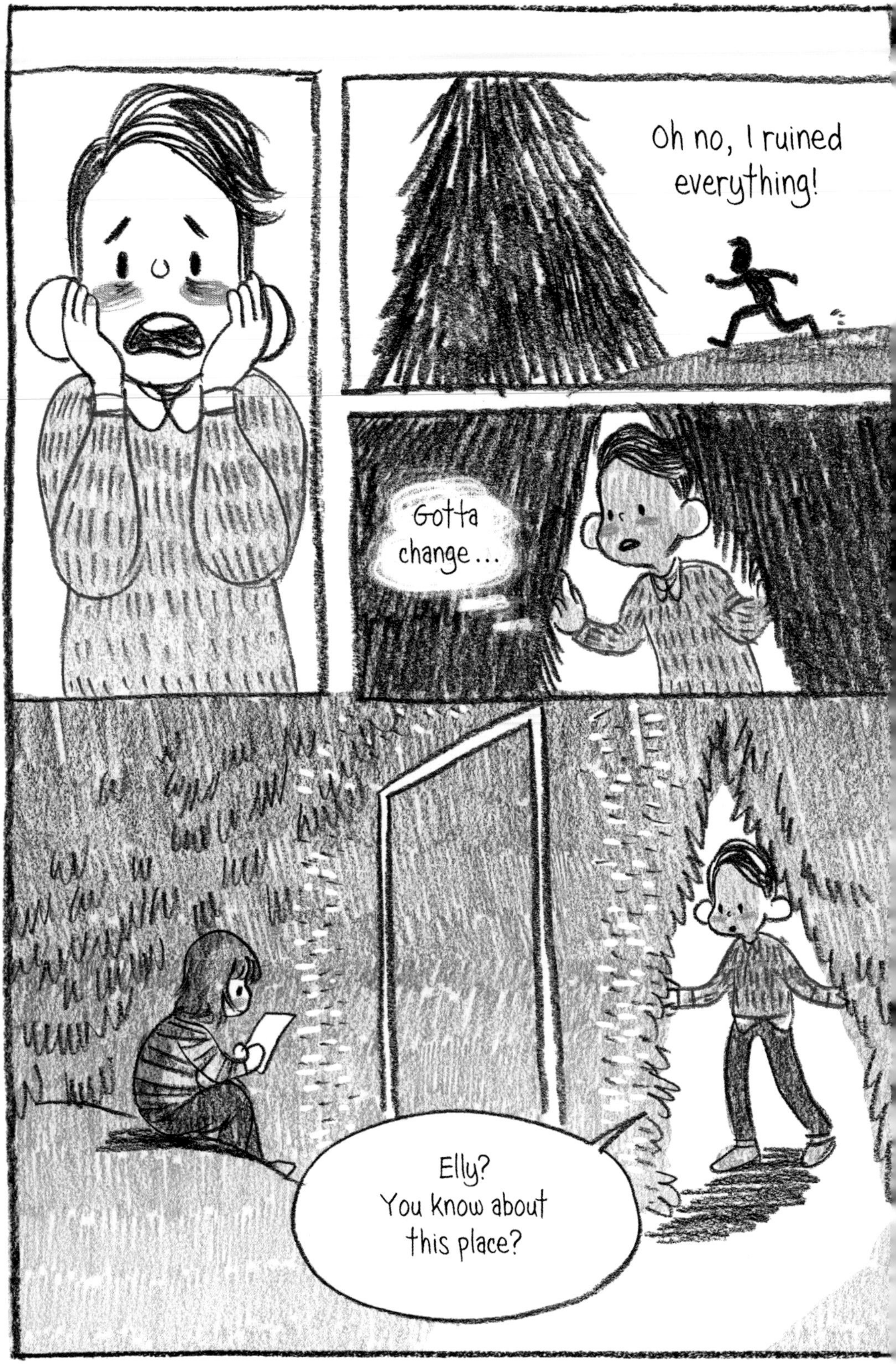
Oh no, I ruined everything!
Gotta change...
Elly? You know about this place?

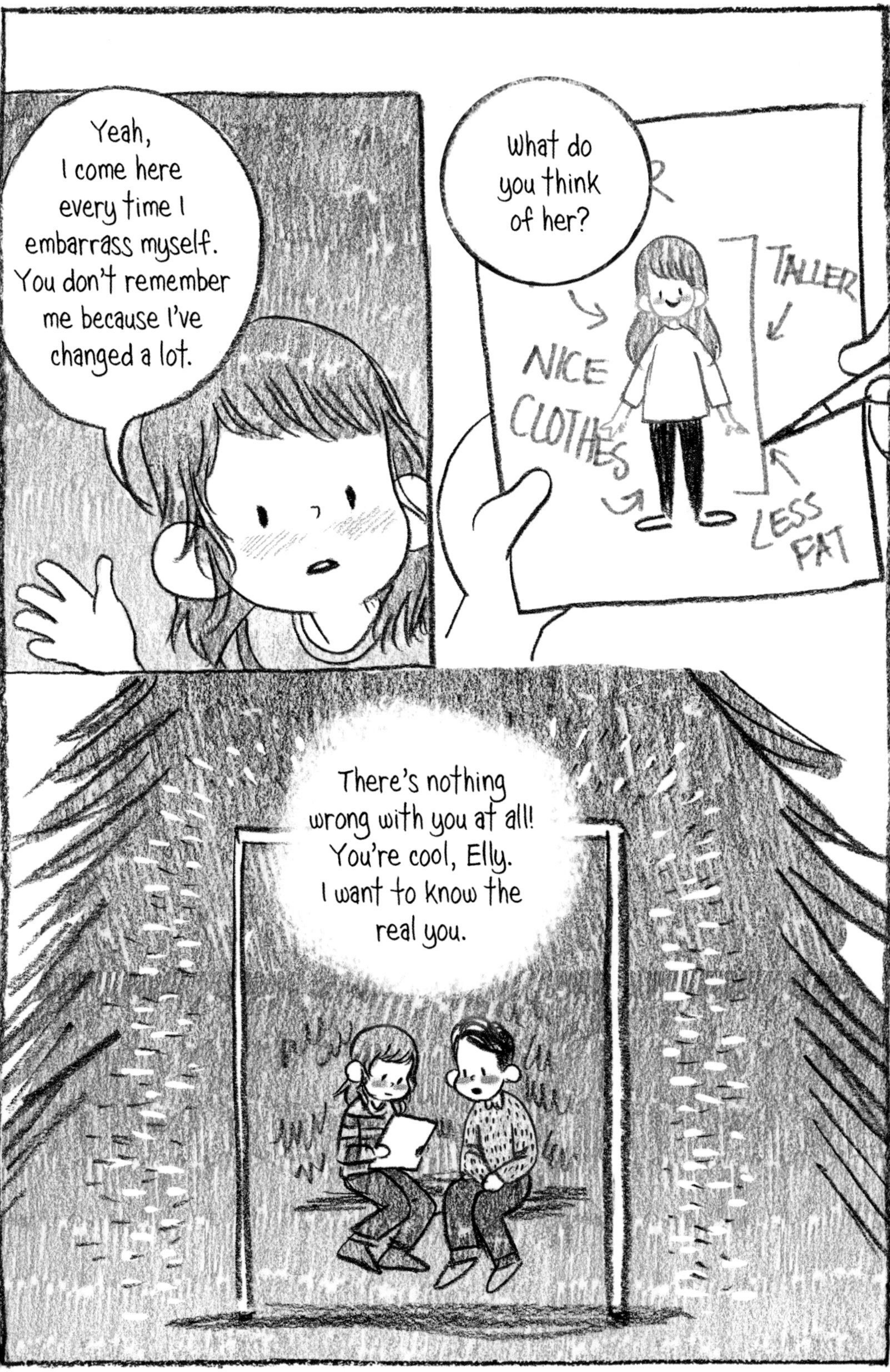
Yeah, I come here every time I embarrass myself. You don't remember me because I've changed a lot.
What do you think of her?
TALLER
NICE CLOTHES
LESS FAT
There's nothing wrong with you at all! You're cool, Elly. I want to know the real you.

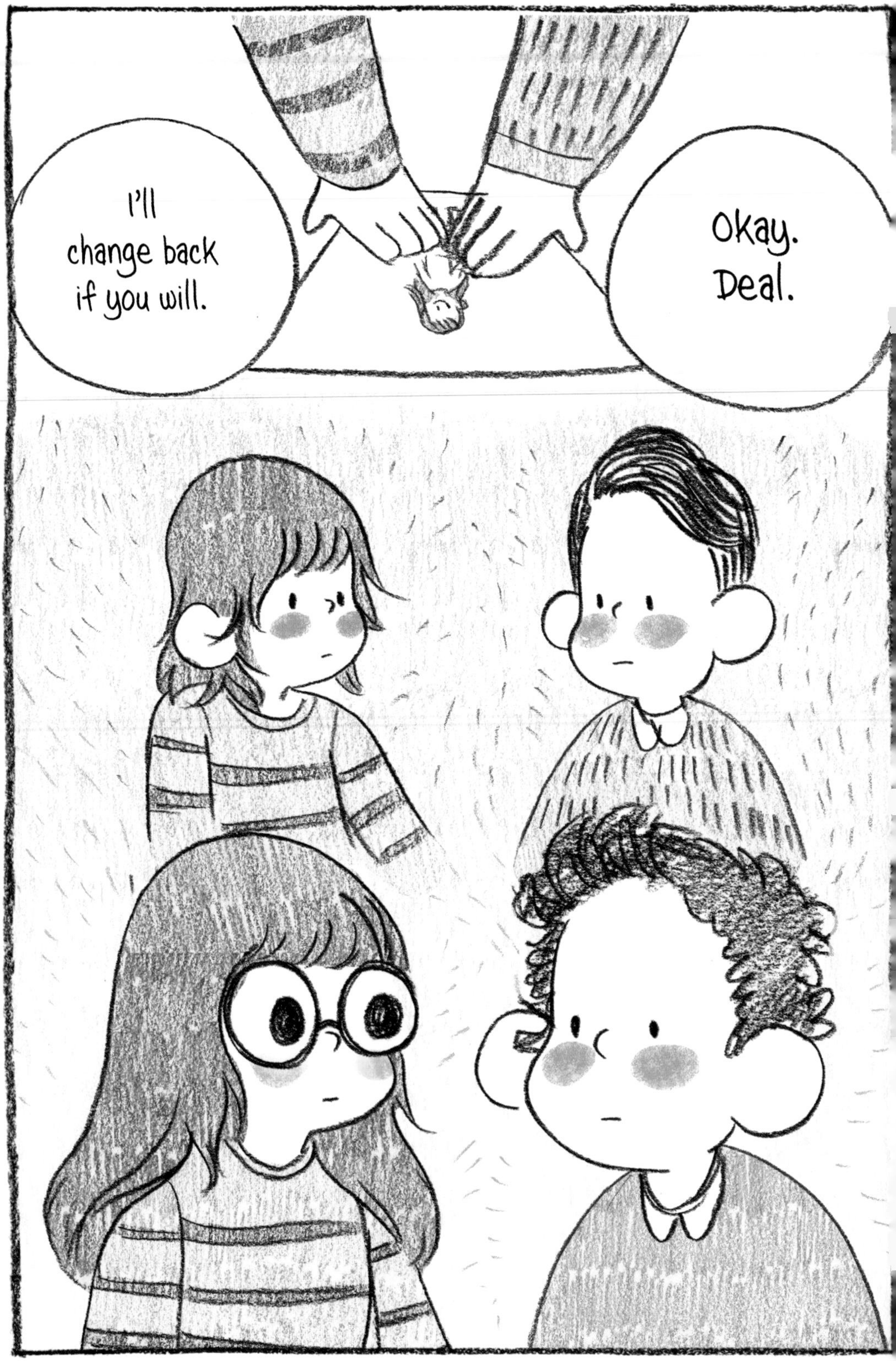
I'll change back if you will.
Okay. Deal.

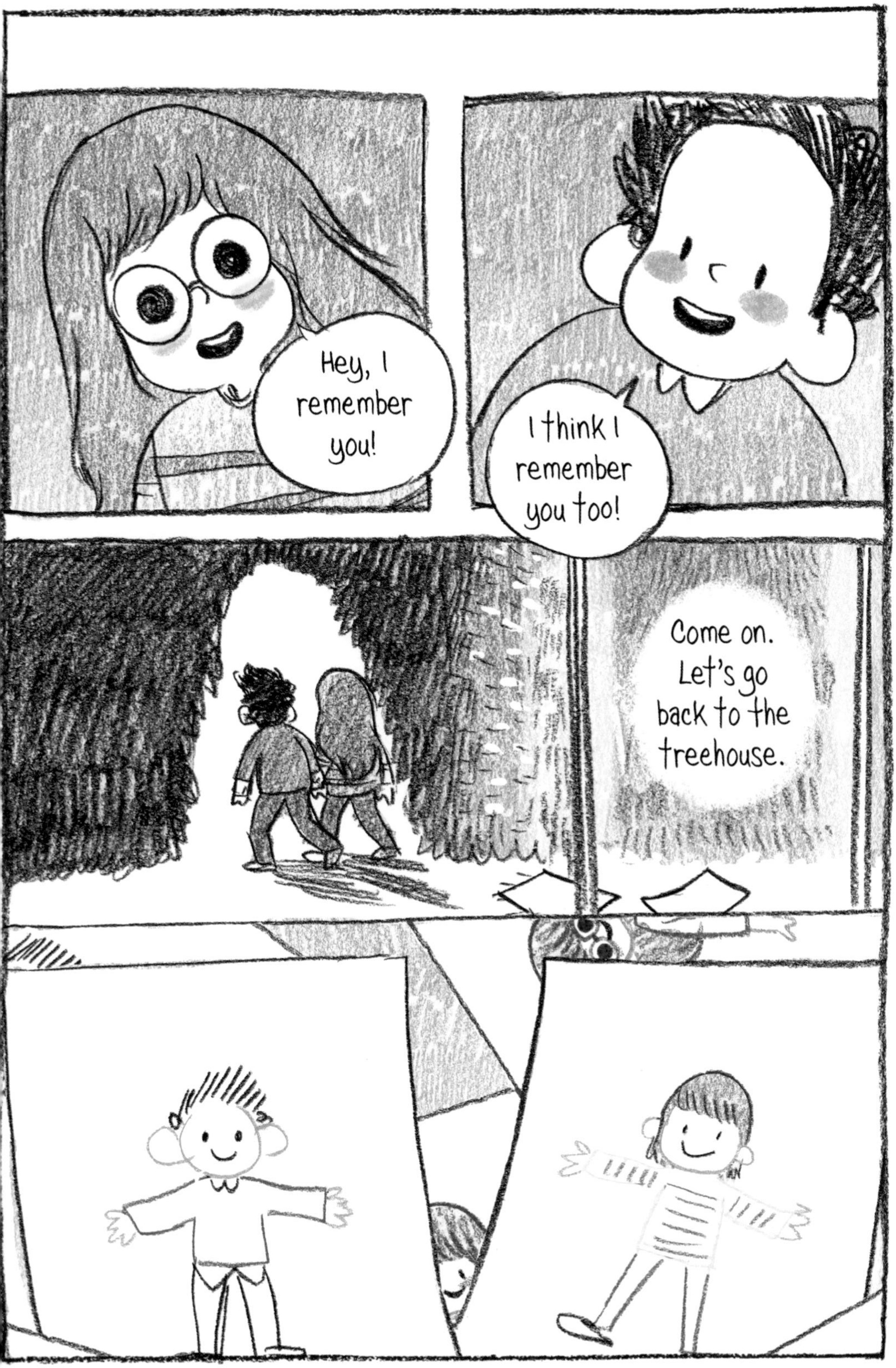
Hey, I remember you!
I think I remember you too!
Come on. Let's go back to the treehouse.

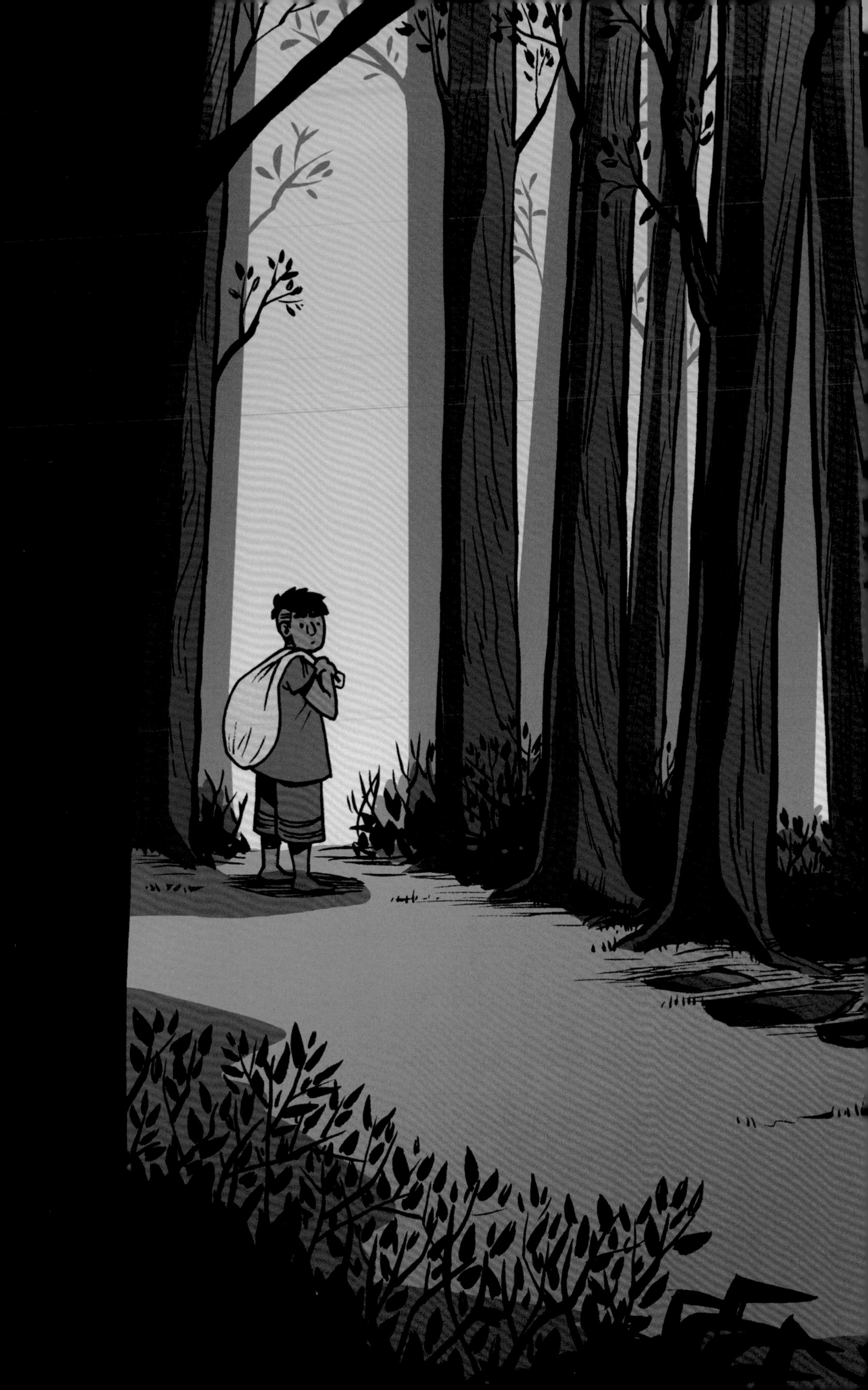

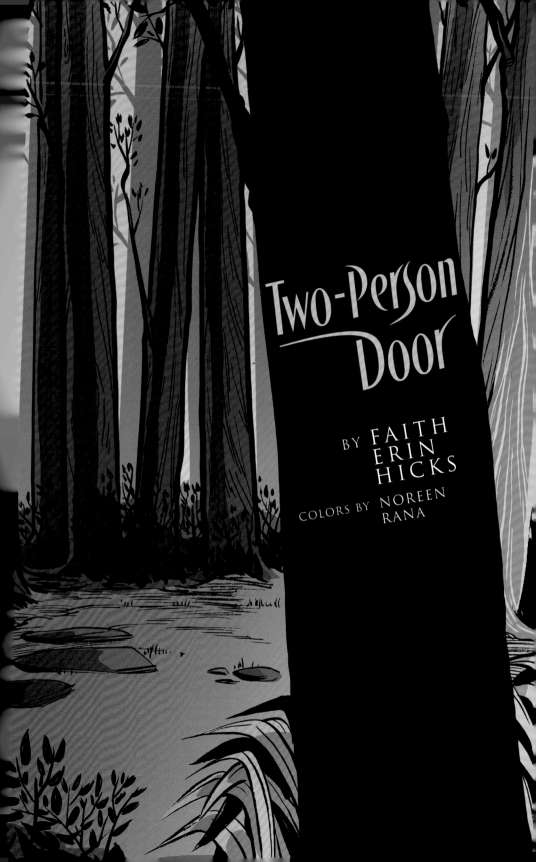

# Two-Person Door

BY FAITH ERIN HICKS

COLORS BY NOREEN RANA

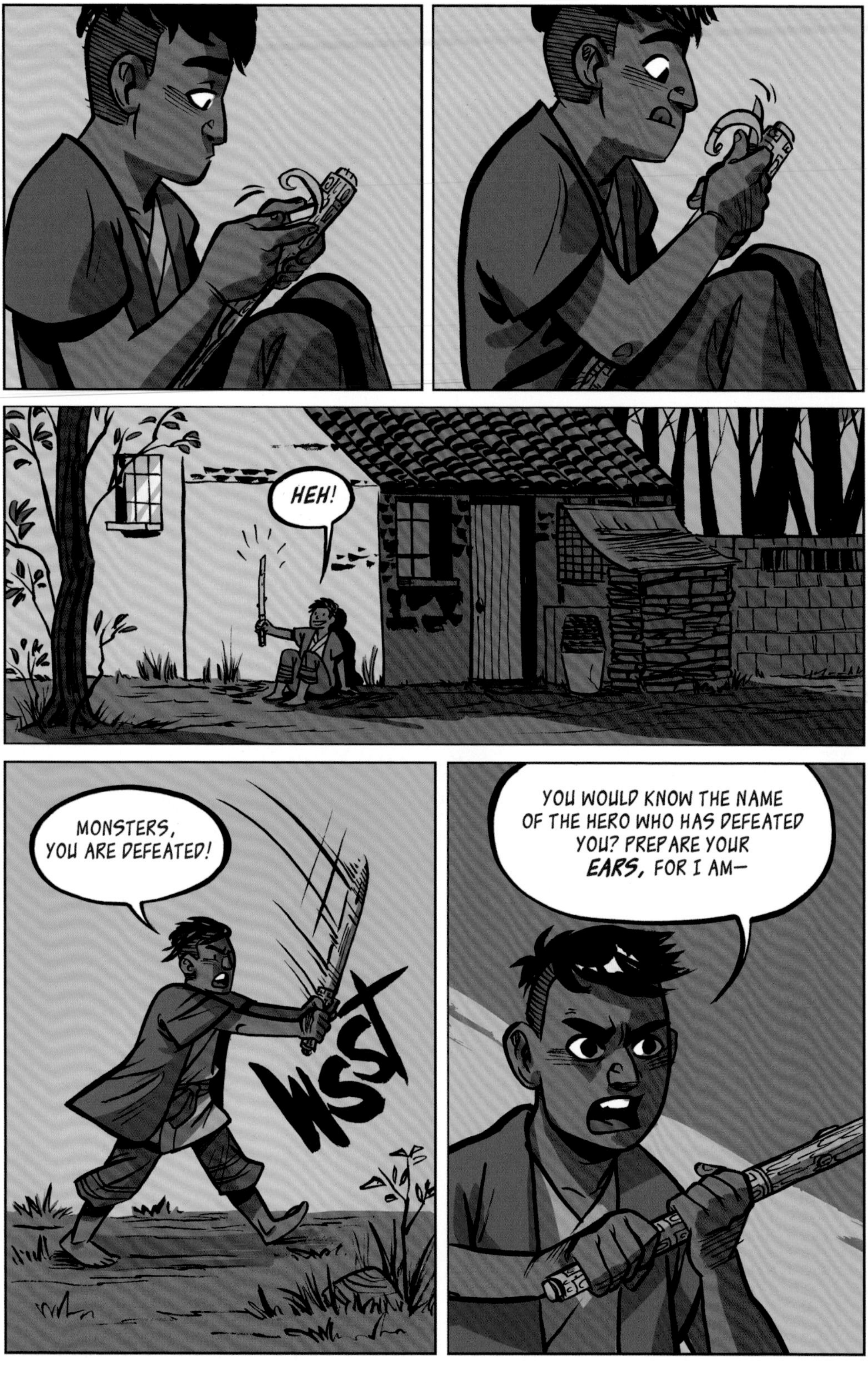
HEH!
MONSTERS, YOU ARE DEFEATED!
WSST
YOU WOULD KNOW THE NAME OF THE HERO WHO HAS DEFEATED YOU? PREPARE YOUR EARS, FOR I AM—

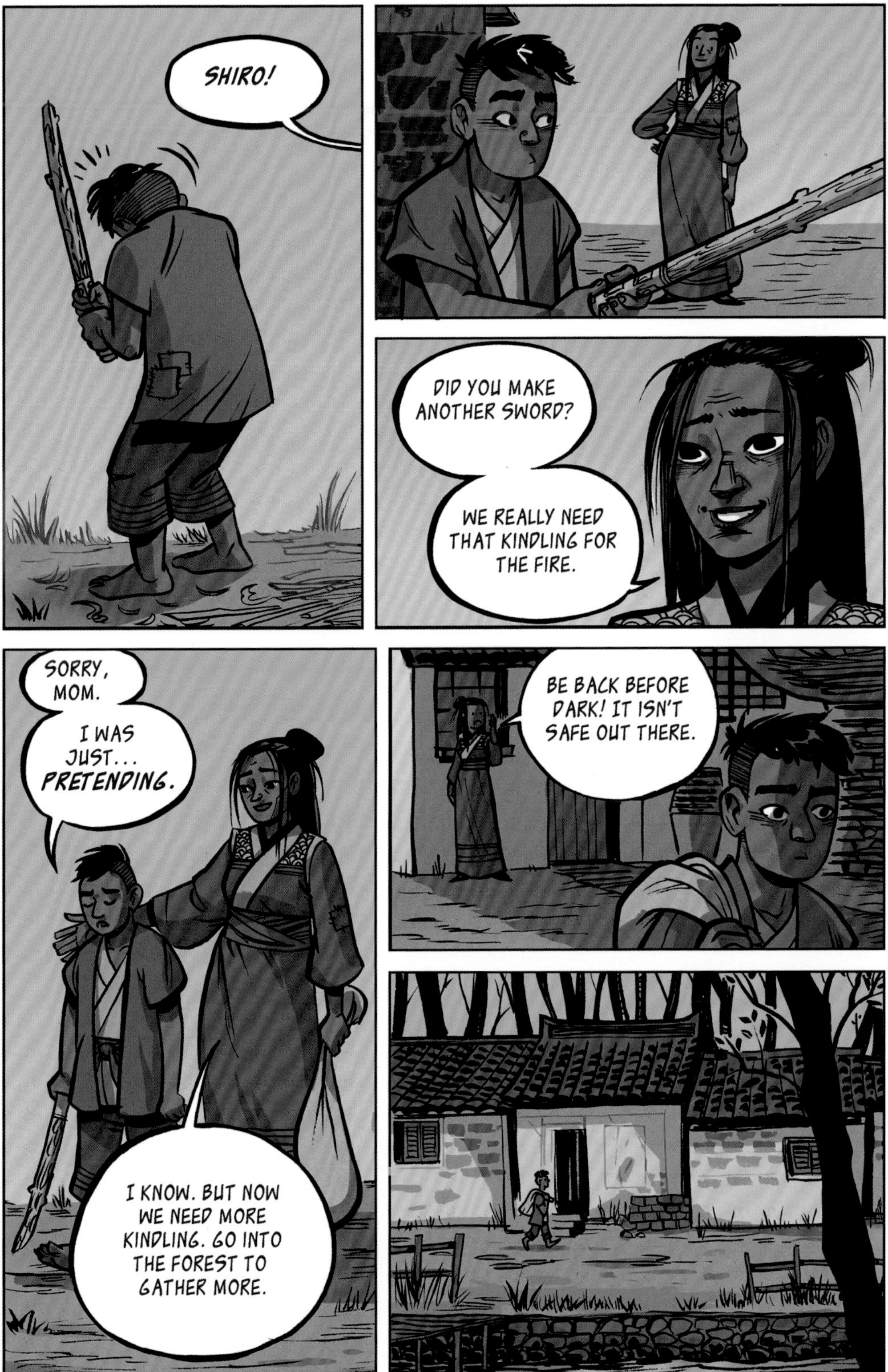
SHIRO!
DID YOU MAKE ANOTHER SWORD?
WE REALLY NEED THAT KINDLING FOR THE FIRE.
SORRY, MOM.
I WAS JUST... PRETENDING.
I KNOW. BUT NOW WE NEED MORE KINDLING. GO INTO THE FOREST TO GATHER MORE.
BE BACK BEFORE DARK! IT ISN'T SAFE OUT THERE.

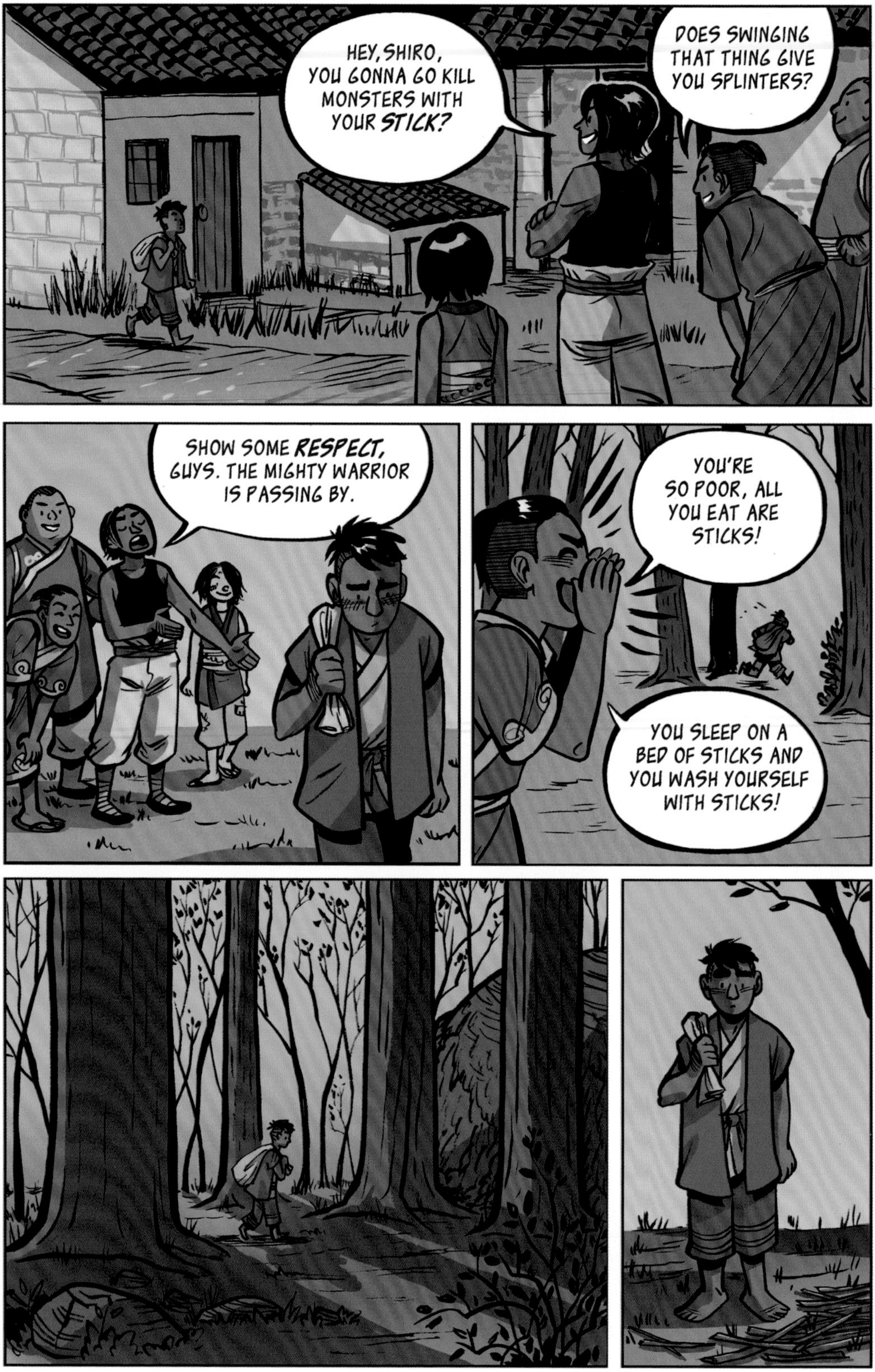
HEY, SHIRO, YOU GONNA GO KILL MONSTERS WITH YOUR STICK?
DOES SWINGING THAT THING GIVE YOU SPLINTERS?
SHOW SOME RESPECT, GUYS. THE MIGHTY WARRIOR IS PASSING BY.
YOU'RE SO POOR, ALL YOU EAT ARE STICKS!
YOU SLEEP ON A BED OF STICKS AND YOU WASH YOURSELF WITH STICKS!

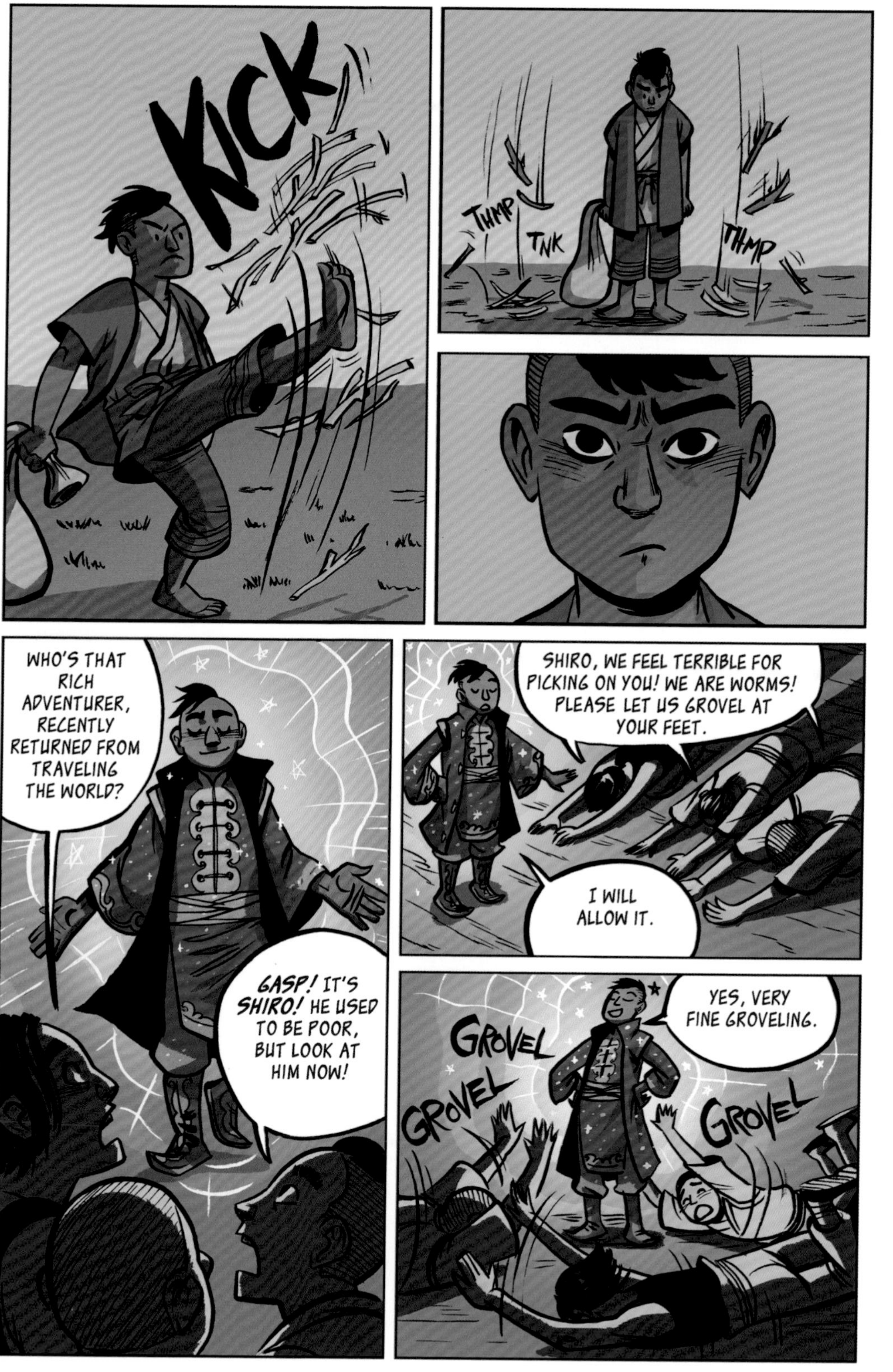
KICK
THMP
TNK
THMP
WHO'S THAT RICH ADVENTURER, RECENTLY RETURNED FROM TRAVELING THE WORLD?
GASP! IT'S SHIRO! HE USED TO BE POOR, BUT LOOK AT HIM NOW!
SHIRO, WE FEEL TERRIBLE FOR PICKING ON YOU! WE ARE WORMS! PLEASE LET US GROVEL AT YOUR FEET.
I WILL ALLOW IT.
YES, VERY FINE GROVELING.
GROVEL
GROVEL
GROVEL

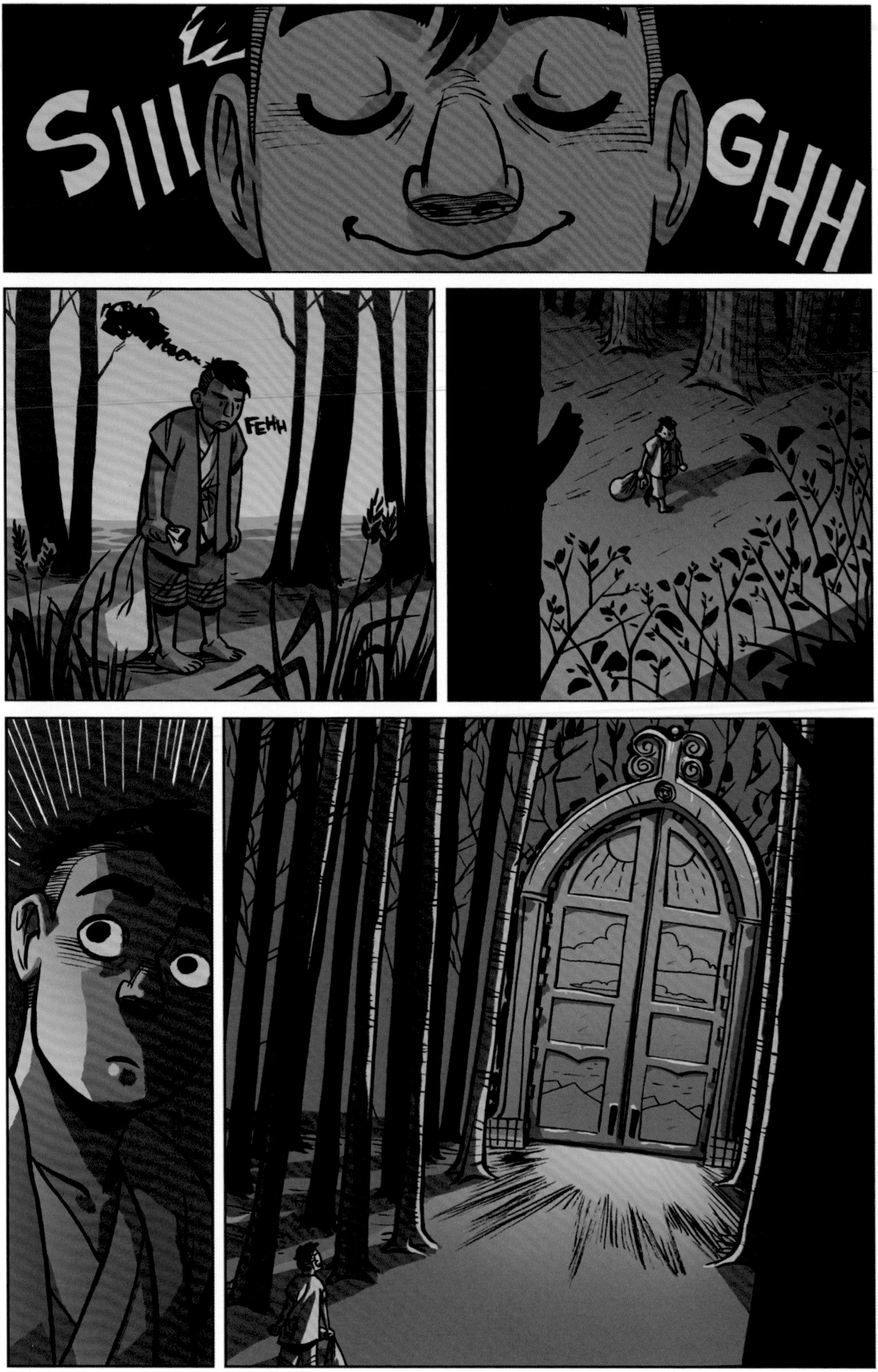
SIIIGHH
FEHH

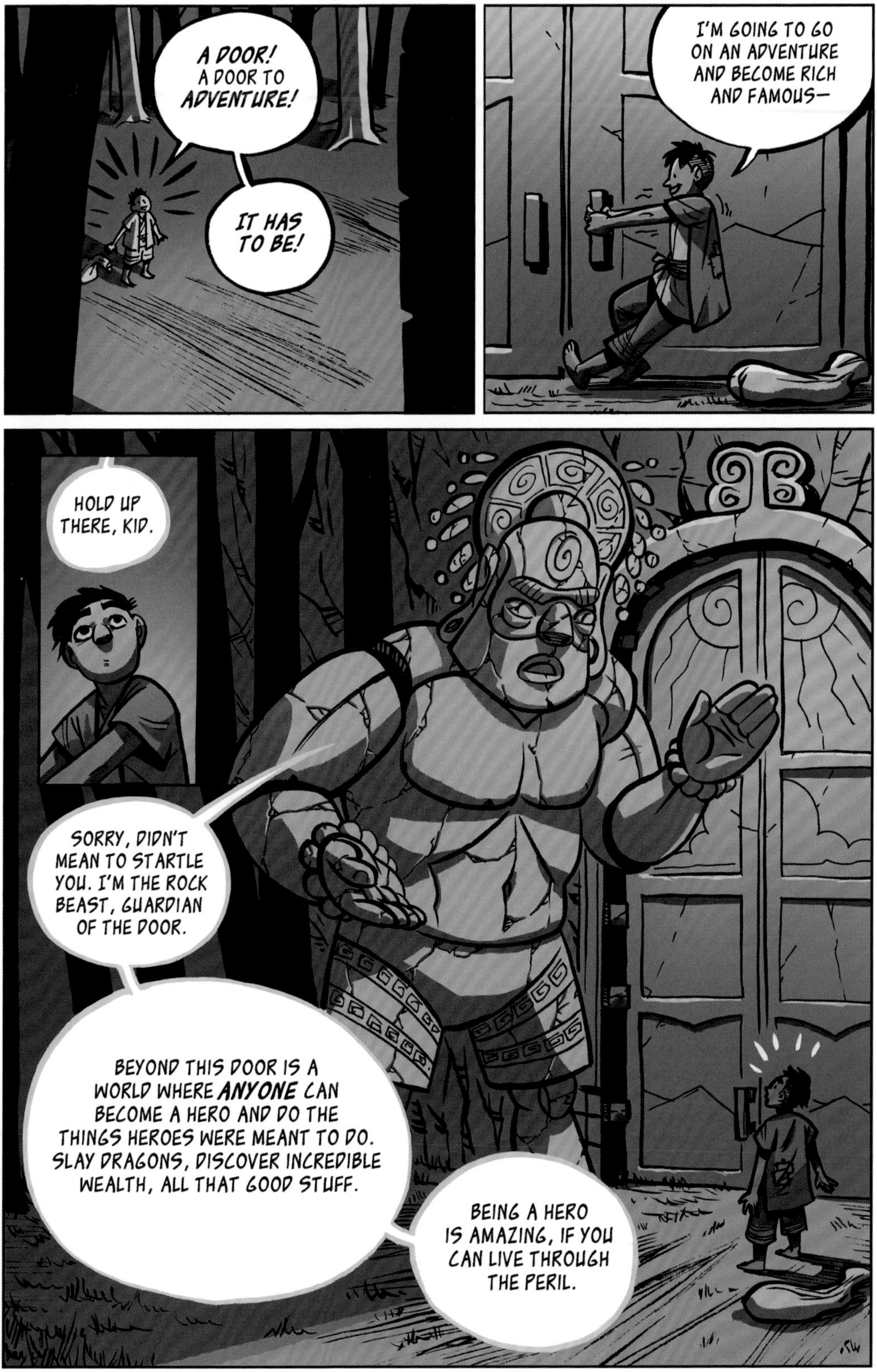
A DOOR! A DOOR TO ADVENTURE!
IT HAS TO BE!
I'M GOING TO GO ON AN ADVENTURE AND BECOME RICH AND FAMOUS—
HOLD UP THERE, KID.
SORRY, DIDN'T MEAN TO STARTLE YOU. I'M THE ROCK BEAST, GUARDIAN OF THE DOOR.
BEYOND THIS DOOR IS A WORLD WHERE ANYONE CAN BECOME A HERO AND DO THE THINGS HEROES WERE MEANT TO DO. SLAY DRAGONS, DISCOVER INCREDIBLE WEALTH, ALL THAT GOOD STUFF.
BEING A HERO IS AMAZING, IF YOU CAN LIVE THROUGH THE PERIL.

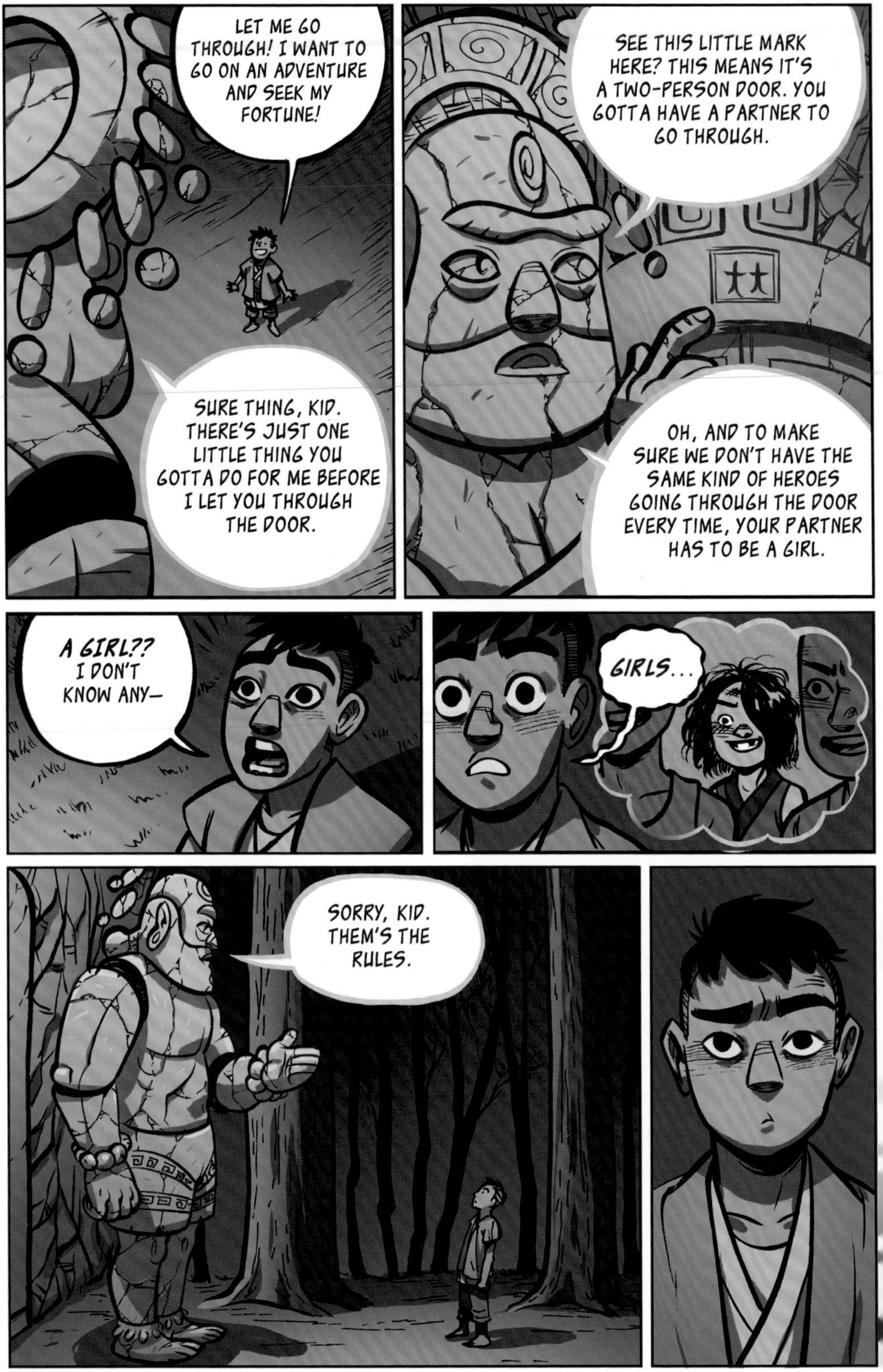
LET ME GO THROUGH! I WANT TO GO ON AN ADVENTURE AND SEEK MY FORTUNE!
SURE THING, KID. THERE'S JUST ONE LITTLE THING YOU GOTTA DO FOR ME BEFORE I LET YOU THROUGH THE DOOR.
SEE THIS LITTLE MARK HERE? THIS MEANS IT'S A TWO-PERSON DOOR. YOU GOTTA HAVE A PARTNER TO GO THROUGH.
OH, AND TO MAKE SURE WE DON'T HAVE THE SAME KIND OF HEROES GOING THROUGH THE DOOR EVERY TIME, YOUR PARTNER HAS TO BE A GIRL.
A GIRL?? I DON'T KNOW ANY—
GIRLS...
SORRY, KID. THEM'S THE RULES.

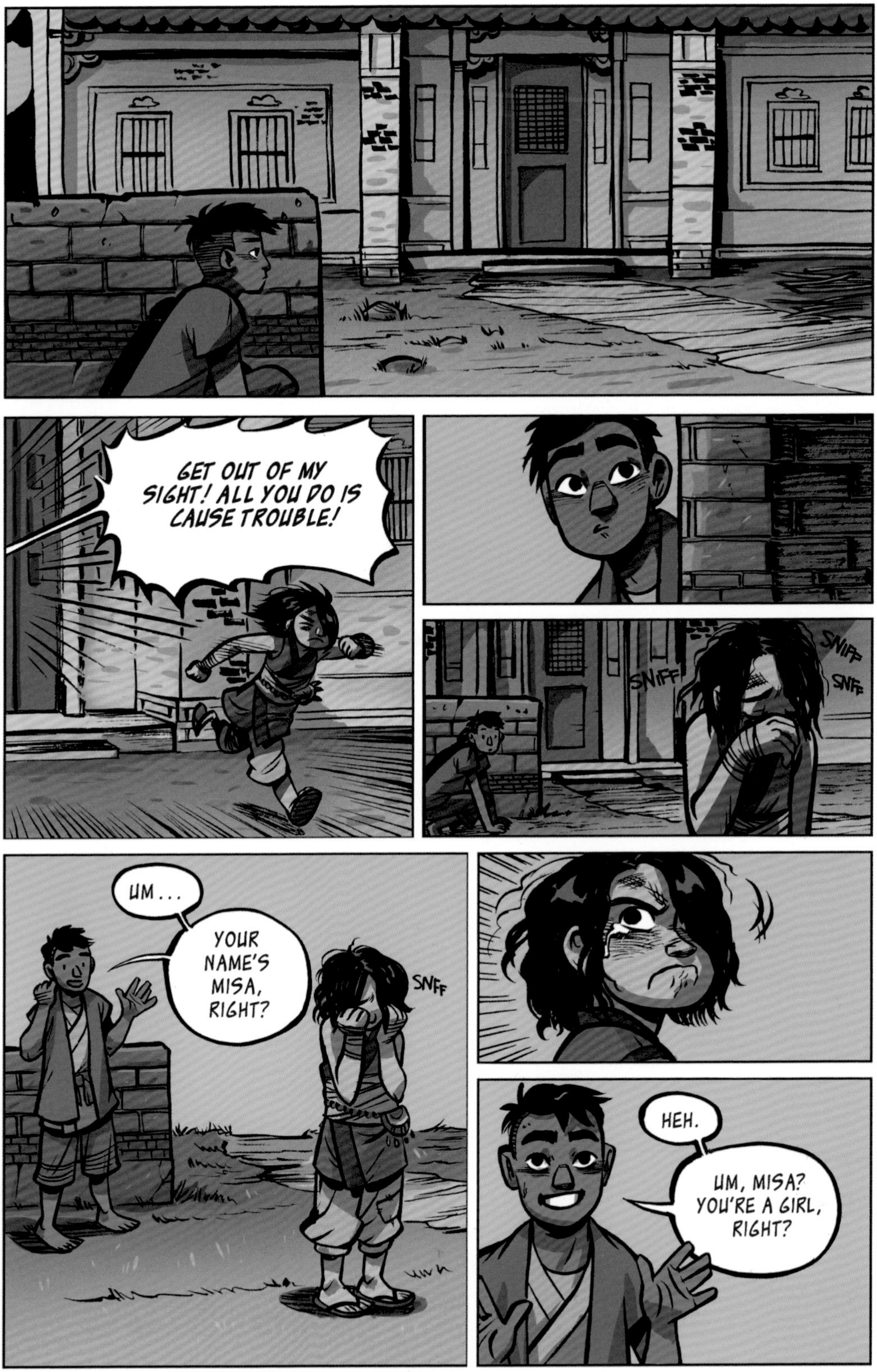
GET OUT OF MY SIGHT! ALL YOU DO IS CAUSE TROUBLE!
SNIFF
SNIFF
SNFF
UM...
YOUR NAME'S MISA, RIGHT?
SNFF
HEH.
UM, MISA? YOU'RE A GIRL, RIGHT?

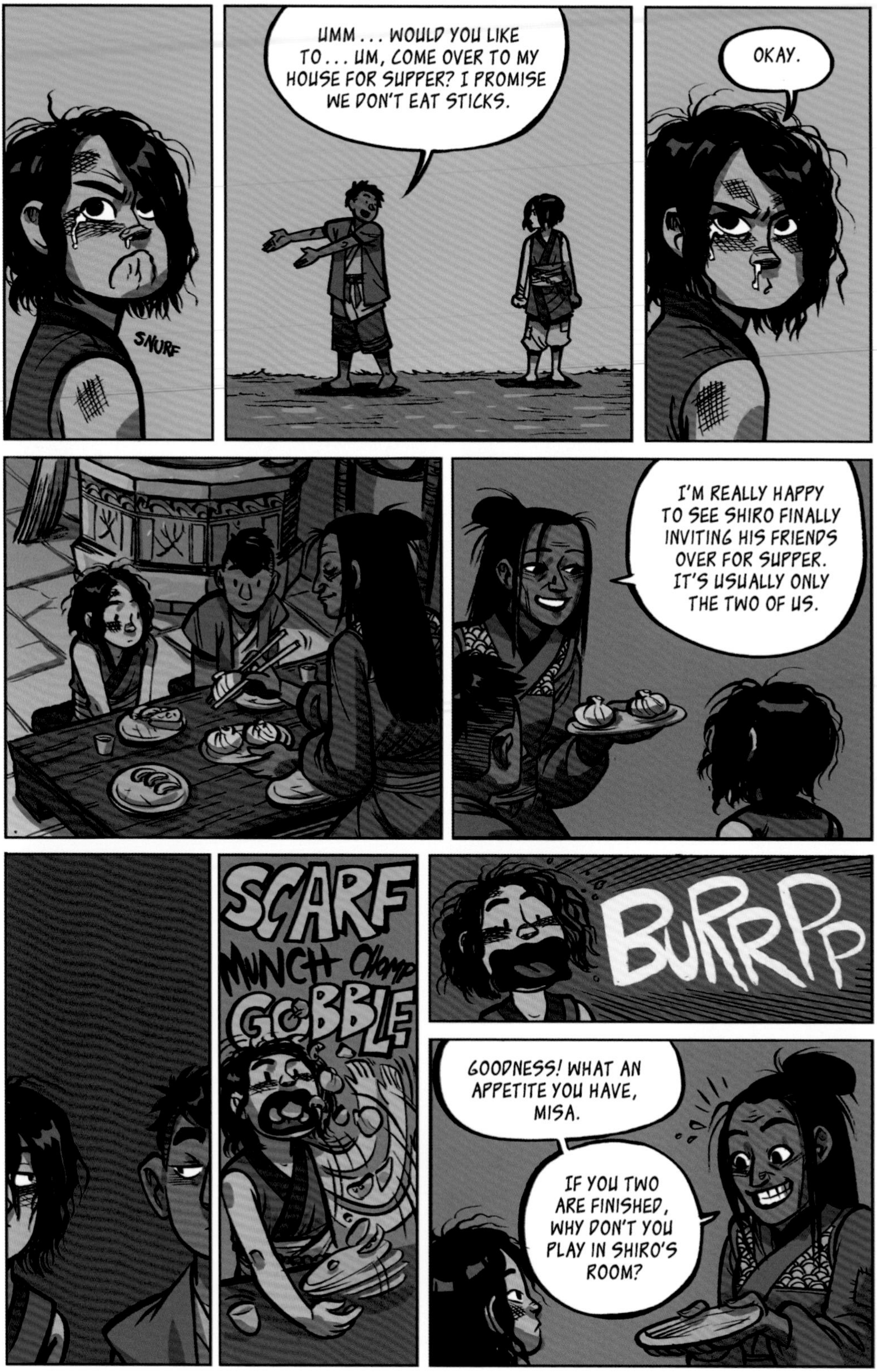
SNURF
UMM . . . WOULD YOU LIKE TO . . . UM, COME OVER TO MY HOUSE FOR SUPPER? I PROMISE WE DON'T EAT STICKS.
OKAY.
I'M REALLY HAPPY TO SEE SHIRO FINALLY INVITING HIS FRIENDS OVER FOR SUPPER. IT'S USUALLY ONLY THE TWO OF US.
SCARF
MUNCH
Chomp
GOBBLE
BURRPP
GOODNESS! WHAT AN APPETITE YOU HAVE, MISA.
IF YOU TWO ARE FINISHED, WHY DON'T YOU PLAY IN SHIRO'S ROOM?

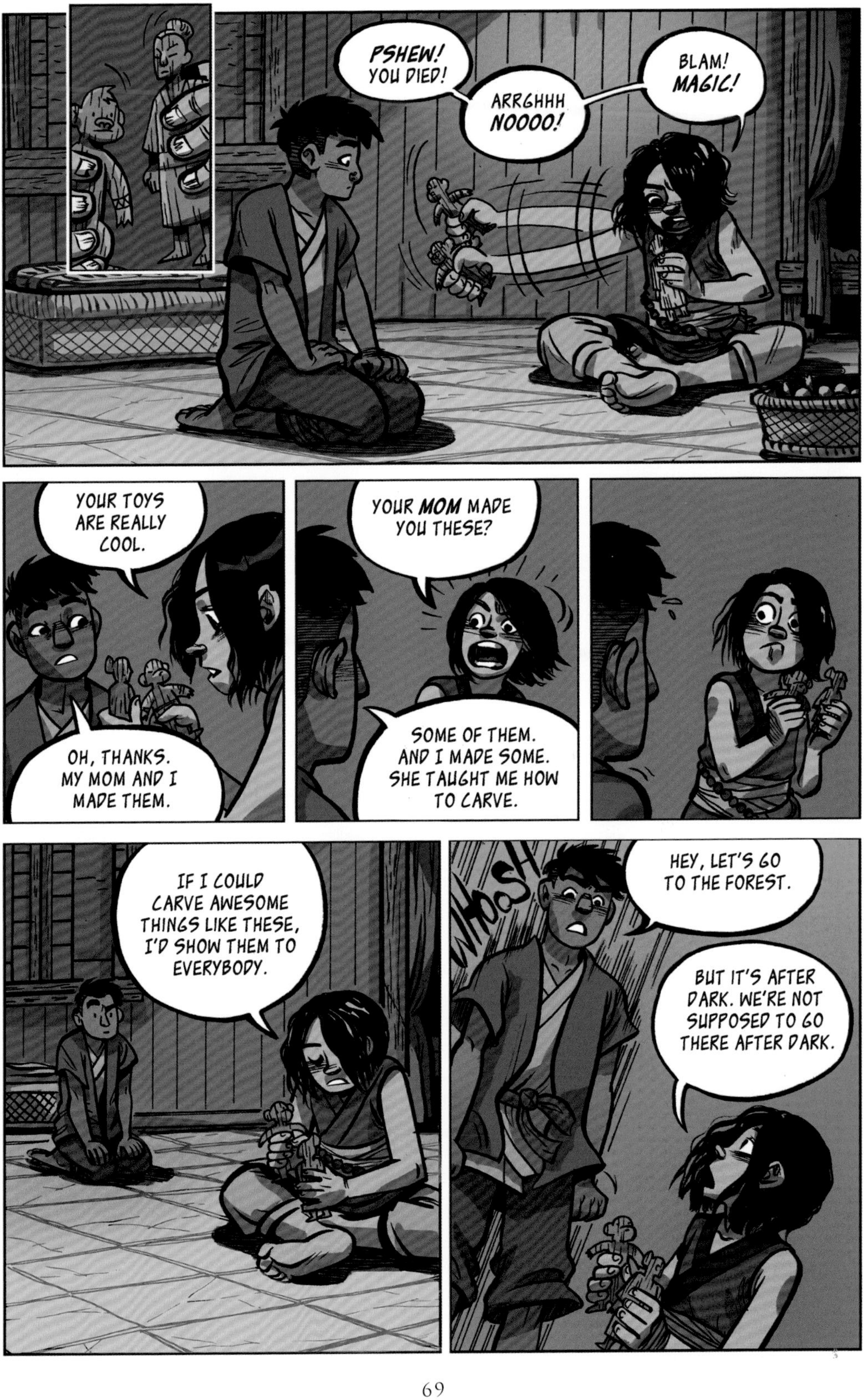
PSHEW! YOU DIED!
ARRGHHH NOOOO!
BLAM! MAGIC!
YOUR TOYS ARE REALLY COOL.
OH, THANKS. MY MOM AND I MADE THEM.
YOUR MOM MADE YOU THESE?
SOME OF THEM. AND I MADE SOME. SHE TAUGHT ME HOW TO CARVE.
IF I COULD CARVE AWESOME THINGS LIKE THESE, I'D SHOW THEM TO EVERYBODY.
WHOOSH
HEY, LET'S GO TO THE FOREST.
BUT IT'S AFTER DARK. WE'RE NOT SUPPOSED TO GO THERE AFTER DARK.

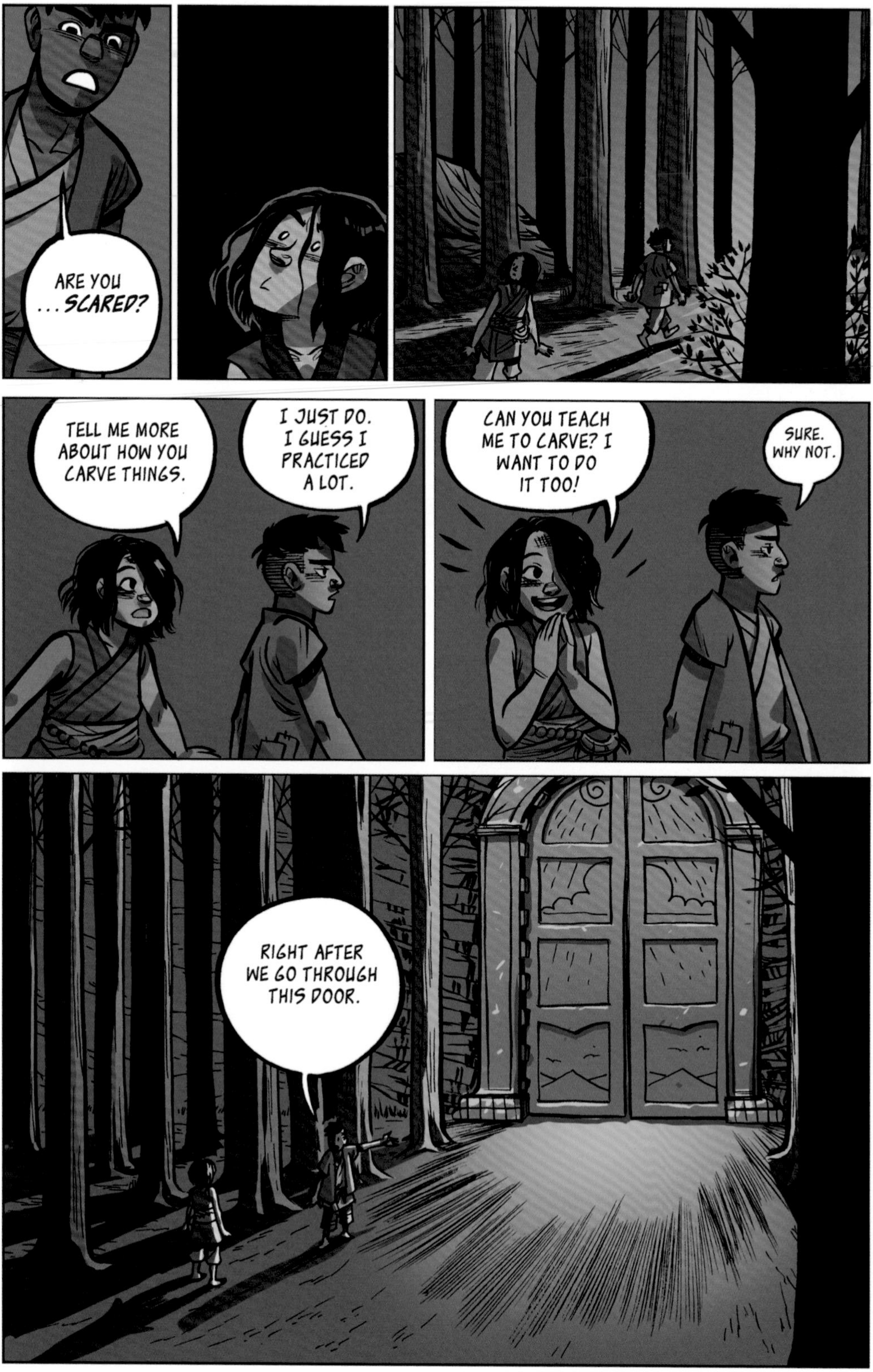
ARE YOU ...SCARED?
TELL ME MORE ABOUT HOW YOU CARVE THINGS.
I JUST DO. I GUESS I PRACTICED A LOT.
CAN YOU TEACH ME TO CARVE? I WANT TO DO IT TOO!
SURE. WHY NOT.
RIGHT AFTER WE GO THROUGH THIS DOOR.

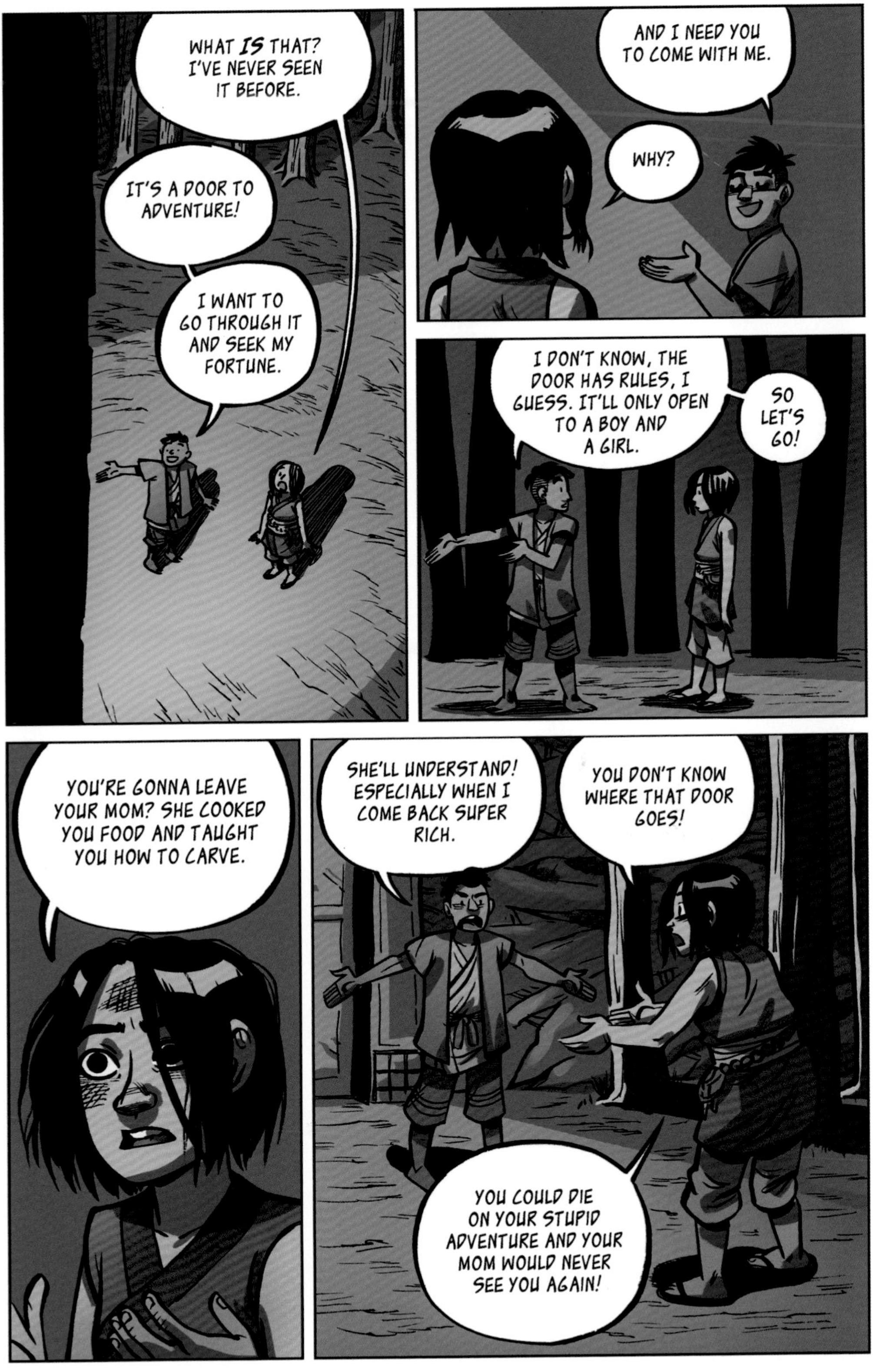
WHAT *IS* THAT? I'VE NEVER SEEN IT BEFORE.
IT'S A DOOR TO ADVENTURE!
I WANT TO GO THROUGH IT AND SEEK MY FORTUNE.
AND I NEED YOU TO COME WITH ME.
WHY?
I DON'T KNOW, THE DOOR HAS RULES, I GUESS. IT'LL ONLY OPEN TO A BOY AND A GIRL.
SO LET'S GO!
YOU'RE GONNA LEAVE YOUR MOM? SHE COOKED YOU FOOD AND TAUGHT YOU HOW TO CARVE.
SHE'LL UNDERSTAND! ESPECIALLY WHEN I COME BACK SUPER RICH.
YOU DON'T KNOW WHERE THAT DOOR GOES!
YOU COULD DIE ON YOUR STUPID ADVENTURE AND YOUR MOM WOULD NEVER SEE YOU AGAIN!

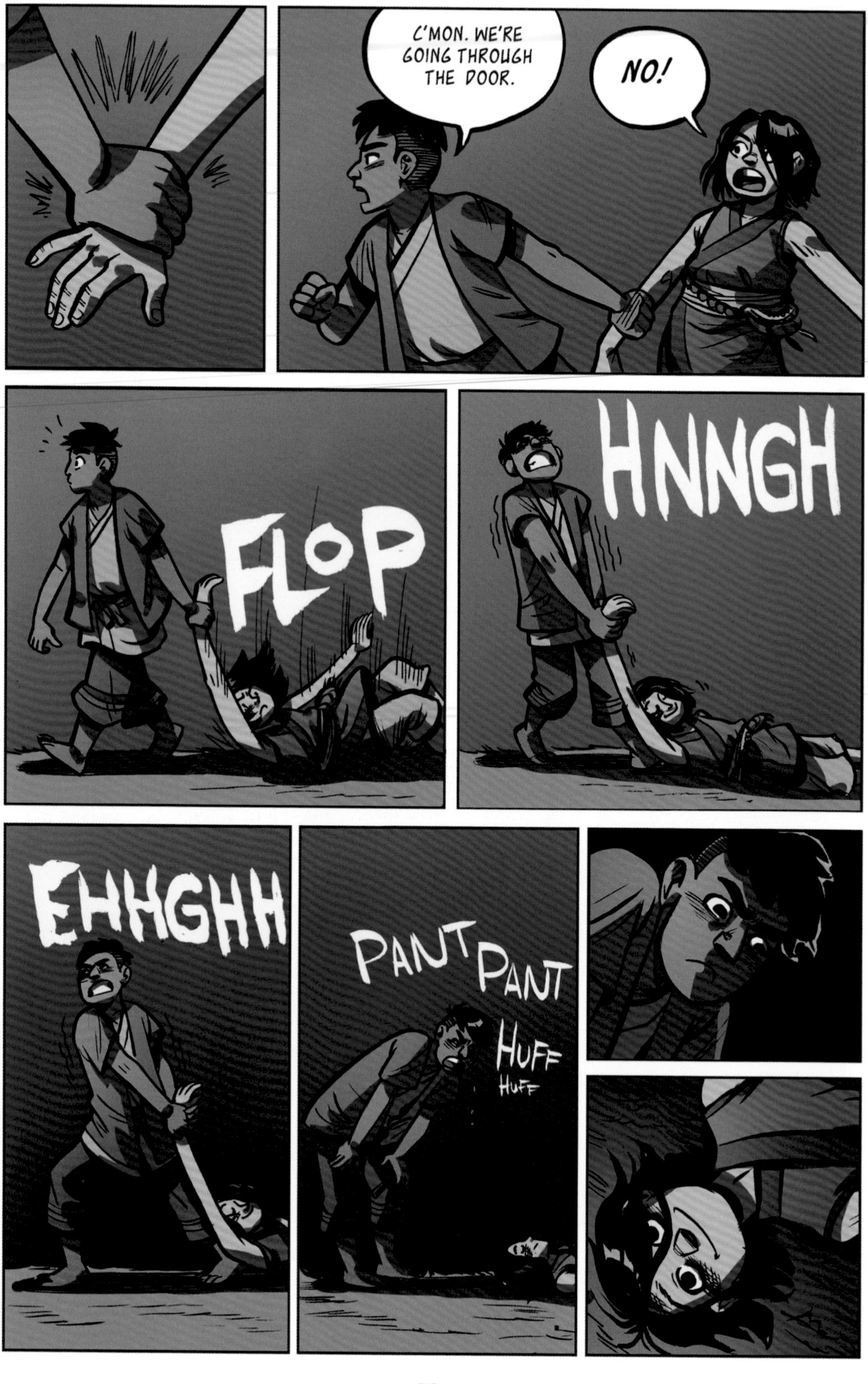
C'MON. WE'RE GOING THROUGH THE DOOR.
NO!
FLOP
HNNGH
EHHGHH
PANT PANT
HUFF
HUFF

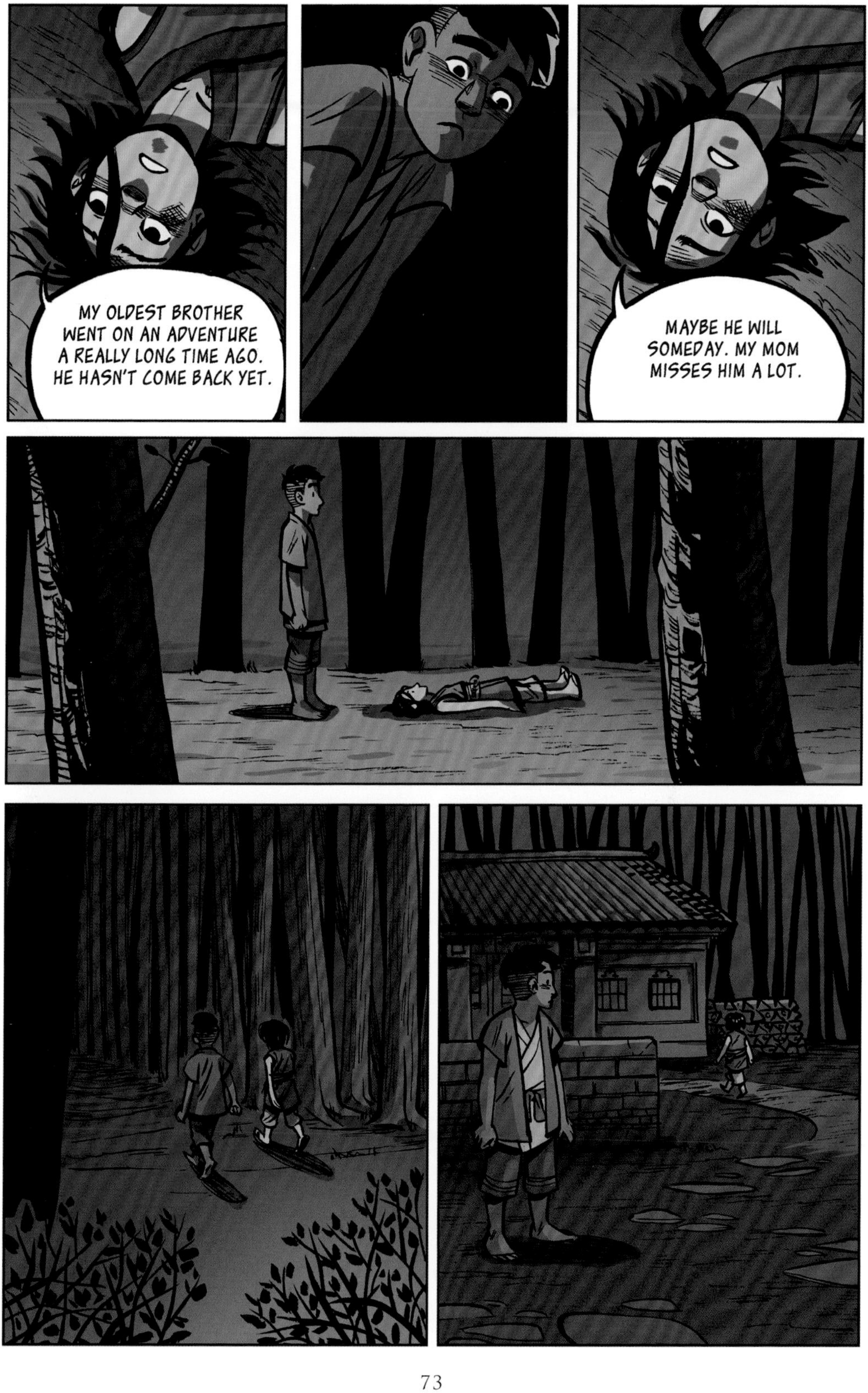
MY OLDEST BROTHER WENT ON AN ADVENTURE A REALLY LONG TIME AGO. HE HASN'T COME BACK YET.
MAYBE HE WILL SOMEDAY. MY MOM MISSES HIM A LOT.

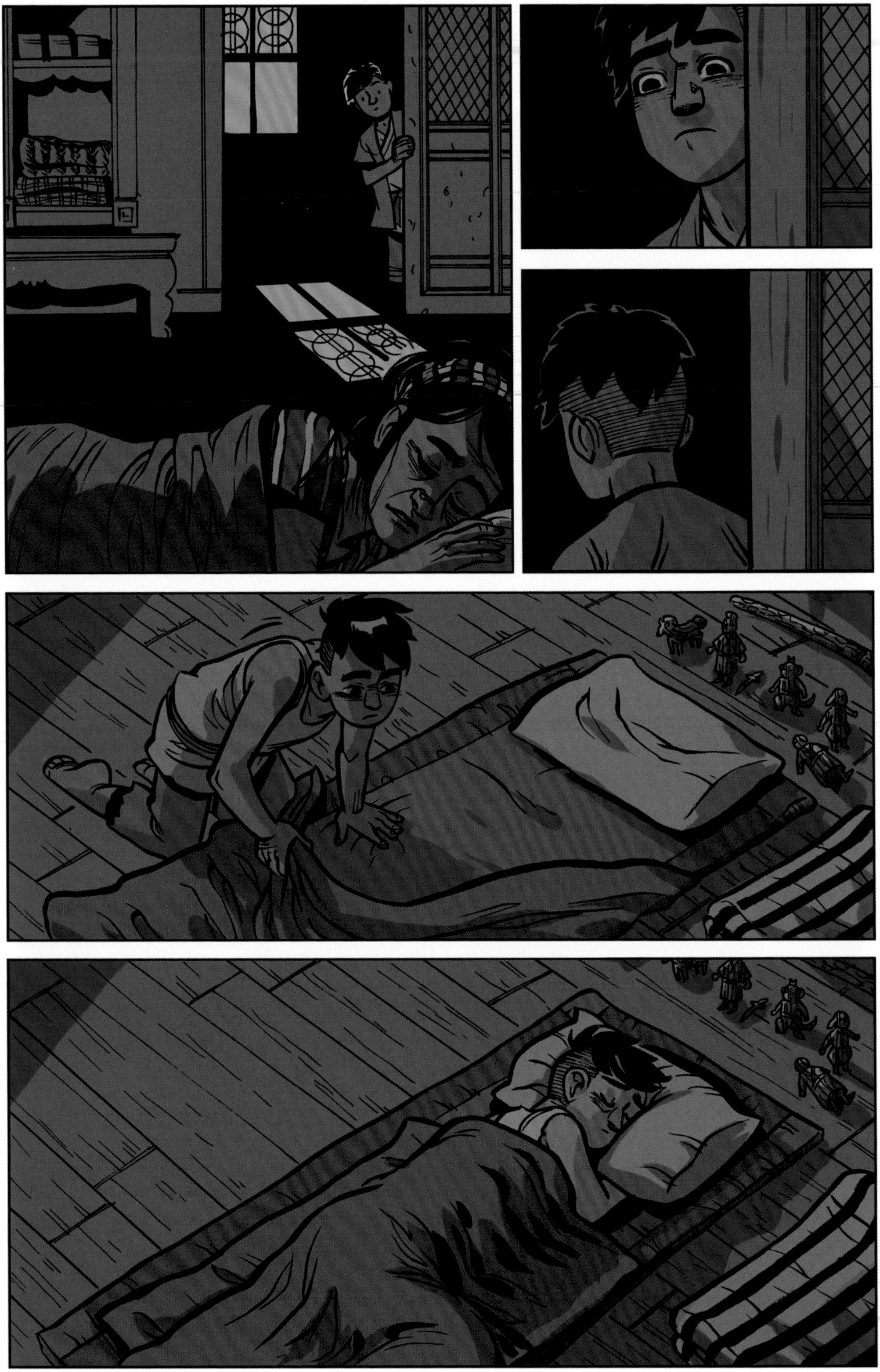

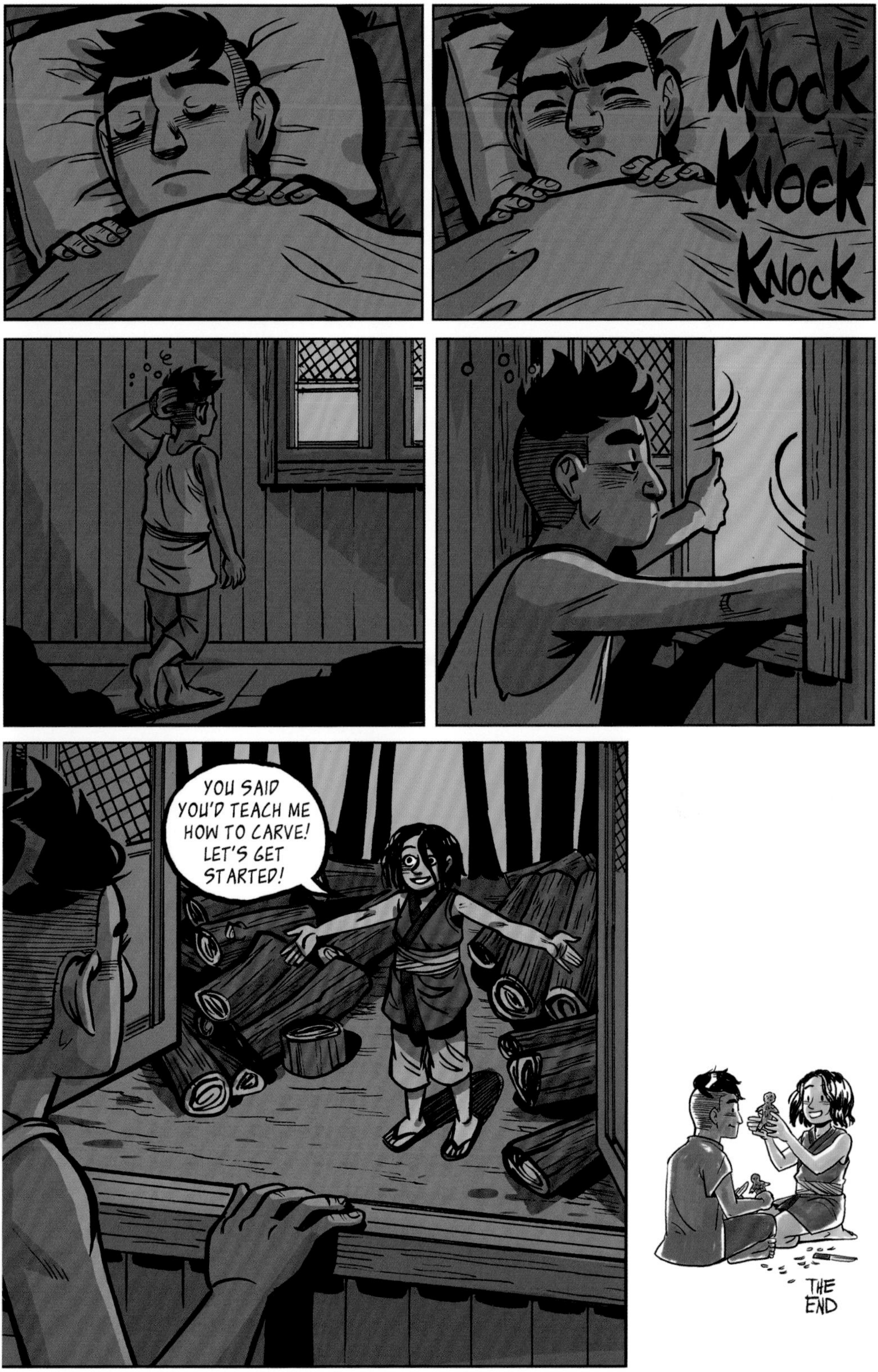
KNOCK
KNOCK
KNOCK
YOU SAID YOU'D TEACH ME HOW TO CARVE! LET'S GET STARTED!
THE END

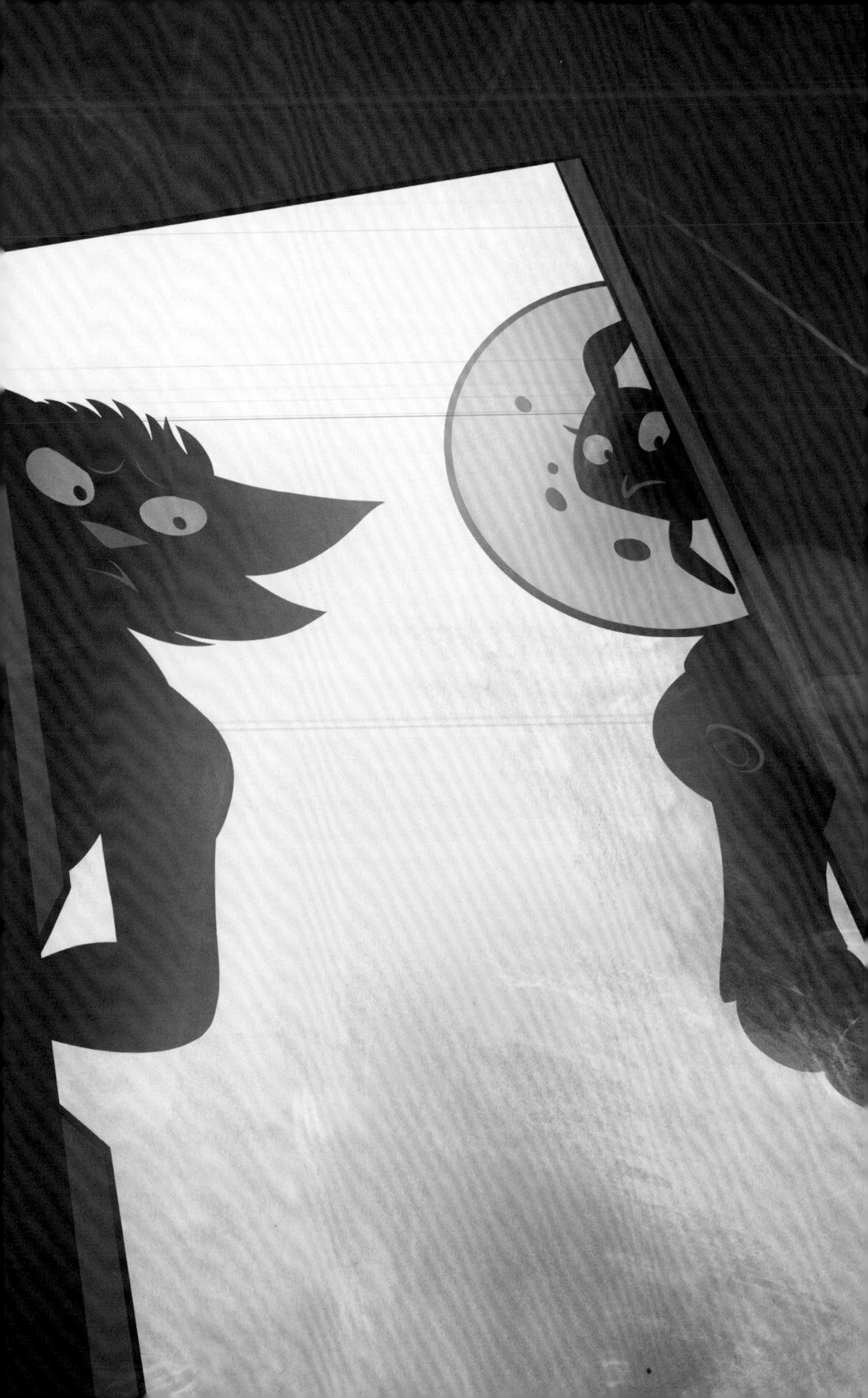

# Fish N chips

### IN
## spring cleaning

### BY STEVE HAMAKER

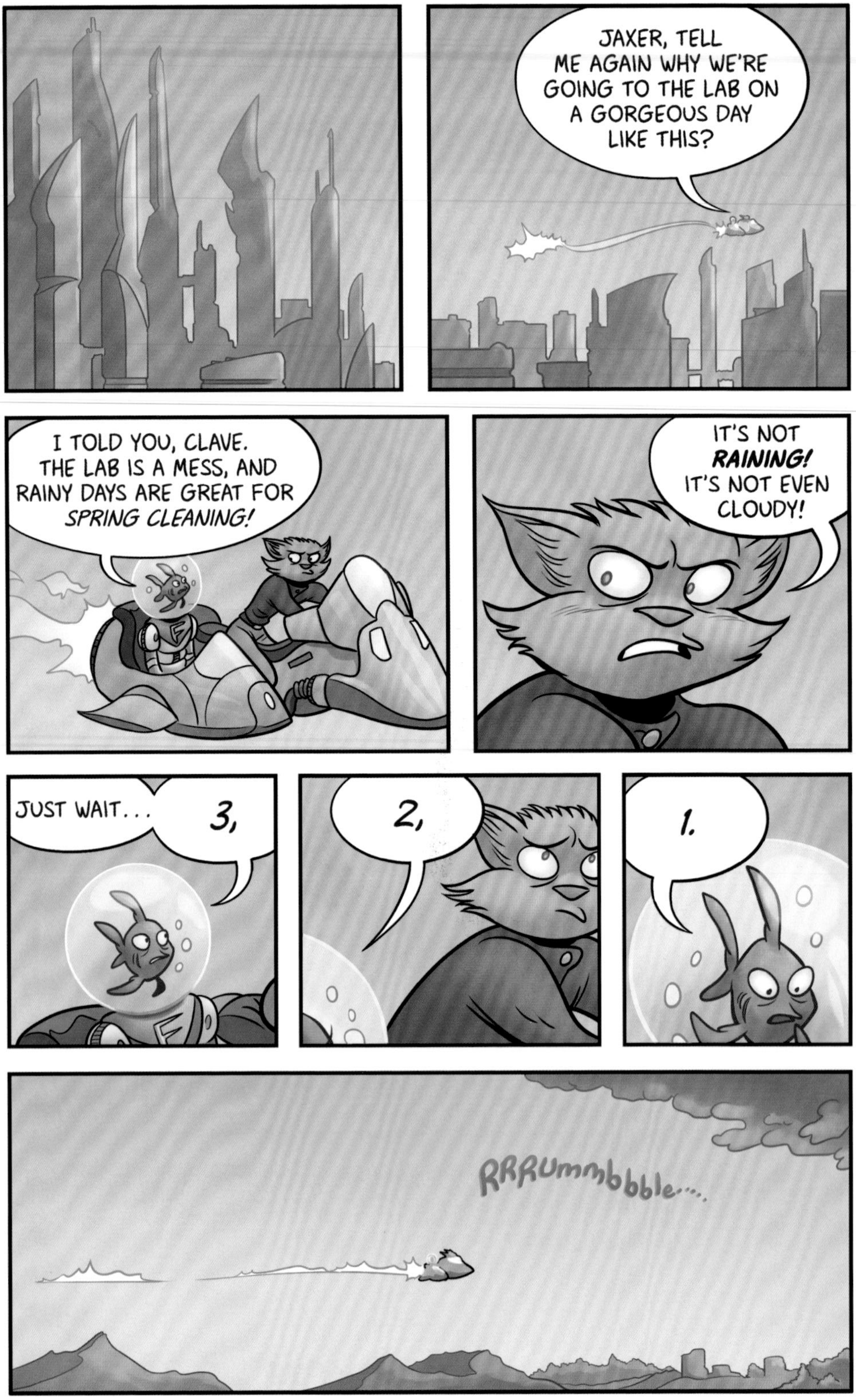
JAXER, TELL ME AGAIN WHY WE'RE GOING TO THE LAB ON A GORGEOUS DAY LIKE THIS?
I TOLD YOU, CLAVE. THE LAB IS A MESS, AND RAINY DAYS ARE GREAT FOR *SPRING CLEANING!*
IT'S NOT ***RAINING!*** IT'S NOT EVEN CLOUDY!
JUST WAIT...
3,
2,
1.
RRRUmmbbble....

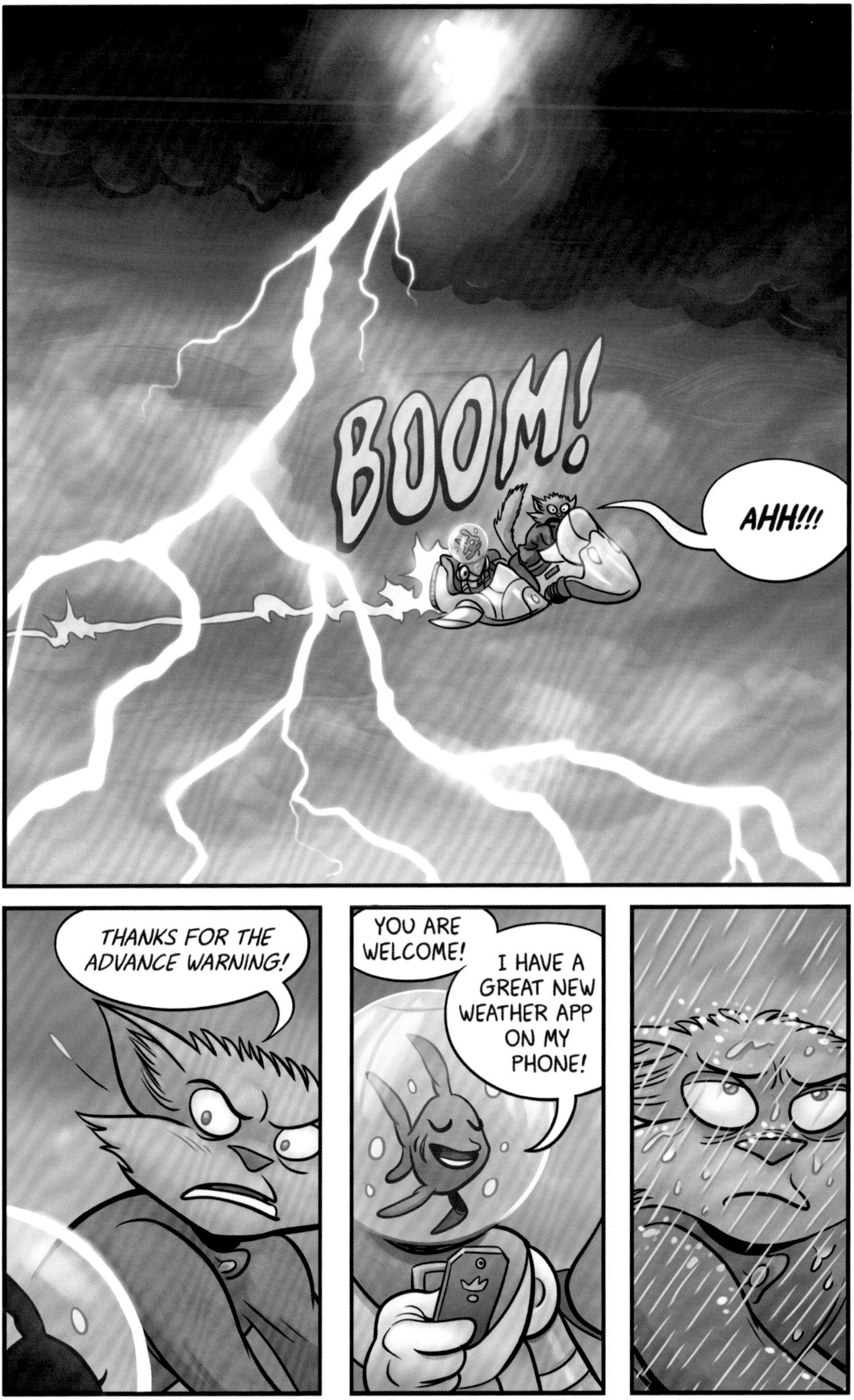
BOOM!
AHH!!!
THANKS FOR THE ADVANCE WARNING!
YOU ARE WELCOME!
I HAVE A GREAT NEW WEATHER APP ON MY PHONE!

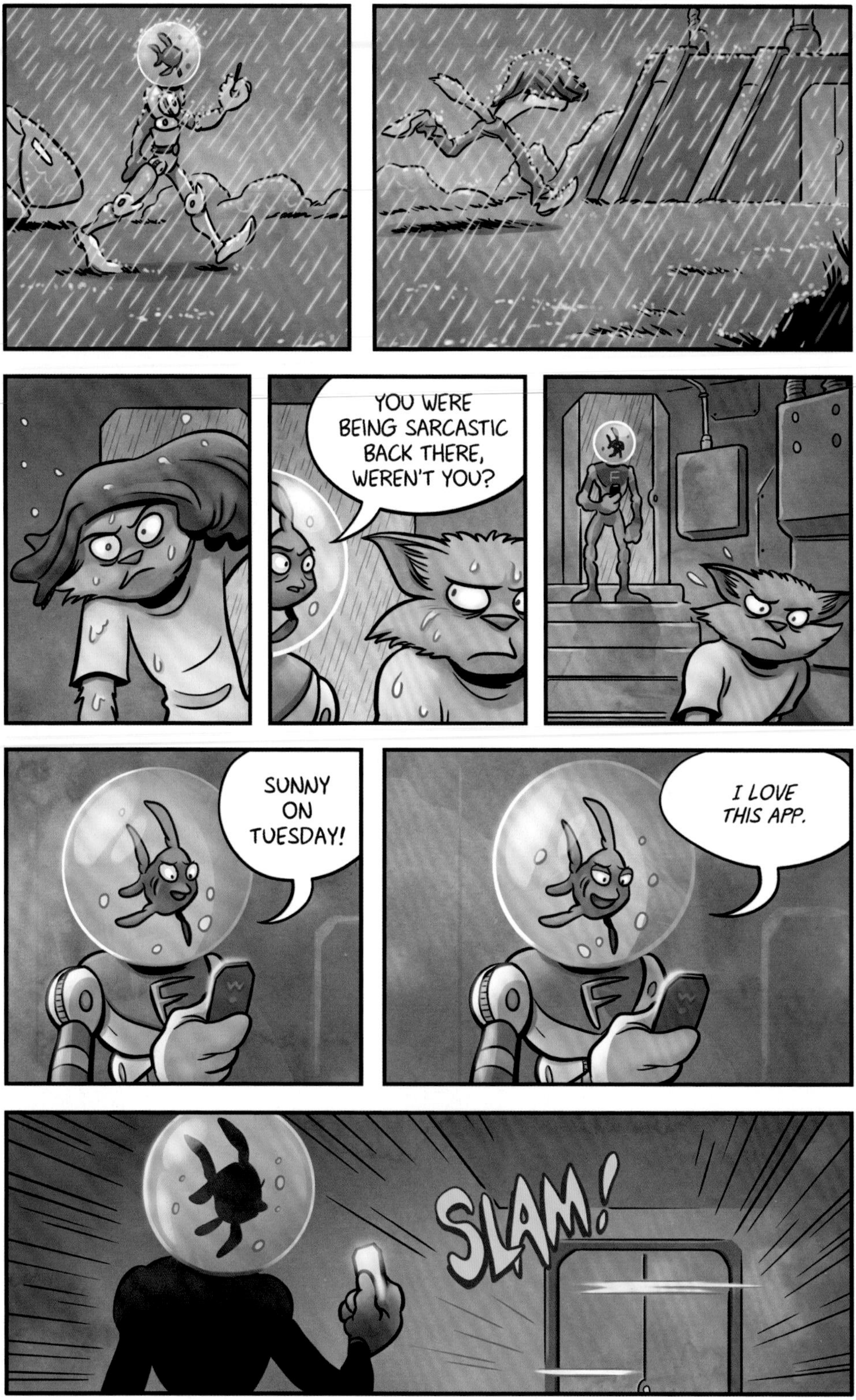
YOU WERE BEING SARCASTIC BACK THERE, WEREN'T YOU?
SUNNY ON TUESDAY!
I LOVE THIS APP.
SLAM!

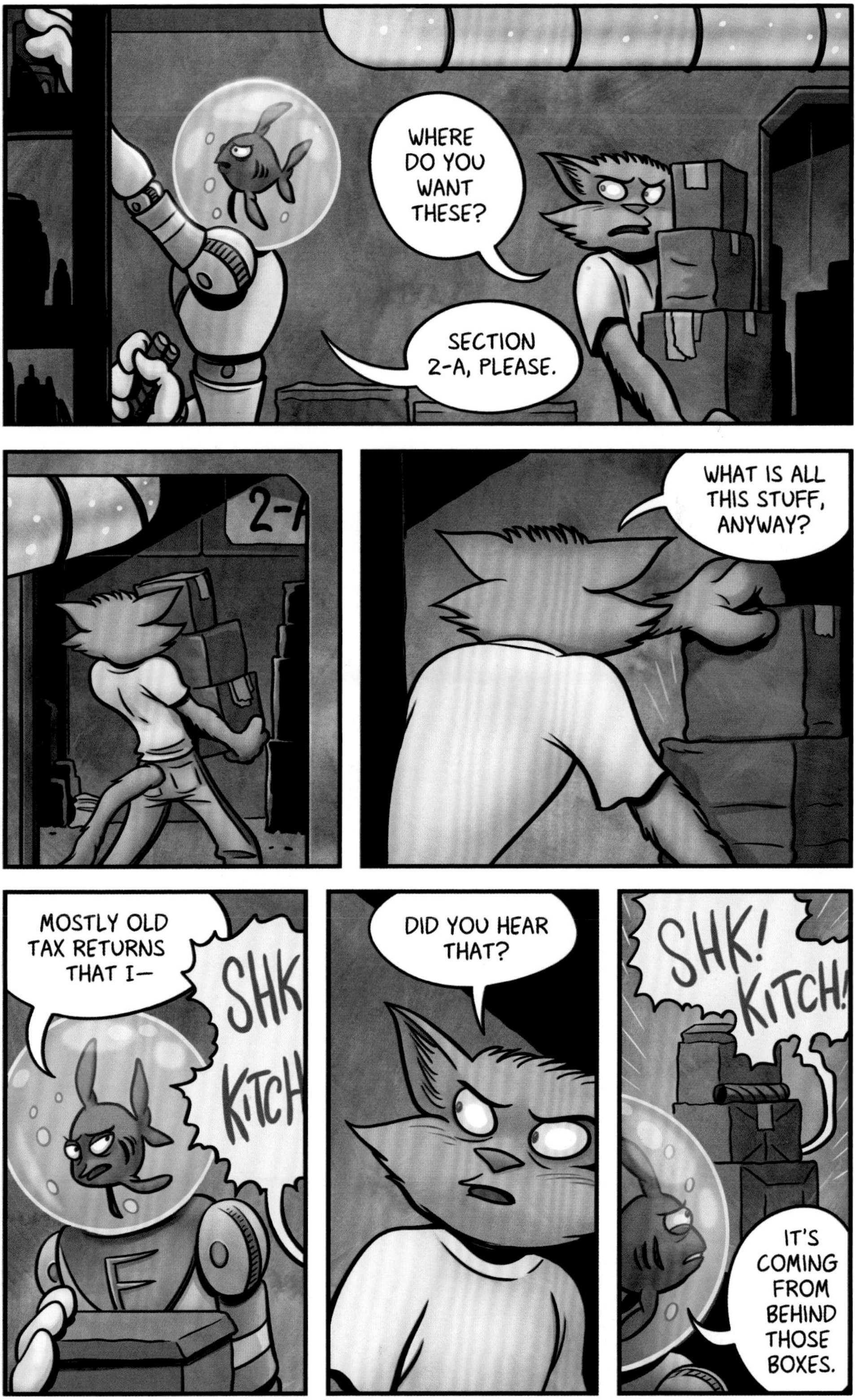
WHERE DO YOU WANT THESE?
SECTION 2-A, PLEASE.
2-A
WHAT IS ALL THIS STUFF, ANYWAY?
MOSTLY OLD TAX RETURNS THAT I—
SHK KITCH
DID YOU HEAR THAT?
SHK! KITCH!
IT'S COMING FROM BEHIND THOSE BOXES.

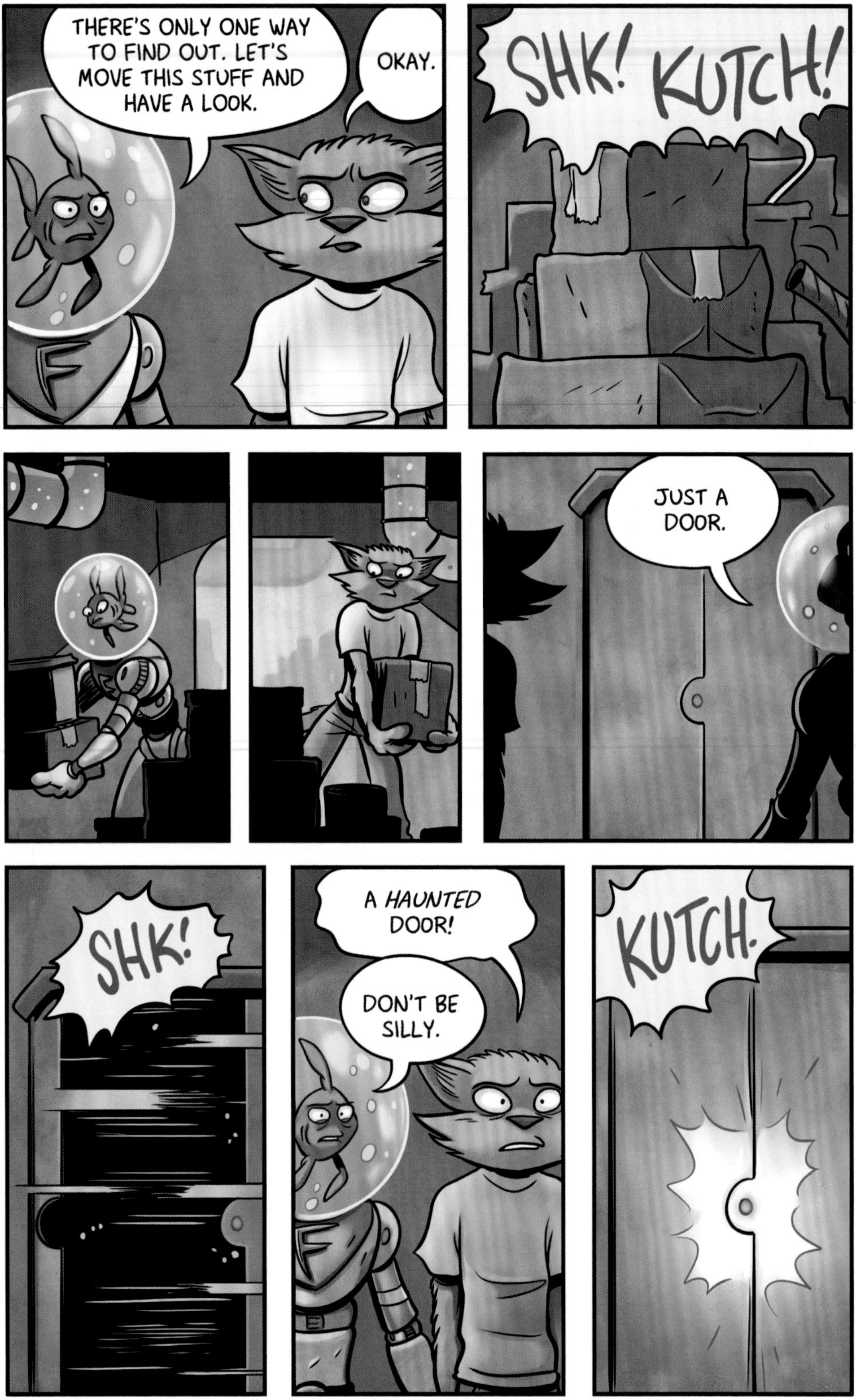
THERE'S ONLY ONE WAY TO FIND OUT. LET'S MOVE THIS STUFF AND HAVE A LOOK.
OKAY.
SHK! KUTCH!
JUST A DOOR.
SHK!
A *HAUNTED* DOOR!
DON'T BE SILLY.
KUTCH.

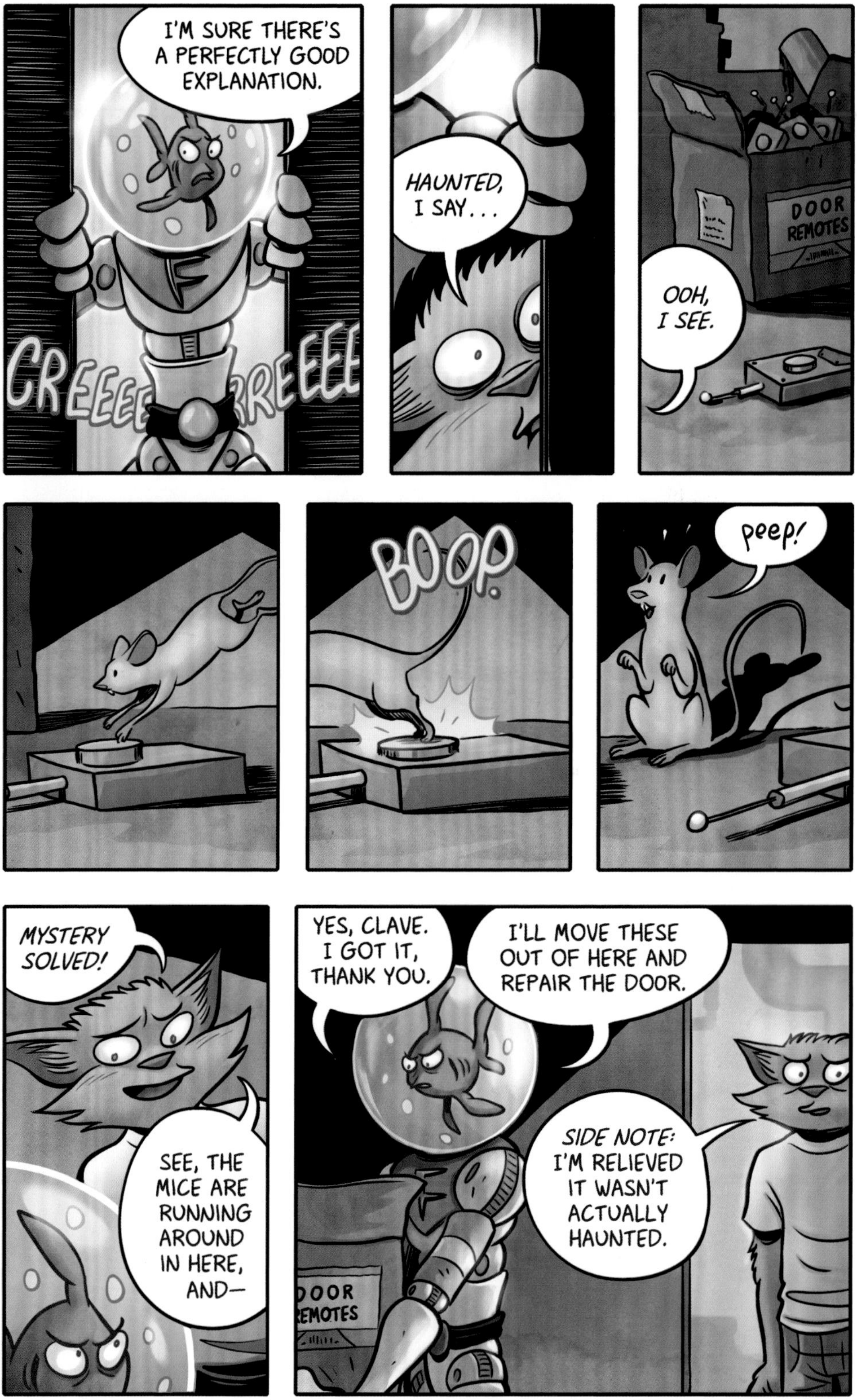
I'M SURE THERE'S A PERFECTLY GOOD EXPLANATION.
CREEEEEREEEEE
HAUNTED, I SAY . . .
DOOR REMOTES
OOH, I SEE.
BOOP.
peep!
MYSTERY SOLVED!
SEE, THE MICE ARE RUNNING AROUND IN HERE, AND—
YES, CLAVE. I GOT IT, THANK YOU.
I'LL MOVE THESE OUT OF HERE AND REPAIR THE DOOR.
SIDE NOTE: I'M RELIEVED IT WASN'T ACTUALLY HAUNTED.
DOOR REMOTES

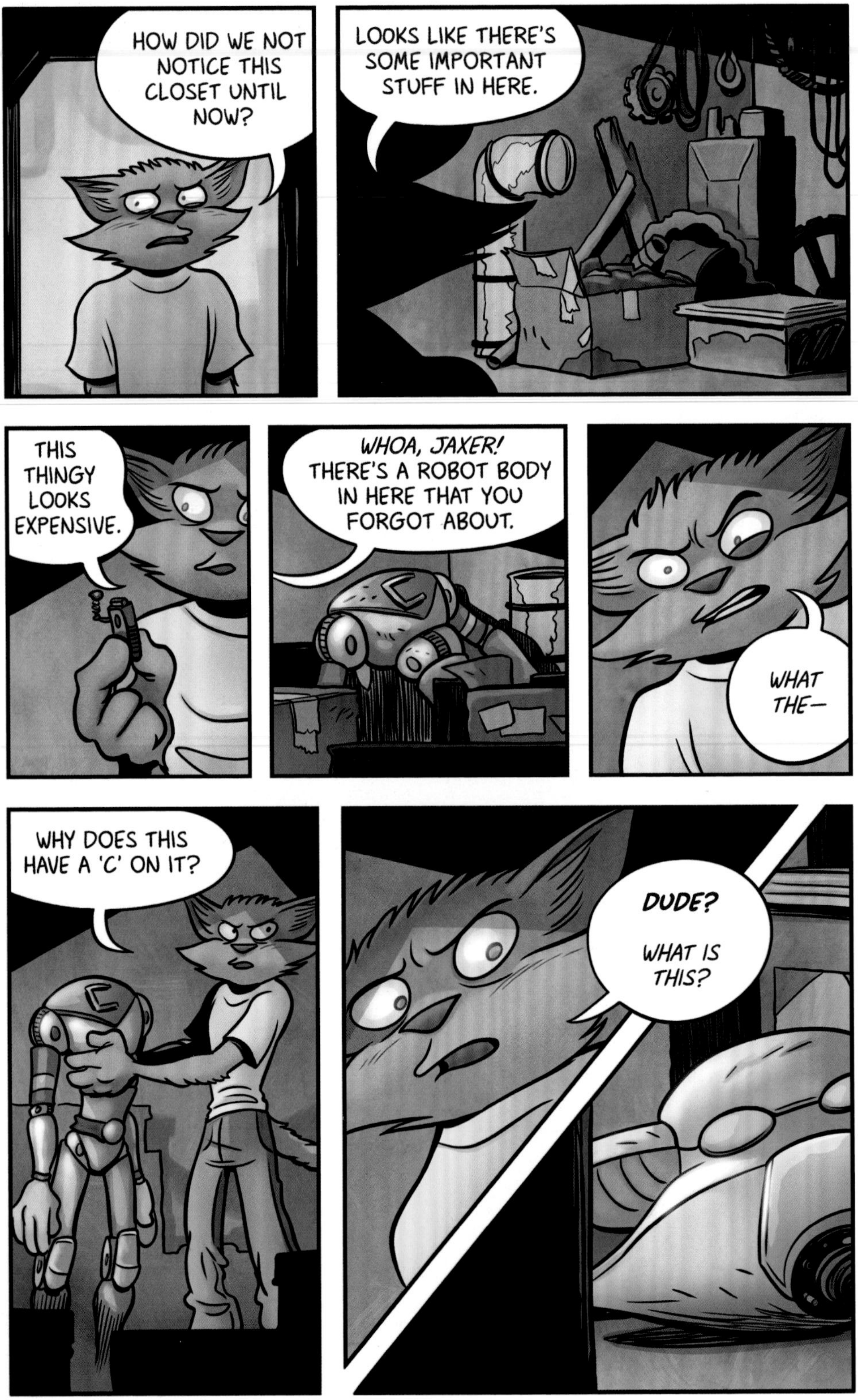
HOW DID WE NOT NOTICE THIS CLOSET UNTIL NOW?
LOOKS LIKE THERE'S SOME IMPORTANT STUFF IN HERE.
THIS THINGY LOOKS EXPENSIVE.
WHOA, JAXER! THERE'S A ROBOT BODY IN HERE THAT YOU FORGOT ABOUT.
WHAT THE—
WHY DOES THIS HAVE A 'C' ON IT?
DUDE?
WHAT IS THIS?

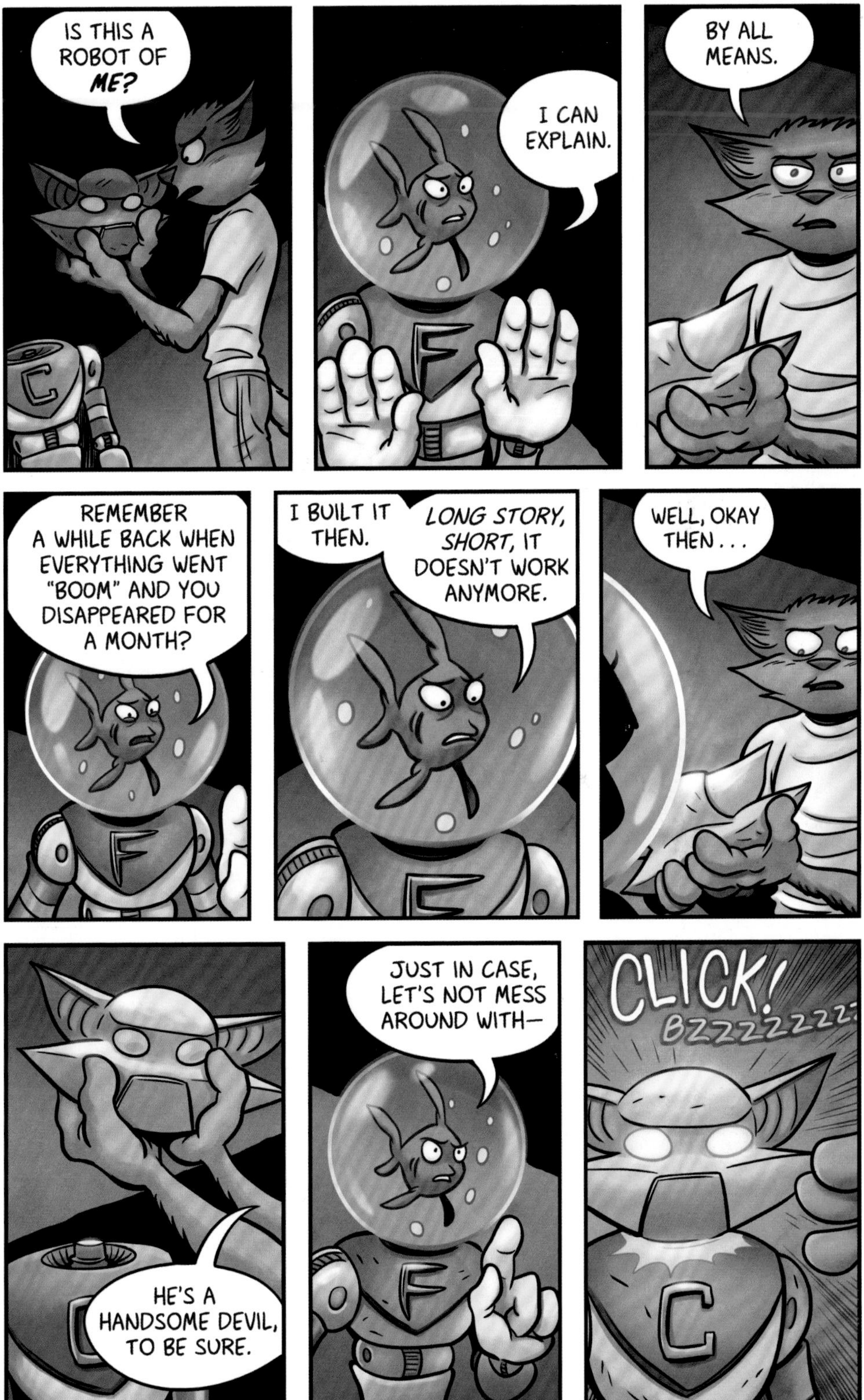
IS THIS A ROBOT OF *ME?*
I CAN EXPLAIN.
BY ALL MEANS.
REMEMBER A WHILE BACK WHEN EVERYTHING WENT "BOOM" AND YOU DISAPPEARED FOR A MONTH?
I BUILT IT THEN.
*LONG STORY, SHORT,* IT DOESN'T WORK ANYMORE.
WELL, OKAY THEN . . .
HE'S A HANDSOME DEVIL, TO BE SURE.
JUST IN CASE, LET'S NOT MESS AROUND WITH—
CLICK!
BZZZZZZZ

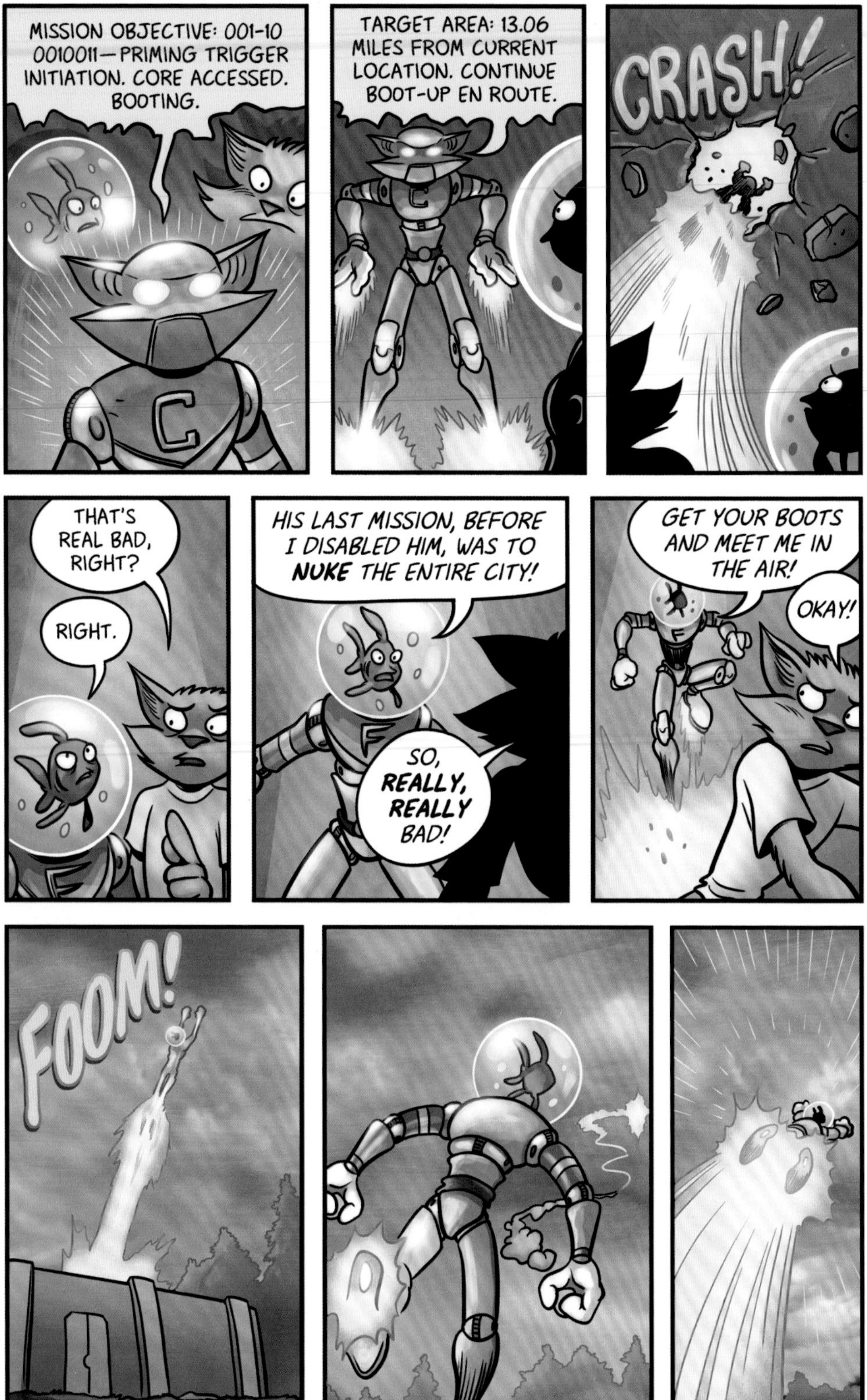
MISSION OBJECTIVE: 001-10 0010011—PRIMING TRIGGER INITIATION. CORE ACCESSED. BOOTING.
TARGET AREA: 13.06 MILES FROM CURRENT LOCATION. CONTINUE BOOT-UP EN ROUTE.
CRASH!
THAT'S REAL BAD, RIGHT?
RIGHT.
HIS LAST MISSION, BEFORE I DISABLED HIM, WAS TO NUKE THE ENTIRE CITY!
SO, REALLY, REALLY BAD!
GET YOUR BOOTS AND MEET ME IN THE AIR!
OKAY!
FOOM!

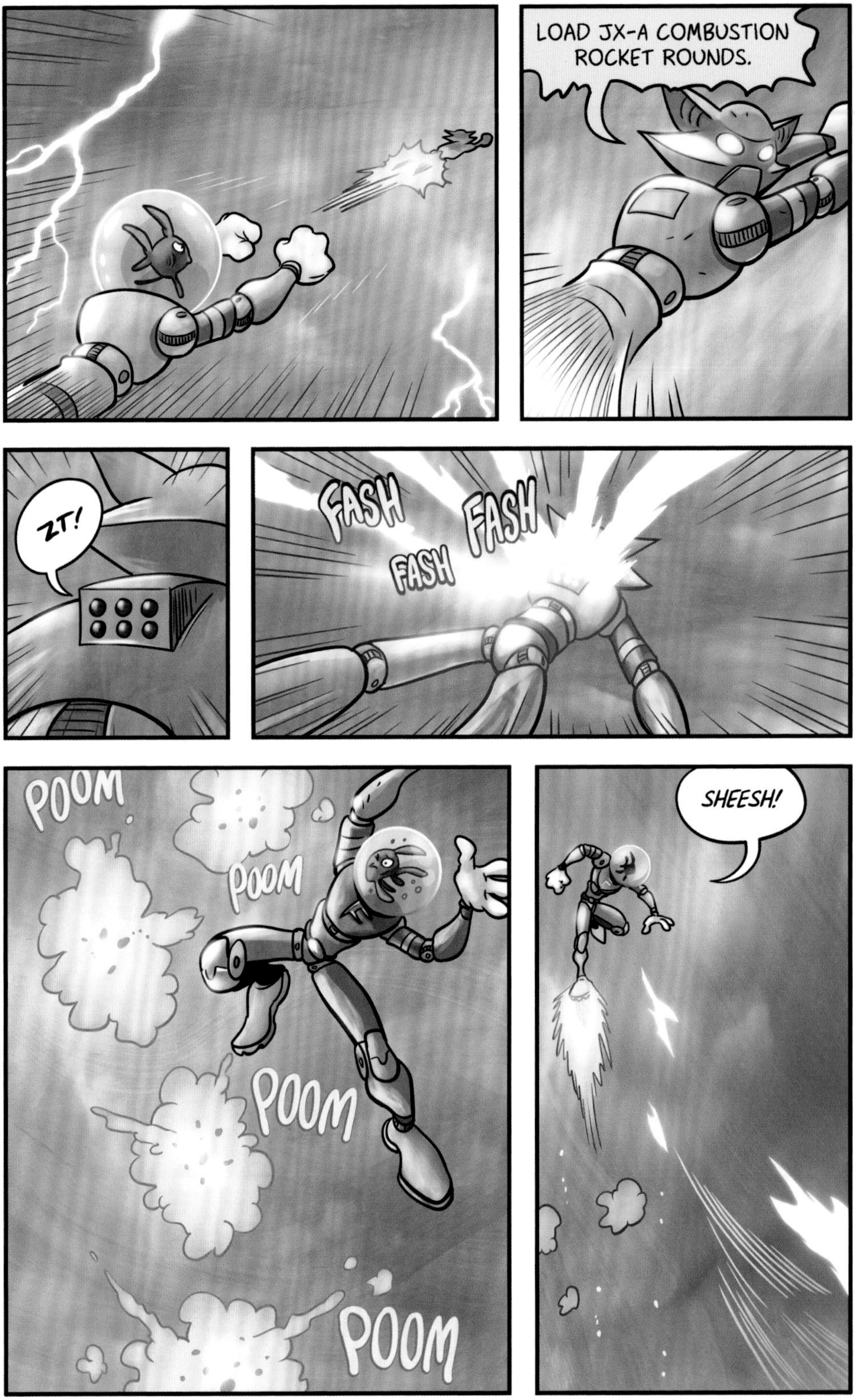
LOAD JX-A COMBUSTION ROCKET ROUNDS.
ZT!
FASH
FASH
FASH
POOM
POOM
POOM
POOM
SHEESH!

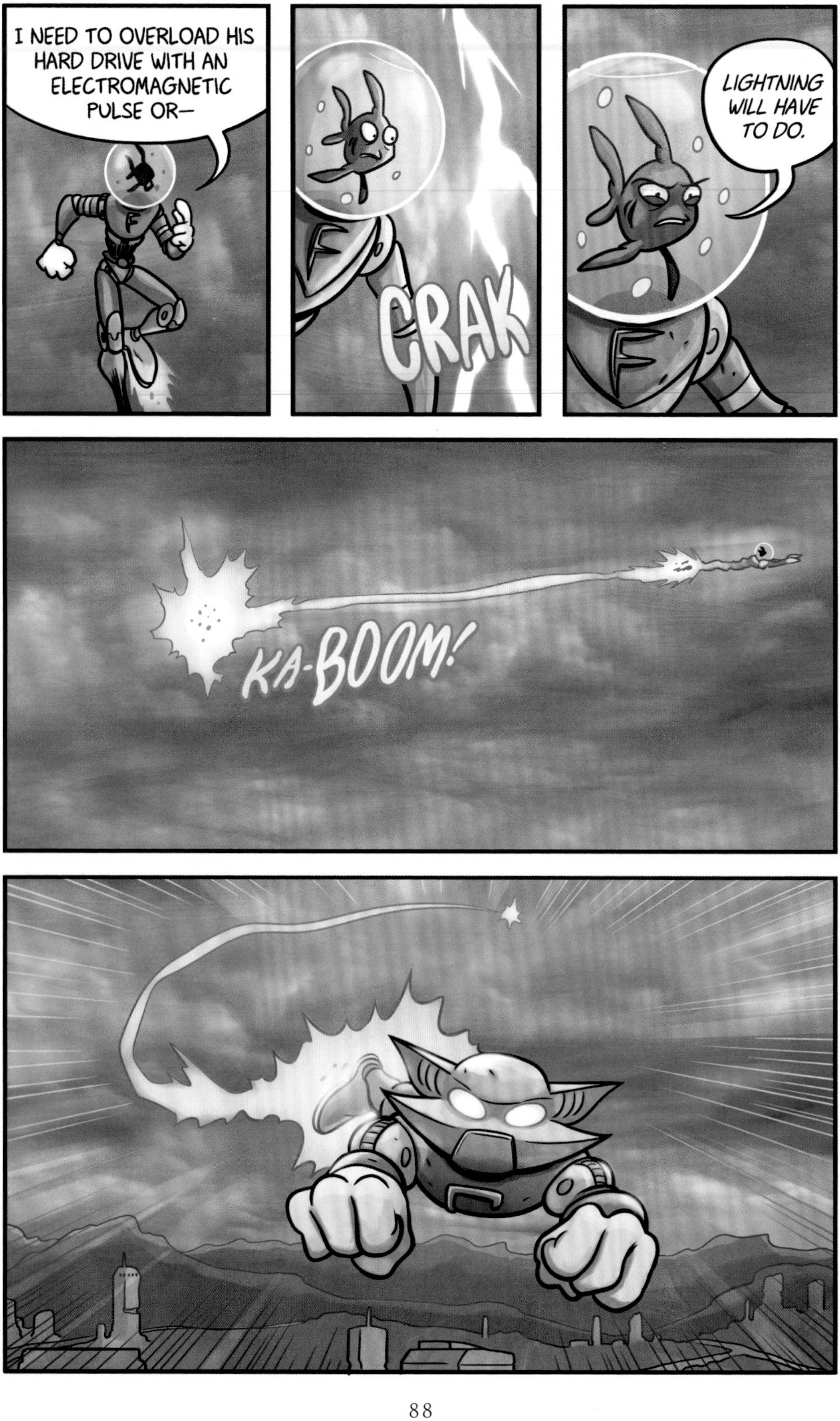
I NEED TO OVERLOAD HIS HARD DRIVE WITH AN ELECTROMAGNETIC PULSE OR—
CRAK
LIGHTNING WILL HAVE TO DO.
KA-BOOM!

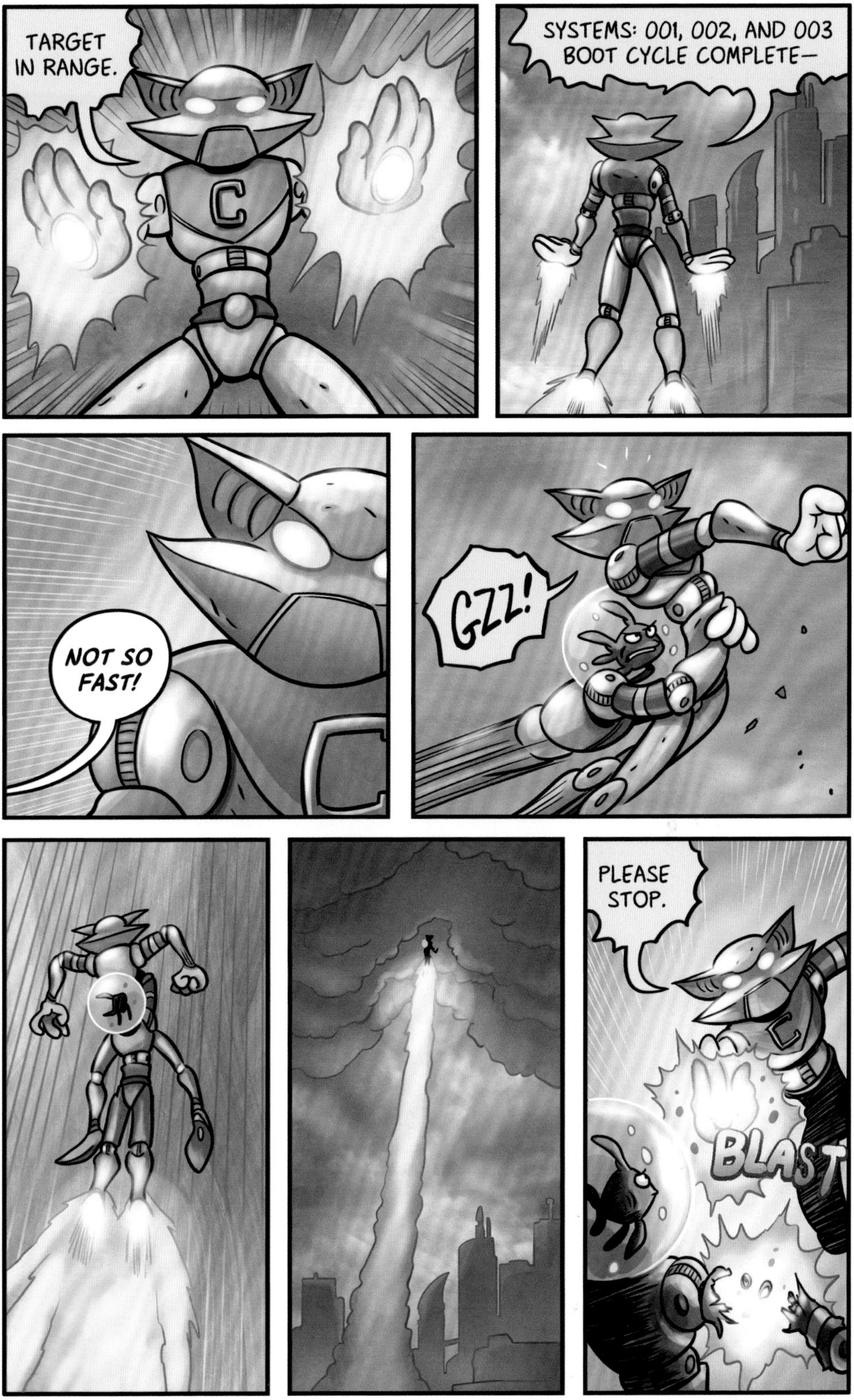
TARGET IN RANGE.
SYSTEMS: 001, 002, AND 003 BOOT CYCLE COMPLETE—
NOT SO FAST!
GZZ!
PLEASE STOP.
BLAST

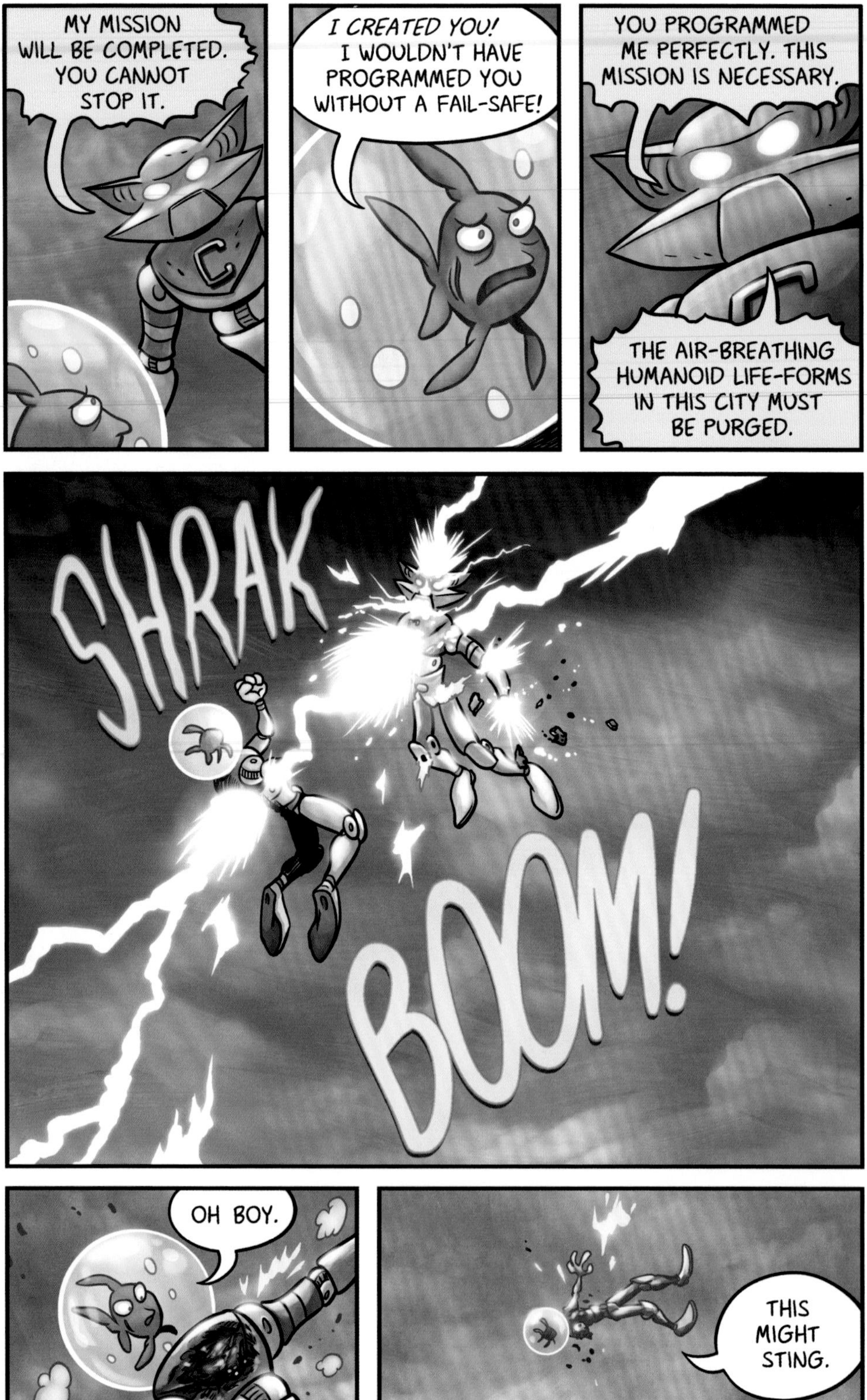
MY MISSION WILL BE COMPLETED. YOU CANNOT STOP IT.
I CREATED YOU! I WOULDN'T HAVE PROGRAMMED YOU WITHOUT A FAIL-SAFE!
YOU PROGRAMMED ME PERFECTLY. THIS MISSION IS NECESSARY.
THE AIR-BREATHING HUMANOID LIFE-FORMS IN THIS CITY MUST BE PURGED.
SHRAK
BOOM!
OH BOY.
THIS MIGHT STING.

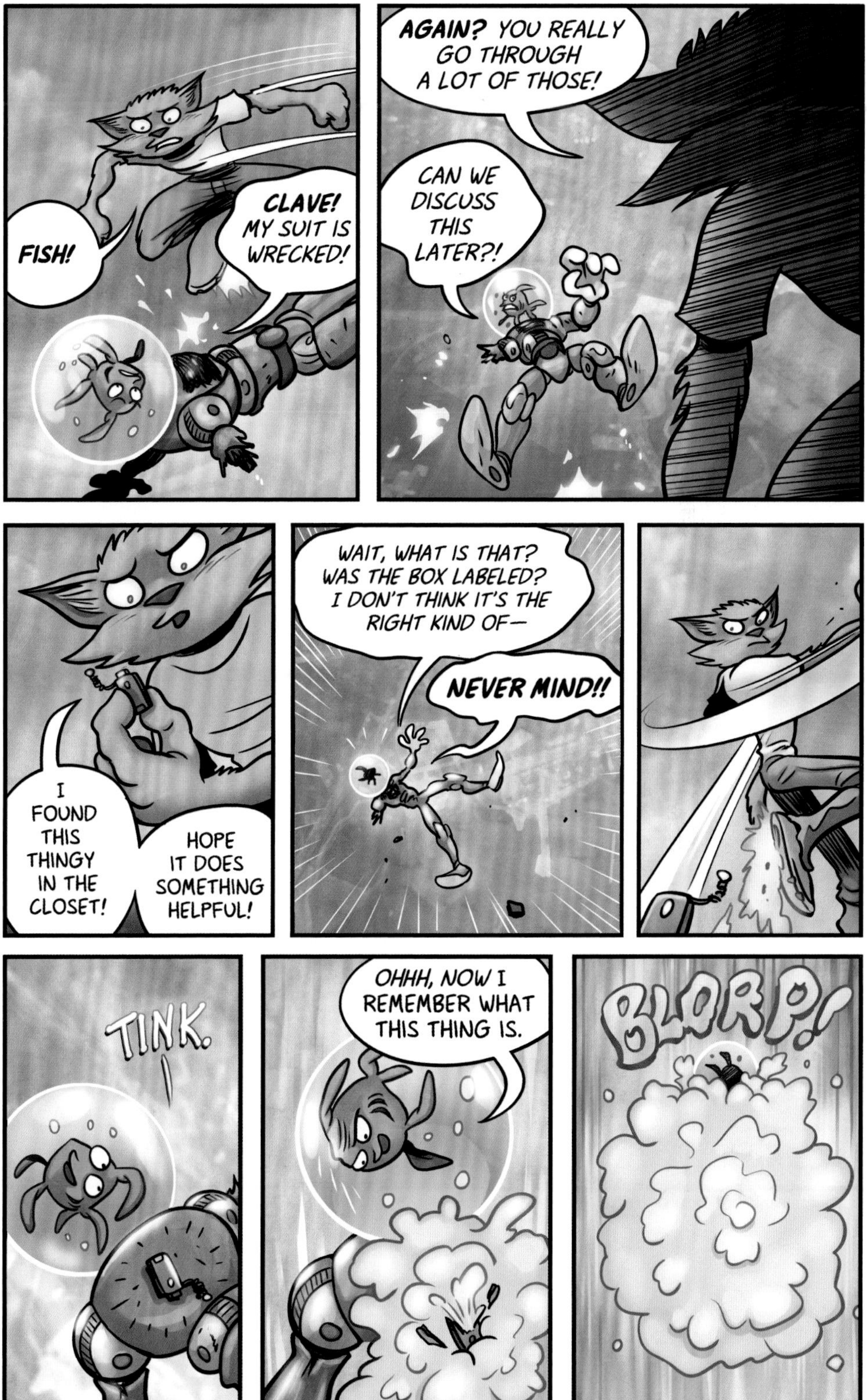
FISH!
CLAVE! MY SUIT IS WRECKED!
AGAIN? YOU REALLY GO THROUGH A LOT OF THOSE!
CAN WE DISCUSS THIS LATER?!
I FOUND THIS THINGY IN THE CLOSET!
HOPE IT DOES SOMETHING HELPFUL!
WAIT, WHAT IS THAT? WAS THE BOX LABELED? I DON'T THINK IT'S THE RIGHT KIND OF—
NEVER MIND!!
TINK.
OHHH, NOW I REMEMBER WHAT THIS THING IS.
BLORP!

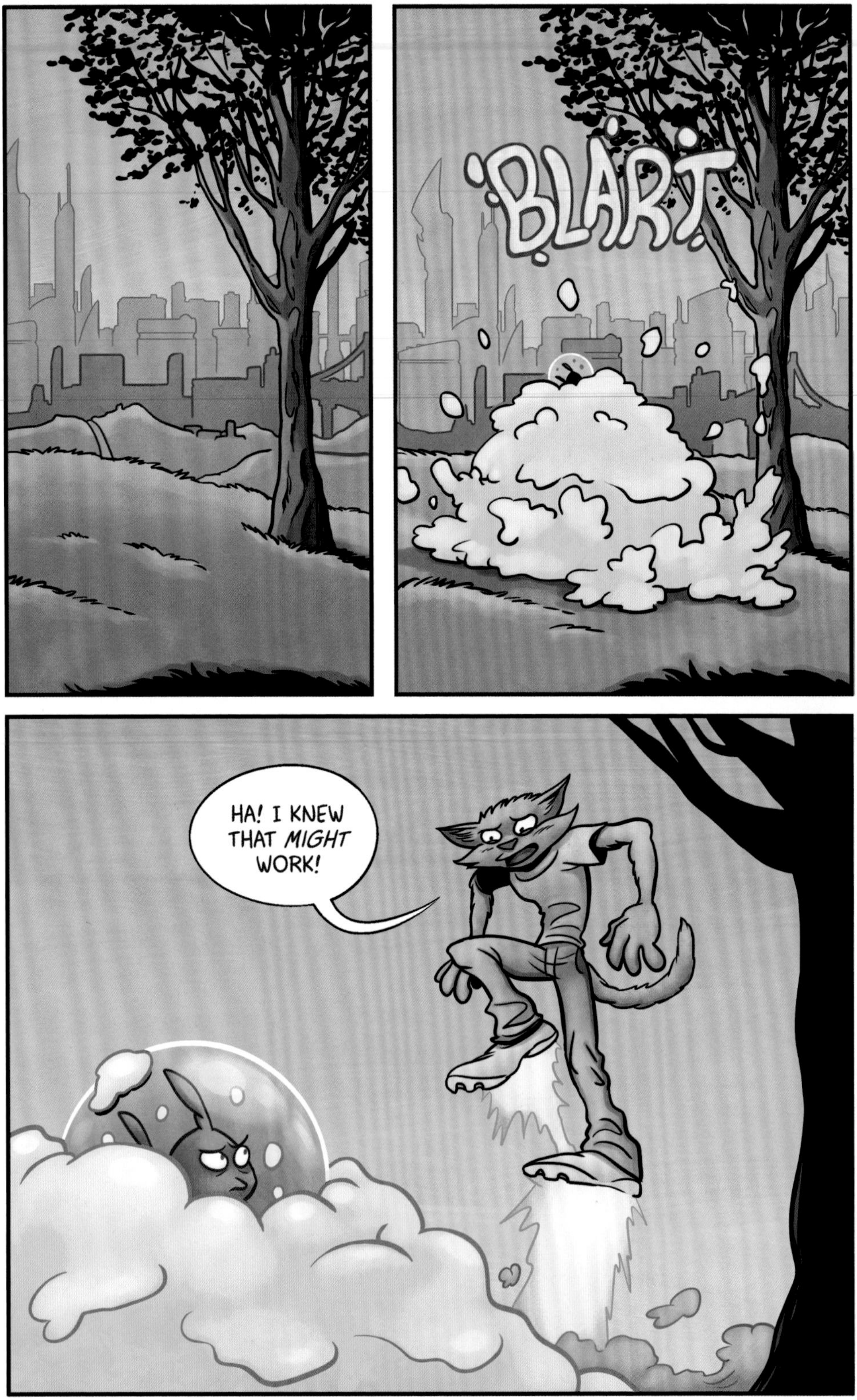
BLART
HA! I KNEW THAT *MIGHT* WORK!

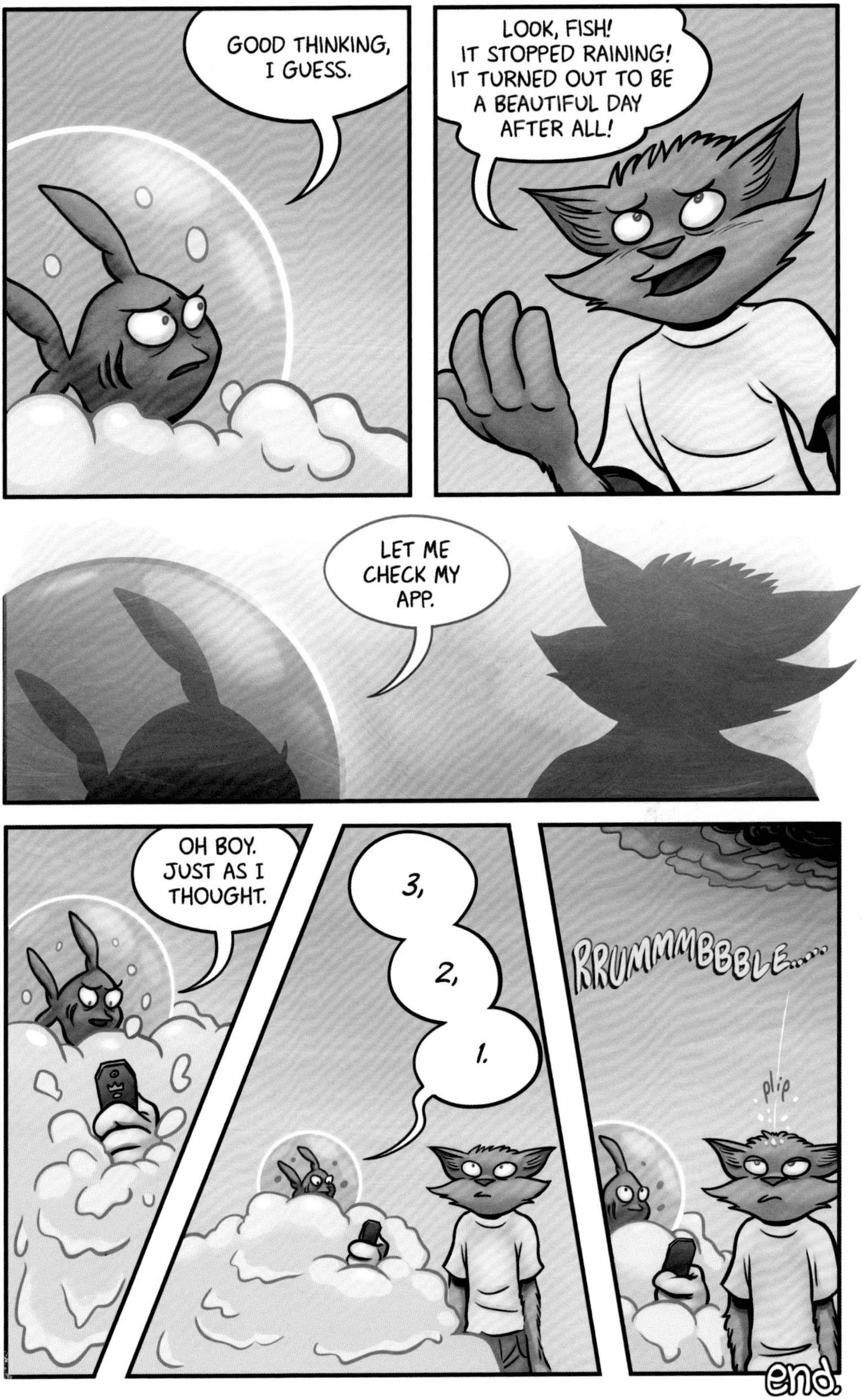
GOOD THINKING, I GUESS.
LOOK, FISH! IT STOPPED RAINING! IT TURNED OUT TO BE A BEAUTIFUL DAY AFTER ALL!
LET ME CHECK MY APP.
OH BOY. JUST AS I THOUGHT.
3,
2,
1.
RRUMMMBBBLE....
plip
end.

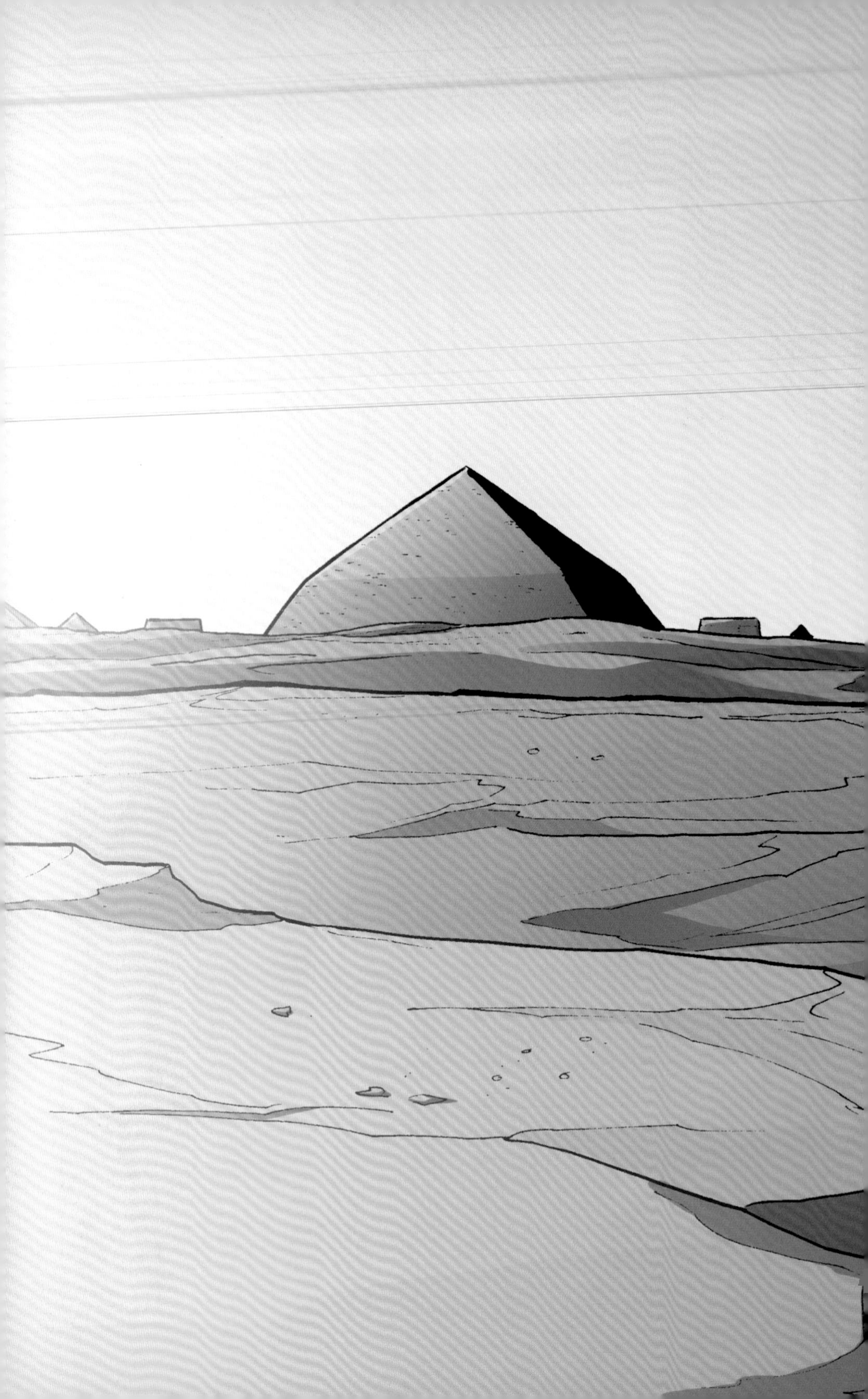

# MASTABA

BY JOHANE MATTE

COLORS BY MARY CAGLE

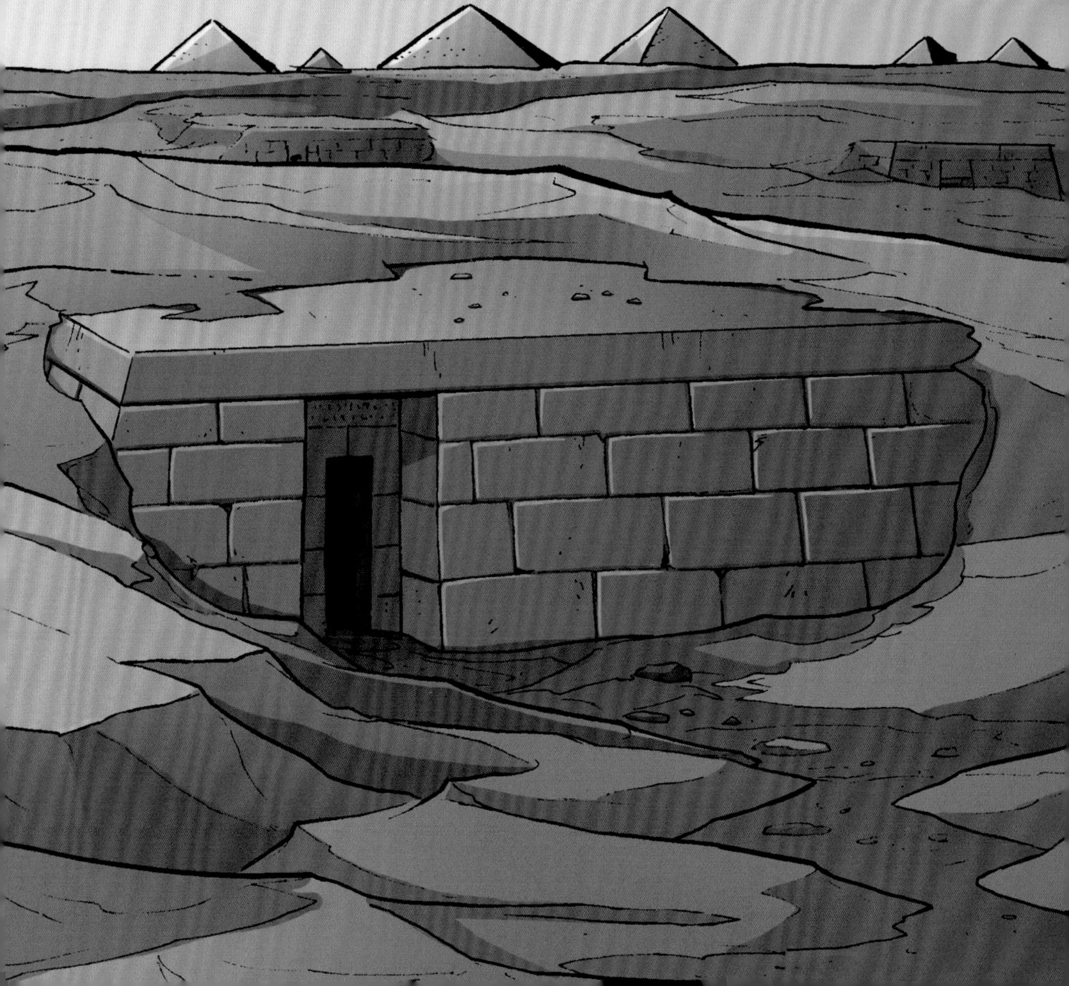

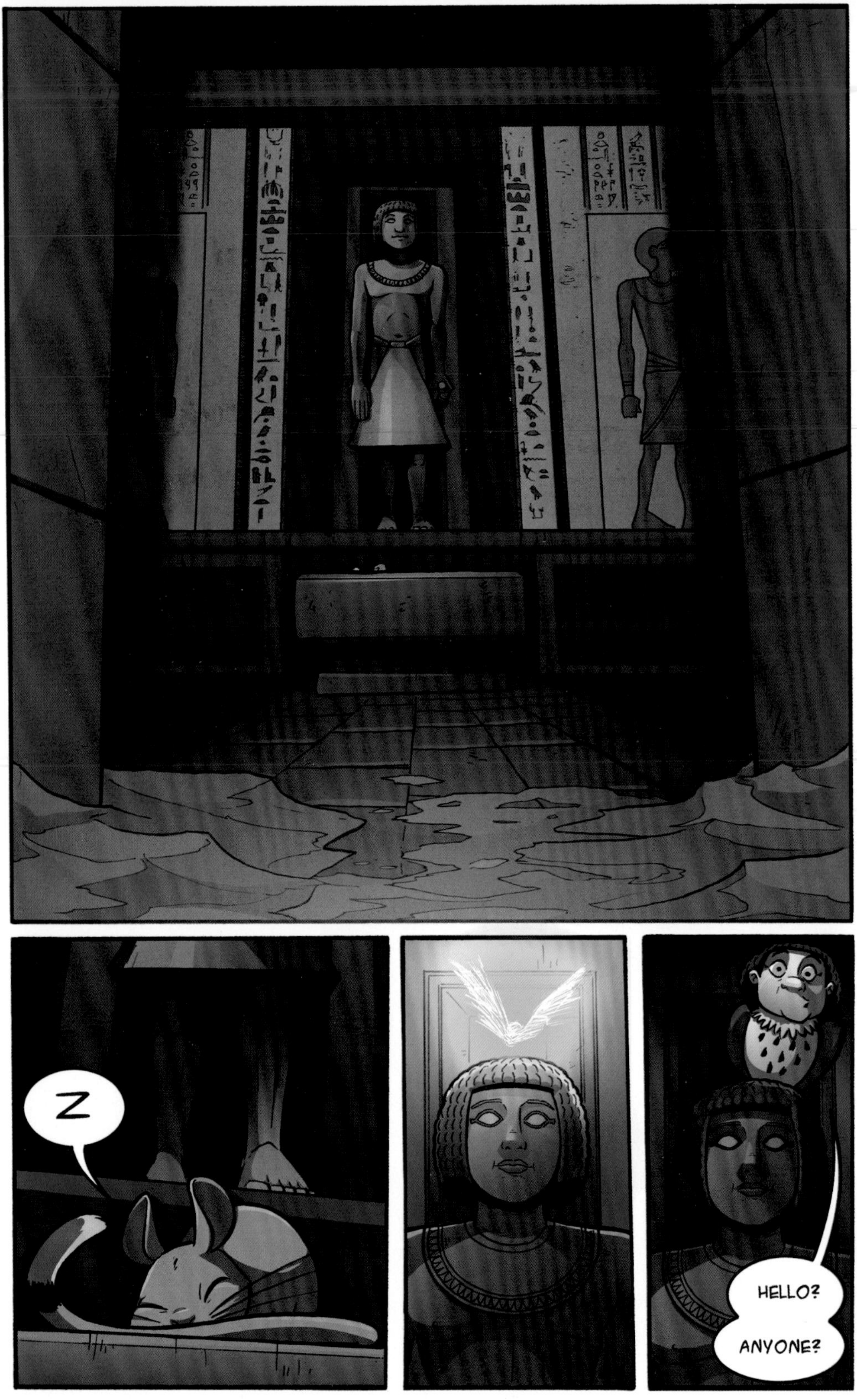
Z
HELLO?
ANYONE?

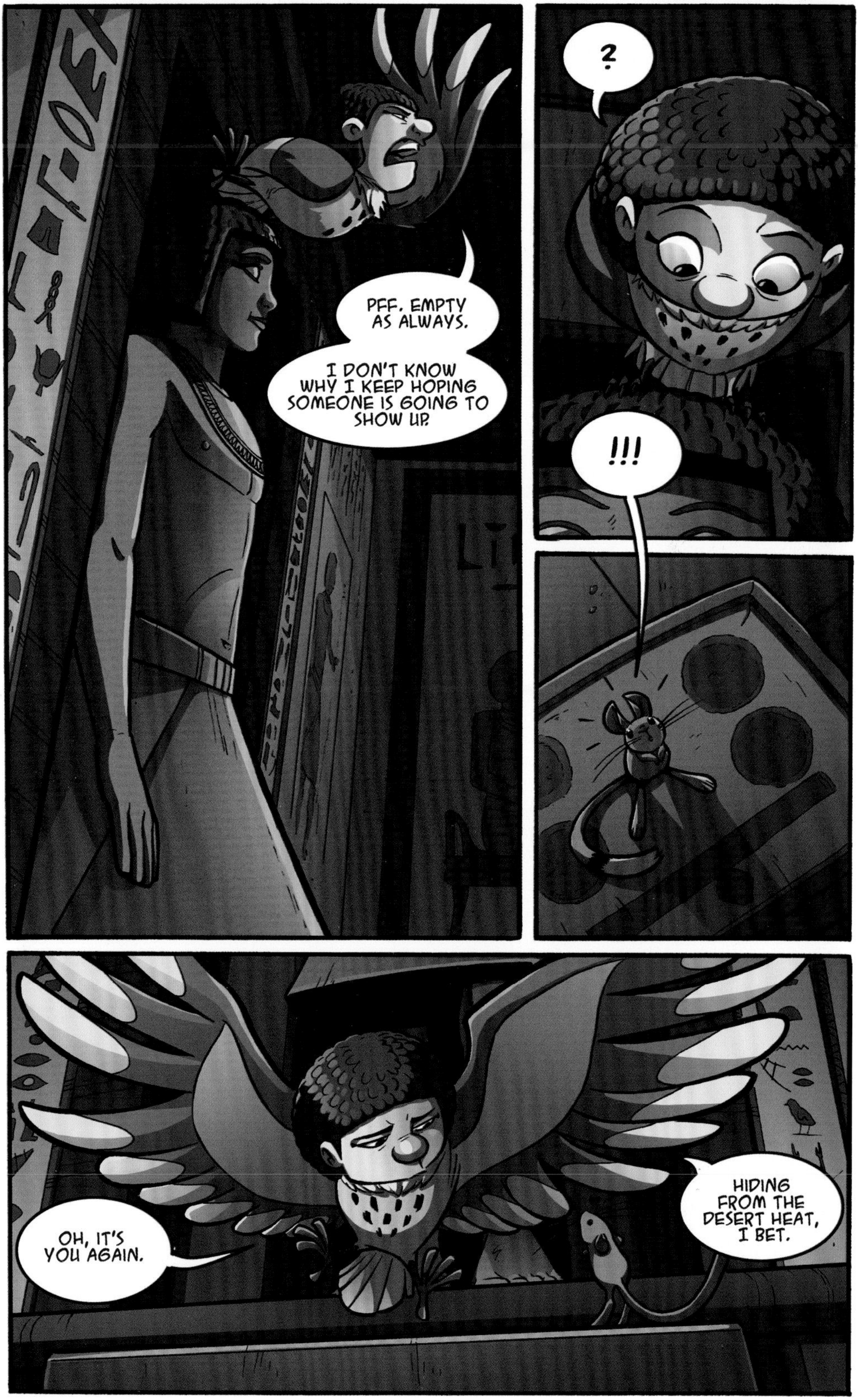
PFF. EMPTY AS ALWAYS.
I DON'T KNOW WHY I KEEP HOPING SOMEONE IS GOING TO SHOW UP.
?
!!!
OH, IT'S YOU AGAIN.
HIDING FROM THE DESERT HEAT, I BET.

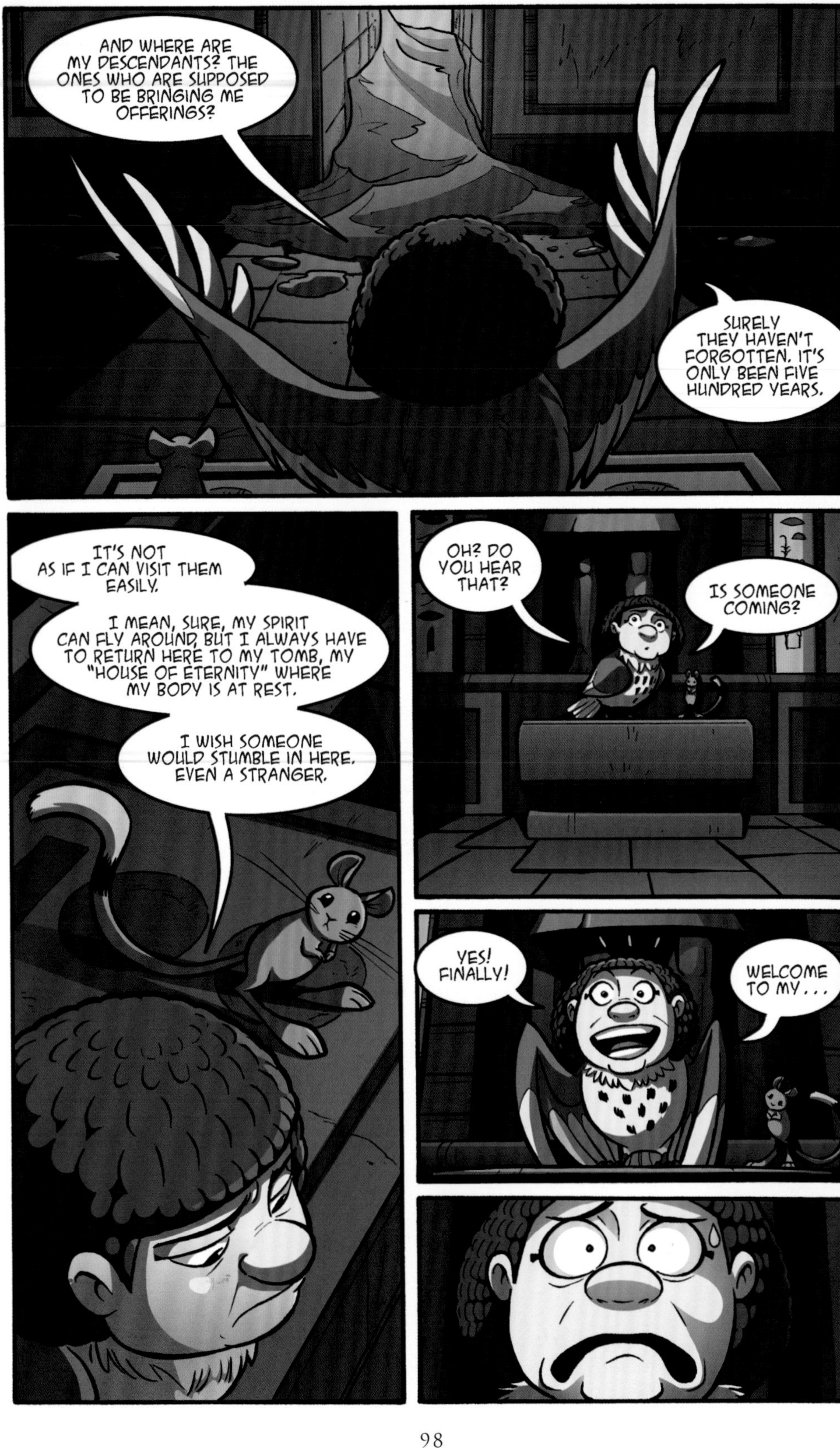
AND WHERE ARE MY DESCENDANTS? THE ONES WHO ARE SUPPOSED TO BE BRINGING ME OFFERINGS?
SURELY THEY HAVEN'T FORGOTTEN. IT'S ONLY BEEN FIVE HUNDRED YEARS.
IT'S NOT AS IF I CAN VISIT THEM EASILY.
I MEAN, SURE, MY SPIRIT CAN FLY AROUND, BUT I ALWAYS HAVE TO RETURN HERE TO MY TOMB, MY "HOUSE OF ETERNITY" WHERE MY BODY IS AT REST.
I WISH SOMEONE WOULD STUMBLE IN HERE. EVEN A STRANGER.
OH? DO YOU HEAR THAT?
IS SOMEONE COMING?
YES! FINALLY!
WELCOME TO MY . . .

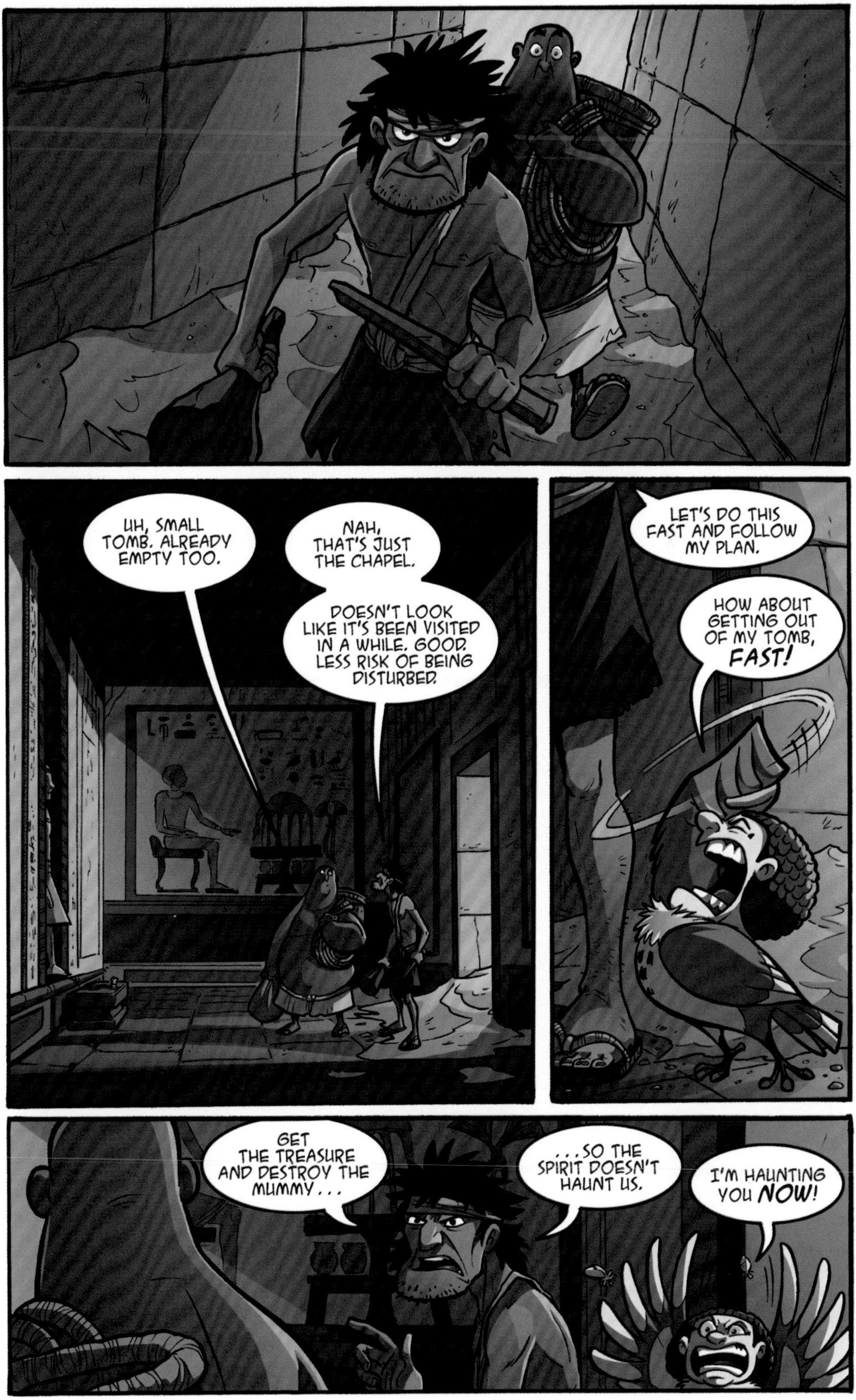
UH, SMALL TOMB. ALREADY EMPTY TOO.
NAH, THAT'S JUST THE CHAPEL.
DOESN'T LOOK LIKE IT'S BEEN VISITED IN A WHILE. GOOD. LESS RISK OF BEING DISTURBED.
LET'S DO THIS FAST AND FOLLOW MY PLAN.
HOW ABOUT GETTING OUT OF MY TOMB, **FAST!**
GET THE TREASURE AND DESTROY THE MUMMY . . .
. . . SO THE SPIRIT DOESN'T HAUNT US.
I'M HAUNTING YOU **NOW!**

LEAVE THE TOOLS HERE. WE'RE GOING OUTSIDE TO LOOK FOR THE TOMB'S ENTRANCE.

WHAT? YOU DON'T KNOW WHERE IT IS? I THOUGHT YOU WERE A PRO AT ROBBING TOMBS.

HOW ABOUT GET OUT AND STAY OUT!

I AM! I'VE JUST NEVER TRIED LOOTING SUCH AN OLD ONE.

OLD, NEW— WHAT'S THE DIFFERENCE?

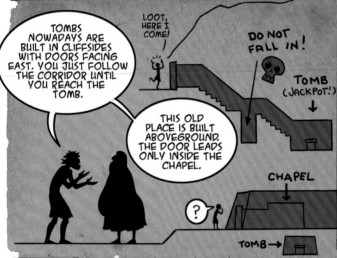

TOMBS NOWADAYS ARE BUILT IN CLIFFSIDES WITH DOORS FACING EAST. YOU JUST FOLLOW THE CORRIDOR UNTIL YOU REACH THE TOMB.

THIS OLD PLACE IS BUILT ABOVEGROUND. THE DOOR LEADS ONLY INSIDE THE CHAPEL.

LOOT, HERE I COME!

DO NOT FALL IN!

TOMB (JACKPOT!)

CHAPEL

?

TOMB →

BAH, THEY ARE AMATEURS. THEY'LL QUIT SOON ENOUGH.

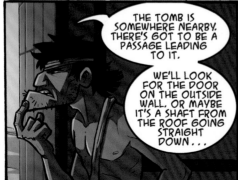

THE TOMB IS SOMEWHERE NEARBY. THERE'S GOT TO BE A PASSAGE LEADING TO IT.

WE'LL LOOK FOR THE DOOR ON THE OUTSIDE WALL. OR MAYBE IT'S A SHAFT FROM THE ROOF GOING STRAIGHT DOWN . . .

FOUND IT!

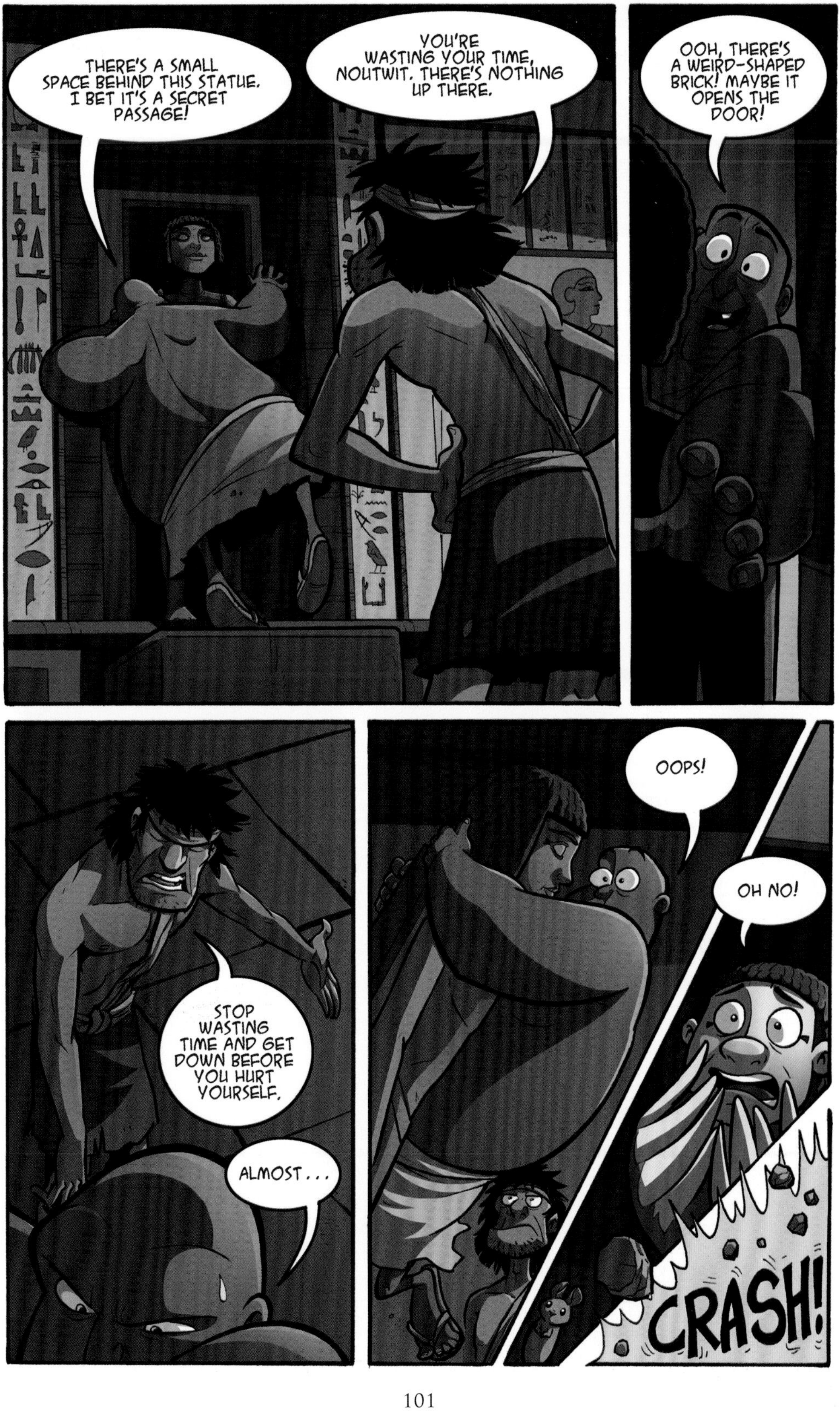
THERE'S A SMALL SPACE BEHIND THIS STATUE. I BET IT'S A SECRET PASSAGE!
YOU'RE WASTING YOUR TIME, NOUTWIT. THERE'S NOTHING UP THERE.
OOH, THERE'S A WEIRD-SHAPED BRICK! MAYBE IT OPENS THE DOOR!
STOP WASTING TIME AND GET DOWN BEFORE YOU HURT YOURSELF.
ALMOST . . .
OOPS!
OH NO!
CRASH!

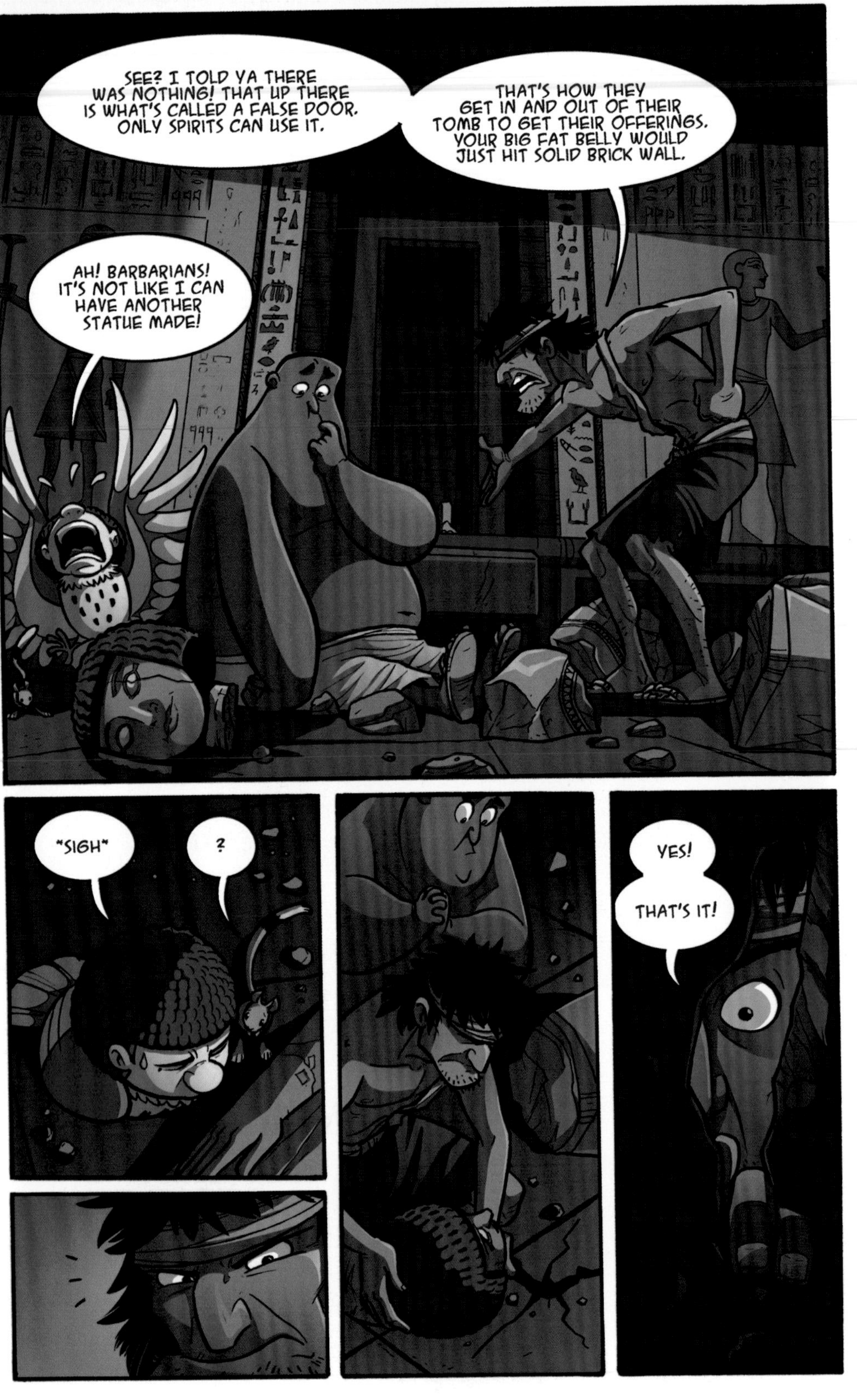
SEE? I TOLD YA THERE WAS NOTHING! THAT UP THERE IS WHAT'S CALLED A FALSE DOOR. ONLY SPIRITS CAN USE IT.
THAT'S HOW THEY GET IN AND OUT OF THEIR TOMB TO GET THEIR OFFERINGS. YOUR BIG FAT BELLY WOULD JUST HIT SOLID BRICK WALL.
AH! BARBARIANS! IT'S NOT LIKE I CAN HAVE ANOTHER STATUE MADE!
"SIGH"
?
YES!
THAT'S IT!

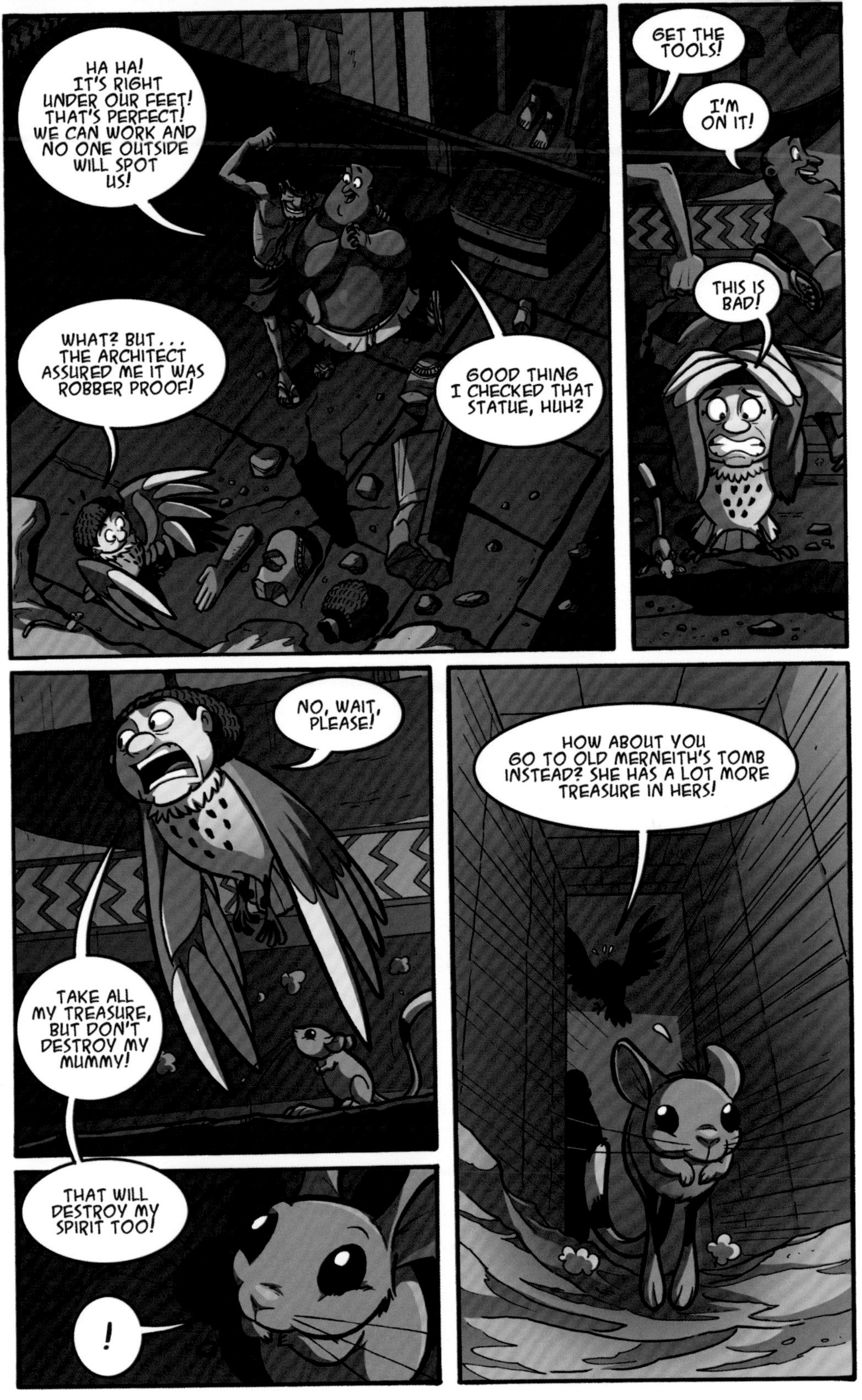
HA HA! IT'S RIGHT UNDER OUR FEET! THAT'S PERFECT! WE CAN WORK AND NO ONE OUTSIDE WILL SPOT US!
WHAT? BUT . . . THE ARCHITECT ASSURED ME IT WAS ROBBER PROOF!
GOOD THING I CHECKED THAT STATUE, HUH?
GET THE TOOLS!
I'M ON IT!
THIS IS BAD!
NO, WAIT, PLEASE!
TAKE ALL MY TREASURE, BUT DON'T DESTROY MY MUMMY!
THAT WILL DESTROY MY SPIRIT TOO!
!
HOW ABOUT YOU GO TO OLD MERNEITH'S TOMB INSTEAD? SHE HAS A LOT MORE TREASURE IN HERS!

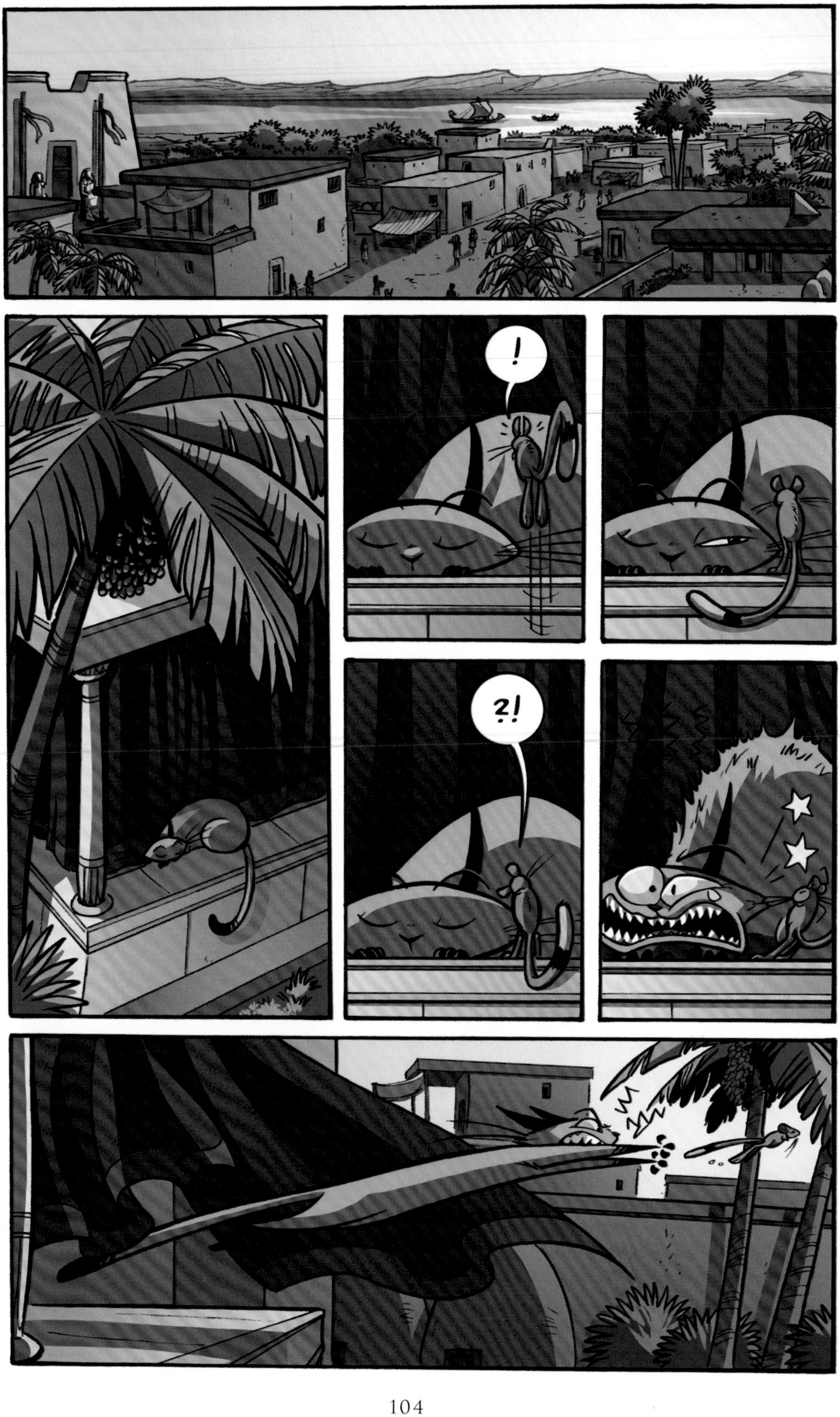
!
?!
ZZ
ZZ

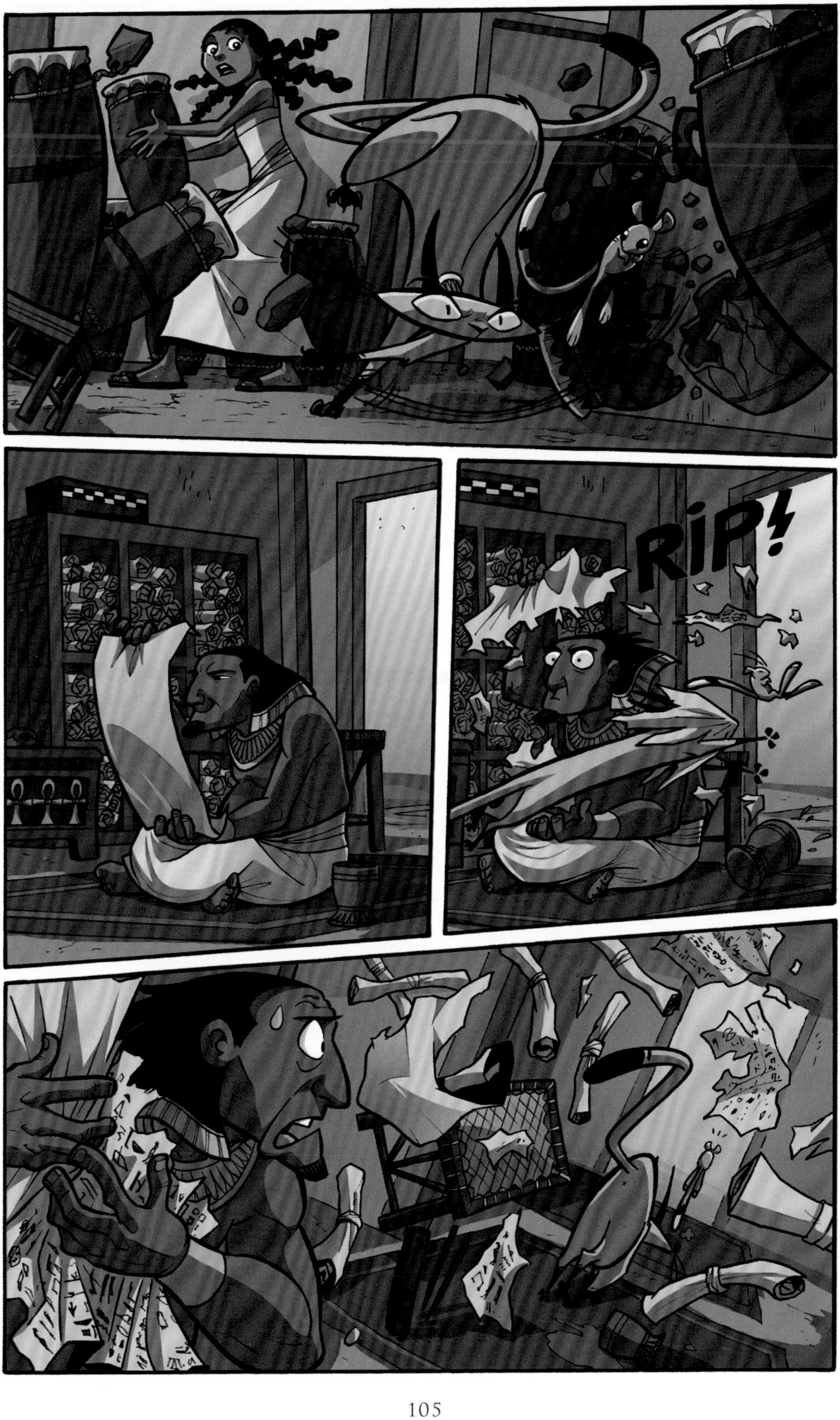
RIP!

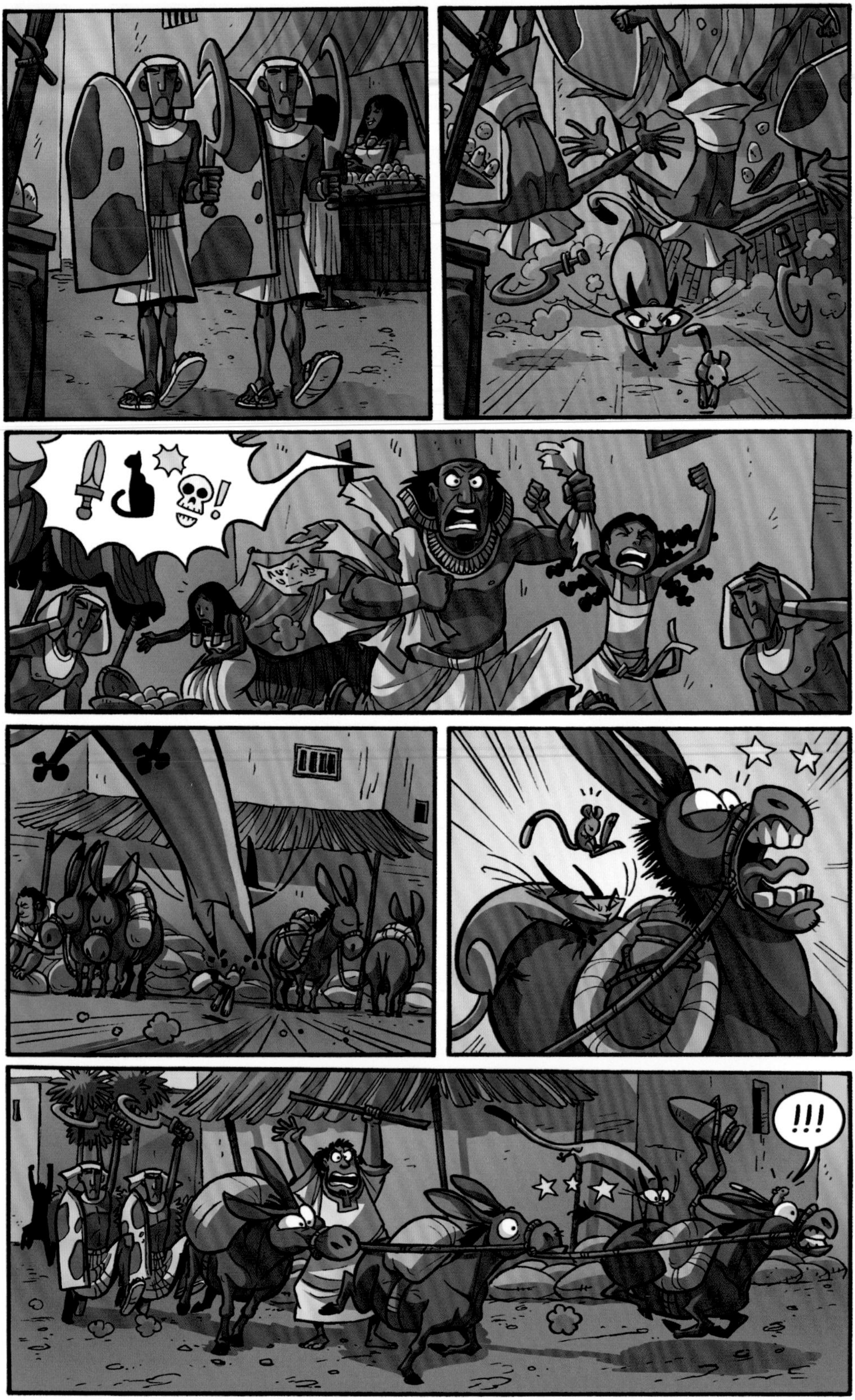
!
!!!

COME ON. DESTROY THAT MUMMY AND LET'S GO!

YOU SURE IT'S SAFE? I WON'T BE CURSED OR ANYTHING?

I AM DOOMED.

I SHOULD HAVE HAD AN ANTI-ROBBER CURSE INSTALLED.

BUH?

NRRR...

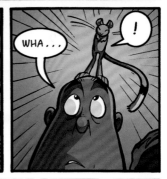

WHA...

!

WAH!

DEMONS FROM THE UNDERWORLD!

WAIT!

IT'S JUST A CAT!

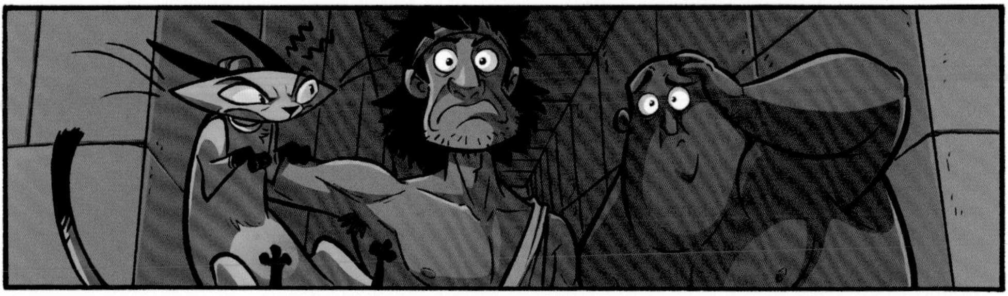

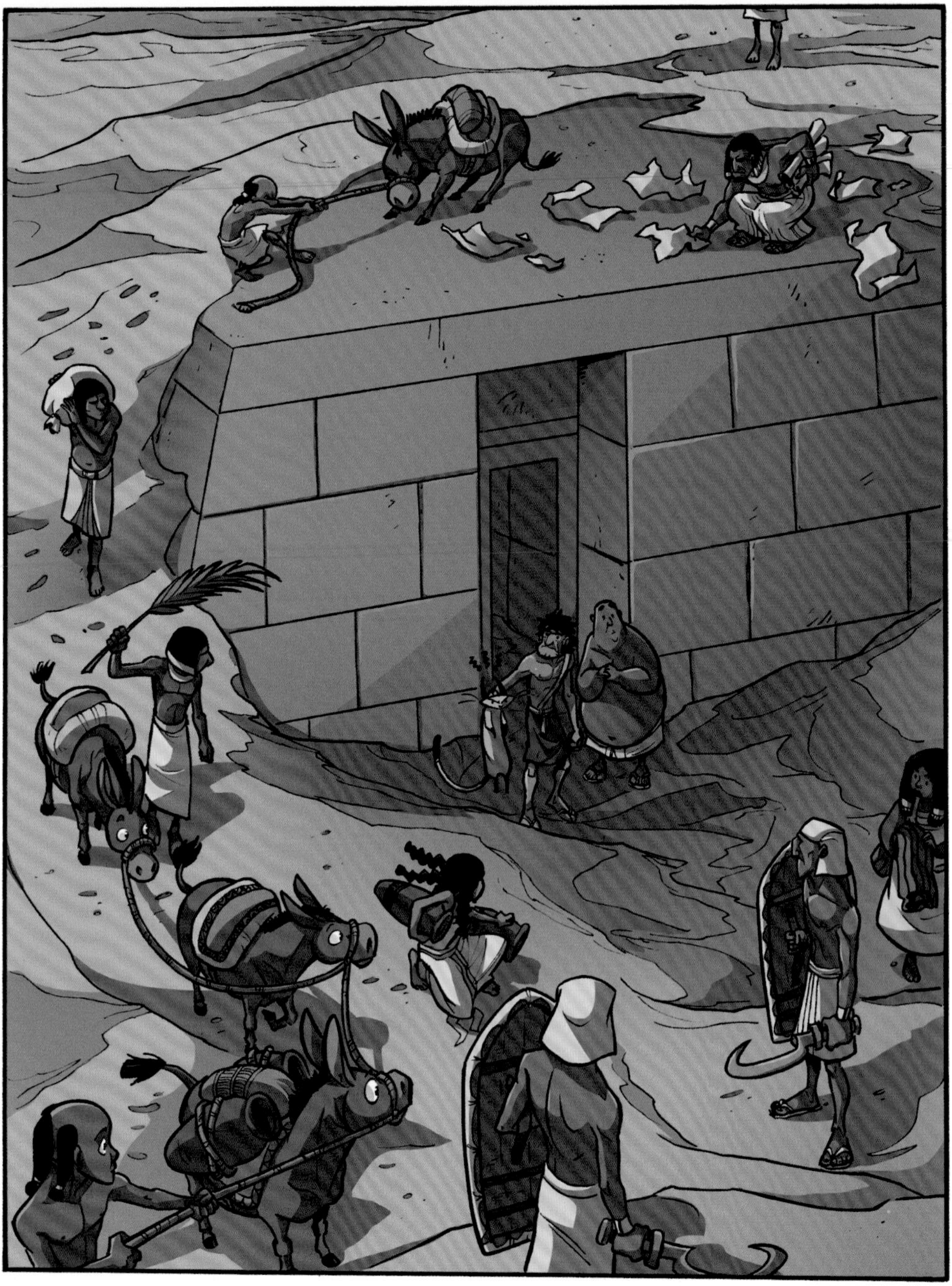

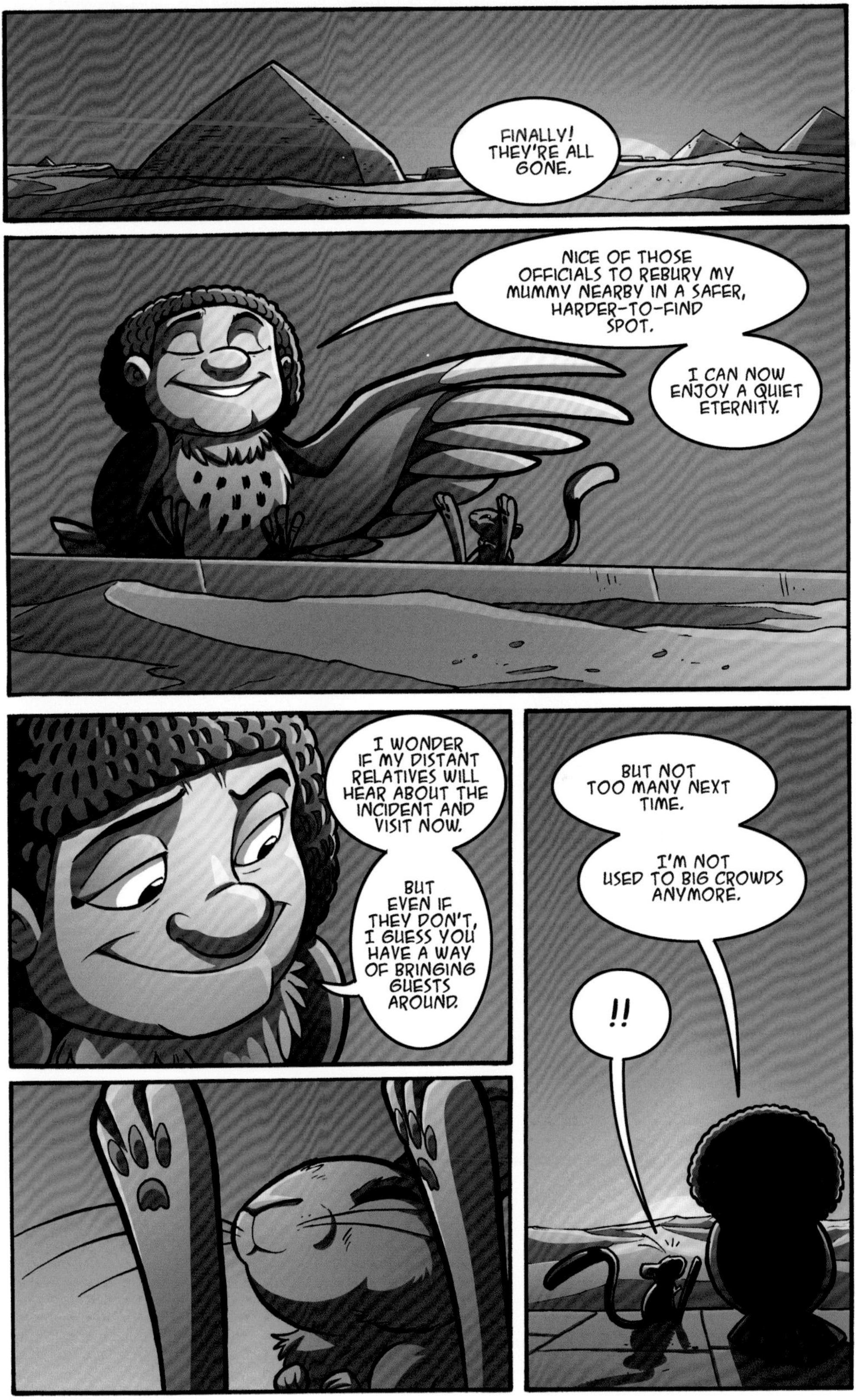
FINALLY! THEY'RE ALL GONE.
NICE OF THOSE OFFICIALS TO REBURY MY MUMMY NEARBY IN A SAFER, HARDER-TO-FIND SPOT.
I CAN NOW ENJOY A QUIET ETERNITY.
I WONDER IF MY DISTANT RELATIVES WILL HEAR ABOUT THE INCIDENT AND VISIT NOW.
BUT EVEN IF THEY DON'T, I GUESS YOU HAVE A WAY OF BRINGING GUESTS AROUND.
BUT NOT TOO MANY NEXT TIME.
I'M NOT USED TO BIG CROWDS ANYMORE.
!!

# WHEN IS A DOOR NOT A DOOR?

BY JEN BREACH & DOUGLAS HOLGATE

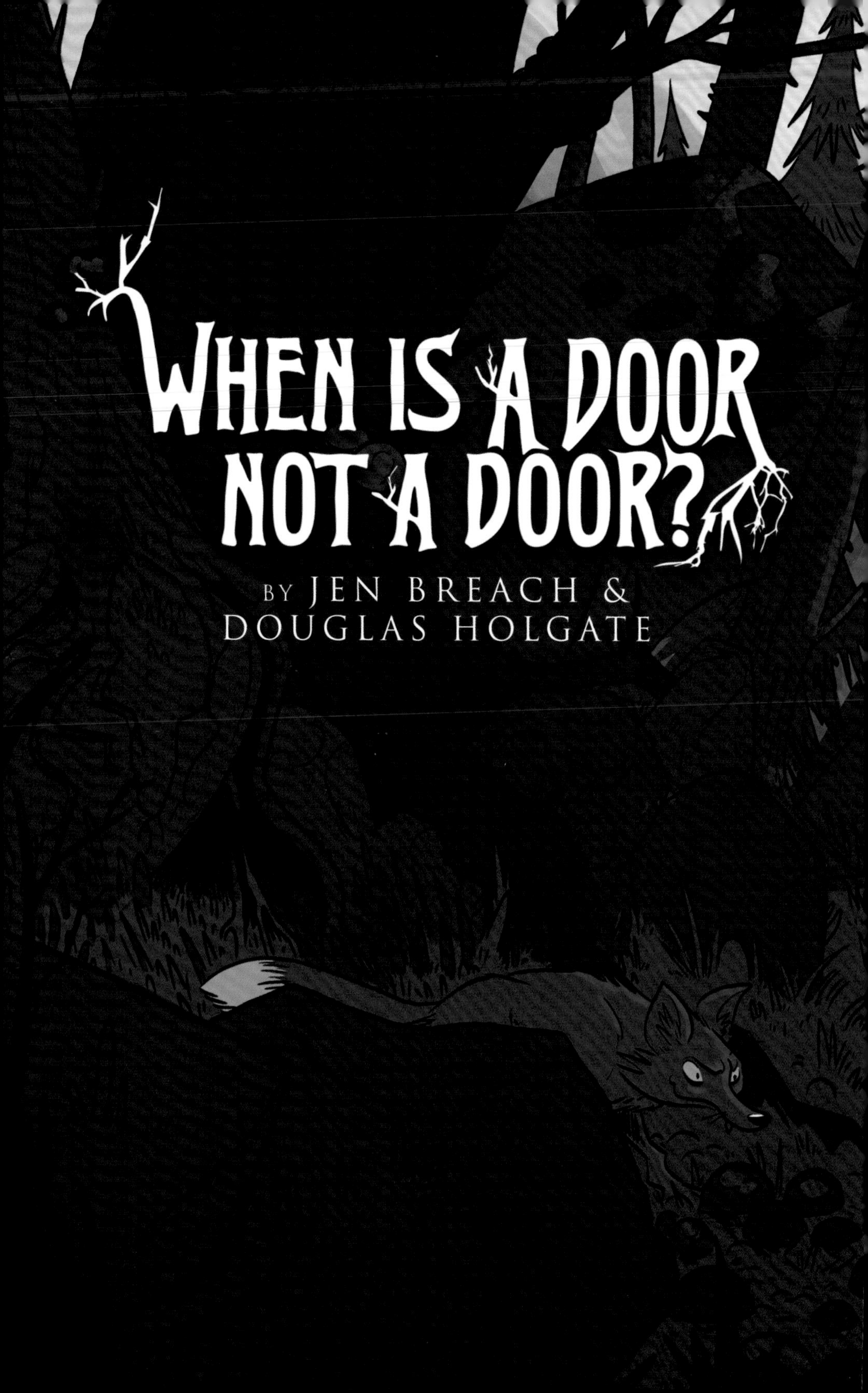

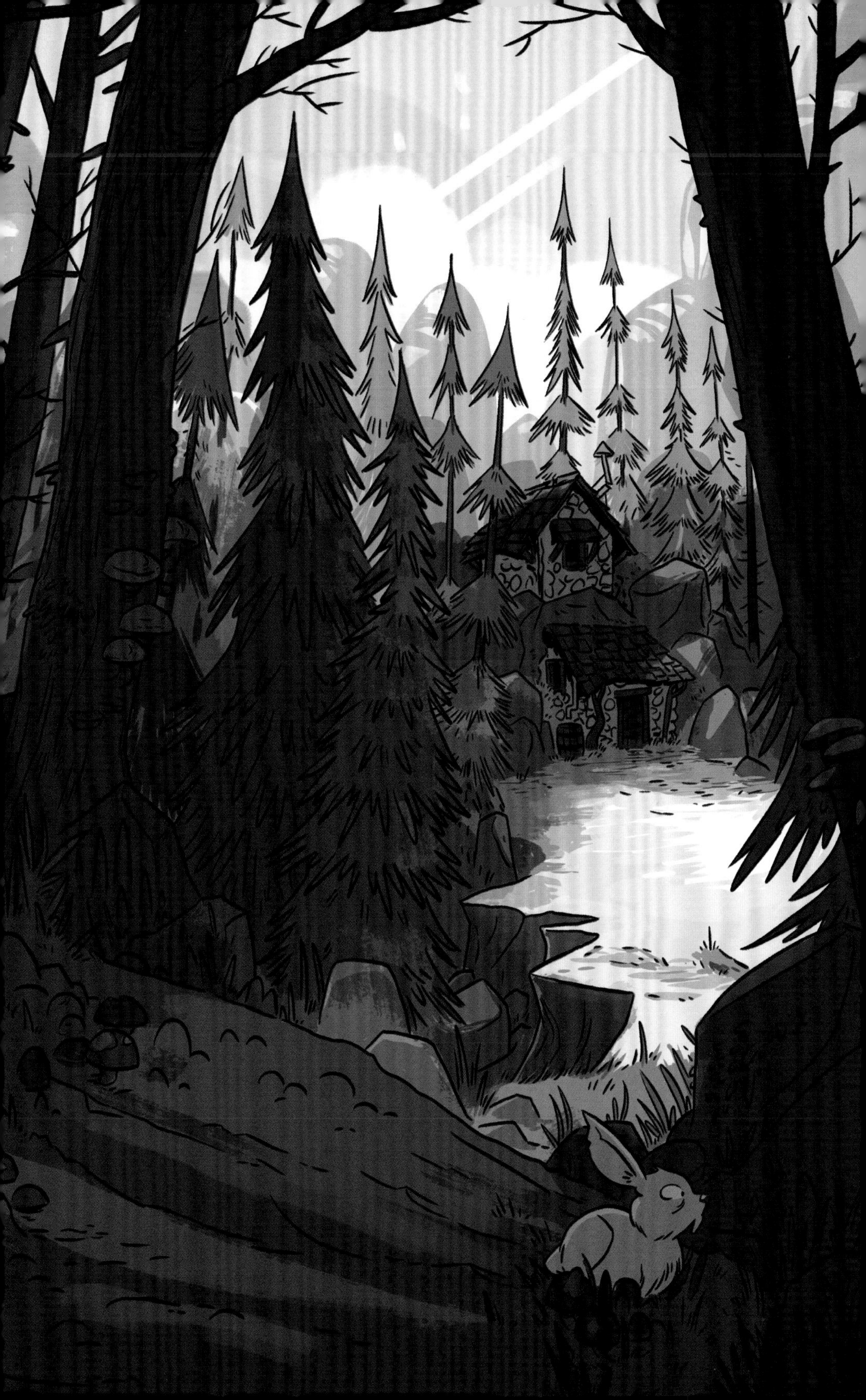

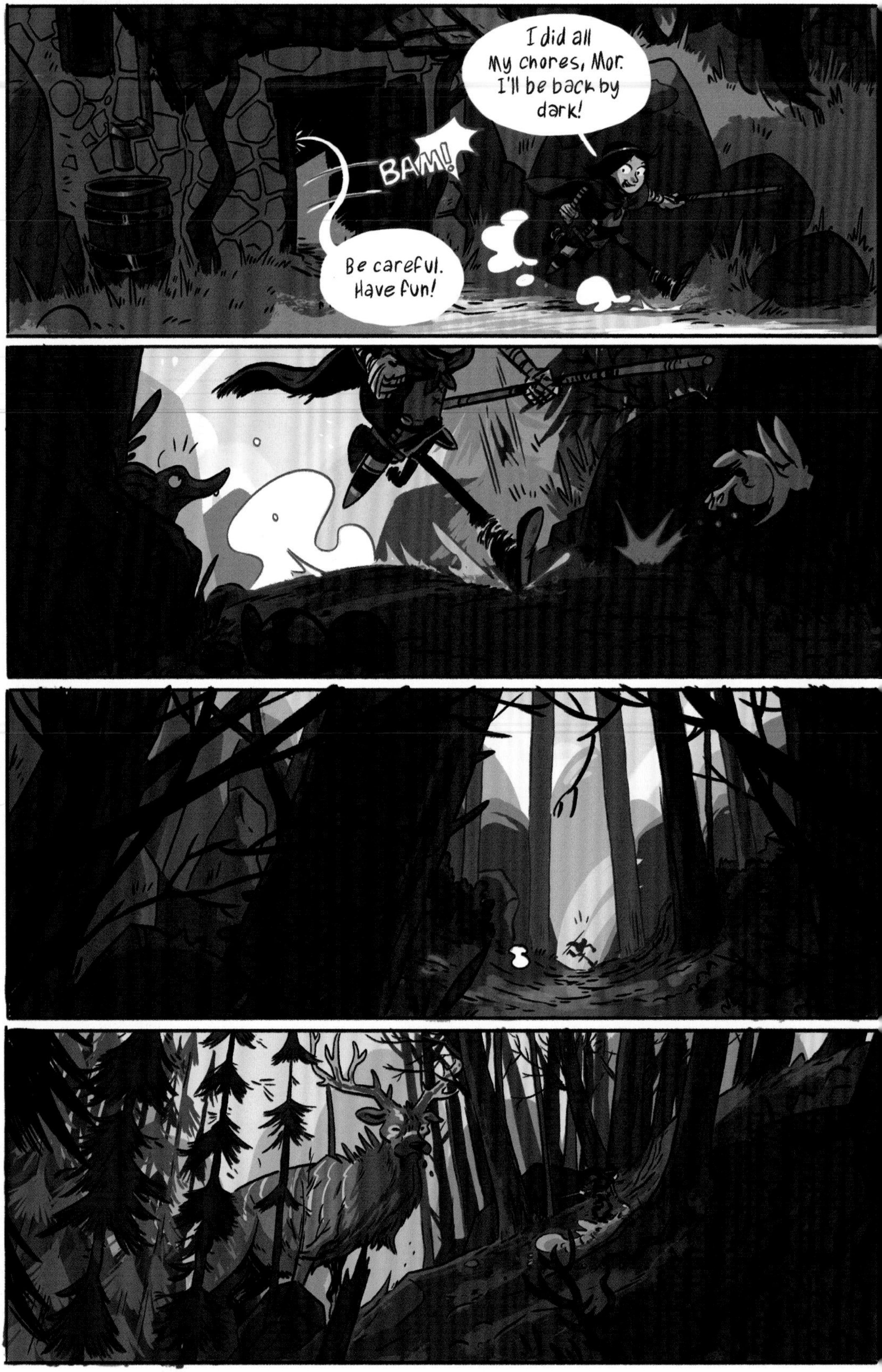
I did all My chores, Mor. I'll be back by dark!
BAM!
Be careful. Have fun!

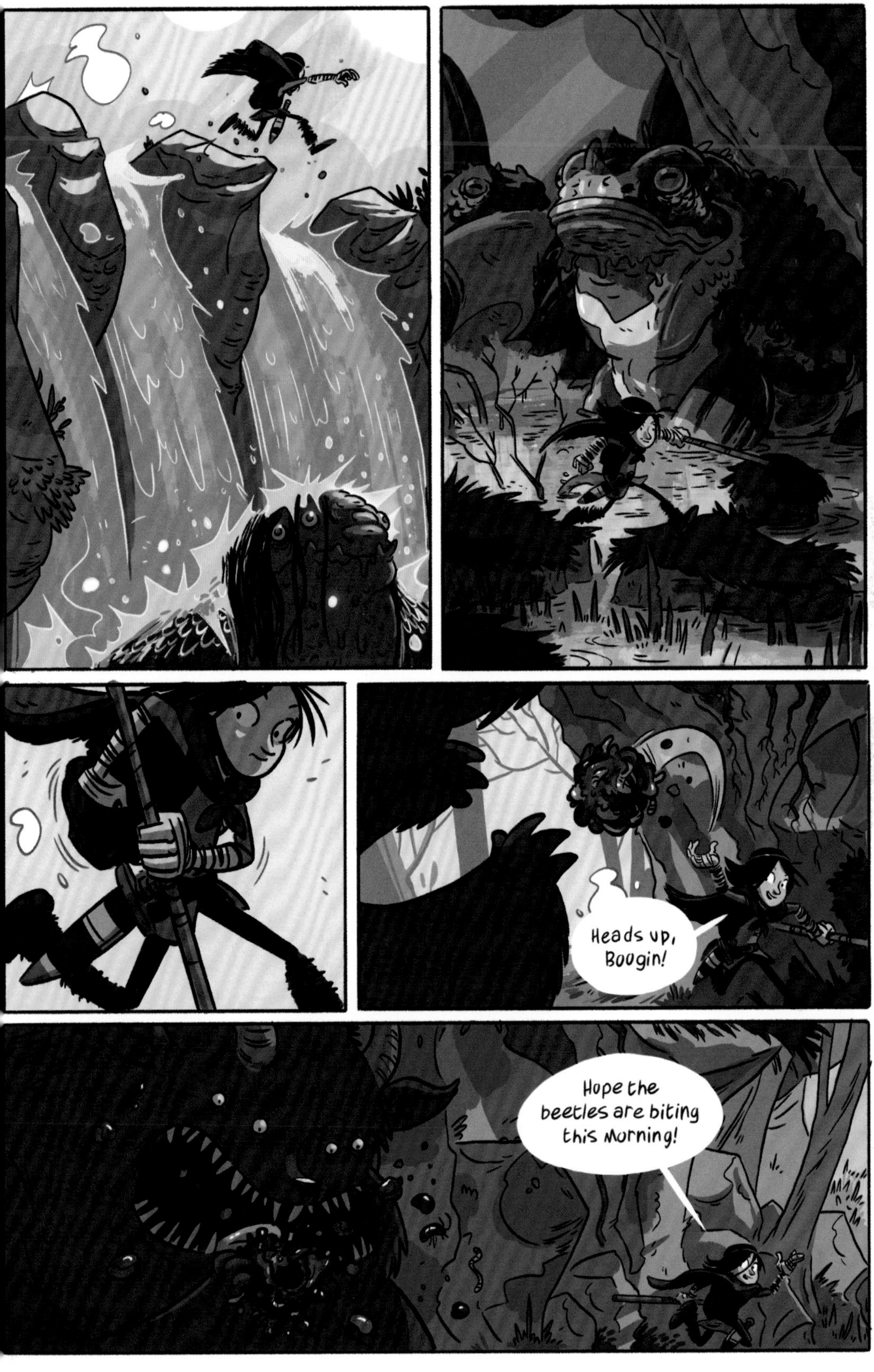
Heads up, Boogin!
Hope the beetles are biting this Morning!

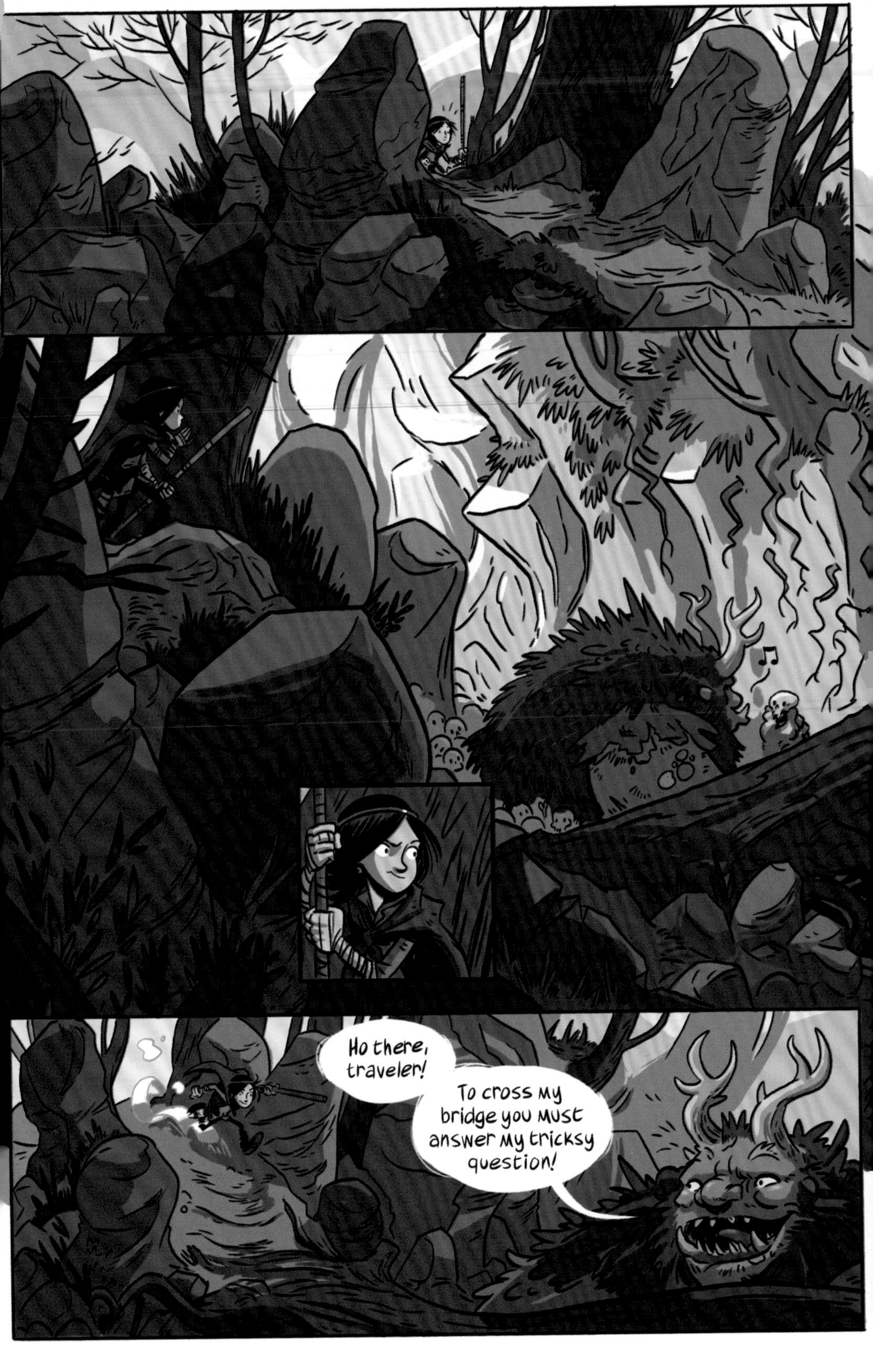
Ho there, traveler!
To cross my bridge you must answer my tricksy question!

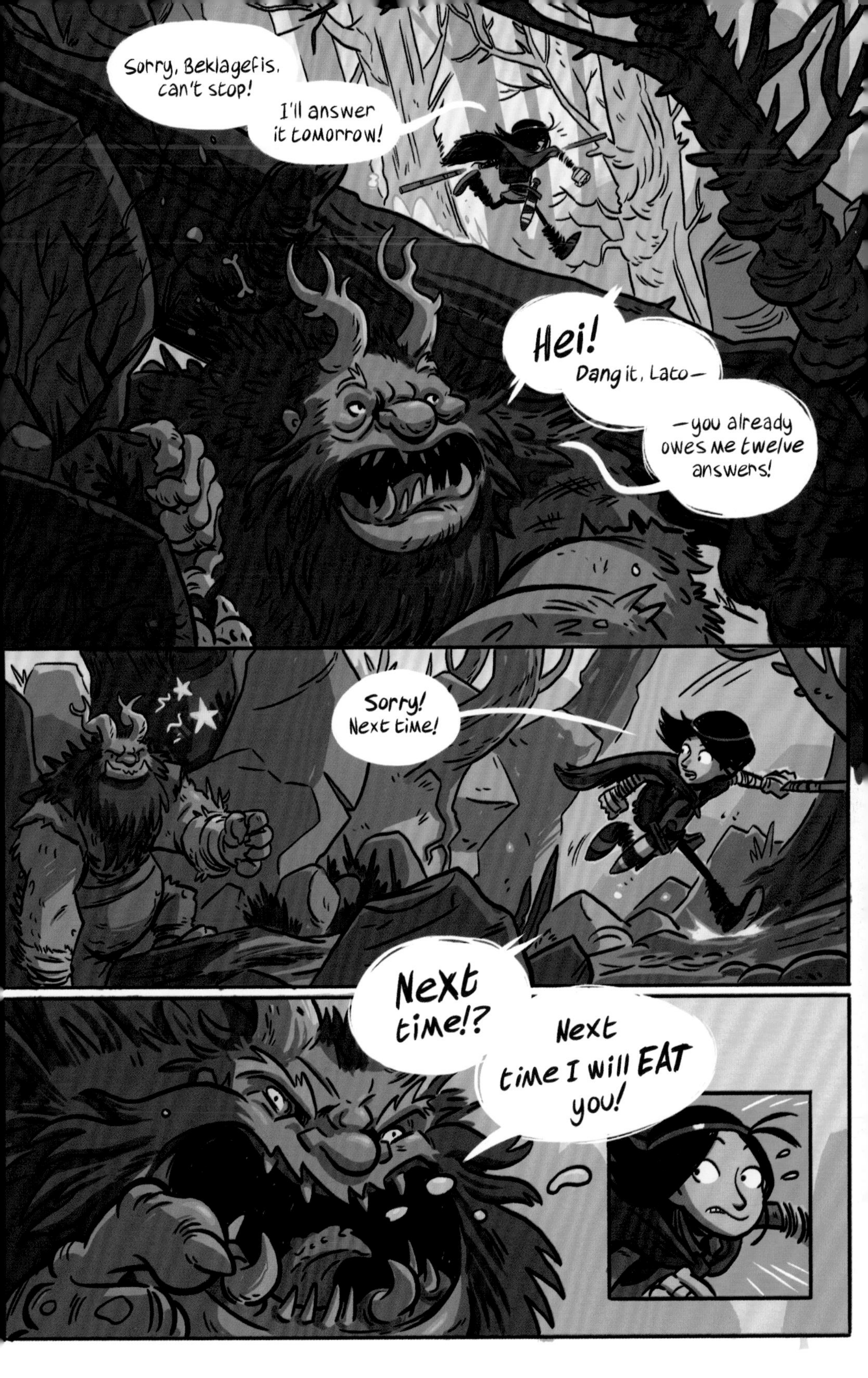
Sorry, Beklagefis, can't stop!
I'll answer it tomorrow!
Hei!
Dang it, Lato—
—you already owes me twelve answers!
Sorry! Next time!
Next time!?
Next time I will EAT you!

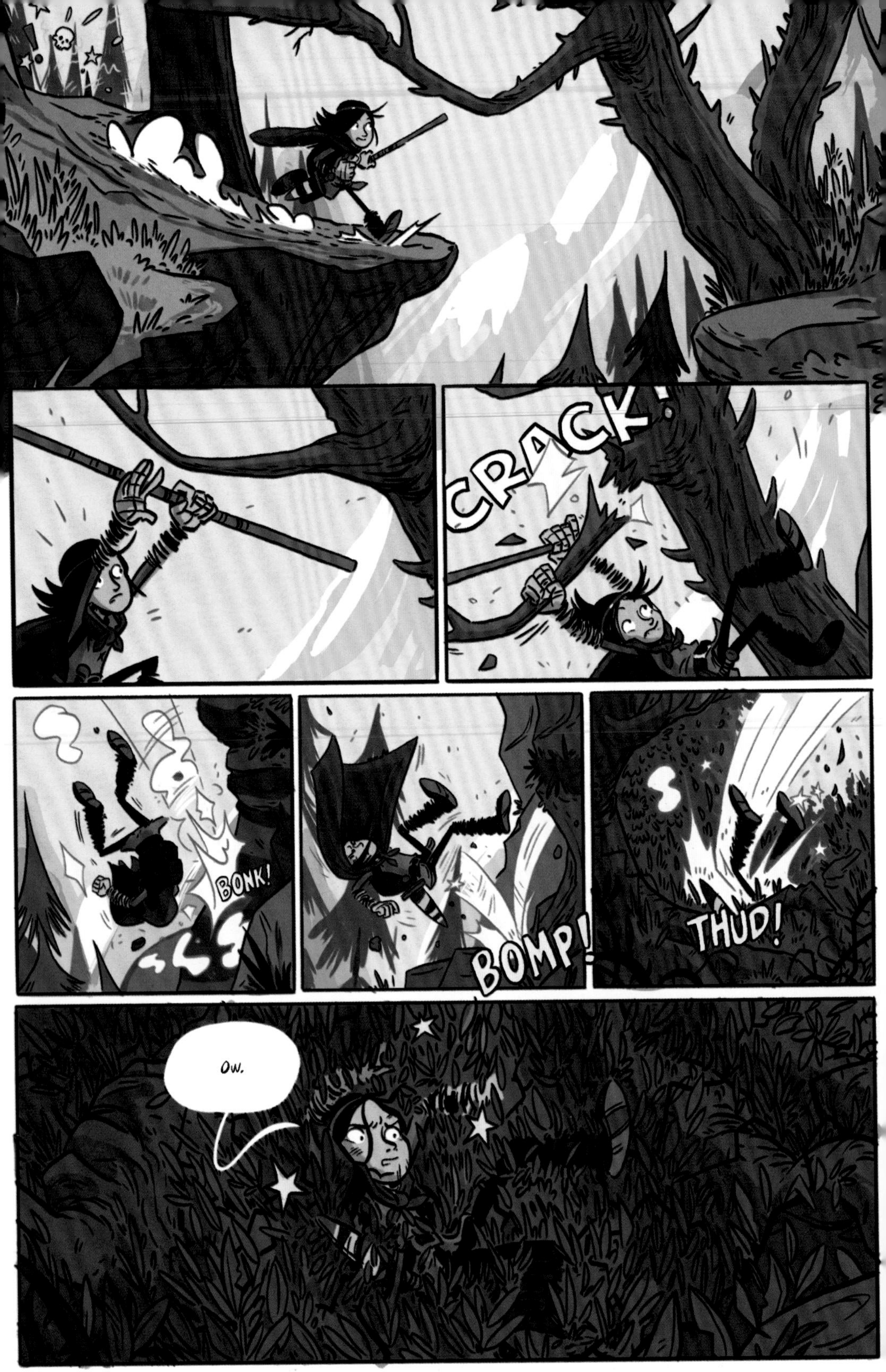
CRACK!
BONK!
BOMP!
THUD!
OW.

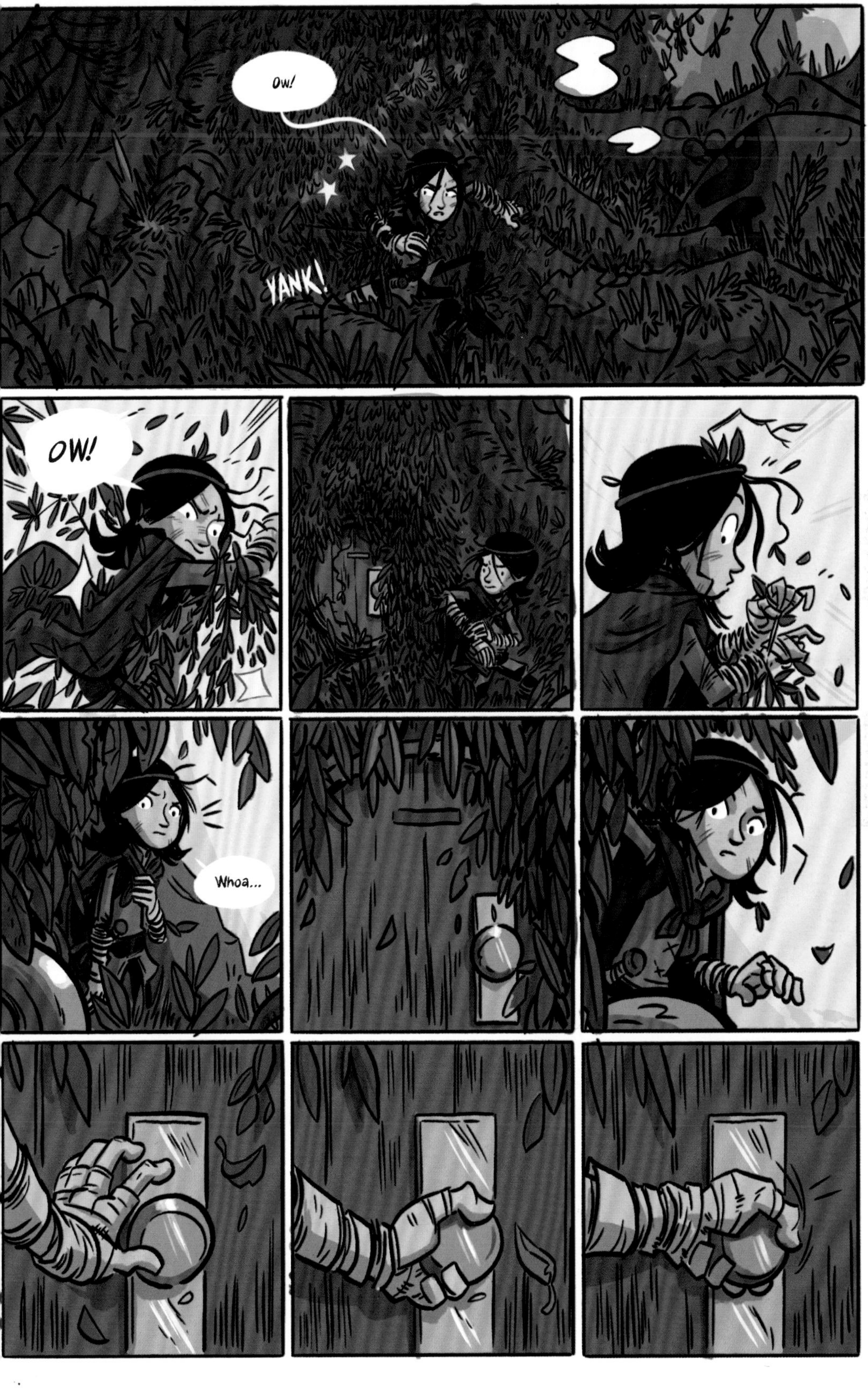
OW!
YANK!
OW!
Whoa...

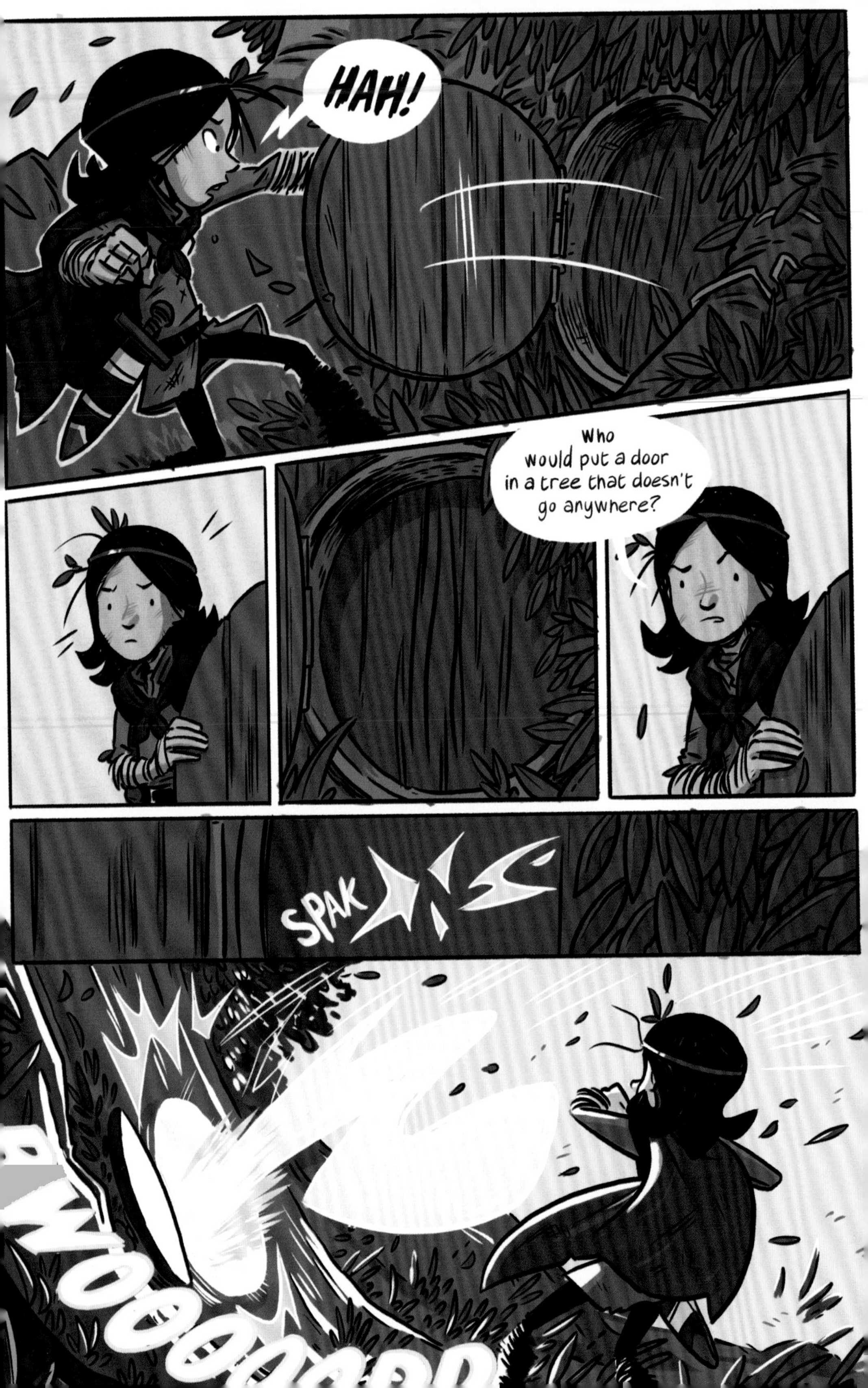
HAH!
Who would put a door in a tree that doesn't go anywhere?
SPAK

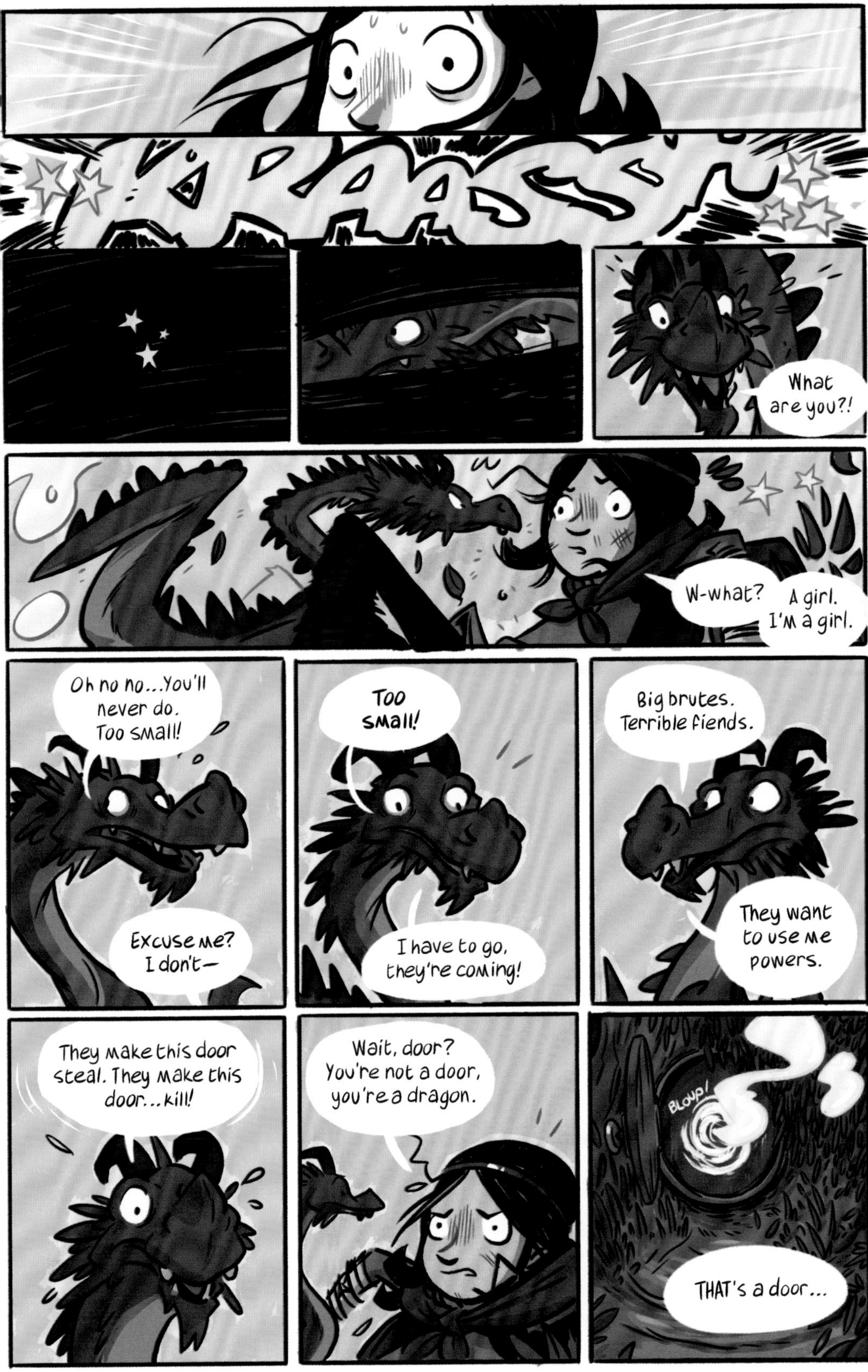
What are you?!
W-what?
A girl. I'm a girl.
Oh no no... You'll never do. Too small!
Excuse me? I don't—
Too small!
I have to go, they're coming!
Big brutes. Terrible fiends.
They want to use me powers.
They make this door steal. They make this door... kill!
Wait, door? You're not a door, you're a dragon.
BLOUP!
THAT's a door...

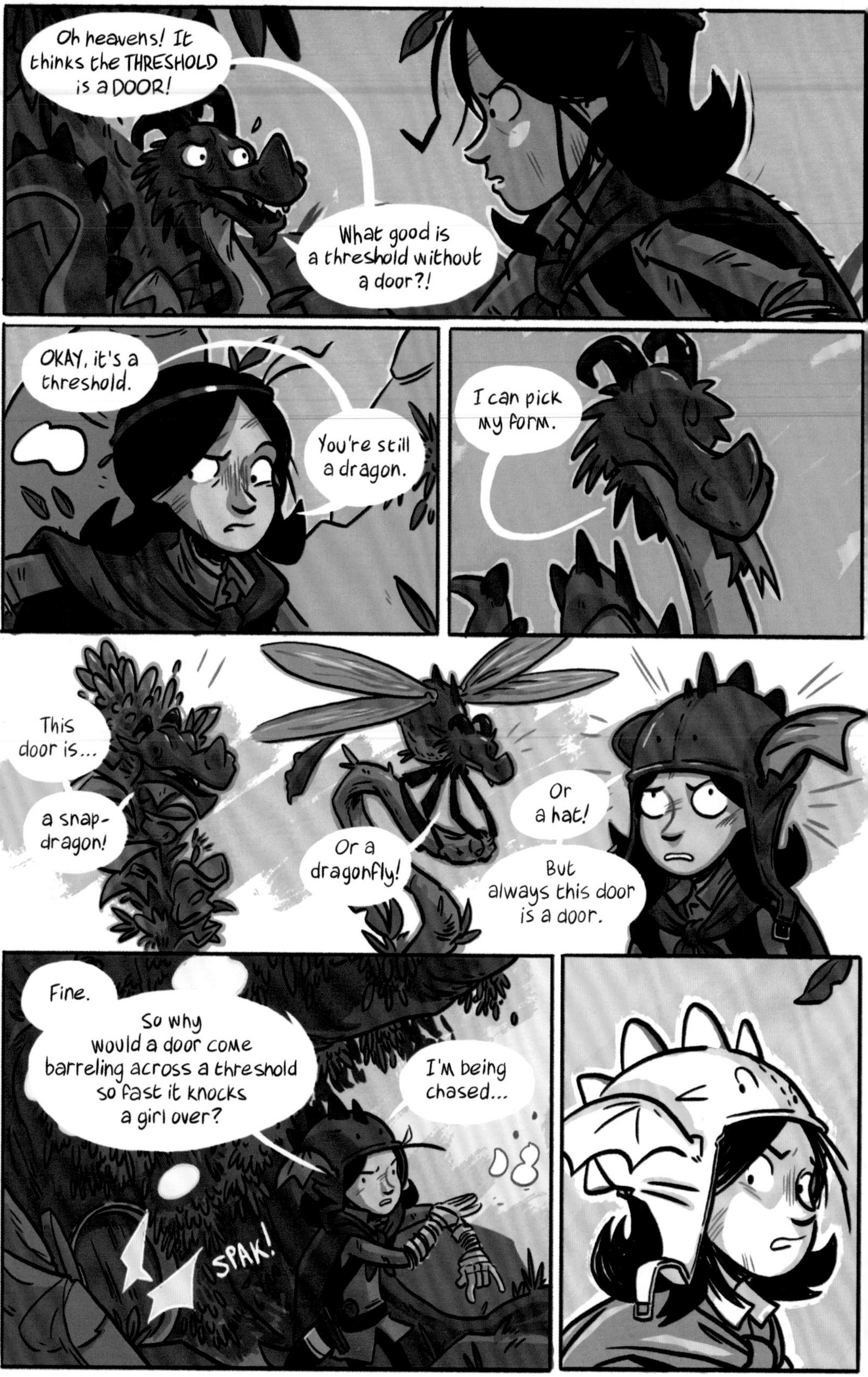
Oh heavens! It thinks the THRESHOLD is a DOOR!
What good is a threshold without a door?!
OKAY, it's a threshold.
You're still a dragon.
I can pick my form.
This door is...
a snap-dragon!
Or a dragonfly!
Or a hat!
But always this door is a door.
Fine.
So why would a door come barreling across a threshold so fast it knocks a girl over?
I'm being chased...
SPAK!

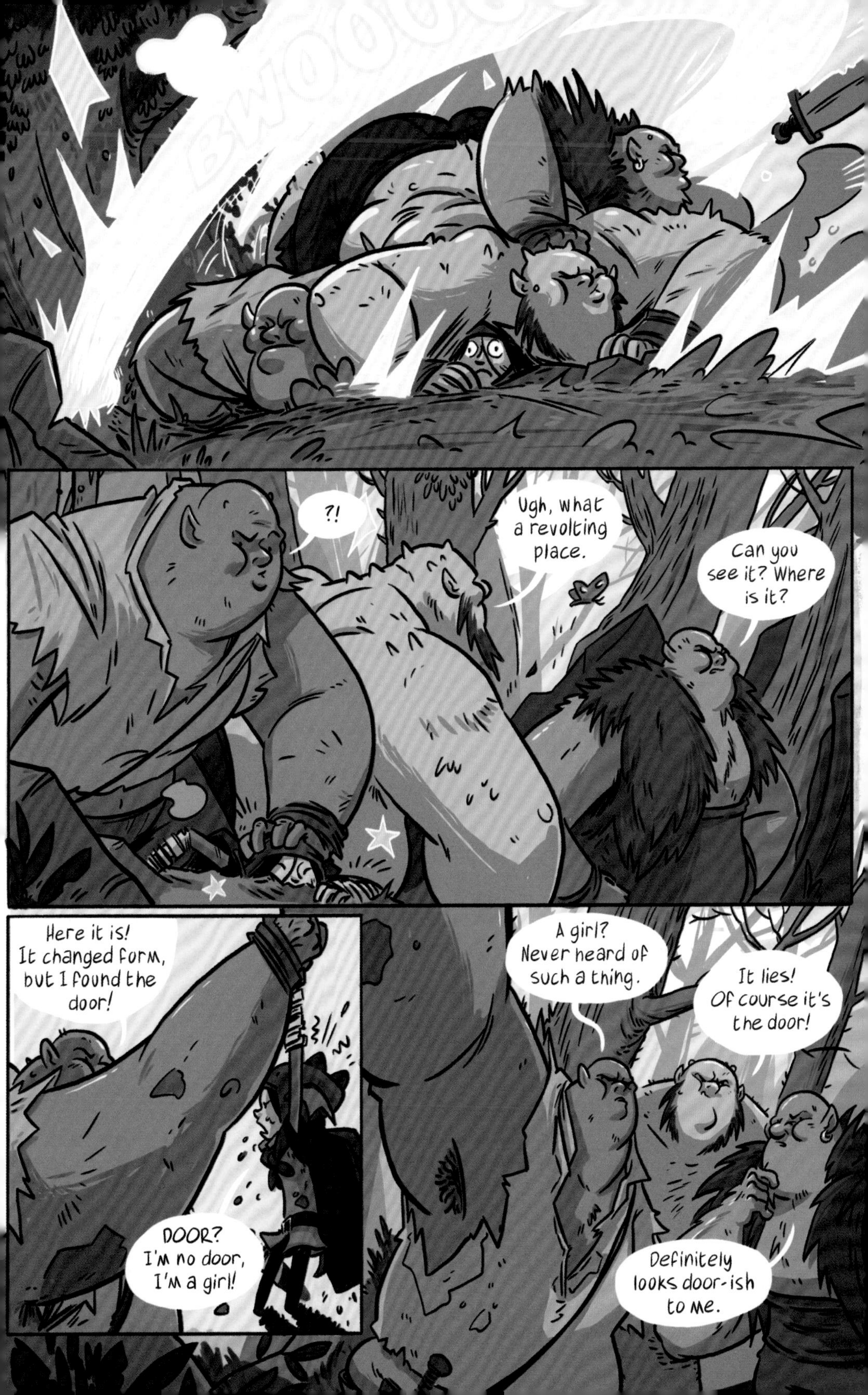
BWOOOO
?!
Ugh, what a revolting place.
Can you see it? Where is it?
Here it is! It changed form, but I found the door!
DOOR? I'm no door, I'm a girl!
A girl? Never heard of such a thing.
It lies! Of course it's the door!
Definitely looks door-ish to me.

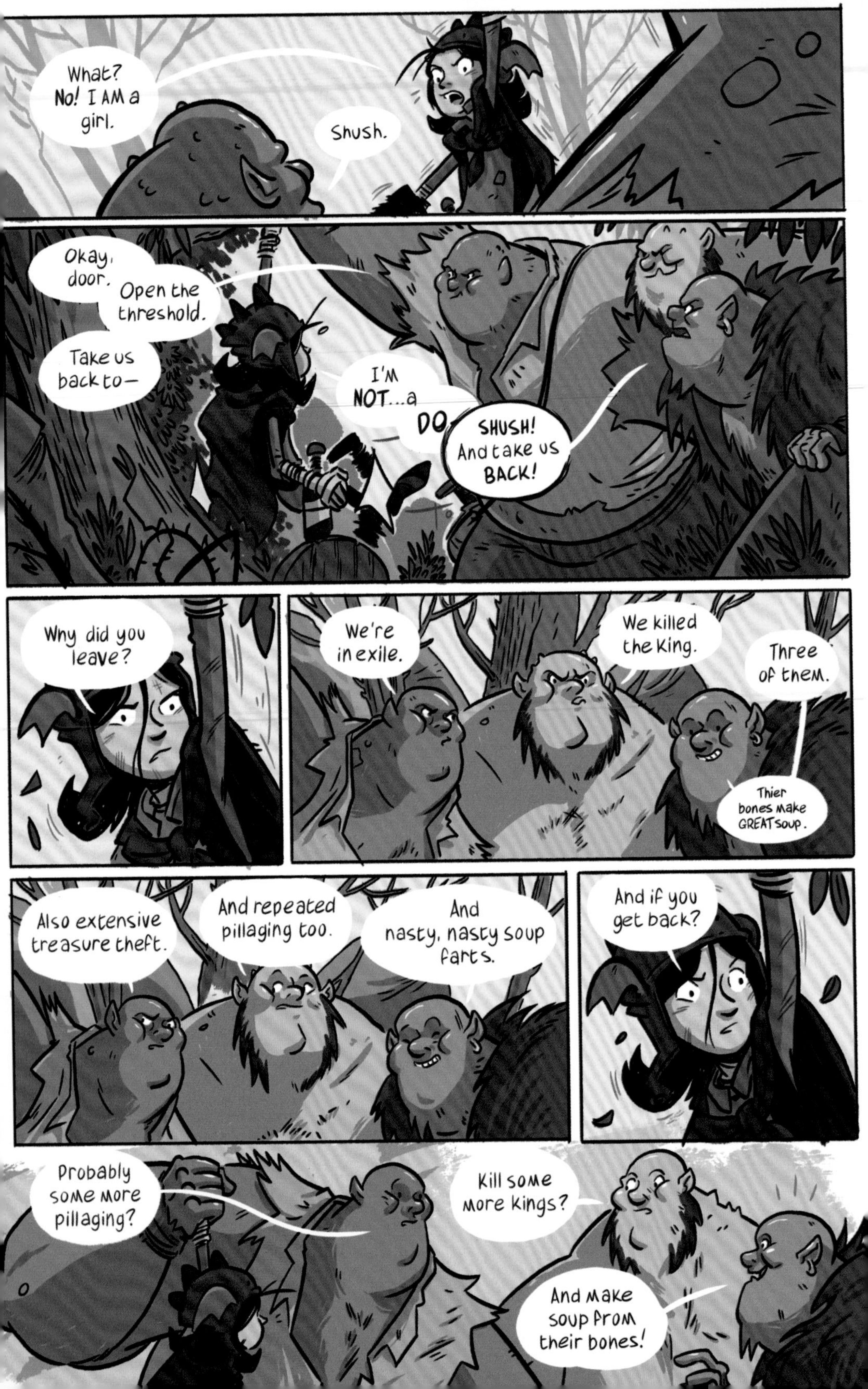
What? No! I AM a girl.
Shush.
Okay, door.
Open the threshold.
Take us back to—
I'M NOT...a DO—
SHUSH! And take us BACK!
Why did you leave?
We're in exile.
We killed the King.
Three of them.
Thier bones make GREAT soup.
Also extensive treasure theft.
And repeated pillaging too.
And nasty, nasty soup farts.
And if you get back?
Probably some more pillaging?
Kill some more kings?
And make soup from their bones!

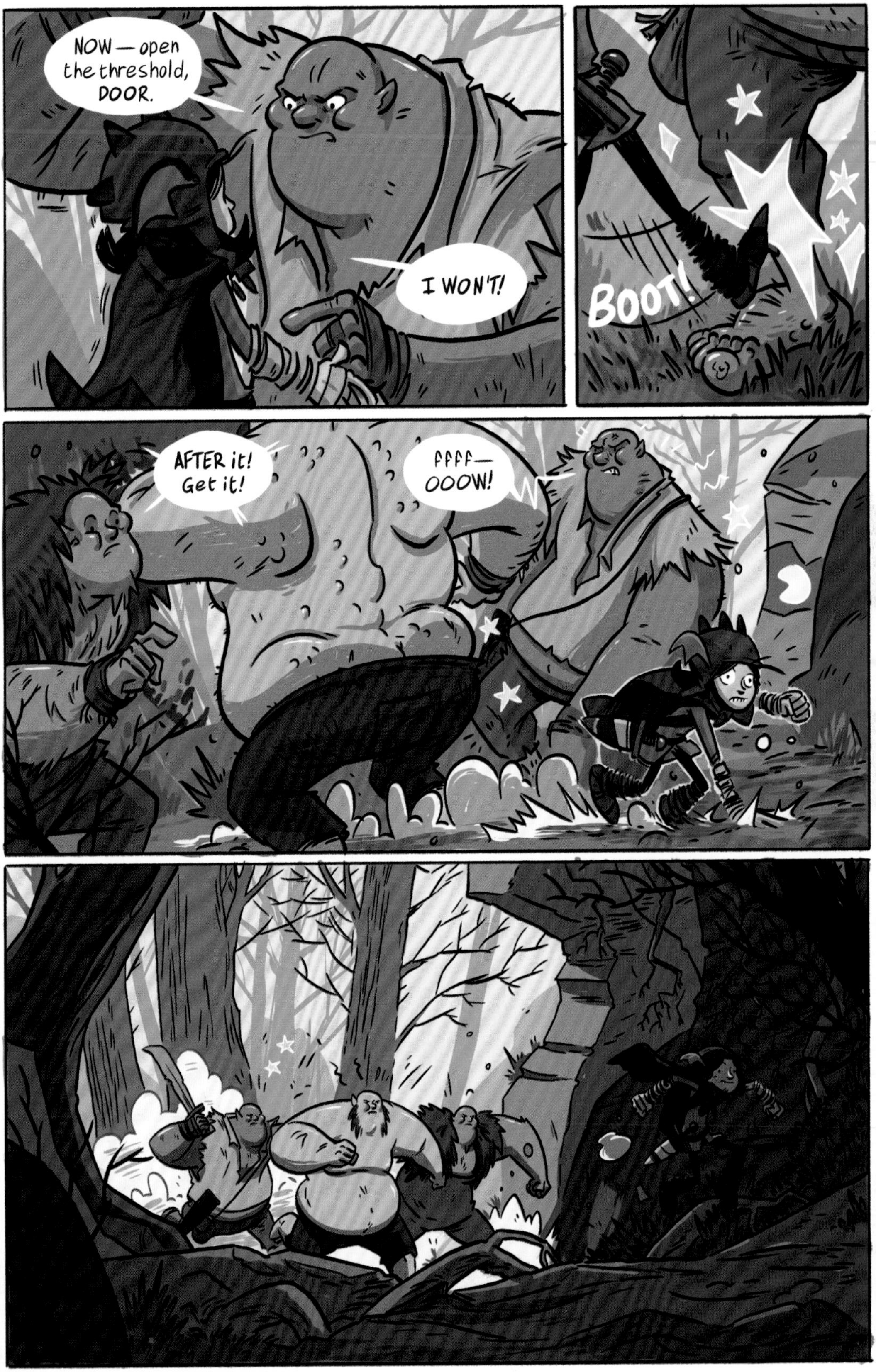
NOW — open the threshold, DOOR.
I WON'T!
BOOT!
AFTER it! Get it!
ffff— OOOW!

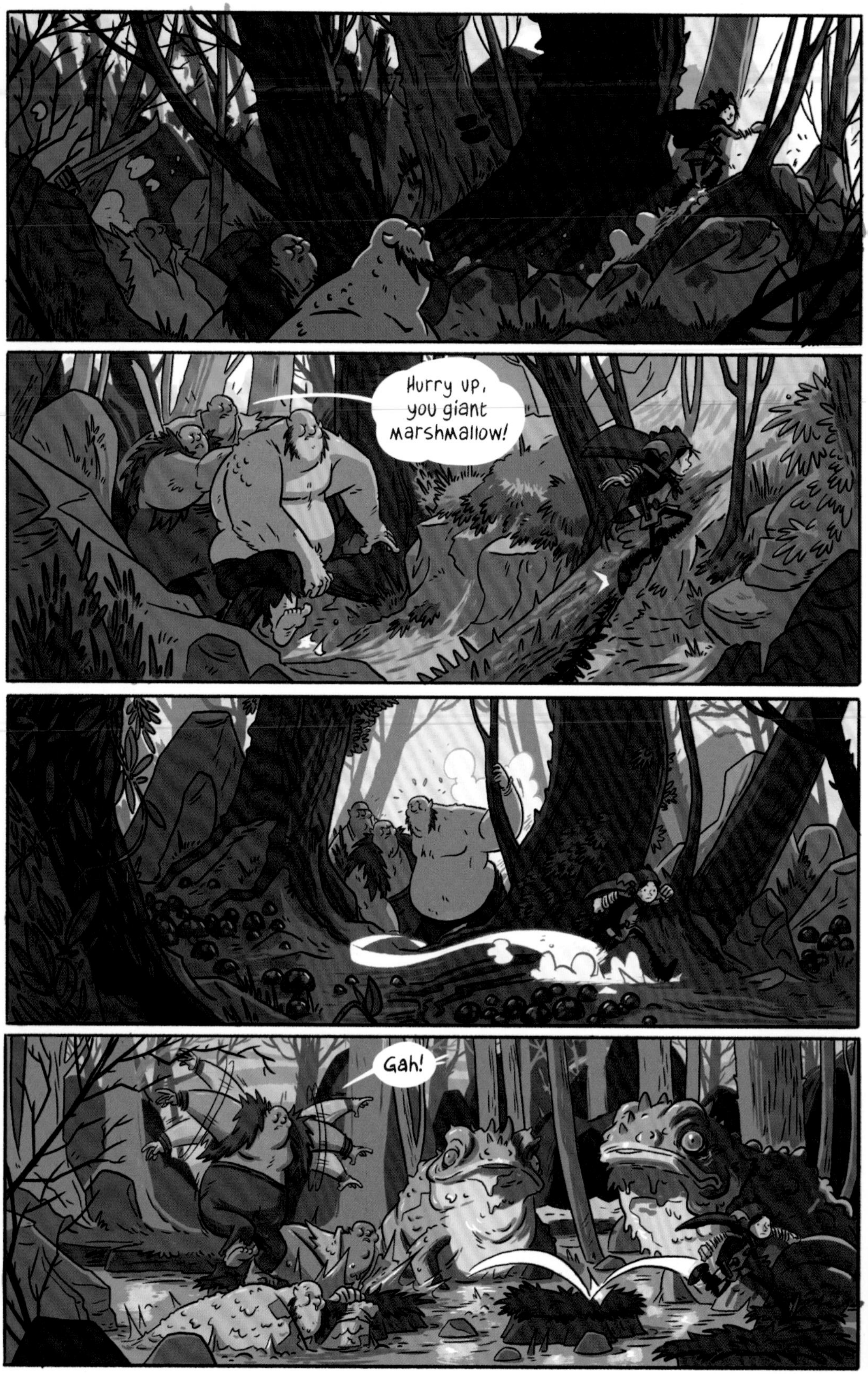
Hurry up, you giant marshmallow!
Gah!

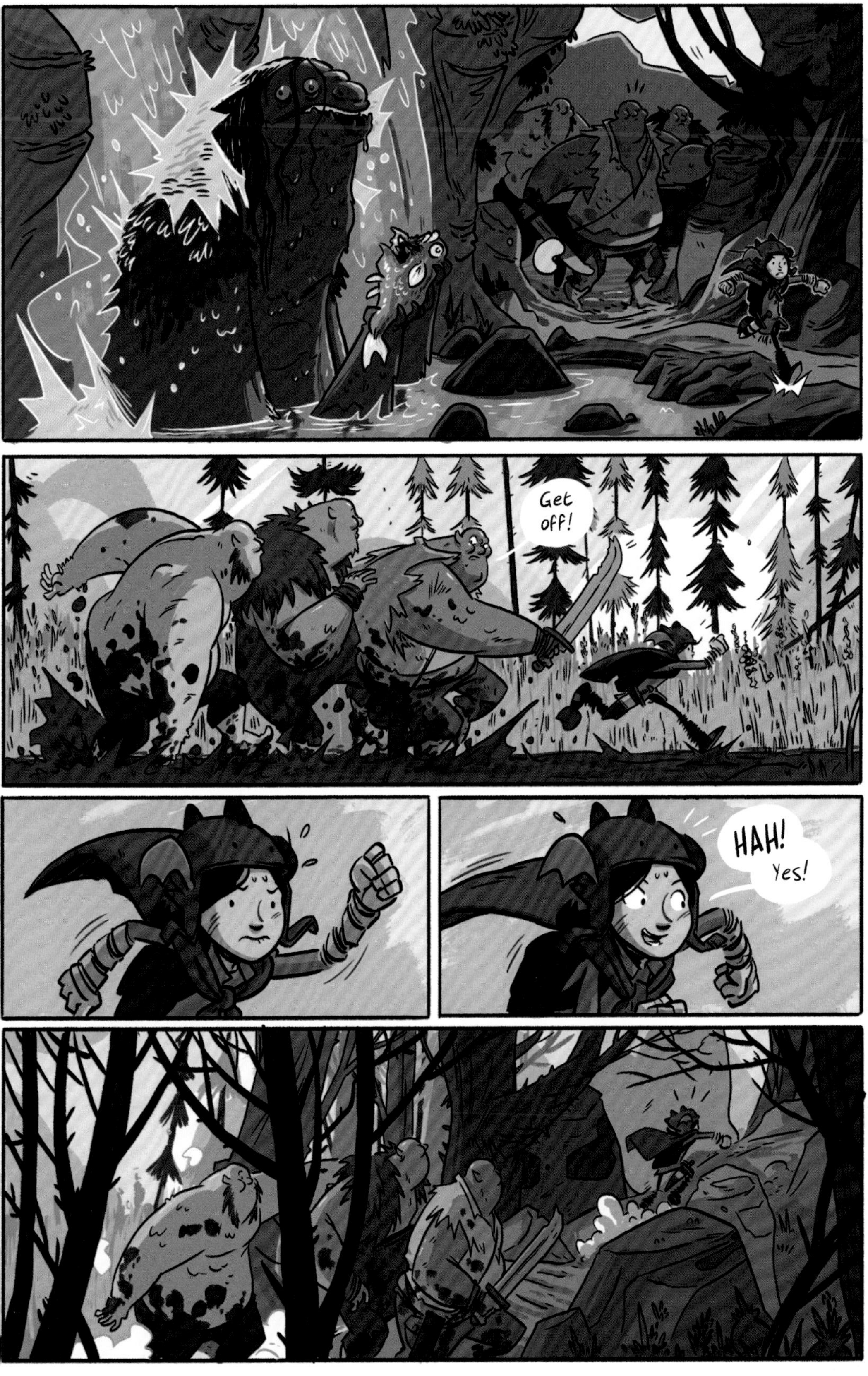
Get off!
HAH!
Yes!

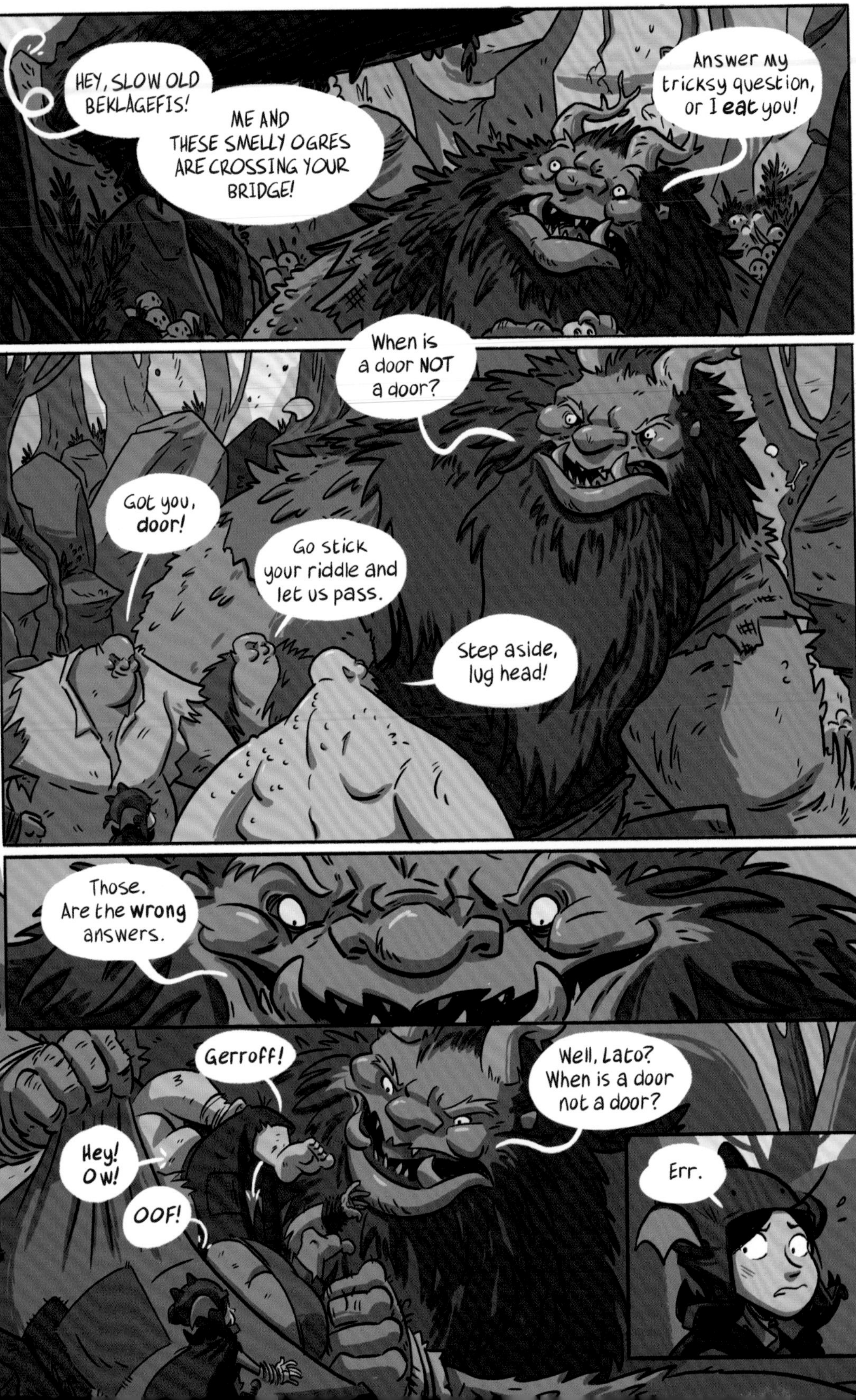
HEY, SLOW OLD BEKLAGEFIS!
ME AND THESE SMELLY OGRES ARE CROSSING YOUR BRIDGE!
Answer my tricksy question, or I **eat** you!
When is a door **NOT** a door?
Got you, **door**!
Go stick your riddle and let us pass.
Step aside, lug head!
Those. Are the **wrong** answers.
Gerroff!
Hey! Ow!
OOF!
Well, Lato? When is a door not a door?
Err.

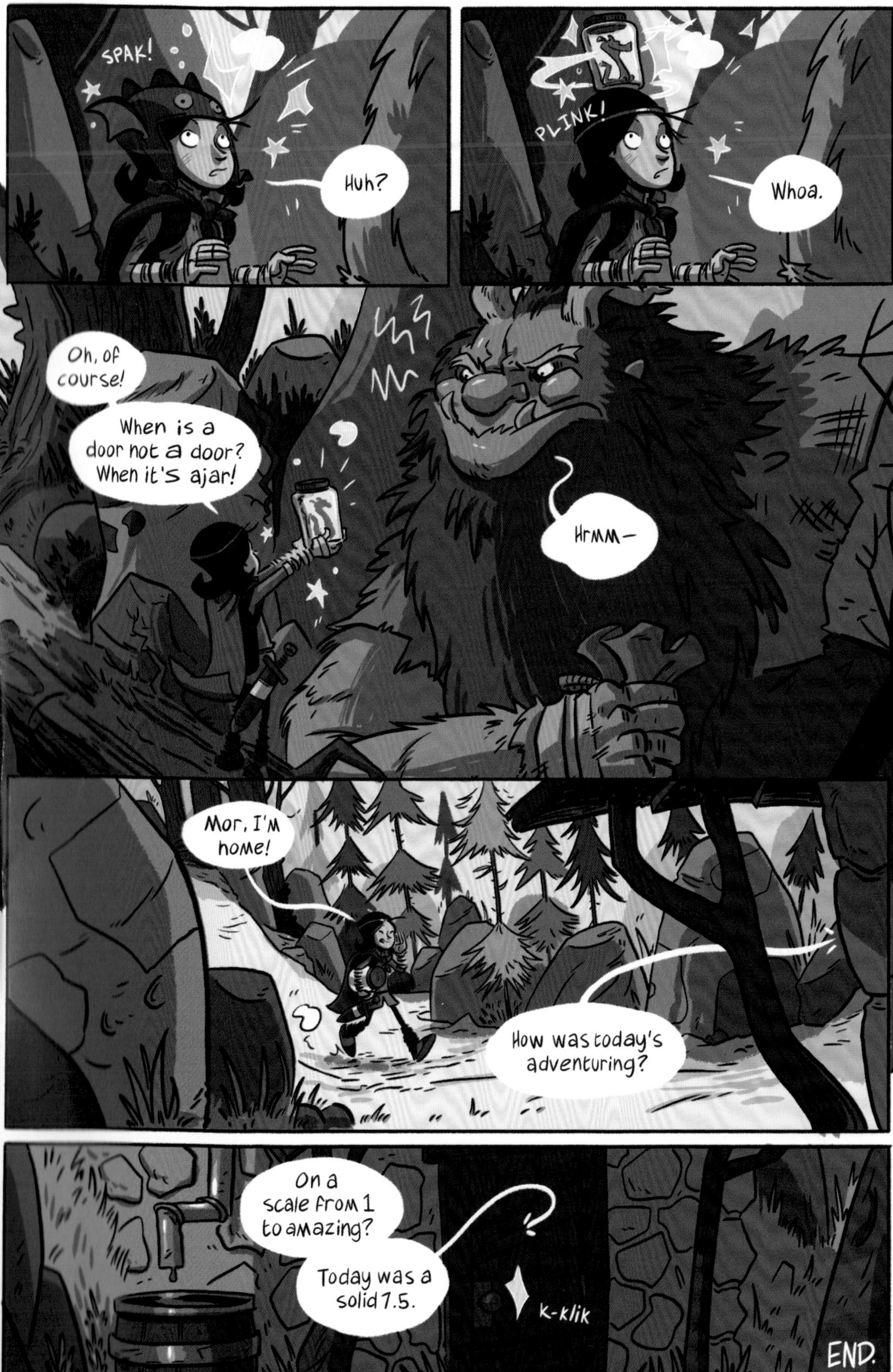
SPAK!
Huh?
PLINK!
Whoa.
Oh, of course!
When is a door not a door? When it's ajar!
Hrmm—
Mor, I'm home!
How was today's adventuring?
On a scale from 1 to amazing?
Today was a solid 7.5.
k-klik
END.

# ABOUT THE CREATORS

**KAZU KIBUISHI** is the creator of the *New York Times* bestselling graphic novel series *Amulet*. He was also the editor and art director of eight volumes of *Flight*, the groundbreaking Eisner-nominated graphic anthology. His comics collection *Copper* was a Junior Library Guild selection, and his debut graphic novel, *Daisy Kutter*, was named a YALSA Best Book for Young Adults. He recently created cover art for the new paperback editions of J.K. Rowling's *Harry Potter* series. Find out more about Kazu at boltcity.com.

**JEN BREACH** is a former archaeologist and librarian originally from Melbourne, Australia. Read more of her writing, including her comics project with Douglas Holgate, *Maralinga*, at jenbreach.com.

**JASON CAFFOE**, coeditor of the *Explorer* anthologies, is also a contributor to *Explorer: The Mystery Boxes*, *Explorer: The Lost Islands*, and the *Flight* anthologies. He is the lead production assistant for the *Amulet* series. Visit him at jcaffoe.tumblr.com.

**STEVE HAMAKER** is the Eisner- and Harvey Award–nominated colorist of the *Bone* graphic novel series by Jeff Smith. Other coloring work includes Coldplay's *Mylo Xyloto* comic series and *Table Titans* by Scott Kurtz. Links to more of his work can be found at steve-hamaker.com.

**FAITH ERIN HICKS's** previous works include *The War at Ellsmere*, *Friends with Boys*, *Nothing Can Possibly Go Wrong* (with Prudence Shen), and the Eisner-nominated *The Adventures of Superhero Girl*. She lives in Nova Scotia. To see more of her art, check out faitherinhicks.com.

**DOUGLAS HOLGATE** is the illustrator of many books and comics for kids, including *Case File: 13*, *Planet Tad*, *Cheesie Mack*, and *Zinc Alloy*. He lives in Australia. Find Douglas on your computer at www.skullduggery.com.au.

**JOHANE MATTE** is a storyboard artist at DreamWorks Animation. Her work appeared in *Explorer: The Mystery Boxes* and several volumes of *Flight*. Her credits as a storyboard artist include the movies *How to Train Your Dragon* and *Rise of the Guardians* and the TV series *Avatar: The Last Airbender*. Check out her at rufftoon.tumblr.com.

**JEN WANG** is a writer and illustrator living in Los Angeles. She's the creator of the graphic novel *Koko Be Good* and *In Real Life*, co-written by Cory Doctorow. Explore more of Jen's work at jenwang.net.

\* \* \*

**MARY CAGLE** colored "Mastaba." She is a comics artist and illustrator and a graduate of the Savannah College of Art and Design.

**DENVER JACKSON** helped color "Asteria Crane." He is a filmmaker, animator, and comics artist from Victoria, B.C.

**NOREEN RANA** colored "Two-Person Door." She is a Toronto-based freelance illustrator and user interface designer.